Hot Spring Honeymoon

A Novel

Dana Smith

Hot Spring Honeymoon is a work of fiction. Apart from the well-known actual people, events, and locales that figure in the narrative, all names, characters, places and incidents are the product of the author's imagination or are used fictitiously. Any resemblance to current events or locales or to living persons is entirely coincidental.

To Eileen, my wife, who has gifted love with laughter...

Characters...

Keefe Kenny	Hot Spring Resort and Café proprietor
Hazel Harwood	Harwood Award Ribbon Co. proprietor
Fletcher McCrea	turquoise mine proprietor
Glenna Goddard	Harwood Award Ribbon Co. employee
Blake Varela	mechanic
Lark Lockhart	medical clinic employee
Garrett Harwood	Chamber of Commerce president
Ranger	highway repair foreman
Jace Brandt	entrepreneur from Salt Lake City
Dotty and Gage	General Store retailers
Gig and Elena	Bakery proprietors
Sal and Mitzi	Hot Spring Café cook and waitress
Bero and Mirari	Basque sheepherders
Dusty	Hot Spring Resort housekeeper
Rory	Mayor and brewmaster at the Brewery
Jolene	Harwood Award Ribbon Co. employee
Sharlene	Harwood Award Ribbon Co. employee
Bunny	Harwood Award Ribbon Co. employee
Tallula	Harwood Award Ribbon Co. employee
Faith	Harwood Award Ribbon Co. employee
Sissy	Harwood Award Ribbon Co. employee
Ruth	Dusty's mother
Bambalina	the burro
Deputy Sheriff	officer of the law
Doctor	physician at the medical clinic
Karl	daredevil

chapter

ONE

The crew boss engaged the transmission to the rotary drill and that is when the accident came to pass. Not a soul within earshot was sure what had happened. The eruption, followed by the concussive explosion and the contrail concocted of venting steam, rock and twisted pieces of metal, could be heard far and wide up and down the valley.

According to the Deputy Sheriff's report the explosion had been witnessed by the naked eye from up to twenty miles away.

It turned out Keefe Kenny had become a passenger upon the world's first flying water well drilling rig. The hot spring proprietor had gone involuntarily ballistic. The gushing water separated the drill from the truck chassis and launched the contraption skyward. The rig arced over the earth, catapulted hundreds of feet from its takeoff point, then plunged and shattered into a riot of industrial-sized confetti upon Nevada's Hot Spring Highway.

On this same morning Blake Varela, hot shot wonder boy, was in the driver's seat of his sand rail road-testing a new engine. He squeezed down on the accelerator with the precision of a marksman. The sand rail launch was emphatic. He concentrated on splitting the broken white stripe right down the middle of the highway when of all things the side of the sagebrush soaked mountain erupted. He was racing toward the blast while closing in on triple digits.

Fletcher McCrae, on account of a date he had with one of his sweethearts, was rock crawling his four-wheel-drive International Harvester pickup truck down from his turquoise mine up on Pipe Dream Mountain. He was hauling Bambalina, his burro, into town, going to put his 'pain in his ass' in her corral. His bond to his burro was as absolute as her instinctive obstinacy was to him. They enjoyed a mutual stubbornness. Fact of the matter was they loved and hated one another; sometimes it was pure love, sometimes pure hate and sometimes, the most complex of all, was love and hate all mixed into one interspecies conflagration

Blake from the highway and Fletcher from the dirt track both converged upon the wreckage. Not now, but later there would be time to figure out what happened and come up with answers while peering into the bottom of a whiskey bottle.

Fletcher leaped out of his truck and ran toward the tangled ruins. He waded into the mangled well drilling rig swinging his legs over the broken pieces struggling to get to Keefe who was pinned motionless beneath the iron scrap.

"Keefe…" Fletcher shouted.

Blake screeched to a halt. He snapped open his five-point harness. He did the high hurdles lifting his legs over the knotted slagheap. Keefe was dead out. The two men tried to lift an eight inch diameter steel pipe off the man. The deformed twenty-foot long steel pipe casing was jumbled up with other twisted pieces. They couldn't break it free. Fletcher took hold of Keefe's shoulders. He feared moving him, not knowing what might be broken and what remained whole, but if they were to revive him, chances had to be taken, second guessing could be as lethal.

Fletcher got a grip on Keefe's arms while Blake used a long piece of scrap to pry, then lever and lift up the demolished well casing. Fletcher dragged Keefe free. They got him rolled over on his back. Fletcher felt for a pulse. There was none. He put his ear to his chest. Nothing… He put the palms of his hands on Keefe's chest and pumped. "You see what I'm doing? We'll trade places. You pump and I'll initiate mouth to mouth." He gave up pumping on his heart. He tilted Keefe's head back, put his ear down to his mouth. "Okay," Fletcher wiped his lips with the back of his hand. He shouted out a "god damn," his hands trembled, then he plugged Keefe's nose with his finger and thumb while he gripped his jaw with the other and gave him the breath of life.

He lifted his lips off the unresponsive mouth. Blake straddled Keefe and pumped again.

Fletcher counted, "… twenty- nine, thirty, let me have a go."

Blake stopped pumping.

Fletcher blew into Keefe's mouth— three quick bursts. Fletcher put his ear to Keefe's mouth.

Sal and Mitzi were coming down from the Hot Spring Café as fast as two old folks could.

Fletcher blew again. Keefe's eyes bolted wide open. He said nothing. He looked his friend right in the eyes, then finally the re-vived man spoke. "Fletch, you kissing me again?"

"Kind of fond of you," Fletcher shook his head; tried smiling. He had never been more relieved. "You know where you are?"

Keefe blinked his eyes. "Looks like I'm in a hell of a mess."

"Blake, go get the sand rail fired up; we're hauling Keefe into town. You'll be the ambulance." Fletcher asked Keefe, "Anything feel broke?"

Sal, a short bald Mexican cook, and Mitzi, his prized taller German NATO bride, waded through the wreckage and hovered over Fletcher.

"Should be dead," Mitzi said.

"You okay, boss?" Sal's voice cracked.

"Fletch," Keefe said. "Everything look like it's still attached?"

Fletcher examined Keefe head to toe, lifted his belt buckle and took a peek. "Looks like it's all there..."

"Thank god. Someday I might want to have a family."

"You already had a family, Mr. Kenny," Mitzi explained.

"I did?" Keefe said. "I had a family?"

"Grown up, and gone," Sal added.

"Fletch?" Keefe asked.

"What is it, Keefe?"

Keefe needed Fletcher to come in closer. "Fletch," he seemed concerned.

"What is it, Keefe?"

"Were they good kids?"

Fletcher looked up at Sal and Mitzi. The three of them were concerned. He looked down at Keefe and smiled, "Keefe, they're the best."

"Was I married?"

"Yep, made it look hard too," Fletcher said.

"Not anymore?" Keefe wondered.

Fletcher shook his head, "No, you're footloose and fancy free. Let's get you to the doctor."

Mitzi was grief stricken. Watching and listening to Keefe, her boss and the owner of the hot spring resort, he seemed disoriented. She pressed her lips together suppressing her tears.

"Sal," Fletcher broke in, "you and Mitzi get hold of his other arm," and to Keefe, "We're going to sit you up."

Keefe said, "Wait a minute."

"What is it?"

"Where are we?"

"Boss, you are on the highway in front of the hot spring," Sal explained.

Keefe turned his head. The wreckage strewn across the roadway didn't make sense. Up on the hillside where the well drilling rig had been set Keefe could see a plume of geothermal water gushing up out of the ground ten feet high. It was a king sized water fountain. The water rushed downhill straight through the heart of the resort. "Do we come here often?" Keefe asked.

Fletcher intervened, "Keefe, there's been an explosion. You were standing on top of the well when the blast occurred."

"You're not making this up?" Keefe thought a second, "Was it a close call?"

"Might be that it still is..." Fletcher said.

The geothermal waters poured by the bucket loads down the hill through the resort and had filled the ditch by the side of the road. The new stream gathered up speed, shot through a culvert pipe to the other side of the highway where it rambled off toward town guided by the path of a dry wash.

Mitzi got maternal. Her accent thickened in the stress. "You need to be quiet and do 'vhat ve' say, boss."

Sal added, "So we can get you back up to the hot spring so you can tell us what to do."

Fletcher smiled at Keefe, "Come on, come on, we're wasting time here."

They sat him up and then lifted Keefe onto his feet, Sal under one shoulder, Fletcher under the other and Mitzi holding onto the belt on his pants.

"You're not going to make me get in that?"

"We've got to."

"That's a death trap on wheels."

"You need to see the doctor pronto," Fletcher insisted.

The men eased Keefe into the passenger seat next to Blake. Mitzi actuated the lever and reclined the seat while Sal began strapping Keefe into the five point harness. Blake's supercharger began spooling up, the sand rail quivered and, when he hit the gas, you could see the machine visibly twist from the torque of the motor.

"Let me get my god damn seat belts on," Fletcher said.

"Kid," Keefe grabbed Blake's arm, "just because I almost died doesn't mean you have to go and kill us all now."

With the tip of his finger Blake tapped his Ray-Bans tighter onto the bridge of his nose, "Mr. Kenny, it's not a good day for dying anyway." When Blake put the sand rail into gear, the machine jerked forward.

"Sal, Mitzi, follow us into town with Bambalina," Fletcher was worried about his burro. He reached down into his pocket, absentminded, then checked his shirt pocket, patted his rear pockets on his jeans.

Mitzi had walked across to the truck. "They're in the ignition."

"Sal, what would we do without Mitzi?" Fletcher asked.

"Look for a woman who likes to tell a man what to do," Sal replied.

"You never do a damn thing she says."

"Si, but boss, she just wants to have her say," Sal winked at Fletcher.

"That's happiness?"

"It's how we are happy. She tells me what to do all day; I tell her what to do all night." Sal could not have been more serious.

Fletcher took hold of Keefe's shoulder, smiled at his friend, "Let's cheat death one more time."

Blake had found his purpose. He'd been commissioned an ambulance driver, with an inaudible siren screaming inside his head. Hard to know, but fact was this is what the good life in Nevada could look like. Velocity as a pleasure was lost on Fletcher. Figured Blake hadn't killed himself yet, then again barreling down the highway in a homemade high powered sand rail shod with street tires, a man is prone to see that there is always a first time and a last time. Chances were even by his reckoning that the three of them might end up a roadside memorial marked with dime store plastic flowers. Fletcher had held out hope for a better fate. Seemed today odds were stacked against that chance.

Blake made the last corner before town somewhere north of triple digits, then eased up dipping into his brakes, bringing the buggy down to twice the town limit. The rig rattled across the cattle guard, shot past the brewery, casino hotel, wedding chapel, general store, bakery, pizza joint, and then pulled into the medical clinic's parking lot.

Fletcher unfastened his safety belts and scrambled out of the rear bucket seat. Blake ran into the clinic. Keefe was feebly trying to unbuckle himself from the five point harness, first pulling a locking mechanism, then he attempted lifting a secondary hasp-like release lever.

The doctor and Lark, his receptionist, rushed out the clinic's front door.

"Fletcher," the doctor grabbed hold of his shoulders moving him aside, "let me have a look." He hunched over Keefe. He looked at his eyes. He put his fresh scrubbed hand beneath his chin and lifted. Keefe's pupils were dilated "Lark, get a wheelchair."

The doctor tilted the reclining bucket seat up. Keefe began trying to climb out of the vehicle. The doctor kept his hands on Keefe. He wanted to keep him right where he was. "That's fine there, Romeo."

"Found him three hundred yards from where the drilling rig blew up," Fletcher said.

The doctor cocked his head looking through his bifocals, "You remember any of that?" he was running his hands across Keefe's body searching for signs of injury.

"Can't say I do."

"What hurts, Keefe?" the doctor asked.

Keefe was matter of fact. "Paying taxes hurts."

"But you don't remember what happened?"

"Remember putting my boots on this morning. Remember having bacon and eggs."

"You don't remember an explosion?"

Keefe was looking right through the doctor, still dazed, searching for any recollection he might have, "You think the IRS is after me?"

"Sometimes these things happen so fast there isn't time to remember."

"He was on the rig when he hit the jackpot," Fletcher said.

Lark, who had gone to school with Blake and graduated four years ago, returned with the wheelchair.

"Let's get you inside, take a look."

"He was out cold," Fletcher said.

"Deader than Easter week..." Blake said.

Doc glanced up at Blake. He decided to ignore Blake's comment. "How long was he out?" The doctor kept a steady eye on Keefe.

Blake and Fletcher looked at one another. Fletcher twisted his jaw, "What do you think?"

"I think I'm glad I wasn't out that long," Blake said.

Fletcher added, "...didn't have a heartbeat when we got to him."

Keefe had a dazed look on his face. He had a pretty good bruise on his temple.

The doctor was cautious, wanted the facts, "Let's get him into the clinic, Lark."

Fletcher and the doctor took hold of his arms. Blake steadied the wheelchair while Lark got hold of Keefe's feet.

The doctor counted, "One, two, three," they lifted Keefe off the bucket seat of the sand rail and set him down in the wheelchair.

Lark was on her knees in front of Keefe. She placed his feet onto the footpads.

Keefe's eyes were perking up. He was gazing down the front of Lark's smock.

Fletcher said, "Looks better already."

Lark looked up at Fletcher. She looked at Keefe; stole a look at Blake. The embroidered edges of Lark's lavender brassiere flashed from under her drab green medical scrubs.

Doctor tried to stay on task, "He's well on his way to recovering."

The sway Lark's figure had on men was still something she was coming to terms with.

Lark wouldn't have minded Blake's noticing.

"I didn't mean anything, Lark." Fletcher said.

"I know, Mr. McCrae." Lark glanced at Blake. He was embarrassed, like some boy caught red-handed.

Fletcher could not imagine Lark being something to fear. He grabbed hold of Blake's arm and tugged. "Come on, Blake."

Lark wheeled Keefe into the clinic. The doctor walked ahead and opened the door.

"Son," Fletcher said with a paternal tone in his voice putting his arm around Blake's shoulders, "Seems to me you got yourself all sidelined. You're sitting on the bench. You need to get yourself into the game."

"Lark's not interested in me." Blake stiffened.

"You need to be interested in her. Take a chance. Make a run at a thing like that." Fletcher was pleading.

"Not my style," Blake said.

"How many people in this town...?" Fletcher asked.

"Three thousand and some," Blake replied.

"How many girls your age...?"

"I don't know," Blake said.

"I do," Fletcher replied, "probably not more than twenty."

"I know them all."

"Maybe you do, then maybe you don't, maybe you don't know what to do about it."

"I know what I'm doing."

"Can't know what you're doing." Fletcher looked up in the sky. "If you did, by now you'd have been doing whatever it is that you should be doing. Now, that fence post doesn't know a thing about barbed wire."

"Yeah, so..."

"So, seems to me you just saw the same thing I did, and I mean seems to me Lark isn't just the best of those 20 others her age, hell, Lark's so damn beautiful makes a blind man in a wheelchair believe he can stand up, walk and see."

"Everybody thinks Lark's a beautiful woman inside and out," Blake allowed.

"Inside and out...?" Fletcher stabbed his finger into Blake's chest, "I'm sure Lark's pretty all the way thru, but when a man goes hunting a woman, he's gotta make plans, set a trap, that's how it's done."

"I don't operate like that." Blake pulled away from Fletcher.

Fletcher was behind him pleading his case. "That's exactly what it is, why all that lovemaking is done after dark. You sneak in, employ your best charms, seduce her, make it easy for her to say 'yes,' don't give her a chance to say 'no.'"

Blake turned around. "Don't push me. I got to do things my way."

Fletcher looked at Blake and could see no resemblance to his own life. He smiled, then lowered his voice and tried to go a bit easier on the young man. "Nothing else you can do. You are in the full bloom of your manhood and I don't know what you were feeling, but I can tell you I know about my oats and, son, the gods were more than generous, they were trying to tell you where to look, telling you where your happiness could be located, they went ahead and gave you the opportunity to admire a fulsome figured woman. That was a lavender clad glimpse of heaven on earth."

"Lark's not interested in me."

"She's just shy," Fletcher was exasperated. "Son, you're all vapor locked, can't just do nothing."

"There's nothing to do."

"Problem with small towns, everybody's all jammed up. You got to learn how to put two words together with Lark, rub them back and forth until they make a fire, look her in the eye and she'll look back, and when she does, you just lean right in and kiss her with everything you got."

"Fletcher, you make that sound like it's something easy to do," Blake said.

"The thought of all that woman being left alone, night after night, that is unforgivable, it's a waste of a precious resource. I'm a turquoise miner, know a thing or two about where to find a good vein, something that will pay out over time and, Blake, my job's to show you where to look and what the hell to do when you find it..."

"You're going to teach me how to mine turquoise?"

Fletcher McCrae stared at Blake. He shook his head, "I'm two decades too late. If I'd met someone like that, why I bet I'd still be married."

"I thought you liked being a bachelor," Blake said.

"A woman like Lark could make a bachelor sing like a canary all the way to the church."

Sal and Mitzi rolled down Main Street and were pulling up in front of the gate to Bambalina's corral, Fletcher began to cross the road when Blake took hold of his arm and stopped him. A pickup truck hit its brakes; the tires squealed.

Fletcher looked at Blake, smiled, "I'm looking out for you; you look out for me."

"For a man who's got a nose for finding turquoise and an eye for the ladies, you sure don't remember much about anything else."

Fletcher smiled, "I'm like most miners, all I'm good for, and when I'm done being good at that, I'll join the rest of the men here in Nevada and be good for nothing.

chapter

TWO

Fletcher was out on the front stoop of Sharlene's double-wide, obliging the dawn, mulling over his list of chores, filling in the nattering holes in his plans for the day with sips from his hot coffee. He had 16 bales of hay loaded in the bed of his pickup. Sun was coming up; bugs were still down. It was clear, crisp spring.

Across the way a door swung open. Tallula, a skinny little thing, was leaving for work. "Morning, Fletcher."

"Morning..."

He set his empty mug on the rail, stepped down off the porch and met Tallula in the middle of the street.

"Sharlene still asleep...?"

"Just getting out of the shower," Fletcher winked affirming what she was puzzling out; it wasn't much of a challenge.

Tallula lived in one of Meadowhawk's original homes. The town's history could be understood as a place born by one brief boom. Ghost town status seemed imminent. The place hung by a thread. But every time someone threw the towel in, some tumble-weed of a soul would come blowing in to try to make work what the last person could not.

"Might be she's just all worn out this morning," Tallula said twisting her head. She waited, kept her gaze fixed dead in Fletcher's eyes.

Kind of woke Fletcher up. He smiled at Tallula's plain dealing, "Well now, you sure you want to get into a middle-of-the-street symposium regarding the appetites of turquoise miners?"

Tallula looked down one end of the block, turned and looked the other, "Hungry man can give a woman something to do."

Sharlene had coffee in one hand and her pocketbook in the other. She was a big boned woman and kicked the screen door open with her generous behind. "Morning, Tallula. I'll walk to work with you."

The vintage of the two women was close to the same. It was a big enough number that it was polite not to ask and common sense dictated a man ought never to hazard a guess. That just gets a man into more trouble than he has already been accused of being in. The two women wore dark cotton pants and buttoned-down-the-middle white shirts, collars open, sleeves rolled up. They both wore less than sensible footwear, but comfort wasn't their purpose. Sometimes a woman looked down and there was a deference earned, good feeling about the way their feet seemed petite, and this could be vital to how the whole of that same human being might feel about the rest of what they were.

Sharlene had her coffee in her hand. She took the last of it up, then handed it to Fletcher, "You put that in the kitchen?"

Fletcher shared an easy smile with Sharlene. She had a prominent chin and jutted it out in pride. She was one of his most rousing lady friends, athletic, broad shouldered, full hipped. Still even after last night's affair it wasn't the kind of relationship where either of them was going to kiss the other good-bye. Sharlene had turned absentmindedly, then stiffened, squeezed her lips together like she was going to blow a trumpet, then glanced to high heaven.

The willowy Tallula wasn't having any of it, "Come on, girl, day's almost over, and kissing Fletcher McCrea in broad daylight in Meadowhawk only gets you gossip."

Fletcher laughed, "Well, there's always that, best and worst thing about living here." He walked back toward Sharlene's mobile home, stood on the porch, turned and fixed his eyes on the sashaying hips of the two women as they headed toward the business district. Fletcher never could make up his mind. Hard to know why he was the way he was; never seemed he had the strength to choose one woman when he had to wash his hands of relations with another.

Bambalina was disappointed. When Fletcher arrived, he backed up next to the corral, pulled one hay bale from the stack on his truck and tossed it down on the ground. Bambalina saw right off it was nothing but cheap hay. Mule headed turquoise miner knew she preferred Timothy hay. Fletcher had a pair of wire cutters on the ledge of the window in the shed. He cut the bale open and tossed two flakes out. Bambalina stared at Fletcher. Looked right through him; thought he could do better.

"What?" Fletcher said as he pulled a bale off the tailgate and lugged it into the shed. He came for a second, "What? Bambalina... you are being contrary," said it like his burro actually understood what the word 'contrary' meant. He lugged another bale into the shed and this time he walked past the tailgate to the door of the cab.

"Everybody wants more! You want an apple, Sharlene wants a relationship, lapidary wants more turquois."

The burro would hear nothing of it. Didn't care what Fletcher had to say. As far as she was concerned, he was just braying. She deserved to be treated right, plain and simple. She'd be a whole lot more cooperative, if he'd get his priorities straight. She wasn't going to tell him twice. He knew full well what he was supposed to do.

Fletcher dug a red apple from the sack. He held it out while his burro approached. She got hold of the apple and Fletcher instead of letting go played a little game of tug-o-war with her. Bambalina's ears pulled back. He could be so annoying.

He laughed and let go. "You are in a mood, girl," Fletcher said. He went around the other side of the shed and filled her trough. Took the wheelbarrow and picked up the spent hay she'd sent packing out her business end.

Fletcher got up alongside and patted Bambalina on her rump. She wasn't having any of it. She lifted her rear hoof off the ground. Pulled her ears back, had that mad jenny glare in her eye.

"You put that gun back in your holster, young lady," Fletcher straightened up, scowled.

Bambalina thought about it, was tempting.

"I'm waiting on you," Fletcher said pokerfaced.

Bambalina stood frozen. Still hadn't set her rear hoof down. She started chewing her hay, ears relaxed, she closed her eyes and set her hoof back on the ground in due course, once she'd made up her own mind. She wasn't going to be bullied into anything.

"Going to stay mad at me for the rest of the week," Fletcher complained as he opened the gate to the corral. "Only prospector in the whole of Nye County I know that's ended up with a burro that pouts." He slammed the gate hard.

In ways a lot of folk might not be able to appreciate, Bambalina acted like the rest of the women in Fletcher's life. She knew Fletcher loved her more when she acted like she loved him less.

Finished with chores, Fletcher walked across the street, and this time not forgetting to look before he did.

Lark was seated at her desk at the window adjacent to the waiting room. The clinic smelled like cotton balls soaked in disinfectant; odor was disagreeable, put a person on edge. The gleaming black haired Lark was filling out forms, didn't bother to look up when he stood at the window. "Be right with you, Mr. McCrea."

"How's the patient?"

"Can't find anything wrong with him that wasn't already wrong with him," she said.

"Oh, come on now, Lark, you sure Doc looked hard enough?" Fletcher stretched a big smile across his grizzled face.

She put her pen down, glanced up from her paperwork. He was as pesky as a yellow jacket at a barbeque. She turned on her swivel chair and stood, "Mr. Kenny is the luckiest man alive."

"Yesterday was a stunner," Fletcher said.

"You see how much water he found?" Her voice rising.

"Got plenty of hot water," Fletcher replied, "should have killed him."

"He seems good to go," Lark said.

"After all that hoo-hah, surprised we're not all out at the cemetery."

Fletcher had other things on his mind. Decided now was the time, he asked, "You ever get out on a date with some of these young men in town?"

Lark froze. She had a near perfect pearl white skin. Her cheeks turned rose. She looked away not sure where Fletcher was going. "Maybe...."

"I'm not talking about me, Lark," Fletcher said. "...talking about Blake..."

"Well, you're too old and he's too young."

"No, he's not. He's perfect age."

"Blake? Mr. McCrea, I don't think two shy people have a prayer of ever going out with one another."

"What if he wasn't shy?"

"And what if horseflies didn't bite?" Lark said. "If you're asking for an answer to a question Blake doesn't have the guts to put to me, then you're not going to like my answer."

"Blake's too shy to put me up to anything," Fletcher said. "I'm just talking. Ordinary thing I'm talking about. See, if two people might be good for one another, then it ought to be right to say so."

"Might... but Blake's a long way from being a good date."

"But the sight of a young lady like you can speed things up. Young man like Blake can find he can say and do things in front of a beautiful woman he'd never thought possible."

Lark stood still. She wasn't sure she wanted to speak her mind. "Fact is, Mr. McCrea, so far I've found men to be about the most confusing things I've ever tried to understand. Makes jigsaw puzzles look simple."

The door in the waiting room to where the clinic's patients were treated opened. Keefe was being released. He closed the door behind him, walked over to the window, "Lark," he said, "Doc said he's through with me, but wants another look, keep an eye on how I'm doing."

Fletcher studied his friend head to toe, smiled at him, shook his head, gave special regard to where he'd been hit on the side of his face. "Swellings way down, hardly see a thing, look good as new. How do you feel?"

Keefe shot back, "Might sound like I'm bragging, but I feel terrific. I'm a brand new man."

"Come on then," Fletcher was perplexed some, "let's go see how good you look riding inside my beat up pickup truck."

Keefe opened the clinic door.

"Thought I was supposed to do that for you," Fletcher wondered.

"Nonsense, Fletch, I'm better than good."

"You check back tomorrow afternoon," Lark said.

"End of the day, Doc's last patient..." Keefe replied.

Keefe looked up and down Main Street. The sight of Fletcher's timeworn mustard yellow pickup had turned into more than something utilitarian. In Keefe's mind the truck had a shine to it he had never before recognized.

Fletcher and Keefe's rugged good looks, if you could call them that, might be best described as two men standing at the gateway to "geezer-dom," the last of their 50's, but there was a fair distance between their mortal destiny and the present actuality. Each man stood somewhere less than six feet tall, their butts scrawny, arms wiry, both had too much sun on their faces. Most folks were of the opinion that these two old friends wore their vintage well.

Keefe grabbed hold of the handle to the International Harvester and swung the door open. He hopped up on top the running board. "I swear I don't remember a more beautiful spring." Keefe basked in the grand expanse of the surrounding desert. "Must be a million shades of green out there..."

Fletcher was looking across the road at Bambalina. Stood up on the running board on the driver's side, two blocks down six women from the Awards Ribbon Factory caught his eye. They were heading toward the town's General Store.

He pushed in the clutch, turned the key, fired up his truck, "Pull in to Dotty and Gage's?"

"Fletch, I don't know... maybe it was my close call, the bang on my head, but Meadowhawk looks like I never have seen her before."

Dotty, a short stout graying woman, was out front of the General Store when the men pulled up. The landmark two-story building anchored the center of town and was topped with a faded turn of the last century sign that read, *Beamster & Otis.*

"Look at Mr. Keefe Kenny," Dotty said greeting the men.

Keefe hopped down off the running board, "Thought it was time I stop wasting all of my hard earned money at the clinic, come on down and surrender the rest of it to you and Gage." He shoved the door closed.

Dotty smiled big. "Oh, come on, Keefe, we're town's best bargain."

Most of what held and still holds the town of Meadowhawk together is something about how folk in town found everything they might need or not need here under the roof of this one place.

"Like going on a carnival ride," Keefe teased. "Turn you upside down and shake all that change right out of your pockets."

"Well, it's for a good cause," Dotty put her hand on the small of Keefe's back as they walked inside. "Won't ever find happiness by being stingy, might as well share those eight bits you got saved up in your britches with me and Gage."

Keefe and Fletcher stood at the entranceway to the store. Gage, the General Store's proprietor and first, last and only husband to Dotty, along with the horde of women on break from the Harwood Award Ribbon Company all quit their small talk the moment they spotted Keefe.

Gage put out his hand, "You look like nothing happened to you."

"I feel fine, feel better than fine. I can't explain how good I feel," Keefe said.

Jolene, one of the women from the Harwood Award Ribbon Company, wasn't looking to shake Keefe's hand. She put her arms out and wanted a hug. "It is so good to see you standing on your own two feet." The bright blonde haired, blue eyed Jolene melted into Keefe. She lifted her head off his shoulder but kept hugging him, "Let me see," she puckered her lips and formed a frown as she scrutinized his face, "look alright to me. How do you feel?"

"I've never felt so alive in my life. Nothing like a close call to wake you right up..."

The women all clustered around the men. Faith, Bunny, Sissy, Sharlene, Tallula and Glenna all waited their turns. Keefe's eyes were bright blue. For a man who might as well be dead after what he'd been through, Keefe by all appearances seemed fine.

Faith and Bunny stepped forward and both hugged Keefe, then Sissy, Sharlene and Tallula. Glenna was last.

"We all went out to the hot spring, saw what happened..." Jolene said.

"What are you going to do with all that hot water?" Bunny asked.

"I don't know. Was thinking I was going to drill a well, install a pump, get some water, I wasn't counting on an artesian gusher."

Sissy, born of Italian descent whose figure cut a fine silhouette, said, "Thought this place was drying up. Not no more."

"How're you going to celebrate?" Gage asked.

"Thought I'd buy a couple of those imported Honduran cigars and a bottle of your finest whiskey. Contemplate my good fortunes, make a new plan, life flashed right in front of my eyes."

"Might have to sell you some of my illegal Cuban cigars for this occasion," Gage said. "Got a high roller from Las Vegas who buys them for me..."

"Keefe," Fletcher advised, "might as well go with the embargoed Cuban, not only do you get a better cigar, you get to break the law at the same time."

"Can't beat that," Jolene said. "It's a two-fer."

"...You trying to pawn off some communist contraband on a law abiding man?" Keefe asked.

"Free traders have a god-given right to enjoy a good handmade Cuban cigar," Fletcher said.

"You ever worry you might get caught?" Keefe asked.

"Hell, that's half the fun right there." Gage urged Keefe, "Let's get you all set up."

"We got to get back to work," Jolene said. "Be out to the hot spring for a soak next few days."

Dotty butted in, "Got a town hall Thursday night. Hope you're all planning to be here."

"Downstairs, 7:30..." Gage explained. "Legislature voted to shut down the fairgrounds."

Keefe looked out the door of the General Store. Across the street the whole of one block in town was taken up by the fairground frontage. He walked out, stood stock still on the sidewalk. He gazed. He shook his head, pinched his eyebrows. Biggest cottonwoods in town grew on that piece of real estate. Most of the teenage boys in town chewed their first tobacco underneath the race track grandstands. Girls got their first kiss and young cowboys sat atop their first bulls.

"We'll be out to the hot spring," Sharlene said.

The women headed out the door. Break was over; time to get back to work.

Jolene stalled a moment. She wanted a word with Fletcher.

"See you tonight?" Jolene asked.

Fletcher, like Keefe, was still accumulating his thinking around the fair closing for good. He snapped out of it.

"Home about six, might barbeque for you tonight," Jolene said.
Fletcher said, "Jolene, never been able to say 'no' to you..."

"Never asked you to do anything you didn't want to say 'yes' to."

"Why we get along, I suppose," Fletcher agreed.

"Get along? I get along all by myself out on a trail ride. But a
man like you can put a little spark in the end of a day." She'd earned
more than her fair share of Fletcher's affections. Jolene took a big
breath. Fletcher let off the musk of dust and sweat. It had a way of
reminding Jolene what is right and good about having a man in her
life.

"I'll see you," Fletcher said jiggering his bushy eyebrows smiling
easy.

Jolene was lost looking at the hair on Fletcher's arm. It was dark
and lot of it. Could have skipped work and been six right now and
that would have suited Jolene fine. Shook her flourishing blonde
hair, tried getting her mind back from elsewhere. Jolene had full lips
and smacked them. She giggled and took off.

He kept looking in Jolene's direction as she caught up with her
girlfriends. Fletcher seemed to spend most of his free time in town
looking at the back end of one girlfriend or another.

Jolene turned around. Sharlene turned too, then Tallula, Bunny,
Sissy and Faith. They all waved.

Glenna paused next to Fletcher. "Squeezing Jolene in tonight?"

"Got a hole in my schedule somewhere for you..." Fletcher said.

Glenna wasn't having any of it, "Oh, I don't think so, Fletcher
McCrea."

"Could be fun."

"I'm afraid that high note you're looking to hit with me would
be my low note."

"Glenna," Fletcher admonished, "I'm not made that way."

"Well that's why we teach a man like you what to do." Glenna
had a false smile on her face.

"Going all in, with all you got with a turquoise miner? Sounds unnatural, a kind of thing just can't happen."

"That's why I don't have a turquoise miner in my life..." Glenna headed back to work. She knew full well if she turned around Fletcher would be contemplating the gifts of those parts of her that he would never be allowed to have. Glenna stopped in her tracks, didn't turn around. She said, "Would you mind, Fletcher, keeping your eyes to yourself?"

"Sure hard to get upset about what I'm missing, if I don't get myself worked up with a good eyeful of it," Fletcher said.

Glenna had her back to Fletcher. She was shaking her head back and forth.

"You're wiggling the wrong part," he chided.

Fletcher McCrea could be so perturbing. Romance in Nevada was a seldom encounter.

Keefe came out front with a sack. Keefe surmised that the two of them were in the middle of the same thing they were always in the middle of.

"You annoying Glenna again...?" Keefe said.

"It seems to be a god-given gift of mine," Fletcher replied. "Gage hook you up?"

"Going to need chest x-ray and aspirin when it's all said and done."

Keefe was watching Glenna walking off. "Only woman in town hasn't given you a shot."

"Suppose every town's gotta have one."

"Makes you kind of wonder, doesn't she?"

"Wonder what?"

"Which one of you is going to give up before the other one gives in?"

Fletcher McCrea and Keefe Kenny had spent the better part of the last decade standing out front of the General Store. Every now and again they'd be in a hurry. Most days they took their time, mull things over, come up with brand spanking new answers to some of life's oldest questions. One of the advantages of living nowhere was there was nothing much to do and so instead you could sop up time going about things at your own pace.

About three quarters of a block down on the other side of the street a woman came walking out of an alleyway right at the edge of the fairgrounds. Keefe found that she commanded his attention. She had an athletic long gated stride, shoulders broad, fine-spun neck, regal chin, a great shock of brown curly hair. Boot heels cut a line to her legs that aroused his carnal curiosities. Seemed to have her belt snugged tight, her pace was feisty, her frame sinewy. She was plenty buxom to Keefe's eye. There was more than enough woman, a veritable bouquet...a banquet...feast to last an eternity. It wasn't normal how he felt. He was hallucinating all manner of gymnastics he'd like to perform right there on the front steps of the General Store. That woman gave the man goose bumps from fifty yards off. His heart was racing. Keefe rubbed his eyes, tried to break the spell. Was a demon set loose inside his mind, a hormonal intoxication, spine stiffened, hair stood on end, and it goes without saying his other most anatomically useful lovemaking body part hidden beneath the buttons on his denims was in full bloom.

"Now, that is my idea of a woman."

Fletcher squinted. He was at a loss for words.

"You slept with her yet?"

Fletcher spit back the answer quick, "No, never, wouldn't, couldn't do that."

"...she from here?"

"Oh, yeah..." Fletcher said.

"That's best god damn news I've heard all day because that is the woman I want to get to know. I don't think I've ever seen anything shimmy so pretty in my entire life."

Blake coming into town down the Hot Spring Highway had been out for more speed trials in his sand rail. The exhaust note made a racket. He waved to the woman as he rolled down the main drag. She waved back. When he saw Fletcher and Keefe standing out on the sidewalk, he braked and pulled up in front of the General Store.

Keefe stepped down off the walkway and approached Blake, "You know that woman?"

Blake was unfastening his harness. He found Keefe's question stunned, "Yeah, I know that woman." He looked at Fletcher, "Everybody knows that woman."

"Everybody?" Keefe looked back at Fletcher, "Why don't I know her?"

Fletcher looked at Blake. They seemed confused. "You know that woman." Fletcher confessed.

"I do? Well that's good, because I'd like to know her better."

"I don't believe that's likely to happen," Fletcher said.

"Why's that? She married?"

"No, Mr. Kenny, that is Hazel; she's divorced," Blake explained.

"Divorced?" Keefe asked Fletcher.

"And that woman there," Fletcher explained, "is the woman who divorced you."

"Why the hell don't I remember any of that?"

"Maybe we should go back over to the clinic have you see the doc. Might be he missed something." Fletcher grabbed Keefe's arm.

Keefe shook off Fletcher's grip. "Divorced? Did I do anything awful?" Keefe asked.

"You weren't any more awful than average; better at being married than a lot of men in this town."

"Well, isn't that just great? Of all the rotten luck, first day back out and I have to go and fall back in love with the woman I was already in love with."

"Might be when you get up close she might look awful."

"I don't think so, looks just about the way I want a woman to look. In fact she looks better than perfect."

"Keefe, wait a second, that's Hazel Harwood, that isn't likely to be a woman prone to changing her mind about things."

"I did."

"But something's wrong with you."

"Nothing's wrong. That's just about the best looking thing I've ever seen."

"We're taking you back to see the doc."

Keefe squinted his eyes, looked intent at the silhouette of the woman. "Hell, Fletcher, can't be anything wrong. I got more feelings of being alive inside wanting to come out than I ever knew."

"But, Keefe, if you don't remember Hazel, must be something serious, be like living with a jack-in-the-box, looking all sweet and sexy and then one day out pop all the old torments."

"Might be I'm remembering the best parts," Keefe said.

Fletcher warned him. "She's hard headed."

"So? The whole damn town is hard headed."

"She's a tough nut."

"I'm a nutcracker," Keefe said.

"That's I reckon more than just a challenge, that's an impossibility. Hazel's got more 'hell no' in her than all of us put together."

"Almost died twenty-four hours ago," Keefe said. "Looks like the gods have allowed me to live so I could fight another day."

"That will be a fight," Fletcher said.

"Might as well throw down for what I want."

"Soon as you get your wits back, this whole project will pass. You'll be okay. Just have to get a grip back on your true self."

"I'm feeling true to my true self right now! I plan to break that hard headed woman down." Keefe ran out into the middle of the street and shouted out, "Hazel Harwood! I aim to peel you like an apple and lick you like a lollypop."

Hazel froze in her tracks. She knew that voice. She slow turned and bent down picked up first thing she could find. It was a rock.

Keefe smiled and waved his arms wild like over his head.

She threw that rock at Keefe as hard as she could.

Keefe was so excited that she'd noticed him. "Isn't she something. . .?"

chapter

THREE

Babbling waters tumbling over rock and cool predawn air smudged with the faint odor of sulfur greeted Sal and Mitzi as they arrived at 5:30 to turn on the working lights and get the day started at the Hot Spring Café. They brewed coffee, set tables, heated the grill, then opened the doors at six. Long haul line drivers who slept in the lower parking lot took breakfast here. Local ranch owners and wage help ate here too. By 7:00 Mitzi had poured coffee for her customers while her short order cook and husband, Sal, stood at his station shaking a skillet with one hand while poking the griddle with his spatula in the other.

Mitzi worked the café. She salt and peppered the tables with waitress banter. Everyone was called, "honey, sugar or darling..." She could be sharp tongued when need be, or smile away a whole world full of worries. She hustled, things got done, nobody waited;

coffee cups were kept full. Still, Keefe's condition was gnawing on her. She kept eyeing the bottle-cap shaped strawberry-soda-advertising wall clock. The customers stepped up on the porch with their boot heels clunking. The screen door opened with a squeak and a firm slap that was near impossible to sleep through. Mitzi was certain Keefe should've been down in the kitchen at his desk by now. Something had to be wrong.

She knocked at his door. "...you still asleep in there?"

"Come on in, Mitzi, nothing you haven't seen before."

She offered a mug of coffee to her boss, placed her hand on his head checking for a fever.

Keefe sipped his coffee. He allowed her fussing.

Blake was in his swimsuit standing on the three meter diving board. He stepped first with his right foot, then left, right, left and thrust his right knee up while swinging his arms above his head gathering his leap upward and then landing both feet onto the tip of the springboard. There was a distinctive *boing* as his weight first compressed the diving board and then once airborne the board *rattled* while Blake executed a one and one-half summersault forward dive

Keefe was in bed looking at Mitzi when Blake hit the water. His blue eyes grew wide. He got a smile on his face. He ran his fingers through his hair. He threw his blankets off.

"Mr. Kenny, please..."

"Well," Keefe bowed rather formally. He was wearing underwear, clad in boxers, bright sky blue. The old woman was shaking her head. He clasped Mitzi's hand, slid his other arm around her waist and began rocking back and forth suggesting the rhythm of a two-step, grinning and flashing his eyes into Mitzi's, "And away we go..." They danced.

"Mr. Kenny, there is something wrong with you..."

"Mitzi, there's something right with me, something fantastic, incredible..."

"I've never danced with you at daybreak. You don't most times want to dance at all."

"Well, Mitzi, things are going to change; life will never be the same again."

Keefe ceased the country dancing. He stood back and bowed.

He grabbed his white terry cloth bathrobe. He cinched it up tight. Keefe walked over to the double doors to the balcony that overlooked the hot springs pools. He turned around and looked at Mitzi, "Don't know if I'm going to believe my eyes."

Keefe opened the doors and the sun poured in; the light of day was in full bloom. "My god, it's our new world, Mitzi; come here, look!"

Blake had climbed back up atop the diving board. He turned when he heard the balcony doors swing open. He waved to Keefe, then put his game face back on as he prepared for his next dive. Steam was coming off the surface of the pools. Keefe had believed he'd never live to see this day.

"Mr. Kenny, the gods must have changed their mind."

"…About what?"

"About whether you should live or die."

"Mitzi, I'm not ready to die."

"But something's wrong; you're not the same man."

"Nothing's the same; whole world's changed." Keefe hugged Mitzi; gave her a forceful squeeze.

She found his whole manner unexpected. "See what I mean, Mr. Kenny. You don't go around hugging people. Nothing like the man I know."

Keefe squeezed her hands. "Mitzi, go on, I've got a hunger for life so strong it's making my stomach growl." He looked at her, this time with a mock stern expression on his face. "Come on, Mitzi."

"But, Mr. Kenny, something's off; you're all hot chocolate and whipped cream, bright eyed and the whole world's yours. You're just naturally a more miserable man; nothing ever seems to work out for you."

When Mitzi turned to leave, Keefe couldn't help give her bottom a puckish swat.

"Mr. Kenny!"

"Sal's a lucky man."

Mitzi looked troubled.

She had that Teutonic talent of self-regulation. Then a smile melted over her face, she tugged on the shoulder straps of her brassiere, "My husband is a lucky man and I am a happy woman."

What Keefe smelled was a new day dawning with the stink of sulphur mixed with a hint of sage. He put his pants on, pulled a t-shirt over his head, stuck a toothbrush in his mouth and went back out onto the balcony. Blake waved to Mr. Kenny, then turned and focused on the tip of the diving board.

Keefe's world had a brand new baby girl, an infant miracle. He'd drilled with the notion that he'd engineer an increase, but the scale of his discovery against the backdrop of the Great Basin framed a vision that burst out bigger than the desert it was set upon.

Keefe came in the back door to the kitchen downstairs and poured a cup of coffee. Sal had an order of pancakes up. He was whisking a bowl of scratch made buttermilk batter then poured it onto the griddle.

"Morning, boss. You're sleeping in; you must have met a señorita," Sal said.

Keefe glanced through the slot into the dining room. "...Slept like a man that didn't have a thing to worry about."

"You got nothing but problems, boss. Hard to know where to even begin."

"Aren't you cheerful?" Keefe said.

"The thing about living half-way between heaven and hell, there's not a damn thing anyone can do about anything."

"Sal," Keefe said, "you sure I'm paying you enough?"

"Hell will freeze over before you'll ever give me a raise."

"What would you do with all that extra money?" Keefe deadpanned.

"Boss, between you and me, let's face it, you're flat broke." Sal was serious, and then smiled, "but no matter, I got to resent something while I'm slaving over this grill."

"Are you picking on me, Sal?"

"Not picking, I'm including..."

"Remind me, why don't I fire you?"

"Because nobody else will put up with you."

"Keep yapping, Sal, might just get a notion to put that up to a test."

"A test... You're self-centered, get angry, yell, never close doors, don't seem to find much of anything that makes you happy. Hell, you don't listen to nobody about nothing; got more problems than most and almost nothing about you that anyone thinks they can make a friend out of."

"Aren't you a sweet talker..." Keefe was looking dead into Sal's tirade.

"Boss, sometimes I think it might just be me making things up," Sal tap-tapped his steel spatula against the grill.

"Making things up?" Keefe said.

"Yeah, but then it hits me like a bull."

"What's that?"

"What a king-sized pain in the ass you really are," Sal was deadpan. He waited. Keefe's hold on stoic gave way to shaking his head, his chest twitching; he was squelching his laugh.

"Why I work for you... See that? A man that won't run from the truth is worth something." Sal poked his boss in the gut with his spatula.

Mitzi was refilling a customer's coffee cup. She kept looking out the café windows keeping an eye on Blake. He was diving alone. It worried her.

Keefe was clad head to toe in denim, long sleeved faded shirt and jeans; had a thin frame, near six feet tall. His long brown hair was in retreat and graying.

Sal had two eggs 'over easy' ready. Toaster popped and he put two slices on a plate. Sal slid his spatula under the eggs, scooped them up and set them next to the toast. The bald, grizzled short order cook handed Keefe his plate.

Blake had spent summers working for his uncle at Lava Hot Springs in Idaho. That's where he'd learned to dive. He was the one talked Mr. Kenny into installing the diving boards. One of the few times in Keefe's life he'd taken someone's advice; turned out to be a teenage boy's dream.

Mitzi came out onto the porch topped off Keefe's coffee. He was sopping up his eggs with his toast. "Blake ought to be careful," Mitzi said.

"You know how boys are always looking for something dangerous to do."

"Life's dangerous enough without looking for extra."

"Mitzi," Keefe shoved the last of his toast in his mouth, "the taste of danger puts a whole new wrinkle on a young man's life." Keefe walked off the porch toward the pools. "You're going to Las Vegas noon today?" He asked Blake.

"Picking up two couples," Blake was toweling his face dry.

"Try not to scare the pants off our guests." Keefe was waiting for Blake to acknowledge him.

"Sure thing, Mr. Kenny."

"Like folk to arrive with something besides white knuckles and a red face."

Keefe pulled his soil stained deerskin gloves out of his rear pocket. He walked across the flagstone pathway toward the rental cabins.

"Morning," Keefe said.

"God, you scared me," Dusty replied as she came out the front door. "How are you, Mr. Kenny?"

"I don't have the whole of my life in front of me like you, but what I got left will do."

"You got a long life ahead," Dusty said, as she loaded sheets and towels into her arms.

"Got honeymooners coming in this afternoon."

"Newlyweds..." Dusty said, "vow your whole life away for two weeks of hot fun."

"You're not ready to settle down," Keefe said.

"Making love to the same person for rest of my life...?"

"Right partner makes a long day short and bad day easier to get over."

Dusty wasn't having any of it, "Only thing I've learned about getting married—that it will make a life seem long."

"...sweet little barrel racer like you...?" Keefe smiled. "Sal and Mitzi seem like they get along."

"But, Mr. Kenny, Sal's got one of those appetites..."

"Maybe, ...maybe Mitzi makes him hungry. They're all snarl and bark," Keefe said.

"Hottest tamale in Nevada's the one Mitzi teases out of Sal."

"It's the dance of love, Dusty."

"Sure does know how to push that man's buttons."

"You got to know how to start a fire and how to put one out."

"I give them their due. They got their game figured out. Most folk don't."

"Those two are fighting to sustain the biggest conflagration of all... lifelong love."

"I never had a man ever look at me the way Sal looks at Mitzi."

Keefe smiled, shook his head, "Don't know what it is about geothermal waters. Might be we all need to go find that one fine day, when we bring that sweet thing of ours here and take a little romp in the hay that's so good, it goes on to last forever." Keefe let his own words sink in. He concluded by saying, "Dusty, why I like my work."

"It's all birds and bees around here, Mr. Kenny."

"For some of us," Keefe turned and spotted Fletcher. He was standing on the porch in front of the café.

"Look there," Dusty said. "King bee for the whole of the county..."

"Next time you are out at the Brewery remind me to buy you a beer. Celebrate being alive. Maybe some cowboy might try to rope you in."

Dusty leaned against her broom, "Wouldn't mind a cute little saddle tramp drift through my life for a day or two. . ."

Keefe walked back across the Navajo sandstone pathways. The lower pool had a long row of teak chaise lounges on both sides and at one end pairs of white painted Adirondack chairs.

". . .you going to work up on the mine today. . .?" Keefe asked.

Fletcher seemed tired, "Hell, Jolene wore me too thin."

Keefe and Fletcher eyed one another then laughed.

"Your friend, Mr. McCrea, ought to try making up his mind," Mitzi butted in. She was listening to the men from the other side of the café screen door.

"Mitzi, what kind of fun would that be?" Fletcher asked.

"Be the right kind of fun," Mitzi said shoving the screen open. "You're too busy having your kind of fun to see how many women you're making miserable."

"Oh, come on now. Must be something else you could improve around here." Fletcher shook his head. "Keefe tell you he's got his heart set on rekindling his relationship with Hazel?"

"You can't mean that, Mr. Kenny," Mitzi exclaimed. "Miss Harwood's just about the most headstrong person I've ever met, makes near impossible look like never going to happen."

"Doesn't matter," Fletcher said. "Tried talking him down but he's made up his mind. Mind still made up. Right, Keefe?"

"Was planning on going into town to try and find her come sunset."

"But, Mr. Kenny, Hazel Harwood hates your guts."

"She doesn't even know me." Keefe was smiling.

"Oh, I'm afraid she does," Fletcher said. "Keefe here seems to not remember her."

Mitzi was flustered, "Mr. Kenny, something's wrong with you. How can you not remember your ex-wife?"

"Might be because everything has changed; time to start my life all over," Keefe said. "Start from scratch."

Mitzi was anxious. "I think she'd sleep with Fletcher with her eyes wide open and the lights left on before she'd even let you talk to her again."

"Oh, come on, Mitzi, there could be worse things," Fletcher said.

Mitzi was concentrated on the problem, "She is determined. Once she set her mind to getting rid of you, Mr. Kenny, wasn't nothing nobody could do to change it."

"Did I try?" Keefe asked. First he looked at Mitzi, then a sorrow cracked the hope right off his face. He appealed to Fletcher. "I didn't try? I let the love of my life go? Didn't anyone have the sense to try to stop me?"

"Mr. Kenny, I tried to tell you."

"Well, my mind's made up," Keefe said.

"There's going to be hell and high water to pay." Mitzi was worried.

"Like rattlesnakes in courtship," Fletcher explained.

"Best thing ever happen to me was that blow to my head."

"But, Mr. Kenny, what you can't remember, she'll never forget." Mitzi was pleading.

"…Oh, you two. How awful can a husband be? Did I hit her?"

"Pushed her once," Fletcher said

"Cheat on her?"

"She cheated first," Mitzi said.

"Yell and argue?"

"Like it was a blood sport," Fletcher answered.

"We ever try to kill one another?"

"No," Fletcher said, "but come close."

"Mr. Kenny," Mitzi explained, "you forgot your wedding anniversaries, never got your wife or kids anything for their birthdays, didn't' even dance with one another."

"Why didn't someone slap me up the side of my head?"

Mitzi was frustrated. "Every time you tried holding a conversation with the woman seemed like it took the National Guard to calm things down between you two."

"I like my odds."

"How in the name of 'until death do us part' can you say you like those odds?" Mitzi asked.

"Sounds like I did everything wrong."

"Everything..." Mitzi agreed.

"Now that I got that out of my system, going to try doing it right."

"But you and Hazel been bad for each other so long, there's no way she'll ever come to believe you could ever be good for her again."

"By the time I get done, that woman isn't going to know what hit her."

"She will never give in."

"And I'll never give up."

"Why the hell didn't you do that in the first place?" Fletcher asked.

"My marriage was a dress rehearsal. Then I got conked on the head and rehearsal's over and the show's opening. I'm going out on the road...got two stars in it, me and Hazel Harwood."

Fletcher shook his head. "Going to be a long spring and miserable summer..."

"Just so long as you accept that no matter how hard you try, might be that it may never ever come true." Mitzi was serious.

"She got a boyfriend?"

"A guy named Ranger."

"Ranger...? What in the hell kind of name is that for a boyfriend?"

"He beat out Buck, Duke and Major," Fletcher said. "It could've been a lot worse."

"We got family in town?"

"Father lives here, has nothing good to say about you," Mitzi warned.

"Because of how I treated his daughter...?"

"Not so much that," Fletcher said, "because you're a 'stinkin' liberal."

"Hates me for the way I vote?"

"He's in the tea party, more than hate..."

"Going to be a whole new world by the time I get done here..."

"What do you think, Mitzi, a hundred to one?" Fletcher asked.

"A ghost of a chance, there's not a prayer written that will change that woman's mind."

"Never liked easy love anyway," Keefe said.

"Going to need a Nevada-sized miracle."

"I'm a big believer in dreams," Keefe said. "Aim to tree that woman..."

Fletcher said, "...and the father-in-law is probably planning to hang you from it..."

"Didn't know loving someone was a hanging offense..."

"Chamber folk are already plenty upset."

"I'm planning on starting 'naked night' out here at the hot spring..."

"'Naked night'...?" Mitzi could not believe her ears.

"Hell yeah, that will wake folk up..."

"You're talking about turning this into some kind of nudist colony?"

"No, folk like soaking in the mineral pools dressed just the way they first arrived here on earth."

"You're turning this whole resort into some kind of biology class." Mitzi was beyond exasperated.

"Hell I am. This is Nevada; do what you damn well please... we're going to find out what these libertarians are made of..."

"They're talking about economic liberty," Fletcher explained.

"Well, good, then I'll charge them double..."

"People are pretty moral around here..."

"Hell they are. Nothing but brothels, polygamists and deer poachers far as the eye can see."

"People are going to push back hard."

"Going to be the good life; honeymoon suites, 'naked night.' Hell, might just be what Meadowhawk needs, could be medicinal, restorative, cure folks of their curiosities, put a spring in their step, a spark in their eye..."

"Mitzi," Fletcher said, "things are going to be different out here."

"Suppose I'm finally going to find out what all those women you sleep with are all fighting over," Mitzi said.

"See what I mean," Keefe was winning the day, "...makes things interesting."

"You think looking at my private parts is going to teach you something you didn't already know?"

"I'm putting the finishing touches on my higher education," Mitzi said. "Suppose if you live long enough, you end up seeing everything. Never thought I'd be in my 80's and last thing I'd be looking at is Fletcher McCrea's big old..." she paused.

"You don't have to look, Mitzi," Keefe said. "You and Sal could just soak."

"There are two things a woman should never ever do: trust a man with another woman, and not take the opportunity to get a good look at the reason why."

chapter

FOUR

"Come on," Gage urged, "can't wait all night." Proprietor of the General Store said to Keefe, "We're full up; town hall's just about underway."

There wasn't a parking place within two blocks of the General Store.

"Looks like the whole county showed up," Keefe smiled. "You and Dotty are going to do some business tonight."

A block down Gage could see Glenna Goddard. The distinguished Garrett Harwood, President of the Chamber of Commerce, was walking with her.

"Haven't seen you at the Brewery," Garrett said.

Glenna was dressed in a turquoise, gray and white plaid, pearl-snap-button western shirt. Broad cut shoulders accented the snug fit at her waist; made an impression on a man. Garrett was the elder in the community. He stood upright, with white hair and a noble gate to his stride. Garrett and Glenna were both fitted out in denim jeans, silver-buckled western belts and fine leather boots. Her hair was more or less still brown with long streaks of gray coming off her temples.

Garrett stooped down and picked up a candy wrapper. He couldn't help finding himself feeling the pull the way Glenna's full figure filled out her jeans. He wadded up the wrapper in his hand. Wasn't any use. Garrett tossed the scrap into a trash bin in front of the entrance to town's one and only casino.

Glenna was sophisticated enough to appeal to an older man and attractive enough to turn a younger man's head. She'd set her boundaries years ago. She'd play along, but she wasn't inclined to go along, not no more.

"Just might ask you for a dance next time the band's playing," Garrett said.

Glenna was easy, "Always have enjoyed a dance with you, Garrett." And that's as far as it ever went.

In the center of the first floor at the General Store an oak-planked cover was folded back laying bare a ten foot wide stairway, it was how the town's citizens entered their community meeting room.

Keefe tapped Blake atop his head as he descended the steps into the hall. The false floor wasn't any kind of secret. It was once used as an alibi to cover for a sheriff who'd been inclined to look the other way back in the days during prohibition.

Fletcher had saved Keefe a place. Faith, one of his lady friends, was waving from across the aisle. She was all cheekbones, long drooping beaded pierced earrings and glamour magazine eyeliner. Then there was the matter of her hifalutin bust she'd swaddled with some kind of extra tight brassiere, intentionally designed to send her breasts leaping out of the top of her low cut sweater. It wasn't fair what she was doing. Faith had arranged herself special tonight so as to stir a man up. She was going to have a beer with Fletcher after the town meeting, and then home to her place where she had promised he would have privileges to certain buttons, snaps and zippers that would free a path into the wilds of her feral frontier. Fletcher McCrea was a brave man.

"Evening, everyone," Dotty said as she banged the gavel at the podium. "We'll bring this meeting to order."

Room of 200 people didn't settle right off. Dotty banged the gavel once more, "Come on, people, a little respect..." She smiled at her speakers who were coming forward and then shook her head scowling at all the talkers in the crowd. "Come on, common courtesy, people, give these good citizens your attention."

Gig and Elena operated the Italian bakery. Gig took hold of the microphone, bent the neck of it up to his height, "We want to welcome you all here tonight. Good to see so many of you." Gig was bald, had a dark complexion, face was smooth, had a dashing thin black and gray mustache. "Settle in, folks. We've got a number of items on tonight's agenda."

Chamber members all sat up front on the left side of the audience. The men were part of the white straw Stetson crowd.

Mr. Garrett Harwood and Glenna Goddard were last to arrive walking down the staircase. Garrett was wearing the fanciest western hat in the crowd. He somehow set his hat upon his head in a manner that appeared more imperial than the ordinary folk.

Discussions had started. The agenda included sidewalk improvements, state highway department's new snow emergency equipment, coyote in the area hunting house cats, and the town's regulations regarding free roaming chickens. They disposed of these items one by one.

Next, Gig looked at Elena then paused holding a dignified patience out over the room as the assembled community came back to order again. "At the fair convention we had our usual breakout meetings. A state government official was there. Long and short of it was that the state cut the county fair money clear out of the state budget."

Rory, the Brewery's proprietor, was also the town's part time mayor, a ceremonial position only. Meadowhawk was otherwise ruled unanimously by passion. The mayor raised his hand, got up off his seat. He waited a moment until the distraction of Garrett and Glenna settled down. Rory was once a redhead now gray, bald, full beard, he sported a gut, but it was an acceptable gut appropriate to his station in life. He said, "Doesn't make even a dime's worth of sense. Who bought those boys' votes? That's what I want to know."

Gyles, seated with the Chamber, stood to rebut, "Nobody's buying anybody anything. Government's trying to stop spending money it don't have."

Fletcher stood. "Hell, everybody that lives in Nevada is paying somebody something. We all came here so we could live free to be as stupid, stubborn and butt ugly as we please. But fact is, shutting down the fair hurts everything we're trying to do."

Garrett Harwood upon hearing Fletcher McCrea's voice raised his hand to speak.

Gig ignored Garrett for the moment and continued, "This is the last fair we got a budget for."

Gage asked, "Then what do we do?"

"What we called the meeting for." Gig looked toward his wife, Elena.

He stood away and Elena stood behind the podium. "Plan is to try to come up with a plan," Elena said. "Biggest problem is all the buildings on the fairgrounds. That's one thing we'll have to deal with. Got a hundred problems to sort out."

Fletcher asked, "How long can we defer maintenance, while we try and figure out which way to go?"

Elena turned and looked at Gig as he approached the mike, "Nothing's going to fall down," Elena winked then added, "except for a few of you men coming home too late for your own good."

Women from the Award Ribbon Factory were seated together. Faith stood to speak. She was all aglow in red lipstick and her Fletcher McCrea attention grabbing outfit. "I don't know about you, but we got to figure something out. Me, Sharlene, Bunny and Sissy, we all want to volunteer and work with the committee."

There was not a grown man in that room that didn't all of sudden believe being on that committee to save the fair could be the most important civic duty they might ever volunteer for.

Garrett Harwood stood up again to address the podium, "Got Otto, Saxby and Rigg available." Garrett turned to appeal to the community, "might be nothing can be done. Fairs might just have to go the way of the horse buggy whip."

"Fairs about the only clean fun thing we do here," Rory said.

Keefe met Fletcher eye to eye.

"Let's take a vote," Gig said, "How many folk want to figure out some way to keep the fair going?"

What seemed like the whole room raised their hands. Those that didn't were seated near the crowd from the Chamber of Commerce.

Garrett Harwood stood up, "Look, the state's out of money. We're going to have to tighten our belts just like any ordinary family needs to do."

Fletcher stood. "That's a big old stew of horse apples and burro dung, nothing to do with what we need to do. We form a committee. We make a plan. We go to Carson City, put the fear of God in our representatives; that's only thing they know. We make them believe they're losing their jobs and they'll make the right vote."

"People in Nevada don't want their taxes going up," one member of the Chamber claimed.

"And folk don't want their fair shut down," Fletcher shot back.

"You'll just run these companies right out of Nevada," another Chamber member said.

"Good, make more room for little guys."

"The little guy isn't the future," Garrett shot back.

Keefe leaped up from his seat. "Everybody here is that little guy, and the little guy's future includes a county fair."

Faith whispered to Sissy, "Honey the cows are about to come home."

Garrett didn't say a word. He was up on his feet motionless, waiting for Keefe's next move. Garrett waited. He'd heard about all he had stomach for.

Keefe continued, "Most all of you know I took a good hit to my head this week, knocked some sense into me." Keefe spoke making eye contact with the whole room. "And I'm a new man. I'm not inclined to just get along anymore."

"Don't believe this town's got to take advice from a man not in his right mind," Garrett replied.

"Think you got the best prayers, right answers to things?" Keefe asked.

"Wasn't aware that you even knew how to pray."

"I'm in touch with the higher powers. Whatever it is conked me on the head kind of cleared my mind, clutter's all gone, see right through things."

"We all know how powerful your penetrating thinking can be," Mr. Harwood said.

"If I recall, it was the Chamber lobbied to sell our water supply to a private company out of Las Vegas, said it would be the best thing we could do. Got rid of our school buses, said it was going to save us all kinds of money. Go up and down the street, not a thing you said we should do turned out in our favor, not one."

"Private sector where these things belong."

"Well, better put your spurs into that idea. Flog that horse. Because best I can tell, this town is tired of being stampeded by the Chamber."

"Don't know anyone here thinks we need bigger government, more regulation or higher taxes."

"If you don't want to save the fair, why should we have you tangled up in the committee trying to do that?"

Another Chamber type stood; it was Gyles again. "We got same rights as everyone here; we ought to be part of the committee."

"We all got rights here," Keefe said, "but some of us got the right convictions for the job."

"We know our way around Carson City."

"And I know my way around a dance floor," Fletcher said, "but that gets me a dance, doesn't save me a fairground."

Gig broke into the back and forth, "We got everyone here agreeing we need to do something."

Gyles said, "Something needs to be done."

"Ask one more time? How many of you want to save the fair?"

Again most hands in the community hall went up.

"Looks to me like most folk want the fair saved."

"Gig!" Garrett Harwood stared with a fiery gaze at the meeting's moderator.

"Mr. Harwood," Gig said smacking the gavel down on the podium, "you can take your seat."

The Chamber's President was not in the habit of being on the losing end of a town meeting. It rubbed his nerves raw. He looked around the room as if he were memorizing the faces of the citizens who had dared to go up against what the Chamber deemed best.

"Mighty proud of you," Fletcher said to Keefe.

"Kind of surprised myself," Keefe replied. "Not going to be too happy when I walk that daughter of his down the aisle again."

"Be a snow storm in July before that happens."

Gig continued from the podium. "We want a committee devoted to saving the fair." Gig lifted his gavel pounded the lectern and pronounced, "We'll appoint you Chamber folk to an advisory group, get to have your full say, but we're sending a committee to Carson City, and they're going to be of one mind, determined to restore funding for the fair." Gig was resolute. "Just the way it is." Gig pounded the gavel once more, "God Bless America, pray the devil stops cursing Nevada. We'll see you all at the Brewery." He banged his gavel one last time, "This meeting's adjourned!"

Glenna Goddard stood. She tried not to appear too pleased. She walked back to speak to Keefe; she all but ignored Fletcher, "Why are you picking a fight with the Chamber?"

"…Just standing up to the man," Keefe said.

"We usually go around him instead of through him," Glenna said.

"Well, it's a new day for Meadowhawk," Fletcher said cocking his chin high.

Faith had joined their knot of conversation. She put her arm around Fletcher's waist. Glenna found Faith's pliability pitiful. Jolene didn't seem to mind; she and the other women knew Faith had dibs on Fletcher for the night.

"You are a man with a newfound voice," Glenna said to Keefe. "Sure didn't take long for you to speak your mind."

"Seems to come natural, feel like I own this place. Like it's home. And if it is, we don't tear it down, we fix it, put a coat of paint on her, water the trees, make a life right here."

Keefe kept looking around as everyone filed up the stairs out of the basement. "Thought Hazel might show her face tonight."

"Hazel? She won't be in attendance at any meeting you might be coming to," Faith said.

"Well, that can't be any fun," Keefe said.

"More fun than cussing you out," Faith replied.

"Pretty thing like that?" Keefe acted surprised.

"Hazel's not a pretty thing; she's your ex-wife," Glenna said.

"Not according to my recollection, she's brand new, prettiest woman I've ever laid eyes on."

"Keefe's head has still got him all mixed up," Fletcher said.

"Could be, maybe set me right..." Keefe said. "I'd kind of like to take a shot at that Harwood woman."

Glenna shook her head, she asked, "Why is it a man seems to always want the one thing he's never going to ever have?"

"Never believe a man when he claims to be happy with what he's got," Fletcher said. "That's a married man talking."

"You are more load than a mule could ever hope to haul," Glenna said.

"Glenna Goddard," Faith was sure, "Fletcher's a peach."

"Keefe," Glenna said, "walk me to the Brewery." She wasn't having any of it.

Keefe put his hands out and held onto Fletcher and Faith's arms, "I'm going to win that woman same as Fletcher McCrea's going to win you tonight."

"I'm fond of your friend," Faith said. "I like how he gets all worked up about things when I put my fancy clothes on for him."

Keefe couldn't help himself. "Way you're all squeezed together kind of kicks up dust in every man here. Have to get a grip on ourselves. There's only one Fletcher McCrea and then there's the rest of us left to wonder, what in the world would a woman like you do to a man like us."

Glenna tugged on Keefe's arm, "You coming? I want to swill beer, not this nonsense."

Fletcher's smile beamed wide. "You're getting yourself all worked up. It's like being at a church that doesn't practice forgiveness."

Glenna hollowed out her smile, "I try to fight it. Just so you know." She turned and started walking away with Keefe. "I ask the dear lord every day," she turned and grabbed hold of Keefe's shoulders and said, "because he knows I got it in for some and not for others. My maker said that it's just not fair, and that's exactly what I told him. It's just not fair." Glenna turned and looked at Fletcher. "And that's why I can never forgive any man that's sleeping with all of my girlfriends; you see, Fletcher McCrea, the reason being that I could never forgive myself, if I allowed you to do to me what you do to the women I call my friends."

Faith and Glenna exchanged scolds. Fletcher, proud of who he was, smiled. Keefe got hold of Glenna's arm and hauled her off toward the Brewery.

Blake had spent most of the meeting looking at the back of Lark's long black hair. He was out front on the walkway talking to some of his hot rod friends. Lark had come upstairs. She was wearing the tightest denim jeans she could squeeze into, borrowed them special from a girlfriend. She had on a white cotton shirt with pair of embroidered red roses, one on each side, gold hoop earrings hung down to and tips touched her shoulders, her dark straight hair all brushed out dangling down her back near all the way to one of the prettiest places any man might hope to set his eyes upon. Lark's figure triggered a fire brigade of desperation in a young man unable to find the means to do a thing about such human physical wonders. Blake shot a glance at Lark then averted his eyes. He was desperate to say "good evening," but could not even risk a smile. Lark knew he'd lose his gumption. His other friends were all knotted up the same. From the direction she was walking, Blake knew she was headed home.

Fletcher had his arm around Faith. He spied the whole thing. Lark's boots murmured crushed hopes against the sidewalk. It was a warm piney and sagebrush scented spring night and one more day in her life she still hadn't been able to put a stop to being alone.

"Blake?" Fletcher inhaled the fine night air. He tried to choose his words so as not to embarrass the young man, "Mighty fine night for a slow walk."

Blake had his game face on, but just below that mask was a stomach running amuck.

Faith got her arm around Fletcher's waist tugged on his belt loop, "Come on, Fletcher, buy me a beer, take me home."

"I got plans, Mr. McCrea," Blake replied.

"Faith," Fletcher asked, "you think Blake's handsome?"

The young man swung his head away, "Come on, Mr. McCrea."

Faith said, "A prized pick of the young men..."

"See that?" Fletcher said. "How about smart?"

"Its' common knowledge he can fix anything; got to be smart to do that."

"See that, handsome, smart... What about brave? Think he's got any courage?"

"Drives like he does," Faith said.

"...Almost got it all. The only thing missing is the guts to take that slow walk." Fletcher put his palm out and pressed against Blake's back. Blake started to straggle down the street.

Lark's walking away was tattering Fletcher's patience. Blake lacked the self-confidence to interpret that Lark had done some considering since speaking to Fletcher. She was calling Blake out. The time for doing nothing was over. She was going to lure this young man into her life.

"Have to walk faster than that," Fletcher said.

Faith asked, "What's that all about?"

Fletcher smiled; put his hand down on Faith's fanny and rubbed it with seasoned tenderness. "Same thing it's always about."

chapter

FIVE

Glenna and Keefe closed the Brewery. They zigzagged along the abandoned sidewalks back toward the General Store. They wandered beneath a night sky making room for the bloom of a cracking new day. Keefe sunk his fingers into his jean pockets, leaned back on his heels, shook his head and sucked the night air in through his nose. He could not take in enough of the surrounding thrall.

Keefe squeezed between Glenna's 1969 Ford station wagon and his 1967 Ford pickup. He pulled a canvas tarp back toward the tailgate. He climbed up onto the rail and hopped down into his bed, his truck bed.

"Keefe," Glenna looking up and down the street said, "what are you doing?"

"Got a sky choked with stars." Keefe swept his hand overhead. "Not a better place to dream great big Great Basin dreams."

Glenna leaned over the side of the truck bed. She wanted a first-hand look. Beneath the tarp free of dust, Keefe had thrown a mattress and bedding into the Ford. "Don't you want to sleep in your own bed?"

"This is my own bed, favorite one."

"If you like it that much, might as well bring it with you," Glenna teased.

"Good bunk in the back of a truck is my idea of fun…"

Might be that Keefe was acting more erratic now, but by nature a hot spring proprietor comes 'dropped on his head hard wired' from the beginning. It is the nature of the beast.

"Hop on up, put your head on a pillow… make a wish," Keefe said flaring his eyebrows with mischief.

"I can't climb into bed with you! Smack dab in the middle of Main Street?"

"Oh, for god sakes, Glenna," Keefe said. "I don't bite." He slapped the bed next to him with his hand. "Do some stargazing. Make a wish. All you're going to do is go home, brush your teeth, put on your pajamas and stare at a ceiling."

"Keefe Kenny, if the sheriff comes by and you get me into trouble…" She tipped her head to the side looking for some reason to see the truth in what he'd said.

"Wishing on a star isn't a crime."

"Making impossible wishes that never come true could be."

"Glenna, I've got my hand on a whole lifetime of ambitions I know I can make come true…"

Glenna climbed up onto the step bumper, "Lucky me, I've got a lifetime to regret doing this…" She stepped over the tailgate, turned and sat down.

"Kick those cowgirl boots off, set those toes free, make your feet at home and the rest of yourself can't help but follow." Keefe was grinning wide. He had swayed Glenna against her better judgment.

"See that, looking more like a woman taking charge of her fate already."

"Why don't men know when to shut-up?"

"Looking right into the center of the Milky Way..." Keefe turned his head, sniffed the air between them, Glenna's scent was doused in lavender. "Smell like some kind of fancy movie star..."

Glenna shot her elbow out into his side. "Save it for a girl who doesn't know better."

"Better spending it on someone who does," Keefe turned his head and tried stifling his laugh.

The star glow was more akin to a cloud than a pin of light. Keefe had a spiral galaxy fire in his eye and a beaming tooth-full grin on his face. He set his sights straight up into the heavens, never lost in his thoughts, aware that Glenna was next to him, still out of sorts, not yet settled.

"What are you looking for?" She asked.

"Looking at one hundred and forty billion reasons why I should be... right there, do you see it? Right in the middle of all those stars... right there, that's the woman I love..."

Glenna scanned the sky, looked toward Keefe. "I don't see anything but a star filled sky..."

Keefe slapped his chest with his palm, "I see her, same place she's always been, same place she'll always be."

"Big fat chance, hot springer; she'll never change her mind..."

Keefe rolled onto his side. "Look, if Hazel could love me once, then it must be proof she could love me again."

"Five years is a long time," Glenna said turning to look at Keefe, "She's torn down that bridge, and Hazel's not the kind to turn around and imagine that she'd ever be going back."

"We never get over someone." Keefe said rolling back to look up into the sky. "Might pretend there's no way back, but there's always a way. I figure she's ripe for the picking, and I aim to pick that woman right off her feet and throw her back into the cauldron of life."

Glenna turned and looked at Keefe. He was still gazing heavenward. "A man like you will have to do what a man has to do."

"Look, I don't remember what happened. I do know how I feel, and I got this thing trapped in my insides, and this feeling, it's stubborn as a stain, been made to work with her. She's the one woman in the wide world for me."

"You're going to need a better game than that," Glenna said.

"Then, that's what I'll go find. I know she's the mother of my two children. I know she is. And that counts for something. I've seen my life flash right in front of my eyes, and the one thing that flashed bigger than anything else was how I feel about Hazel Harwood..." Keefe was waiting for an answer that wasn't going to come. "Aren't we a pair, me in love with the same woman for the whole of my life and you can't seem to find anyone to fit the bill?"

"I came close; just never had the guts to jump in with both feet."

"Probably didn't even know what they had." Keefe said, "Might be, that you already know him; all you got to do is open the door and invite the man in."

"They'll fight all night trying to undo the buttons on my blouse. Sun comes up and whatever they were fighting for goes right out the window lost in the light."

Keefe rolled over on his side, propped his head up with his hand and sunk his elbow into his pillow. He rubbed Glenna's shoulder. He could feel her worries.

She looked at Keefe for a moment, then looked away. "More comfortable than I thought it would be," she said.

Keefe yawned, let off some tension; he was tired. His eyes were starting to close. Glenna pulled the blanket up. Keefe's eyes opened and he continued gazing at the sky.

"You're still in love with her," Glenna said.

Keefe's eyes fell shut again, "Feels more like some sort of mental illness."

Glenna's eyes fell closed too. She muttered, "It's never going to work."

Keefe's eyes were closed; he mumbled back, "I'm incurable."

"Feel sorry for you..." Glenna turned over on her side away from Keefe.

"No need. Man's got to do what a man's got to do." Keefe rolled over on his side and cuddled up with his bunkmate.

Glenna was almost asleep. Keefe slung his arm around her waist.

"You're a good man," Glenna said.

She pressed his arm in close. In the next breath Keefe fell asleep, and in the breath after that so too did his ex-wife's best friend.

Like clockwork, six in the morning, Elena would unlock the front door to the bakery. She would leave her loaves of bread baking in the ovens. Gig would remain in the kitchen to mix pastry batter while she stepped out front and swept down the front walkway.

Keefe's eyelids fluttered. The bakery's chimney stirred the liminal edges of his waking. The aroma of the baking bread dough addled his dreams. He pressed closer to Glenna. She was gone, out, breathing deep. They'd stayed up too late. It took a moment to put everything together; he glanced at his wristwatch. He sat up.

It startled Elena, "Keefe! Is something wrong?"

Keefe said. "I did some stargazing last night..." Glenna elbowed Keefe. She didn't want Elena knowing she was there. Keefe flinched. "Is Gig baking?"

"Like his life depended on it," Elena said, "come on in, I'll pour you a cup of coffee."

Glenna poked Keefe in the side again. When he glanced down, Glenna gestured with a finger across her lips for silence. She was desperate for him to get out of bed and go before she was found out.

"Do you want any coffee?" he asked Glenna.

She winced. Her eyes widened. She whispered, "...shush."

Elena stopped sweeping. "What's that, Keefe?"

Glenna pointed with her finger, grit her teeth, crossed her eyes.

Keefe pulled his boots on, "You and Gig get up early every day?"

Elena shook her head, "You don't even want to know..." Elena was younger than she appeared, like Dotty down at the General Store she was not so thin, gray. She waited gripping the broom in one hand, her other against the backside of her hip. "It's what we do."

"When do you two sleep?"

"...Sleep?" Elena giggled. "Not in any baker's life I know of..." she held the front door open for him, "let's get you a cup of coffee, getting to be a little long in the tooth to be closing the saloons down."

"Well, there was that," Keefe allowed, "I've been kind of unpredictable."

"Gig is unpredictable. You seem to be a man dancing to his better natures." She closed the door behind him. "Come on in back into the kitchen, say 'good morning'."

Gig holding a knife was lancing the tops and sifting flour over pastries he was preparing for the ovens on the maple-top work table. At hand were cooking sheets, pans, timers, measuring cups, whisks, spatulas, rolling pins, and mixing bowls.

"Good morning," Gig said plucking hold of a dish towel wiping his hands, then setting it down atop the very same place he'd picked it up from.

At the rear of the building their driver was pulling on a chain to hoist the roll up door. Loaves of bread were being readied for delivery.

"You make a lot of bread," Keefe said looking around the back room where they worked.

"Make it fresh every morning," Gig explained.

"Where's it go?"

"This goes to Ely," Elena said.

Keefe hadn't seen the back end of their operation before.

"How'd you land in Meadowhawk?"

"...Broke down here on vacation," Elena said.

"Stop..." Keefe didn't believe them.

"There was a bakery on every corner in Boston," Gig said.

"At least it seemed like it," Elena said.

"By the time Lou had fixed our car, said we could be on our way, it was too damn late." Gig laughed. "It was the biggest mistake of our lives."

"And the best thing to ever happen to us," Elena said.

Glenna waited. She was desperate not to be found out. She sat up. The sound of a truck coming into town from the Hot Spring Highway could be heard. She slunk back down on the mattress. She listened as a vehicle rolled down the street. The truck pulled up in front of the bakery. Glenna pulled the blanket over her head. The big diesel pickup truck motor made a racket.

Door opened. She heard Hazel's voice, "coffee, pastry, bread?"

"Coffee," the man replied. He remained in the truck, engine left running.

Hazel once on the sidewalk turned and looked up and down the block. Hazel didn't quite know what to make of Keefe's pickup and Glenna's station wagon parked out front. She didn't see Keefe through the windows inside the bakery. She was getting sick and tired of dodging him anyway.

A bronze bell on the door jingled announcing a customer had entered the shop. Keefe looked through the kitchen door window. He turned back toward Gig and Elena. Keefe grabbed hold of his head with both his hands. "...Oh my God...!" He stole a second peek through the window. Hazel was browsing the pastries in the display case. The same thing was happening to him as the day he got out of the clinic. Hazel's dark eyes were all full, part pretty, part eternity, lipstick and heartbreak, moody midnight walks and tingling sensations that shot up the back of his neck. Her face set upon him like the best day of his life. He became fixated upon her curly brown hair swirled up and sculpted into a shape and set in place with a turquoise and silver barrette. One more time, inches south of his belt buckle and right behind the buttons on his denim trousers, a kind of one man inmate riot of a prisoner sentenced to solitary confinement was attempting to breakout and escape into a favorite part of who he was.

"Give me your apron." In his eyes he had that spark of a prank playing boy. "I'll help her."

Elena peeked through the small window and surrendered her apron, protesting in a whisper, "Keefe, I don't think Hazel's going to want you helping her."

He was quick to put on the apron, seized Gig's baker's hat and set the rim square upon his head cocking the top off to one side. He winked at Elena, pressed down on his apron against his involuntary and out of his control private parts. He begged in a whisper for hope and asked, "...How do I look?"

"You look motivated," Gig knew he was before a man on a mission. He glanced at Elena, then looked back at Keefe and smiled. He pointed at the door, "Go on!"

Keefe pressed the swinging hinged door open and walked behind the pastry case. He stood in silence. Hazel was concentrating on the baked goods pointing to her selection. "Morning Gig, two coffees, ciabatta, pair of 'brioche'..."

Keefe's eyes took hold of Hazel's finger. That finger lured him deeper into a sea of human scented cravings he believed would never visit him in this life ever again. His mind went off into all that finger might mean, all the things that finger could do, how it was thin, the nail polished bright red, agile and steadfast, it could touch and hold, express desire, point to wishes, sensual and capable, it was Hazel's finger, the one finger in all of kingdom come, what a glory it would be to be touched by that finger again.

Keefe selected a loaf of bread and rattled the loaf into a jittering bag. Time felt like forever. When was she going to look up? He took waxed paper and plucked the two breakfast pastries into a smaller sack, walked to the end of the counter and stood at the cash register.

Hazel looked up. She lifted that finger, the one Keefe moments before had been enraptured with, and she pointed it at him, as if pointing to a criminal in a line-up. She spit out between her teeth, "...YOU!"

"Miss Harwood," Keefe smiled, "how are you this morning?"

Hazel dropped the coffees on the counter. She turned and retreated. Keefe chased her out the front door as she fled to Ranger's truck. Keefe pursued her holding out the pastries and bread.

Hazel hit the button to the electric window. Ranger got out of the truck on the driver's side.

Keefe froze dead in his tracks, "Ranger?" It was all a topsy-turvy dream. "You're going out with Ranger?" He'd known about Ranger, but that fact like so many things was misplaced in his mind.

Ranger came around the other side of the truck. "The lady doesn't have to speak to you."

Keefe wasn't feeling that another man had a right to explain Hazel to him, "I'll keep that in mind."

Gig and Elena had come outside. "You two boys, settle down," Elena pleaded.

"Ranger, you get back in your truck," Gig said.

Hazel was wild eyed. That finger pointed. She grabbed hold of the handle to the door. She banged on the dashboard with the palm of her other hand.

Ranger took hold of Keefe's arm and pulled him away from Hazel's door.

Keefe shook off his grip on his upper arm. "Get your hands off me."

Ranger got hold of Keefe's arm and pulled a second time. He sent him flying back against the rear of his own pickup truck.

Gig shouted, "Keefe! Hold your temper..."

Keefe was serene. "I got hold of every hair on my head." He kept his eyes on the other man. He waited.

Ranger was a big shot, told men what to do, hired and fired, accustomed to being in charge. He was a blue collar executive, three inches taller and twenty pounds heavier than Keefe. Drove a new truck and wore fine boots and fresh laundered shirts. He was a working man, plain short hair, an uncomplicated face.

Ranger reached out and tried to get a hold of Keefe's shirt collar.

Keefe, the quicker man, clasped hold of Ranger's wrist. "You shouldn't do that."

He swung Ranger's arm one way until the bigger man flexed his muscles and began to offer resistance and then like that Keefe spun him back the other way knocking him off balance. Using Ranger's own momentum, he tossed the man away. Ranger stumbled backwards against Keefe's pickup truck bed. Until now Ranger had not made a fist.

"First you start grabbing. Now you want a fist fight?" Keefe said.

Glenna tossed off her blanket and popped up behind Ranger and grabbed hold of his shoulders, "Ranger, you punch that man and me and a posse of women will hunt you down and scratch your eyes out..."

Hazel rolled her window down, "Glenna," infuriated she hopped out of the truck. "Are you having an affair with my ex-husband?"

Glenna spread her arms out, assuming being fully clothed was proof otherwise, "Do I look like I'm having an affair with your ex-husband?"

Everyone froze. Glenna looked quick, first to Elena, next to Hazel, then Gig, Keefe and last of all Ranger. "Please... You'd think you were talking to some teenage girl just out of her training bra."

Hazel looked down into the pickup truck bed. She sized things up, "You're making love to Keefe Kenny in the back of a pickup truck on Main Street?"

"Wish I had, might at least had the pleasure of doing something I've been falsely accused of."

Glenna hopped down onto the pavement. "Go on," she told Ranger, "...get back in your truck before you do something stupid. Acting dumb is dumb enough." Ranger didn't move, "Go on," she shoved Ranger. Glenna was steamed.

Elena got between the two women. "Go on, Hazel, get back in the truck."

Gig tried getting Glenna to back off too. "Come on, Glenna, easy does it."

"Easy does it?" Glenna shot back, "Hazel, what are you doing with this man?"

"I'm not sleeping with him in the back of pickup trucks."

Hazel had been a better cut of woman than Ranger had known. Glenna knew he was a class of man that had a habit of saying one thing and doing another.

"I know your kind, Ranger," Glenna said. "I know what hotels you stay in, where you drink, what time you go to bed, what time you get up."

"You're nothing but trouble, I don't ever want to speak to you again," Hazel said to Keefe, "every time I try being civil you just can't help ruining my day."

"I'm sorry, Hazel," Keefe said. "Sorry you gave up on me."

"You ought to do a better job of blaming yourself. Beats sleeping with my best friend in the back of a pickup truck out on Main Street."

"Hazel," Glenna said, "we weren't sleeping with one another."

"That's god's truth, we weren't sleeping with one another; we were just plain and simple sleeping. And that's all."

Hazel tapped the side of her head, "You're too full of yourself, Keefe. Idea hits you and next thing you know you're shooting off and taking the whole world with you, whether the people in your life want to go or not. I couldn't do that anymore." She turned her attention back to Glenna, "And I thought we were friends, thought you were on my side."

"I am on your side," Glenna said.

"Come on, Hazel," Gig approached. He stood in the middle of the arguing women. "Let it go..." He plucked his baker's hat off Keefe's head. "Please..."

Keefe unfastened the string he'd tied around his waist to hold his apron tight. He pulled the apron off and surrendered it to Elena.

"Hazel Harwood, I am sorry if I was too busy trying to make a living. Now I know that's only part of what a husband is supposed to do."

"Well, that other part was a flash in the pan."

"Well, I say something deep inside my soul has changed..."

"Call your son or daughter; share all that change with them."

Hazel got back into Ranger's truck. He put the truck into gear and began backing out of the diagonal parking space.

"Do I still have a job?" Glenna asked.

Hazel rolled her window down, "You still want a job?"

Glenna's pride swelled up, "...maybe..." she looked right through Hazel.

"Maybe...?" Hazel got wild eyed. "There's a maybe, and maybe never ever again."

"Guess we'll just have to see what we see," Glenna lifted her chin to add pride and backbone.

Ranger began to pull away then stopped dead in his tracks. A flock of sheep was headed toward them. Bambalina, Fletcher's burro, was in the lead, Bero and Mirari on horseback were just behind, then the two hundred sheep. Last was Fletcher in his International pickup truck, driving the rear of the flock to new pasture west of town. Bambalina by instinct was inclined to protect the herd. About the only thing she found more annoying than Fletcher were coyote.

Gage and Dotty came out onto the front of the General Store to watch the driving flock coming down the center of town. They waved good morning.

"Another beautiful dawning day in Meadowhawk," Fletcher said waving to the General Store proprietors.

Ranger rolled at a snail's pace toward the flock. He was taking Hazel to work come dust storm or sheep herd stampede. He was determined to drop her off. They forged halfhearted smiles, galled and annoyed, as the herders and flock surrounded the truck and drove past.

Bambalina gave Ranger a careful glare. Something about that man didn't sit right with her. Bero and Mirari, husband and wife, had their hands full with the flock and were oblivious to the circumstances.

Fletcher veered off to one side of Main Street and as the last of the sheep passed Ranger's rig he paused alongside. "Morning, Hazel," Fletcher knew right off how infuriated Hazel would be. "Have you ever seen a more beautiful daybreak?" He smiled trying to break the ice.

Hazel wasn't having any of it, "The best ones I've ever found are the sunrises you aren't in."

Fletcher shook his head and laughed. He looked out in front of the bakery, saw Gig, Elena, Glenna and Keefe standing in front. "Auspicious beginning to a whole new day," he laughed, "You know about the fairgrounds being closed?"

Ranger spoke up, "We heard."

"Did you?" Fletcher said laughing again. "Did you hear about Hazel's ex-husband getting blown up Monday?"

"Oh we heard that too," Ranger said

"He seems to have survived," Fletcher laughed. "Only thing is he's got this notion of winning Hazel back. Doesn't just want a date, wants the whole thing." Fletcher laughed so hard it hurt. "He's coming for you like a prize bull. Great big stubborn animal like that can get what it wants."

Hazel gave Fletcher that look, the one that burns right through a brash man's words. "Only bull is the one in his head, and bullheaded only takes you so far in life, until that's all that's left."

"Hazel, he's not headstrong. He's in love." Fletcher laughed harder.

"I hate you, Fletcher McCrea," Hazel said. "I never want to see your face again." She swung her head, Ranger pulled away.

Keefe and Glenna were standing dead still watching the whole encounter. They watched Ranger and Hazel roll off down Main Street toward Hazel's Award Ribbon Company.

"I didn't mean to get you into trouble," Keefe said to Glenna.

Fletcher had a big grin on his face. He waved to his friend as he rolled by. His hubris gored Glenna.

"He gets under your skin." Keefe said.

"Why Hazel and I get along so well, she can't stomach the look of you and I can't bear the sight of Fletcher McCrea."

"I'm sorry I got you into trouble," Keefe said.

"I'm sorry too." Glenna said. "I hate missing out on things I'm accused of doing, but never did."

"Might be you're right, maybe we ought to go over to your place and put some truth to Hazel's accusations."

"That's sweet of you, Keefe, but you know I kind of like you having strong feelings for Hazel, gives a girl hope, almost better than sex.

"What could be better than sex?"

She was looking at the tailgate to Fletcher's truck heading off out of town down the Hot Spring Highway. "Not giving any to Fletcher McCrea."

chapter

SIX

Keefe was pounding stakes into hard ground with a sledgehammer. A raven was twenty yards off hopping in the sagebrush hunting a cricket. Five miles up Pipe Dream Mountain Fletcher was underground at work freeing more turquoise from the earth's grip.

"Made lemonade for you," Jolene shouted into the mineshaft.

"Maybe... in... a... while..." Fletcher's voice echoed back.

Clark's Nutcrackers were flitting between the pinions and junipers. Bambalina was standing dead out asleep in her corral twitching her ears. How a burro does that remains a mystery. Fletcher tolerated Jolene doing chores when she came up to the mine. His bright blonde haired blue eyed lady friend had pulled the bedding and hung it on a clothes-line in the fresh air. She'd swept out the Airstream trailer, and then she sat out on a chair on the deck basking in the sunshine reading her romance novel.

A lurid story was a guilty pleasure; put her in a mood. She unbuttoned her blouse a notch further, let the sunlight shine on her
cleavage. Jolene read her book thinking she might learn a trick or
two. The mine was up at 7000 feet. Late spring had been bursting
wide. There were moist spots with grasses and sedges and fresh
blooms. Painted ladies, swallowtails and blue butterflies were on
wing flitting in the air. From up here Jolene could look out over
the valley and spot Keefe's place, then the Hot Spring Highway
and beyond, Meadowhawk.

Keefe on account of all the hot water he'd found had decided
time was right to put up the unused sections of his greenhouse.
He'd constructed one 24-foot section two years back. He had three
more same sized unused sections.

Keefe put his deerskin gloves on, took hold of the hickory handled sledge and used the whole of his upper torso to bring the head
of the tool down on the top of a new stake. He had broken into a
sweat. He removed his shirt and wiped the dust off his face with his
red paisley bandana. Days were growing stinking hot.

Mitzi had come out onto the front porch of the café. She would
never be caught dead without her mascara and eyeliner on. She
pinned her hair up neat. She wore glasses now, frameless, gold. She
was no young thing, but sketched out across the old woman were
the remnants of a fine figure. She cleaned off tables, poured coffee,
and swatted flies. She was as always on watch pretending to look
for things that needed doing, while in fact keeping her eye out for
what was really going on. She believed that there were things people
ought not to be doing. When she could, she tried to save the misguided from their weaker selves. It was a thankless task, but Mitzi
while not a church going woman tried as hard as any evangelical

Christian going door to door to help lead folk along the way to a better world.

It didn't take any time at all for Mitzi to see the short haired Dusty, the housekeeper, all smiles loading fresh linen onto her cart. Daytime hours the young woman dressed plain. Man had to look twice to notice things about her she didn't choose to feature until sun had set. She didn't need makeup. Had a chisel face, mischief in her eyes, brown in color, shoulders and hips strong enough to buck hay, keep up with any man. Up on higher ground a crackerjack well drilling crew had come in from Beowawe, Nevada. Must have been six big trucks parked up that hill and twice that many men in hardhats. It seemed that for every one man that worked it took two to think things through and one man more to finally decide. Still, you couldn't complain. This elite crew had succeeded where other men had failed in capping a geyser north of here. They had a proven record with geothermal wellheads. Dusty sorted the men according to age, physique and temperament. She selected from this rowdy and firm plentitude a bald square-jawed man for recreational romantic purposes. Mitzi knew which man Dusty would choose even before she picked him, how she'd bait the trap and where she'd take her prey after she got the man tangled in her web.

Mitzi walked down to the end of the porch where she could get a look at how things were progressing at the greenhouse. Blake was taking his shirt off. He was going to try his luck at pounding stakes with the boss. If not for Keefe's newfound sprightliness for life on earth, Blake, the younger man, ought to have been hired to do the whole job. As it stood, Blake was leaving for Las Vegas to shuttle guests to the resort. He would return with the newlyweds late this afternoon.

The men were between stakes. Strapped onto the rear of Keefe's pickup truck was a 5 gallon water jug filled with ice and fresh drawn spring water. Keefe and Blake each took a good long drink. They took turns dousing their heads beneath the faucet, then shook the water out of their wet hair. Looking out over the valley they counted twelve mustangs grazing on the other side of the highway. The stallion lifted his head while his herd browsed. The wild horse treated man suspect. Keefe took another thirst quenching slug of water out of the metal cup, then wiped his mouth with the back of his hand. The stallion startled. Dirt and dust fell off as the stud trotted away. The herd raised their heads off the brush they were grazing, sensing a breach into their space, turned and bolted with the stallion.

Late that afternoon in town Hazel had stepped out back of her Award Ribbon Factory. There was a pack of cigarettes, lighter and ashtray full of lipstick smeared cigarette butts on the picnic table underneath a cottonwood tree. It wasn't stinking hot in Meadowhawk, but creeping up on a long afternoon working hard the whole day was reason enough to have a bottle of ice cold beer. As long as she'd had to work for a living, as long as it was her company, and not in small part because it was in Nevada, and a person did as they damn well pleased, Hazel had set as policy that coffee breaks in the afternoon ought to be beer breaks. Some of the girls that worked for her had to count their calories, but most indulged, smoothed out last few hours before quitting time.

Hazel opened the box and lighted a cigarette.

Glenna opened the door to join her on the afternoon break, "Hazel, you don't smoke."

"Do now,"

"Since when did you start smoking again?"

"Since Keefe Kenny hit his head." Hazel puffed and inhaled. She blew out the smoke.

The two women made up a few weeks back on the same day they got into it in front of the bakery.

"I'm not of the mind that any man had the cunning for getting under your skin."

"Keefe Kenny is more miserable than a case of chiggers," Hazel said.

"He's just a man." Glenna replied.

"That's not a man; that's an ex-husband. Not the same thing, whole different animal."

"Pretty much over that, I mean there isn't anything we don't know about men at this stage of our lives."

"You reverse engineer a woman and what do you get? Not a man I can make sense of."

"Must be job related stress, working deadlines, getting things boxed up, shipments that have to go out," Glenna said. "It is good work we do but, Hazel, it will take its toll, put a furrow in a woman's brow."

"Last week, after you and rest of the crew called it quits for the day," Hazel was nervous, "last Wednesday..."

"Yeah?" Glenna said.

"Delivery came in from Ely," Hazel took a swig of beer from her bottle, "just got off the phone with my daughter in Tucson. She was trying to get me to come down for Christmas." Hazel put out her cigarette, dug one more from the box and lighted it right up. The cheeks on her face began glowing red. "It was that young man; has a face right off a postage stamp, a face you'd like to lick, probably twenty-five years younger than either one of us."

"He could be a handsome man with a few more years of sunburn and bad habits."

Hazel gave her best friend the eye. Glenna put two and two together; she raised her hand to her mouth.

"Yes, I did," Hazel said.

"You did?"

"In my office..." Hazel puffed on her cigarette to relieve her anxieties. "Don't know if I was getting even with Ranger or trying to get my mind off Keefe."

A beer was no longer out of the question. Glenna popped the cap off a bottle and took a good long drink.

"It was fun," Hazel said. "Not sure I'd do it again, but I did not disappoint that man."

"God almighty, Hazel, I know your office." Glenna's eyes got full of thought. "Hazel, your office doesn't have any curtains on the windows."

"I kissed him," Hazel said.

"That's why you're upset?"

"It got me all worked up, confused my mind."

"Hazel Harwood," Glenna laughed, "you are a work of art."

"I thought I was supposed to be grown up by now." Hazel took a long medicinal puff off her cigarette. "Instead of spending winters with my husband growing old south in Yuma, I start a business in the middle of the one place in the whole world that'll talk my sex life to death long after I'm buried and gone."

"You got to have the courage of your convictions," Glenna said. "Young men aren't anything but an old man in a boys' clothing."

"Young men got more nuts and bolts south of the border," Hazel said.

"Might have the hardware, but older man, he knows how to use the tools," Glenna said.

Hazel stopped laughing. "So, I got my lips pressed up to this young man and he wraps his arms around me and squeezed me harder than a tube of toothpaste."

"Only live once, might as well mix in a few wild squeezers."

"So, he's kissing me and starts rubbing my back end like he's making a wish and my mind goes wandering off, I'm thinking this isn't all that it's cracked up to be, kind of left me feeling empty."

"So what did you do?"

"Didn't want to disappoint him, kiss was good enough, no better or worse than Ranger's kisses," Hazel explained, "and that's what rattled my cage."

"That's why I don't like stirring things up," Glenna explained. "Empty kisses turn being single into being lonely and the only thing lonely gets you is a pity party without a shoulder to cry on. I got better things to do than waste my time on a man doesn't have a knack for riling me up beyond regret."

"...Was a time in my life, if a boy slapped me on my rear end and poked me with his lips, I'd be finished before he was done unfastening the buttons to my blouse."

"You are such a bragger..." Glenna said.

Hazel shook her head, rolled her eyes. "...Full time job being me."

The women both sat up on the table with their feet on the bench. Glenna took a drink then said, "The best jar of pickles at the Nevada State Fair, with a first place ribbon taped on the lid? That's a minor miracle in this modern world. Never knew a jar of pickles could mean so much."

"All those kids, all that they need is a helping hand to lift them up... First place ribbon for best-in-show can turn a young good life into a great life." Hazel put out her cigarette and fetched another from her pack.

"It's been good, Hazel. Got a good business..." Glenna laughed, "have a good crew working here. Put a lot of food on the table for some good women in this town."

"Who in the world would have ever believed, that this would be the thing that makes me happier than anything I've ever done in life? Must be something wrong with me..."

"They keep closing down fairs, won't need ribbons anymore. Then, you'll have reason to believe something's wrong."

"They're never going to close the fairgrounds."

"Your father, Garrett Harwood ... too many men think like that man."

"Don't know that what they're doing is called thinking." Hazel said.

"I can keep a house clean. I can do a good job. And I do have some happy days," Glenna said. "But, when it comes to supernatural powers, there's not a woman on earth that can turn a fool into a man."

"Maybe they're just the weaker creature. They can't control themselves." Hazel took a long drag off her cigarette. She was lost chasing thoughts through the air. Then Hazel declared, "It's that fanny of yours." She tried smothering her laugh.

Glenna tapped her bottle against Hazel's, "I used to pretend it was my clever conversation that men found so interesting."

"The sweet talkers are just bootlickers," Hazel cracked. "I wasn't counting on men thinking what I got stuck to my backsides was something that they still might want to get all worked up about.

"We are two of Meadowhawk's natural wonders," Glenna said.

"Honey, Lark is a natural wonder."

"What's that make us?"

"We're more like an adventure."

"An adventure...?"

"It's best to sneak up on yourself in the mirror, and don't do it first thing," Hazel waved her finger to make the point. "Have a cup of coffee; too soon can scare a woman our age."

"Seems like I find something new to worry about on my face every day..." Glenna said.

"Those are just character lines," Hazel said.

"I must be turning into a Broadway musical..."

"Why they invented make-up," Hazel said.

"Start out so pretty you don't need any."

"Those days are so long gone; you can't see them from here."

"Ain't that just grand? Don't just need make-up; now we need glasses too."

Blake pressed the vintage '59 Chevy Suburban stretch airport shuttle at breakneck pace down the Hot Spring Highway. This was a five-door model with a fire engine red paint job. There was one door for the driver, four on the passenger side. From the look of the two couples in Blake's rear view mirror, time was of the essence. The youngest bride seated in the second row had put her hand between her brand spanking new husband's legs just outside the Las Vegas city limits. Her fingernails scratched against the tender part of his inner thigh for the better part of 100 miles and had induced a spectacular form of post nuptial spousal arousal. The shuttle was infused in a sea of pheromonal vapors. Fertility was palpable. Privileged intimate acts, between man and wife, were as of this moment not more than ten miles distant. The more progressive couple, seated in the third row, had planned ahead. Faced with a long flight, they elected to perform a consensually conjugal, digitally inspired libidinous maneuver in their car in long term parking before take-off. This was a testimonial to their maturity.

Mitzi spotted the shuttle. Newlyweds tugged at this old woman's heart. After all the ups and downs she'd gone through with Sal, and they'd weathered some tough times as man and wife, one thing she'd never forget was first time she made love to that man after they'd gotten married. Took the guilt out the things she let her husband do to her, and felt not one iota of shame for things she had been holding back and now, as his lawfully wedded wife, felt free to try.

Keefe sat down with Fletcher and Jolene out on the front porch taking in the late afternoon glow of a warm Great Basin day. Two teenage boys were playing on the diving boards, a few long haul drivers were up in the soaking pools, inside the restaurant lazy ceiling fans swirled above diners eating Sal's roasted chicken and fresh from scratch mashed potatoes.

Dusty handled the registration desk. Blake got the two couples' bags. He carted them across the hot springs and set the guests' luggage on the front porch of the honeymoon suite cabins. The younger man pulled his bride. He took the shortest path at the quickest pace toward the biggest moment of his life.

Mitzi thought he seemed too anxious. He was doing things all wrong.

"Young groom looks like he is on a mission," Fletcher said.

For Keefe, the young man's urgency was perfect, "What life's all about."

Jolene said, "Other couple looks like they already been on their honeymoon."

"Never know when a woman might change her mind," Fletcher smiled.

Mitzi wanted to have a word. "Young man…" Mitzi called from the porch. She slow hustled down the steps and fast limped out onto the patio between the pools.

Keefe, Fletcher and Jolene had a pretty good idea of what Mitzi was going to do. She pointed toward the door of the cabin and sent the man off to his room. She got hold of the woman's hand, and after her new husband closed the door, Mitzi pulled the bride back to the café and up onto the porch.

"You just sit down here, this is the owner of the hot spring, he'd like to buy you a drink," Mitzi's accent showed some, "...vouldn't you, Keefe?"

Jolene jumped in, "Sure, he would."

Keefe smiled, "Don't you look like a prize?"

"She's fine, her husband's in some kind of hurry about things he ought to be taking his good time about..." Mitzi said, looking back across the courtyard checking to be sure he'd remained in the cabin as she'd told him to do. "Vhat vill you have?"

The young woman wasn't sure what to do. She said, "Glass of white wine..."

"Got a good glass coming right up."

"Big night...?" Fletcher smiled.

The young lady blushed. Jolene thought the bride was full of expectations; eyes glowing, cheeks beet red, long natural blonde hair, fancy city clothes.

Mitzi returned. "Here you go, simple but good."

The groom came out onto the porch of the honeymoon suite. Mitzi pointed her whole hand, indicating to the groom, to get back inside. "He'll just have to wait one more lovemaking minute."

Jolene lifted her bottle of beer up for a toast, "Here's to a happy marriage."

Keefe chimed in, "A long life and fat babies..."

Fletcher was scratching the graying whiskers on his chin. "Matrimony, honeymoons, and family life set a man like me off on pins and needles."

"Fletcher's our prize bachelor." Jolene winked at the new bride. "Single man's same as married man, only difference one's scared of vowing."

"Best drink that wine quick," Fletcher said, "if you don't rush on over there and cure that groom, he might not make it one more hour on this good earth."

Keefe, Jolene, Fletcher and Mitzi all watched the young bride drink up her wine. There was unanimous approval.

Mitzi refilled her glass. She got behind her chair and began pulling it back to stand her up, "Now, come on, you take this glass with you."

Jolene got on her other side and the two women spontaneously reckoned they'd best escort the young bride to her cabin door.

Keefe closed his eyes and shook his head. "I've been waiting for this day, Fletch, it's like first day of school, best day of my life, makes me feel there's a glimmer of hope for a world gone mad."

"I don't know what you know; don't know what you've done before," Mitzi said.

"None of our business," Jolene wanted to back Mitzi up.

They stopped below the front stoop. Mitzi looked to be sure the door wasn't cracked and her groom wasn't eavesdropping on them.

The young bride took a drink from her glass of wine. She drew in a breath, squared her shoulders and stuck her chest out ready to leap headlong into the most important moment of the rest of her new married life.

"I like that," Jolene said. "Bride's got to have the courage of her convictions."

Mitzi said, "I want you to go in there and first thing you got to do is not let him get off on a bad habit on your first night together."

"That's right, never break a good man if a bad habit is allowed to set in," Jolene said, "...like dressage, got to rein him in, trick him into believing that he's in charge."

Mitzi added, "Even though men act like they're the boss...truth be told, they never are!"

Jolene got all bright eyed, "And, honey, that is the beauty of the thing."

Keefe and Fletcher, with Mitzi and Jolene distracted, high-tailed it to the backdoor of the honeymoon suite. They knocked at the threshold. The young groom answered.

"I'm Keefe, this here, is my friend, Fletch," the two men had Nevada wide grins on their faces. "Son, the best days of life on earth are on the other side of that door."

Fletcher said in a whisper, "and hired help is giving your wife her final instructions."

The young man almost spoke when the two men pounced; they got their hands around his mouth.

Fletcher put his finger up to his lips. "Shush... listen up, this is secret men's business!"

Keefe slowly released his grip on the groom's mouth. "We thought since she's getting advice from two seasoned practiced hands, we best give you some hard earned, man-like wisdom too."

Keefe opened the gate to the hot spring sluice box and started filling the soaking tub on the rear porch. At the same time, Fletcher pulled a silver hip flask filled with whiskey out of his boot and took a good slug down and then handed the flask to the groom.

"Just a little nip, you look too hungry, kid; virtuous bride will concentrate a man's thunderbolt."

"That's right; got to be cocksure of yourself." Keefe said

"Best thing to do is keep your eyes on her eyes."

"And don't look down," Keefe warned.

"You'll just lose control if you go looking at that pair of pas-sion's playthings."

"And don't try anything on your own..."

"That's right; just go along with whatever she has in mind..." Fletcher was so enjoying the moment he took another nip from the flask. He handed it to Keefe. He took a snort. The groom reached for the flask. Keefe thought better of it and handed it back to his friend. Fletcher said, "Things are so exciting we need the hair-of-the-dog more than you."

"Now," Keefe explained waving his arms like an umpire, "you just go along and get along, don't force a thing…"

Fletcher became serious, "Then, when it happens…"

The groom's eyes got wide and full of wonder.

"Why, when the gates of heaven open and the light of love shines from her eyes…"

The groom confused, first checks with Fletcher, then with Keefe.

Fletcher could see the young man was inexperienced. He puts his arm around him and puts the flask up to the groom's lips and poured more whiskey into the man, "…you'll know what to do, let instinct take over, God-given human behavior will be your beacon, your guiding light…"

"Don't try too hard," Keefe said.

"Don't clench too tight," added Fletcher.

"Go slow; be gentle. You'll seem like you're trying to be a good groom; a bride will admire that."

"…Even if you don't know the first thing about what you're doing."

"Once it gets going real good, go ahead and take the lord's name in vain," Keefe advised.

"If you find yourself on the bottom, take that free hand of yours and swat her on the behind,"

"But, gently, just enough to show her that you're the boss,"

Fletcher agreed, then said, "After you have fulfilled your duty as husband and soon to be father, act satisfied, talk slow, say something sweet…"

Keefe, as the proprietor, added, "When it's all over, bring her on out for a soak and some stargazing…"

"Light a candle," Fletcher said.

Keefe added. "Tell her how long you have dreamed about this moment..."

The groom got a far off look in his eye.

"And if you're smart, never let go of that dream for the rest of your life, not for one second." Keefe said. "That's a fool's game..."

Fletcher and Keefe paused and studied the groom's face for any sign of doubt. Once they were convinced that their hard earned wisdom had all sunk in, Fletcher said, "Good, that's all there is to it..."

Fletcher and Keefe turned the man around and pushed him back into the cabin.

Mitzi got behind the woman and gave her final instructions, whispering sage wisdom into the bride's ear, "Walk in slow, calm like, when he touches you, tell him to keep his hands to himself, that this is the most important night of your entire life, and you need to take things at your own pace."

The bride turned back, surprised by Mitzi's advice.

"You take charge, when you think the time is right, take his shirt off one button at a time. If that goes the way you like, take his pants next..."

"But, don't give away the bank." Jolene looked her dead in the eye. "Stay calm. Pretend you are doing your solemn duty. Bring a man to his knees, if you play that card right."

Jolene kept a steady gaze into the bride's eyes. She nodded her head at Mitzi, wanted a woman to woman word with the bride. "Give us a moment of privacy." Mitzi turned and walked off. Jolene said, "Now, I'm just saying, don't be afraid, put those pretty lips of yours to work. You are a married woman now, and there is no shame in doing as you see fit."

The bride blushed and almost spoke. Jolene put her hand up to keep her quiet.

"It's okay, know just how you feel, it's an unspeakable pleasure we're talking here, it's between you, your man and God. There is no shame in giving your husband things he has always dreamed of."

Mitzi couldn't help but overhear every word. She said, "Might just inspire him to go ahead and make a real impression on his bride."

"Whole idea is to give as good as you get," Jolene explained. "And if he doesn't give the next time, then he don't get."

Mitzi spoke like a prizefighter's manager into her ear. "Get him on his back and get on top of him on the bed. He gives you any trouble, you just yell out and we'll be right outside until we're sure he's going along. Don't take a thing off. You'll know what to do. Make him fight for you; make him struggle."

Jolene stood in front of the woman like she was a beautician making the final touches on her big combed out puffed up hair. She used her fingers to tease the woman's hairdo. She unfastened one of her buttons on her blouse, got hold of the lace on the edges of the bra and got the fabric to peek out some. Jolene was smiling. "That groom, poor man, those things peeking out, almost isn't even fair."

"Remember, you make him earn those," Mitzi advised. "A married woman or not, never wants to serve those up for free."

"They are priceless parts," Jolene said. "A gateway, a thing a man has spent the whole of his youth tossing and turning in bed wondering when he would ever get the chance to have his way with."

"Jolene is an experienced woman. A new husband will appreciate the happiness you are offering to bestow upon him, if you'll take the time and make him earn his way into your charms." Mitzi looked at Jolene, "I say she's ready," Mitzi swatted the woman on her behind and said, "Congratulations..."

Jolene stood aside while the young bride walked up the porch steps. With the door knob gripped firm, the young bride took a deep breath, holding her chest up; she was ready to show her teeth. She waited a moment, gathered her resolve, then opened the door. And like that, the door closed; the biggest deed needing being done in the life of love was at the brink of the one moment a man and woman will hold dear for all eternity.

Mitzi and Jolene looked into one another's eyes and listened with all their might. Mitzi was dreaming of that long lost day in her life, while Jolene by this point wondered if such a moment might ever hit town for her. Right here on the side of the Hot Spring Highway beneath the shadow of Pipe Dream Mountain in the Great Basin, a place where a husband and wife have come to set down in memory the consummation of their marriage, things were too quiet at first. Jolene thought she'd heard the groom say something, heard the bride say, "no," and "don't do that," and next thing was the sound of a squeaky mattress and then a man let out an, "oh, my god," and Jolene thought she might've heard fabric ripping.

Mitzi had no doubt that the new bride was getting her way with her man. She tugged on Jolene's arm and turned.

"What are you two doing?" Mitzi said.

Keefe and Fletcher had snuck up right behind them.

"Same thing as you..."

"What are we going to do with you two?" Mitzi asked.

"Jolene can have Fletch; you go see Sal," Keefe said.

A bride's shriek came out of the honeymoon suite.

"Poor bride, I hope he's not rushing the dear thing," Mitzi said.

The groom sounded like he was stifling a great big sneeze. It was so loud the four of them looked back at the cabin door. They all turned shocked. One by one, first Jolene, next Fletcher and finally Mitzi, they all looked at Keefe.

"What are you going to do?" Mitzi asked Keefe.

He smiled, "Going on up to my room, close the door, put on a little music, close my eyes and have myself a little Hazel Harwood honeymoon."

chapter

SEVEN

Remote ranchers making their way to the county fair overnighted at Keefe's Hot Spring. It was a chance to soak off the dust kicked up on those long lonesome dirt roads. They'd get out of the mineral pools, walk back down to the parking lot, gather in their trailers and small talk with neighbors. It gave them a cocktail hour to worry out loud about this season's hay crop yield, and quarrel like coyotes about the federalized evils of the Bureau of Land Management. Bellyaching was the glue that held together the backbone of their rural spirit.

Horse competition preceded the fair's official opening. The dance on Saturday night was near best thing to happen to the county all year long. Sunday's rodeo was the grand finale. By Monday the whole thing would be over, but for the bruises the cowboys nursed.

Dusty, dressed plain in a flannel shirt, denims and packer trail boots had a sorrowful glow on her high cheeks. She was back in her working woman disguise. That man from Beowawe had made a mark on her heart. He'd taken off back north with the rest of the crew. Turned out, that while they fixed the hot spring well, that man Dusty had entertained busted a piece of her happiness off inside her. She had the bittersweet taste of longing clogging most all her thought. He was the first man in memory Dusty could count that she'd found worth being with for more than just a good romp after sundown.

Mitzi understood the woman's gloom. She could see into life well enough to foretell Dusty's fate. She knew it was only a matter of time until a fresh infatuation hijacked Dusty again and drove her down that winding road of makeshift infatuation. Still, wallowing in her sorrows didn't much suit this young woman. She was not inclined to long bouts of man suffering.

"Honey," Mitzi said. "…looks to me like the scientist that's come down from Reno is going to be put to good use."

Dusty squinted her dark eyes, studied his silhouette, "Best cure for what I got is more of the same medicine."

"Might be good to go through a rough patch," Mitzi thought it made some kind of spiritual sense.

"Hell, my whole life's been nothing but a rough patch," Dusty was trying to buck herself up. "What I don't have is enough smooth sailing."

"I'm not sure what you have in mind is what my grandmother would have described as smooth sailing."

"My grandma told me I ought to make the most of each and every day, and do that with a clear conscience, and not one whit of shame until something even bigger and better comes along." For the first time today Dusty grew a smile made of mischief on her lips.

Even with the greenhouse up and near ready to begin operations the circumstances were still the same; the fact was that Keefe knew next to nothing about farming. So, he got advice. A real scientist who had earned a doctorate in horticulture had come down from University of Nevada in Reno. He was part of the Extension Services' Master Gardeners Program. He had firsthand geothermal farming technology experience. The scientist had been brought in from the *Biggest Little City in the World* to sort things out, rope the right way in. He had a load of dank loamy river bottom soil hauled in from Fallon. Next Keefe witnessed with his own eyes the miracle that sprung from flats of germinating seeds. Birthing life from scratch out of soil was a means of witnessing creation itself. He loved every root, every leaf and every part of these fresh new blooms.

The scientist had a pair of wire cutters in his hand, sweat pouring down his face, "Your planthouse is going to be a first class operation once we get her all wired up."

Keefe had been hard at it with a wheelbarrow hauling soil inside, "Doc, I got strong feelings for all those seeds, hope to help turn them into something good."

"You already got something good."

"Never really have spent much time thinking about what's waiting dormant inside a seed."

"Hard to look the other way, especially when that seed might need you."

Keefe referred to his *Farmer's Almanac* like it was divine guidance. The sage reference book had wonder and intuition scaled to same size as Keefe's.

The scientist had been trained to do everything by rote. He strung misters across the top of the greenhouse. He had set up an electronic timer so that he could control the temperature and humidity. They'd found a second hand swamp cooler that had been advertised on a local radio station. Folk could call in and could give a description and phone number for a thing they wanted to get rid of. It was kind of a rural bulletin board classified-ad community service. Nevadans had an affinity for buying, selling and trading their useless things to one another. Citizens could take pride in stealing something they needed right out from under the noses of their neighbors for near next to nothing. Wasn't just the buying or selling that counted, it was an opportunity to really stick it to someone that made the bargain best part of the reward.

Keefe asked, "You still get excited about your work?"

Standing on the top rung of the ladder, straining to wire in the servo motors that actuated the greenhouse louvers, the scientist chuckled, "Sure, folks' lives are going to be made better because of what you're doing here."

Keefe said. "Wouldn't that be something?"

"Already is," the scientist said again. "Whole community is going to eat fresh vegetables, be nutritious food, right kind of livelihood, right here, out here on your land."

That scientist did skillful work Keefe reckoned. And come sundown Dusty hoped to employ the man to help her sand on that rough patch she needed smoothing out. Life at the hot spring was more than a full time job for the people who came to work there.

"Let me have a look," the scientist said examining the side of Keefe's head. "How do you feel?"

"I see things now I didn't see before. I hear things I never listened to." Keefe explained, "Five years ago, our kids were gone and I was all caught up out here trying to make this place work. I had priorities backwards. Life's nothing but love, and you take that love of your life and the rest of what life has to offer, you and her, both together. I'm nothing but a piece of vulture bait without my wife."

"You think something's wrong?"

"There's always been something wrong with me. But, since I got bonked on the head I see an eternity of beauty in a thimbleful of whiskey. I love this hot spring; know what I'm doing now. It seems to come natural to me. And I got to tell you, man to man, I've never seen anything, in my whole life, that has roused my thirst more than the sight of that woman they call my ex-wife."

Fletcher's past was all classified 'top secret;' wasn't anything he wanted to talk about anyhow. All people needed to know, so far as he was concerned, is that he was a hard rock miner. He'd first come to Nevada in the 1980's by way of the Atomic Test Site. He never spoke about his work there. Hard to brag about how good you had been at devising the means of ending life on earth. It was common knowledge that the most qualified man in the county for blowing things up was Fletcher McCrea. Out of the blue, more than two decades ago, just like that he lost his stomach for enabling a worldwide thermonuclear Armageddon. Just wasn't as much fun as he thought it would be. And that is why he had been deemed sane enough by the National Security Agency to be licensed to set off conventional explosives. A modest sized demolition project put the fun back into the thing. Of course conventional demolition work didn't pay near as good as nuclear annihilation, but Fletcher rightly calculated that there wouldn't be much use for money in a world that no longer existed. Fact was, his freedom to seek peace on earth added up to most of what was left of what this man wanted. He believed in his bachelor freedom, the company of a woman and last, and most of all, he preferred the freedom to entertain the company of a wide range of women.

Bambalina preferred explosions of temper. She detested sudden surprise and loud bangs. She had no use for any of that kind of thing. If that was what Fletcher McCrea, her sorry excuse for a keeper, wanted to do with his time allotted here on earth, best leave her in town and go blow the hell out the world without her.

The herd of mustang spotted Bambalina. She was being hauled off Pipe Dream Mountain in the back of Fletcher's all-wheel drive International pickup truck. Captivity grated against mustangs' instincts. There was something even more than unnatural about that burro being trapped in the bed of that truck. It set all wrong in a mustang's mind. It was an equine blasphemy. It was something like the current state of human beings and their believing, when compared to other animals, that they were superior living beings. From Bambalina's reckoning the man who took care of her didn't even make horse sense.

Fletcher rolled into Meadowhawk. The town was easy on a citizen's eyes right smack in the prime of the leafy season. Shade was soaked and slathered in fresh green shoots. Fletcher waved to Dotty, dressed in her working smock, out front of the General Store. He unloaded Bambalina into her corral. Watered her, threw a few flakes of hay, tossed an apple into her feed, then much to his burro's chagrin slapped her hard as all get out on her rump as if that was something she enjoyed.

He didn't need to tell her, she could smell it all over him. *You are going to go blow all hell out of something.* She knew. He tried to sneak the fuses, the blasting caps, and the rest of who knows what into the truck without her noticing. The whole thing stunk. She wanted no part of it. No amount of explaining could convince Bambalina that the human species was even one lick more intelligent than the burros she'd known over her life.

"You just stay here." Fletcher explained, "Come on back for you after I'm done doing my work."

There wasn't a word of truth to what he was saying, Bambalina knew all too well he'd be coming back, stopping at the Brewery, leave with one of those easy women he ran with. All she had to look forward to was switching her tail and twitching her ears until that man has had his way with another one of his so-called girlfriends.

Might not be whip smart, but a burro has a keen sense of when a master was not being forthcoming. This miserable fate befell her when she was auctioned into an involuntary interdependence. Her welfare was in shaky hands. The whole of life depended upon what time he finished his all-important secret man business. Bambalina was certain that there was not a God concerned with her welfare.

Fletcher stood on top of his truck's running boards. "Don't give me that look."

Bambalina knew she'd be stuck in this no good miserable dirt lot with nothing to do but count pickup trucks driving up and down the Hot Spring Highway. She looked right through the miner she had cast her whole lot in with. Might fool some of those women he ran around with but not this burro.

"There's too much dog and too little cat in you," Fletcher complained. "I don't want to have to explain myself to nobody about nothing. All I want is a burro."

Bambalina's head drooped, she was inconsolable. She lifted her sad eyes and looked up and down the highway, must be a better miner to devote her life to. The burro turned and walked away; last thing she had to say came out of her business end, a greenhouse gas exclamation mark. That's what disappointment can do to a relationship.

The sheep ranch was five miles beyond Keefe's Hot Spring. A decade ago Bero had left Nevada and traveled to the Basque region of Spain, the Pyrenees; it was there that he courted and married. He returned with his bride a happy man. Bero left his wife, Mirari, towel drying her hands on the ranch house porch. She had a look on her face. Fletcher McCrea was nothing but worries to any kind of woman.

The men drove out to the base of the hard rock bluff on the north side of the ranch. Rock was near hard as granite and the hole they were punching was going to take the better part of the day.

"Bero, I need to go on over to Spain and try on one of those Basque women."

Bero shook his head in doubt, "A man does not test Basque women."

Fletcher was amused, "Kind of high strung?"

Bero looked up to the highest point in the sky. "A Basque woman," he snorted out a laugh, "they are the confusion of all men."

"Stormy, fiery...?" Fletcher was hoping, "shoot, I knew it. You're a lucky man, Bero."

"I have a wife, I have my health," Bero was a practical Basque sheepherder. "God has given me more than I could have hoped for..."

"You have sheep, you have Mirari and you make cheese, and soon enough you will complete the first cheese cave in all of Nye County."

The drilling went as reckoned. Late in the day, Fletcher chained the rotary tool to the bumper of his rig and had Bero back the truck and drag the tool off 200 yards.

In demolition work, the best plan was that the single man would be responsible for setting the explosive charges into the bores. Even if the single man had a more exciting sex life, it was the married man's wife that counted most. So, Fletcher pushed the charges ten feet deep in with a long piece of plastic pipe. He rubbed the end of his nose to fend off even the chance of a sneeze. No matter how many times in his life he'd set a blasting cap into a load of explosives, he'd get the urge to urinate; just how it was in the demolition business. Fletcher came off his knees and backed away from the hard rock hillside uncoiling the detonation wires. At about fifty paces he kneeled once more, this time attaching the ends of the wires to a radio controller.

Things had been known to go wrong at this stage. Bero had taken his position on the other side of the truck and raised his head over the hood to keep an eye on the county's most mortal man. Bachelors came a dime a dozen. Fletcher knew the score. He didn't take his eyes off the detonator until he got about twenty paces further back toward the truck. Fletcher stopped, tried to swallow his fears and when he turned toward Bero, plastered the best smile on his face he could muster. He walked on the tips of his toes through the sagebrush as if one false move might set the explosives off and end his life right then and there.

Once he got around the safe side of the truck, he got down on one knee. "You pray?" Fletcher asked Bero.

Bero knew fear in a man's eye. "Pray for healthy sheep?"

"I pray when I'm setting fused explosives into a bore hole. Squeeze the juice out of every little prayer I know."

"Prayer is no friend of a man from Nevada."

"Don't say that, Bero. I got my heart set on a happy ending."

"Death is the end."

"Yeah, but if there's an afterlife I'd like to arrive in one piece, just in case I might get a date with one of those cute little Basque women."

Fletcher reached through the window of the truck, opened the glove box and grabbed hold of the remote radio controlled detonator.

Bero had a belly laugh, "You think you're going to have sex when you get to heaven?"

Fletcher was holding the detonator, first turning the safety switch on the actuator. He scanned the blast zone one last time, the men squatted down behind the truck. "Bero, I figure closest thing to heaven on earth is making love to a good woman, now, if you were stuck in heaven for all eternity, what do you think God has got planned for us to do?"

"All we know is that God does have a plan..."

"Figure what's planned is some kind of eternal orgasmic event that will hold us in a kind of everlasting rapture." Fletcher was dead serious.

Bero gazed at Fletcher. He didn't speak English well enough to know what in tarnation the man was talking about. So he played along.

Fletcher offered the knob for Bero to twist. "Go on, makes a man feel omnipotent..."

Bero grabbed the knob, "What's omnipotent mean?"

"Means you get your way about everything,"

"But, that's not how life works."

"And that's why you're married and I am foot loose and fancy free..." Fletcher laughed. "Go on twist that knob! We got a cheese cave to create, hell even a man who has thrown his life away and got married deserves to live it up once or twice before he dies."

Bero flipped the switch. Fletcher winced. First, one second passed, and then what seemed like forever, two seconds ticked off, Fletcher shook his head back and forth, couldn't believe he had such rotten luck. After about ten seconds Fletcher said, "I hate when that happens." Fletcher stood up and marched mad as all get out toward the rock wall they'd set charges in. "You stay right where you are..."

Fletcher stomped off straight and for the first twenty paces cussed with a creativity seldom heard.

"Fletcher, don't go out there..." Bero said.

Fletcher raised his hand in the air and swung it down. He was furious. "Bero you are a married man, you got something to live for." He kept marching and cussing, and this was with cussing's most choice derivations; he shouted exasperations; suspected a conspiracy, intoned contempt for near all things in the universe, and repeatedly blamed the higher powers as he stomped through the sagebrush making his perilous way back to the remote controlled radio detonator... "...of all the goddamn lousy miserable... why, in the name of goddamn life, is it that nobody in this goddamn miserable lousy world, can manufacture a goddamn reliable blasting cap...?"

Bambalina stopped dead in her tracks. She lifted her head. She thought she'd heard something. About the best fun she'd had all day was when she got the chance to chase two school boys off her pasture. She didn't trust them for nothing.

Keefe swiped his finger in the remains of the bowl of pesto.

"And it's good for you..." Sal said.

Keefe licked his fingers, "We can make pesto pretty much any time we like." He continued poking around the stove.

Sal swatted Keefe with his dish towel. "Go on, get out of the way."

Sal had heated a skillet and browned pine nuts to a golden roasted succulence.

Keefe swiped his finger a second time in the leftovers in the mixing bowl. He picked up a spoon with his free hand and scooped a helping of pine nuts.

Sal, irritated by Keefe's renegade style, froze. He awaited Keefe's verdict.

Keefe dabbed the tip of his pesto covered fingertip into the spoonful of nuts. He placed his finger into his mouth closing his lips around the pesto and pine nut encrusted tip. His eyes were squeezed shut. He shook his head groaning, "ummmmmmmm...."

"Does it need more salt?" Sal wondered.

"It wants for nothing..."

"Then, out of my kitchen..." Sal barked.

Keefe walked toward the back door; he tightened the belt of his terrycloth bathrobe. He filled a disposable cup with water at the sink where Sal was washing the lettuce. Screen door slammed shut behind Keefe. He walked around the side of the building went through the wood gate. He walked the flagstone pathway to the upper pools.

Glenna had got off work from the Award Ribbon Company and had lied through her teeth, wasn't any good that could come from telling Hazel that she was going to come out and soak here at the hot springs. She was wearing her imported bright vermillion one piece swimsuit. She wore a floppy wide brim straw hat. She tucked her long hair up into it. Her lipstick matched the suit and her oversized sunglasses made her seem like she was a somewhat fuller figured fashion model out of a big city publication; Glenna Goddard was all Vogue Magazine glamorous, made a man's eye rove and a wife's other side of her mind tattle about the strength of her husband's character. Except for Hazel, who was still at work, the rest of the crew she'd usually come soak with had gone to Carson City. This was the committee to save the fair made up of her workmates and the men that had volunteered to go to the state capital with them.

Keefe kicked off his flip flops, set his towel and bathrobe on a chair. He waded down the steps into the hot spring waters tightening the string to his swimming trunks. He had a grin, and a grizzled beard, after hauling soil all day he needed a good long soak. He knew most everyone by name, winked at one friend and flinched his eyebrows at another, exhaled and hooted as he bent his knees swimming a velvet paced breaststroke across the mineral pools. He spit water and took air, floated over to Glenna, rolled over and sat on the submerged bench seat next to her.

Keefe wiped the water from his face. Glenna sat deadpanned. Her sunglasses hid her eyes that she kept fixed on the sky's dusky highlights. Keefe was rubbing the ends of his hands regarding the dirt he'd got stuck under his fingernails.

"Not a better time of day for a soak," Glenna didn't so much as move her head.

Keefe looked at her. "Look as if you come dressed for best day of summer."

"I like feeling special about how I look even here, emptiest county in Nevada."

"I'm going to have to paint my fence and polish my tile so as to keep up."

Glenna's stoic face broke into a smile. She took a handful of water and drowned her lips and cheeks in a helping. "I do get pleasure from playing dress up."

"Almost too good to be true..." Keefe said. "Look like you belong at some high end luxury resort."

She smiled, "Like keeping my life simple."

Keefe was mighty proud, "We're not too bad, cute little rural hot spring."

"Greenhouse is looking real fancy, walked up to the wellhead, looks like you have a plan. If I didn't know you, Keefe Kenny, I'd say it was as if you know what you're doing."

"Wouldn't fit in here, if I knew what I was doing."

Glenna mocked. "Might be light goes off any day now."

Keefe wasn't having any of it, "That day's long gone, time in my life to have a soak, see and feel things, right here, things you didn't even know were locked up inside of you."

"Like truth serum, a long soak makes a mind pliable," Glenna claimed.

"Can anyway, get in the water thinking one way and get out thinking another." Keefe dunked his head underwater. He came back up for air. "When I was twenty I had passion, and I got even more of it now. I forgot the rules to life. You got to show a wife that you want what you have."

The mineral waters soothed Keefe's bones. Sparrows hopped about at the edges to the gardens. Swallows were in the air playing in the daylight's last thermals. Sun was low and shadows stretched clear across the valley. The muted sounds of the teenagers splashing and teasing, laughing and leaping off the diving board vanquished the solitude.

Glenna baited. "Don't suppose you heard about Ranger getting into trouble."

"Not a bit surprised."

"Playing eight ball in a tavern," Glenna said. "He ended up having words with a man thirty years his junior."

Keefe seemed amused. "He seems to find trouble more than most."

"One man gets punched, ends up on the floor. The other lands in a chair explaining himself to the deputy sheriff." Glenna splashed a bit more water on her face. She tried washing the smirk off her lips.

"Deputy let him go. . .?" Keefe asked.

"Tea party," Glenna explained. "Nobody's messing with Ranger."

"Called in a crony favor, one of those fake judges he donated to." Keefe said.

"Acted like he got off scott-free," Glenna said. "Young man up in Ely was a UPS driver. From what I hear he got under Ranger's skin and then some."

"Life has a way of catching up on a man." Keefe's eyes grew alert. He sat up on the bench he'd been slouching on. He kind of went somewhere, like he was across the valley on the other side. Glenna thought he'd put two and two together.

Keefe reached toward Glenna, his hand floating on the water, absentmindedly he started patting what he thought was her arm.

Glenna looked down at Keefe's hand on her breast, the one closest to her arm, the one he had been patting with his hand.

"Glenna," Keefe was mesmerized, "You know what that is?"

She pushed Keefe's hand away, "I'm not sure I know what you're looking at."

"Those dark patches," Keefe said. "Pinion trees..."

Glenna settled back deeper into the soaking pool. "Hard to believe what can keep a man's mind occupied."

Keefe had a smile break wide open on his face. "I've been looking at those mountains since first day I arrived here in Meadowhawk." Keefe stood up in the pool. "Been looking right at them this whole time."

Glenna flinched. Sound of an explosion reverberated throughout the valley. "What in the name of creation is that?"

Bambalina knew what it was. It was the sound of Fletcher McCrea, and he wasn't ever coming back. Only thing worse than his loss was waiting to find out what kind of miserable son of a bitch was going to try and buy her at auction. Burro like her wasn't worth much anymore. Miners had radios they could listen to, books they could read. Just wasn't as lonely as it once was. Goodbye and good riddance. Bambalina could hardly believe she'd been orphaned and that Fletcher McCrea was gone from her life for good. The only thing waiting for her in the future was some half-witted sorry assed pretend hard rock miner with too much hope and too little luck. Being a burro was never easy. There wasn't a thing to do but go graze at the cemetery, and when she found her miner, piss on his grave.

chapter

EIGHT

Keefe dusted off his white straw Stetson. He'd spent most of the afternoon polishing his Tony Lamas. The finishing touch was his satin finished silver and turquoise bolo tie.

Fletcher was whittling off a piece of licorice with his pocket knife out front of the General Store. The curb was kept clear during the fair for customers. Dotty came out the door and lost her breath as she looked across the street, where they'd right then turned on the red, green, and yellow neon lights of the revolving Ferris wheel.

"How many carnival ride tickets did you buy?" Dotty asked.

"Got one ticket for every one of my sweethearts," Fletcher said.

Dotty looked up and down the street, "Didn't know they made pockets that big. You got one for Sissy?"

"Sure do," Fletcher said nodding his head, "...got her a birthday card and a fresh deck of playing cards."

"Hard to believe you play cards with your ladies."

"That's all Sissy and I do when we share time is play gin."

"That's a tall tale. All you and Sissy do is play cards?"

Fletcher snipped another chunk of licorice off and stuffed the piece in his mouth chewing, "Finds my card playing the only part of me that agrees with her."

Keefe rolled up and turned into the parking space in front of the General Store. He kicked his parking brake down firm, left his radio on and hopped out of his Ford, singing along, "...and no one *knows*... what goes on *behind*..." and with a flourish, he bent down on one knee and tried to sell the last two words with all he's got, missing the mark of the note, but not by so much, he belted out the long finale "...closed...doors..." and for his razzle-dazzle finish, he pushed the door to his pickup truck shut.

"How about that? Only the second blown up man- to live and still tell- comes rolling into town right out of the sagebrush," Dotty said.

Keefe stood up, reached inside the cab of his pickup and turned off the key to the ignition. "I'll tell you who's excited. Mister Hard Rock Miner here scared the hell out of the whole county this week."

"I am a man never been easy to tame; lose my temper pretty near every time I'm out working with explosives."

"Hell, you could have taken your time; didn't have to make the whole cheese cave in one blast."

"Oh, come on, Keefe, half the fun is blowing the thing up."

Keefe laughed, "Fletcher McCrea, you're going to need to learn how to sneak up on a thing."

"I been sneaking up on things for a month's worth of full moons. If I keep sneaking, going to need a mortician put makeup on me." Fletcher smiled sly at his friend.

"Way it's been going, might want to think about ordering that custom fit pine box go along with that makeup."

Fletcher snipped off a piece of licorice and threw it at his friend. Keefe snatched the chunk of candy out of the air. He shook his head with a smile blooming across face, then puffed on the licorice like he was smoking one of those fine Cuban cigars.

Glenna happened into Lark at the General Store that afternoon. She invited her over. Her place set on the southernmost street in Meadowhawk next to a fathomless sweep of sagebrush. From the deck out back, on a clear day, an eye could wander off into the yonder until the mountains vanished beyond the horizon's edge. Plan for now was to help each other get ready for the dance. Glenna talked Lark into sitting on the stool at her armoire. It was an antique, black lacquered authentic piece of furniture, made special for a woman. She stood behind Lark and fussed over her like a for hire hairdresser.

"Growing up, seems to my mind, you were *always* playing with the boys," Glenna said, while holding Lark's long black hair with one hand and combing it out with the other.

Lark was looking into her own eyes in the mirror. Her likeness vanished as memories appeared. "My mom always said I must be part boy."

"The first lucky man to plunge his nose into that hair of yours tonight, all he's going to smell is woman. Go on, close your eyes," Glenna brushed a layer of blue-green makeup on her eyelid. "Blake's going to be in a world of hurt when he gets a look at you."

"He's got handsome eyes, but best I can tell they don't seem connected to anything."

"He's doesn't know," Glenna said. "Pretends like he knows, but he doesn't understand the first thing about nothing, unless it's got oil in it."

Lark was discouraged, "Are you dancing tonight?"

"Sure, but it's not the same thing. Too many lonely men in this town think I'm something they want to try and take home. I enjoy being their disappointment." Glenna shook her head. She pinched Lark's shirt at the shoulders. She went to her closet. "I've got a shirt that has your name on it. Try this on just for fun."

Lark snapped the pearl buttons and then tucked the midnight blue gabardine shirt into her jeans.

Glenna unbuckled Lark's silver belt buckle and cinched it up two notches more. "...that too tight...?"

"Tight as a lock," Lark complained.

"Then, suck your tummy in some more," Glenna said, "...like you got any tummy to suck in."

Lark by habit tried hiding her curves. She regarded herself in the mirror from the front, then the side. "Makes everything else on me stick out."

Glenna turned to her side and looked at her own silhouette. "Lark, a woman's figure needs to speak to a man," she squeezed her hands tight against her own waist, "when you go dancing, best to dress up in something more than a whisper."

"Men don't need encouraging."

"One day you are going to walk into a room and nobody's going to sit up and even notice; ought to enjoy yourself while you have what a man still wants."

Lark looked straight ahead regarding herself in the mirror. She squeezed her lips tight, took a deep breath, smiled into Glenna's eyes behind her in the mirror.

"Why do we have to wait for some man to make the first move?" Lark asked.

"It is written down in human nature; way it is."

"Thought we had equal rights in this world."

Glenna got a serious expression on her face. "You want to make short work of Blake? When you find him looking at you tonight, look back and doesn't matter what else is happening, don't take your eyes off of him. Don't look away, no matter how much you might feel like you should. Keep looking right through him, stay calm, tilt your head like you're curious, keep looking at him, then wait for what will feel like the longest few seconds of your life, it will feel like you are waiting for a kettle to whistle, like time is standing still, then blink those eyes of yours and smile, a real smile, don't say a word... let your heart tell him the truth."

"I don't have the nerve."

"Not a better night for it than going to the dance and finding yourself in the arms of a man you want. A good dancer is almost better than being in bed with the man."

Lark looked up at the ceiling. Dancing was about as much fun as she had nerve to hope for.

"What I do is wait to see how close my partner tries to hold me. If he's tense, likely he'll hold me back. So what I do is I go ahead and sneak on in... I slide my arm up a little closer on his shoulder, hold his lead hand a might bit tighter, I let my breath blow warm on his ear... he'll know he has got hold of something he might not want to let go of."

"You make it all sound like you have it planned out."

"Just nudging fate; a dance with an attractive man can be an epiphany. Man like that... he might have the answer. All those midnights you couldn't sleep... looking out some forlorn window, wondering when you were going to get that first chance in life."

"I don't think a young girl from Meadowhawk dares dream..." Lark said blushing.

"Lark, we got to pry a man off the fence, give him the courage to take a chance."

"Then what happens?"

"*Fourth of July*, once you get a man where you want him, best day of a woman's life."

Sharlene had friends over for a cocktail party. Since what to wear could be a fateful decision, they all came with extra garments. One by one they'd try things on and model them for one another. Sharlene, Sissy, Tallula, Faith, Jolene and Bunny couldn't quite fit into one another's clothes, but was a riot of woman-fun trying.

After a cocktail or two they'd sneak off into Sharlene's bedroom and make their grand entrance into the living room for the big fashion show. Jolene started the whole thing. She had come out in Tallula's sequin dress. She was all big blonde hair, ample busted, good, loving, honest-to-heaven country girl, teetering atop spiked high heels. Of course, there was a lot more Jolene in that dress than Tallula.

"My goodness, Tallula's going to need a few extra meals," Faith laughed.

Jolene swung around so her lady friends could admire her derriere.

"That fanny of yours ought to bring a good price at auction," Faith said, as all the women snickered and giggled.

Jolene wiggled her hips back and forth, pushed out her chest and stuck out her butt, "I'm bringing top dollar."

Bunny was a big enough woman to fit snug on a king-sized bed, "Leave one of those little skinny cowboys for me."

Faith picked up her cocktail glass, "Here's hoping, I got my heart set on a slow dance with a steer roping champion."

"I'm through with bareback riders," Sharlene said.

"They're not ever going to grow up and be the kind of cowboy to settle down," Tallula explained.

"They're just tumbleweeds with bruises." Bunny was the only one of the ladies that wore fake eyelashes. She fluttered them and said, "...but sure is fun while they're here."

Jolene put one hand on her hip and the other up to the side of her head, turned and sauntered back to the bedroom, daring to speak what was on her mind, "I'm saving the last dance for Fletcher McCrea."

Faith threw the pillow on the sofa at Jolene, and the rest of the women all chimed in.

"Jolene!" Bunny shrieked.

"You are always cutting in line," Tallula complained.

"Just not fair..." Sharlene and Faith agreed.

Bunny rose up from her seat. She tried with all her might to be convincing. "I don't believe that it's right to bring some cowboy we just met home and hop in bed with him."

Jolene walked out of the bedroom her blue eyes wide. She could hardly believe her ears. Sharlene and Tallula were stunned.

Bunny's game face broke. She laughed and fluttered her fake eyelashes, and soon the laughter had the women in tears, and ten minutes later they had to go do their makeup over because of the thing.

Tip Top Tom and His Band of High Country Haymaker's had come in by tour bus. Smooth singing was Tom's best card in his deck of talent. "Been drinking whiskey," he sang, "alone most every night..."

"Come on Keefe," Jolene tugged on his hand.

"My pleasure."

Keefe cocked his hat off to one side so as he could place his cheek on Jolene's. "Heard the ladies come back from Carson City with terrible news."

Jolene closed her eyes. Keefe was a good dancer. "Last time we'll ever dance here."

"Garrett Harwood and Chamber folk seem a might bit too happy about that."

"I didn't grow up in the same America as those folk," Jolene said. "Seem like they're stewed in venom..."

Keefe squeezed hold of Jolene a might bit tighter, "I got no quarrel with how any man votes, but will not sit by and have the place I love be dismantled right in front of my eyes."

Jolene said, "We're not even two-bit poker chips; sit out here pretending like what we got means something, the whole while, the rest of the world's taking everything we hold dear, and shipping it off to China."

Hazel had come in the side door. She had no intention of missing the dance. Until Keefe had hit his head, didn't even know she still existed. She worked it out and was sitting off in the corner of the dance hall with Ranger. She was using her father, Garrett Harwood, and the rest for protection. An ex-husband wasn't going to spoil her night.

Keefe stood deadlocked. Jolene knew Keefe's chances stood contrary to reason.

"Isn't she something though?" Keefe said. "I'm going to dance every song with her."

"That so, Keefe" Jolene laughed. "Maybe, in another life..."

"They used to be kinda normal," Keefe said, "like the rest of us; whole side of the dance hall isn't anything but a bunch of high blood pressure types now."

"Well, don't go over, all you'll find is hot water."

Keefe walked Jolene back to her seat.

Sharlene never missed a thing. "Hazel Harwood's keeping an eye on you, Keefe."

"She won't speak to me."

Tallula butted in, "Oh, Keefe, come on, none of us are too complicated. Give us a dance; buy us a beer. Walk us home... never know what good fortune could come from a plan like that."

Keefe bent down on one knee, put his arm over Tallula's shoulder, "I been scuffing my boots on this dance floor since the end of never, and there's not another table of women that has done more to give the men in this county a shot at a night they'll never forget."

Tallula was heartbroken. "Of all the rotten no good luck," Tallula complained, "last thing we need is an *in love with another woman man* one knee at our table."

Keefe kissed Tallula on her cheek and stood up. He tipped his hat. One of the cowboys in town for the rodeo was behind him.

Tallula's night took hold of steer roping hope. Wiped that sober look off her face and replaced it with encouragement. She got up off her chair and took that man out to the dance floor. They slid so smooth to the tune, was hard to believe they'd just now met.

Glenna and Lark were seated at a table at the edge of the dance floor talking with Dotty, Gage, Elena and Gig.

Glenna excused herself. "Keefe...Come on, take me out to the fairgrounds for one last ride on the Ferris wheel."

Keefe was gazing into the shadows of the back of the room where Hazel was trying to ignore her so called best friend and ex-husband. "I was thinking about asking a lady for a dance."

Glenna turned; she knew Hazel was mad as the dickens, "Got about twenty men between you and that dance."

"Why do I like those odds?"

"Because you are a stubborn flea bitten fool; it's what we love and hate about you. Won't listen to a thing people say."

"Well, come on, might as well make the town talk."

Keefe put his hand upon the small of Glenna's back. Ranger watched as they walked out to the door toward the carnival rides.

Garrett Harwood had his eye on the same thing. "What's that friend of yours think she's doing with that man?"

Hazel lifted her bottle of beer, closed her eyes, she took a drink to soothe her temper. She set her beer down. She shook her head. "She's all fancy fingernails and rotten as two day old road kill. If it wasn't for her makeup, everyone could see right through her." Hazel bobbled her head, "She said I have no right to tell her who she can and cannot talk to."

"Would you put your arm around my shoulders?" Glenna asked, as she took her seat on the ride.

"Be my pleasure."

"Ferris wheel's always been a tummy tickler," Glenna said.

"I thought it was because of how I felt about the girl."

Glenna up at the high point of the ride gazed out across the fairgrounds, casting her search as far as her eyes would allow, "Hard to believe all this is going to be swept away."

"Meadowhawk's got nine lives," Keefe said, "only two, three used up so far."

Out at the furthest edges of the fairgrounds, where livestock paddocks were set, Glenna spotted Bambalina. Fletcher had put her leather show halter on. She was aching for an airing out. The bitty burro had spent most of the afternoon braying. She was desperate. She had to see everyone at the dance. She would never forgive her keeper, if he did not allow her the pleasure of at least one look. Every year it was the same. When she heard the band strike up their first tune, was like a meadow of sweet grass was waving in the breeze of her heart. The scent of all that desire wafting out the front of that dance hall gave her a newborn faith in humanity.

Blake had been avoiding Lark. More than once she tried making eye contact, but then he'd lose his nerve, blush and look away. Of all the rotten luck, a young cowboy approached her table. Blake discouraged, dropped his head and cursed the pointed toes of his boots. He braced his nerves in his gut, and finally took off— slow walked over to Lark.

"You want to dance?" Blake asked.

"Go on," Elena urged.

"Clean up real nice when you try," Dotty said to Blake.

Lark got up off her seat smoldering; she was so irritated. Blake flushed and looked as if he'd done something he ought not to have done.

Lark took three steps toward the bar and turned to Blake. "I can't dance with you now."

Blake had not seen Lark so worked up; she was all lightning and thunder. "You can't dance with me?"

"You want to dance, you got to be the first one to ask."

"I didn't know that."

"You spend too much time working on your cars and not enough time working out how you ought to treat a woman."

Blake took off his hat and put it across his heart like he was going to say the pledge of allegiance. Ran his free hand through his black shiny hair, and looked off as if he were getting ready to read words off a chalkboard, even opened his mouth, but words did not come. He did a full circle on the heels of his cowboy boots and put his hat back on.

"If you can't dance with me, maybe you can let me buy you a beer."

Lark took a deep breath, exasperated, she paced off toward the bar; as she passed Blake, she took hold of his hand and tugged him along behind her.

Struggling to dig money from her tight-fitted pocket, Lark raised a twenty dollar bill into the air.

"I'm buying." Blake said.

"You can buy the next round." Lark was steamed.

While she was ordering, he kept looking at how she was all different— like Lark was changed by something, her fair skin shined, black hair was all combed out, when she'd grabbed hold of his hand her touch had meaning to it, was a force, seemed like thoughts were installed inside his mind— like she was the same, but seemed all different.

"How you two doing tonight?" Dusty asked.

"Going to teach Blake how to two-step."

"Could be rewarding work, if Blake wasn't so bashful," Dusty was standing between them but had her eyes, all jazzed up with dancing makeup, locked on a cowboy across the room. "Blake, I bet, could make a good project for a woman."

Blake took a long drink from his beer. The idea of dancing was a thing for a young man to be jumpy about.

Dusty's aim was higher; dancing was only prelude. She had her mind made up on a bull rider across the room. From the look he shot back, didn't appear her man was worried about drawing some toughnut bull at the rodeo tomorrow, or dancing with Dusty tonight.

"You two have fun out there," Dusty was looking straight at her cowboy. She cocked her short haired head off to one side and sent the least innocent smile to the man she had hoped was the one might make the cut. She'd come dressed for the dance in her country girl's finest denims and tight fitted blouse. The time had come for Dusty to go hunting her one and only.

The whole moment went lost on Blake. The band was playing; everyone in the hall was talking; was hard to hear much of anything. "Lark, you look like someone I never met."

Lark took a drink of her beer. It occurred to her to wipe her lips with the back of her hand. Blake would have recognized her then. She resisted the urge, instead licked her lips with her tongue. Blake there and then got stiff. Like Lark had mesmerized him, like there was something wrong.

"Are you scared of me, Blake?"

He never had anything like this happen. Lark's lips were all of all things, the pair of prizes most on his mind right now.

Lark did not understand this man, "I got something wrong with my nose?"

Blake aimed to find the courage to kiss those lips.

Lark tapped him in his gut, "You alright?"

"I don't think so," Blake had a case of shakes in his voice.

Lark drank down more of her beer. Her patience was running thin.

Lark was flustered. "We can take our sweet time, or we can rush right through it..."

"You want me to kiss you now?"

Lark put her beer down on the bar. She plucked his beer out of his hands drank some and set his down on the bar too. "I aim to have the man who has me for the first time unfasten every button, every zipper, down to the last hook on my bra. The man who can persuade me to do that, I'm making that *man* the luckiest *man* in the world."

Blake blushed dumbstruck, "Never heard any woman talk like that, not even in a movie."

"This is you and me, stuck in Meadowhawk, trying to make a life before clock strikes twelve."

"So," he asked, "how much time we got?"

"You haven't got any time left, at least no time left to not be trying."

Blake was not clear in his mind about whether he had the courage to take this next step. His jitters had made Lark's nerves jangle too.

He leaned toward her. He was aiming for her lips, he tried kissing her. She leaned back and tapped him on his gut again. She saw the bartender caught what happened.

Now she was blushing. "Buy me a beer, ask me to dance, walk me home after, and if you even so much as try anything..."

Blake was confused, "I thought you said..."

Lark tried to calm down, "Any way you cut it, going to be a big challenge," Lark drank the rest of her pint. She set her glass back down on the bar.

He was trying to keep up. "What do we do now?"

Lark dragged Blake behind her, "Got to be good at something besides making each other nervous."

"I don't ever dance," Blake said.

"Might just take first place ribbon in the amateur division of the two-step contest."

Lark spun around into the ballroom dance position. Blake let his hand be coaxed over hers and took hold. That was more excitement than near anything he'd ever tried with a woman. Lark's hand was the hand he wanted to hold, even if it had been his secret. Then with his other hand he pressed firm up against the small of her back. Blake could not believe it had only taken as long as he could ever remember to get Lark in his grasp. He had a far off look in his eye. One more time he found himself gazing at the lips on Lark's face.

She blew a puff of breath to wake him from his daydream. "Blake, tonight, if, and it's a big if, if I make the biggest mistake of my life and I let you kiss me on the way home, don't press on my lips too hard, and don't call me tomorrow, and don't go avoiding me, if you see me at the General Store!"

Glenna paid fifty cents for one throwing ball. Keefe had to knock all three milk bottles down. Keefe took the top bottle right off and left the bottom two standing where they were.

"Never win," he said.

"Not supposed to win," Glenna replied, "...you're supposed to be a big spender and good sport while you go down trying."

They wandered more, bought an "exclusive only at the county fair" deep fat fried Hostess Twinkie; it was a fad like specialty item from one of the chow wagons, biggest thing since pig racing.

Keefe took the first bite, "Now, that'll land you in the hospital."

"Better than a corndog," Glenna cracked.

"Can't have a proper childhood without a dog on a stick and a genuine county fair..."

They walked around the front of the dance hall. Fletcher was grazing Bambalina on the lawn at the entrance to the hall.

Ranger had come outside. The burro's grazing offended his sensibilities, "Fletcher McCrea, why don't you follow the rules like everyone else. Livestock's supposed to be grazed out by the barns."

"Bambalina asked me special bring her over here, so she could get a look at what all the fair folk look like."

Bambalina was first animal to pick up the scent in the air. Human beings never could stop what was in their minds from oozing out of their skins.

Garrett Harwood all gray haired and red faced was standing up on the stoop in front of the dance hall. The elder of Meadowhawk smiled, but it had been hollowed out by time.

Best part was not a soul in the crowd, but for maybe a seasoned cowboy or two, could read the burro's eyes well enough to know what it was that was running through her mind.

Ranger walked down off the front deck steps, "Maybe, you might be considerate enough to remove that animal before she fouls this area."

Fletcher stood his ground as the other man approached. "I'd say any fouling been done here, might well have already come to pass."

"This is a dance, not a stinking parade."

"Bambalina's just pulling me along; I'm her parade float." Fletcher grinned.

Ranger moved in close. "Maybe you ought to move along."

"Impressive, Ranger, you telling the truth; hard to believe."

Ranger clenched his jaw. The muscles on his face showed.

Fletcher continued, "One thing I got to say about *my* lady friends is that when I speak to them, I tell them nothing but the truth, and I don't change it to suit the audience."

"I don't see you Sundays at church."

"I don't believe we pray to the same God," Fletcher said. "Best I can tell is Hazel Harwood has no idea what you worship, and who you're practicing prayers with."

"You're stepping across a bright line."

Fletcher laughed, "I'm just passing through; I mean no harm. You see the life I'm enjoying isn't the same life as your kind. Mine is an open book. I'm afraid you got yourself one of those secret books, those stories are bound to catch up with you one day."

"I don't know," Keefe interrupted. "Fletch, way I understand things, what a woman doesn't know won't hurt her."

Glenna took hold of Keefe's arm. She tried to pull him back.

Fletcher was enjoying sticking Ranger's life out into the open, "I don't win any awards for being a bachelor. My life leaves much to be desired, but there is one thing I aim to do, work at it each and every day, I don't pretend to be something I'm not."

Garrett Harwood had about enough of Fletcher's sass, he let blow in anger, "Get that jackass out of here..."

Fletcher took his eyes off Ranger, looked at Garrett Harwood. Bambalina knew what was coming before Ranger did. It all happened in slow motion. There was maybe this one cowboy in the crowd with the reflexes quick enough to see the burro's striking out. He saw her spin around, just like that lickety-split. She was the quicker animal in the brawl. Her rear hooves hit square against

Ranger's jaw, while his coldcocking fist wilted short of its mark. One blow was all it took Bambalina. Stood him stiff and felled the man like a pine tree. Bambalina wasn't to be trifled with. Fletcher watched his assailant splatter in a heap on the lawn. A man never wants to not see it coming. A burro's rapier like kick driving the full force of its pack animal passions home will cost a brawler a victory.

All that the town folk in the crowd could remember was witnessing Ranger's head snap back from that prize fighting burro's knockout blow. Hazel Harwood's date was sprawled flat out cold on his back.

Garrett Harwood stormed down the steps of the front deck in a fury and got hold of Bambalina's harness. The beast had control of the burro. Garrett jerked her head down hard. A cowboy up on the porch let out a sharp whistle and must have been twenty of his kind rushed off the dance floor so they might participate in the impromptu frolicking out on the front lawn.

Bambalina knew the kind of man she was up against. Time had not been so kind to him and he'd turned mean; she could smell the sourness in his soul. He cocked his hand back in a fist to deliver a punishing blow. Bambalina was pulling, hard as all get out, trying to escape the man's grip. The rodeo cowboys could see that there was nothing fair about the man's technique, was going to administer ordinary lopsided kind of beating; the kind Bambalina's species had endured all too often by a breed known all too well for a kind of cruelty beyond anything made any kind of sense. If she wasn't wearing a halter and it was just the two of them in a field, she'd make quick work of this bitter pill of a man. She'd have him cornered in a corral or leaping for his life over a fence.

Garrett double clutched. He aimed to inflict pain and suffering with his first blow. Keefe shoved Fletcher aside and come up from behind, he was a more able fighter; he took hold of the old man's fist and with the other grabbed hold of his opposite shoulder. He used the man's anger and effort against him, taking him to the ground; tried putting him on his back as easy as he could.

Rodeo cowboys come as a mob off the deck into the scene. Everything went so quick the men were not sure who had laid out Ranger or why?

The fall broke Garrett's grip on Bambalina's harness.

Fletcher took hold of her. He got between his animal and the mob. Fletcher put his arms out like he was trying to halt oncoming traffic. The clan of Chamber types had all gone to Ranger's aid, but one by one they had turned and were readying an attack on Fletcher.

Keefe continued restraining Garrett and that only infuriated his ex-father-in-law even more.

"Get your hands off me," he said with a boiling anger pouring from his face.

Keefe and Garrett were being pulled apart. Each man had three cowboys holding him. Keefe was not near so upset, had a kind of serenity to his person. "Now, Mr. Harwood, I'm just not going to allow you beat that burro. Not becoming a gentleman of your stature."

Hazel had come out the dance hall doors. She hurried down the steps to her father's aid. She slugged one of the cowboys that had a grip on her dad. "Let go of him, for God's sake, he's an old man."

Keefe put his arms up. He tried to surrender. Hazel pushed him with her hands against his chest.

"He's a mean man, Hazel. So is that man there." Keefe pointed to Ranger.

Fletcher was still rattled. He never was a fighter. "Hazel Harwood, what's become of you? Running with a pack of Chamber types, Chamber of god knows what they have turned into, angry at everybody and everything; they been infected with some kind of disease."

"Don't tell me who I'm supposed to be with." Hazel lit out toward his sharp wit. Two cowboys got hold of her, each from one side. "I don't much care for your advice, Fletcher McCrea, a man with your habits, telling me, who I'm supposed to keep company with; that is a fool's errand, all you are is a sun addled prospector, owe more money than you're worth."

Garrett was straightening himself up, "It's all over. Fairground is closing, town's changing, got to get with the times, going to be a new day here. You two are nothing but old news; got about as much of a future as a day old newspaper."

Fletcher said, "Wasn't so long ago Chamber was all about giving the little guy a hand up; not no more. It's like somebody come from main office, come out to Meadowhawk and poured *Drano* right down your throat. All you can do is spew out high minded jingo, bunch of talking points, and truth be told, you wouldn't know how a fair and square world worked if it came in the mail with your name written on it."

Most everyone at the dance had come out to bear witness to the brawl. Rodeo cowboys were inclined to watch Keefe and Fletcher's backs. The men that traveled in Garrett Harwood's circle, people from the Chamber, they were shoulder to shoulder considering whether or not to test their brawling skills.

Fletcher was disgusted with what was becoming of his town, "You believe you are making this town a better place to live, you getting any happier in your years?"

"Fletcher McCrea," Garrett said, "you are a quitter. Quit working at the test site. Quit trying to make this country a safer place for its people,"

"You think Ranger's the kind of man bring happiness to your little girl?"

Garrett spit out his response, "He's got twice the wallet you'll ever have. Look at you two, a couple of pathetic broken men, living dreams never going to come true. Neither one of you have even an inkling of what the world is all about."

"Chamber types," Fletcher said, "you and your people all infected with some kind of big shot ideas— Las Vegas style make everyone out to be a sucker kind of poison—don't like this kind, they speak Spanish; don't like that kind, man's wearing an earring, everyone's an atheist or a traitor."

"If we don't open up this place to the way the world is," Garrett said, "won't be anything left of her but another dried up ghost town."

"I don't know who you are talking to," Keefe said. "Just never seems to include those of us who live here, like you're trying to help somebody that doesn't exist. Something's wrong with you if your side's winning and you're still not much more than miserable."

"You had your chance, Keefe Kenny. And you couldn't even keep my daughter happy enough to sleep under the same roof."

"But I'm man enough to know when I've made a mistake, and fate opened my mind when I took that blow to my head. Now, you see, I not only know how to change, but I know what to change. And I know that the change I got in my heart will make all the happiness Hazel could ever hope for."

"Should have given up on you first day I set eyes on you," Garrett said. "I knew in my bones you're not even a nickel slot machine worth of a man."

"Biggest mistake I ever have made was letting the mother of my children slip right through my fingers. And I aim to do something about that."

"You are never going to be a lick different, same man you were when I met you...You're nothing but a full-of-himself-pillow aimed at smothering the breath right out of my daughter's life."

chapter

NINE

"Gage you better come here for a minute." Dotty's husband walked out the front entrance to the General Store.

Dotty busted the silence, "You know anything about this?"

"Know as much as you do."

Dotty was wearing her denim work smock. It was eight o'clock straight up. She turned the sign over on the window sill; they were open. Across the street a boom truck had come in first thing from Ely. Two men were hanging a commercial grade *For Sale* sign atop two pressure treated poles on the fairgrounds.

Gage walked out to the edge of the sidewalk and looked up and down the business district. A late model Mercedes-Benz, fancy type, the kind seldom seen in town, set parked down the street out front of the Meadowhawk's 1950's vintage Sundial Motel. Gage looked back at the men putting up the sign; they had thrown him for a loop.

The Harwood Awards Ribbon Company women were straggling to work. Hazel had already stopped for her coffee and pastry at Gig and Elena's. Ranger was out of town. He had a contract for road repairs north, on the Idaho border in Jackpot. Never mind that it was a government funded project; work was work, excavation and paving business was one of those so called public-private partnerships. Since Bambalina had rung his bell and Ranger had been picked up off the grass in front of the dance hall, seemed that something important to a man not too far north of his knees had gone all wobbly.

Dusty's fortunes had turned a might more workable. Her cowboy dancer had drawn a bull with something of a benign disposition. Aside from a tender tailbone, he was more than good to go. What bucking he hadn't had to contend with in the rodeo arena he had brought with him and used to good purposes, and to Dusty's delight out at the hot spring. But, after quenching her thirst and as the days passed, first one week, and then two, her frisky saddle tramp was more dull conversation and whiskey than an independent minded woman had time for. The day had come for her cowboy to go try his luck at the next rodeo. Dusty put her best effort into mustering sorrow about his leaving, but the fact of the matter, it was time to put an end to her annual county fair romance.

Mitzi answered the phone when Dotty called. She was watching through the café's back windows, when Dusty swatted that cowpoke on his behind and sent him packing out to his pickup truck. Mitzi and Sal's cabin set next to Dusty's. But for the fact that the two of them were so hard of hearing, the last couple of weeks might well have been remembered for how rough it was to sleep from the racket coming out of Dusty's place.

"Dotty," Mitzi declared, "I'll get off the phone and go tell Keefe right away." Mitzi was concentrating more on gleaning the details of Dusty's sendoff of her cowboy than she was of the news of the fairgrounds. "That's just terrible; be a sad day in the history of this county when that fairground is sold." Mitzi listened to Dotty a minute. She shook her head disgusted. "Those boys up at the state capital... hope that thing between their legs falls off, put it on a hook and use it for fish bait."

"Fletcher McCrea..." Sheriff Deputy shouted. "...want to have a word with you."

Tallula came out of the trailer on Fletcher's claim in a bathrobe. She looked down the steep hill to where the deputy had parked his vehicle before hiking up. "Morning," she said.

"Suppose you don't work for Hazel no more."

"Still do," Tallula explained, "I'm on company sanctioned Fletcher McCrea turquoise mine holiday."

Deputy Sheriff looked around Fletcher's claim. It looked nothing like a resort location. Then again, Fletcher's animal spirits were lost on men like the Deputy Sheriff.

Tallula was reading the lawman's judging mind and wasn't having any of it. "I'll go call Fletcher, take him a few minutes to climb out of that hole he's dug."

"It's that burro of his that's dug him that hole," Deputy Sheriff said. "But, I've been directed by the Sheriff to have words with Fletcher, so I'd appreciate it if you told him that I'm here."

Tallula was a skinny woman. But, even if she didn't have the same sized features as the rest of Fletcher's girlfriends, she went ahead and wagged that tail of hers all the way up to the mine, knowing full well that deputy was concentrating on more than official business.

Bambalina had been enjoying her morning with a pair of Clark's Nutcrackers. The birds and burro were feeling frisky and making fun. The birds had been swooping down from the tops of the pinion trees playing a favorite game of keep away with their burro friend, Bambalina. The Nutcrackers trusted burros twice as much as man. Bambalina, with the Deputy Sheriff's arrival, was playing dumb. The Nutcrackers alighted upon the burro's back and same as Bambalina, six eyes in all, two birds and one burro, were gawking at the human curiosity that come up to the mine with the shiny star pinned on top his heart.

Bambalina was nobody's patsy. She knew full well why the officer had four-wheeled up Pipe Dream Mountain. A burro has instincts tuned twice as sharp as regular folk when it comes to a hunch. It wasn't fair, but was how human law was applied in such circumstances. Even if Bambalina could prove that Ranger was going to coldcock Fletcher before she coldcocked him, justice was not on her side. There wasn't a deputized soul alive going to give a burro the benefit of the doubt, when a man of Ranger's community stature was involved. Still, if there was any solace to her predicament, was that word of Ranger's malady because of that kick, traveled like wild fire across this region of Nevada. Was an accomplishment that Bambalina was so rightly proud of, she'd felt her fateful trip to a glue factory was something she could not bring herself to fear. Furthermore, Bambalina trusted Fletcher McCrea would petition for her exoneration. She believed in her innocence and had full faith in her cause. With hooves dug in, she would remain defiant to man's burro bigotry until her mortal fate's last breath and final chapter.

"Now, come on," Fletcher appealed to the Deputy, "look at that burro; Bambalina wouldn't hurt nobody. Simple fact of the matter is Ranger ought not to have come at me the way he did. I brought that burro up to be peace loving."

Tallula was sitting on the stoop behind the two men. Deputy kept pointing toward the defendant, Bambalina... "I have my orders, and Sheriff has instructed me to tell you to keep that nuisance up here in her corral. And Sheriff wanted you to know in no uncertain terms, if you do come to town, you are not to bring that animal with you. The Sheriff said he doesn't want to see that sorry miserable mangy face in Meadowhawk ever again."

Fletcher crossed over to the fence. The Nutcrackers took flight off the burro's back as Bambalina approached, performing her best version of a death march; quivering her lower lip, there was remorse in her eye, and wasn't nothing alive more sorry about what had been done to that pillar of the community, Ranger. It was a fine moment in the remains of this beast of burden's life.

The Deputy, naturally suspicious, smelled something. "Don't think for even one second you can fool me," he said to Bambalina. "Next time you kick a man I will personally come hunt you down, stick ginger so far up your behind it will make you dance like a 'drunk Jezebel' touring in some two-bit Wendover, Nevada revue. Do I make myself clear?"

"Last time I checked," Tallula said, "...burros I know don't speak English."

"This one does," Deputy said.

Bambalina was almost panting, then her chest started twitching, and next thing she goes off, braying at the top of her lungs.

"She understands every stinking word..." the Deputy shouted over the burro's racket.

"You'd be braying too if someone told you that you had to stay up on this mountain for the rest of your days," Tallula said. "A girl has got to be allowed freedom to roam..."

Deputy hiked back down to his four-wheel drive patrol vehicle. "She stays up here or that burro gets shipped off to the rendering plant..."

The phone rang all day long. Citizens concerned about the fairgrounds being put up for sale were planning to meet at Rory's Brewery. Keefe drove into town in his pickup truck. Dusty hitched a ride. He made good on his promise and bought the hot spring housekeeper a beer. First off, they celebrated being alive, and for a close second, the departure of her rodeo cowboy. Dusty had come near as she could to a 'steady' in her life, and was grateful to have her 'free as the wind' life back again.

She was reading a letter her mom sent, "Driving all by herself from Montana, she's coming to see me."

"Like to meet your mother, find out what kind of stock you've been cut from," Keefe said.

"She never leaves the ranch; been ten years since she's gone more than fifty miles any direction," Dusty said.

"Well, she can enjoy soaking with her grown up girl out at the hot spring."

"She's a piece of boot leather," Dusty said. "Still rides, tough as nails, works twice as hard and just as long as ever since dad passed."

Rory's Brewery was furnished with a nineteenth century solid oak western back bar. The show piece had come scarred with 'honest to god' pistol playing bullet holes. The oak back bar stood near ten feet tall and stretched twenty-five feet across. The canopy had a solid carved Indian chief in feathered head dress set atop dead center.

Rory worked day and night. Didn't much matter whether he was out back brewing, tending to his inventory in the cellar, or standing behind the bar serving customers. Whole town was a tug-o-war. Whole mess was either a stand-off or a stalemate. Consensus among citizens was for some other place.

"Try a taste, ready today, it's Meadowhawk IPA."

Keefe took a drink. "Rory, that's best Indian Pale Ale I've tasted since the last IPA you poured me."

"Keefe, that's the taste of the sweat of my brow."

Up and down the bar folk were filling up the bar stools. More citizens stood behind the seated patrons. Rory and a part time second hand off duty fireman were pouring pints, trying to keep up with town's customers.

Dotty and Gage, both were cut the same, short and stout. They shut down the General Store, same time end of every day, eight o'clock. Dotty removed her smock, turned the sign in the window over, then locked the front door. She put her arm through Gage's. They'd hurried all day helping customers. This was their chance to slow down. They were joining the rest of the town folk for a beverage. The time had come to commiserate over the fairgrounds being put up for sale.

Women who worked at the Harwood Award Ribbon Company were accounted for. Members of the Chamber were knotted up as was their custom, sitting at tables congregating among one another.

Glenna finally showed herself. Keefe had hoped she might not have come alone. She waved from the door. Glenna was looking around the Brewery committing to memory every face that was there.

Keefe stood, "Go on, Glenna… take my seat. Take a load off."

"No need, I've been sitting all day," she said.

Keefe finished his pint. "You and Dusty hold down this end of the bar. Save my stool."

He walked out front and checked the sidewalks up and down the block. Sun had set and Meadowhawk's street lights had come on and formed pools of light in the business district. Glenna knew full well where he was headed.

When he had come around the block, he caught Hazel at the Harwood Award Ribbon Company turning around and slamming the front door. She nearly knocked the old wood door off its hinges. She didn't have a thing to say to that man. Keefe looked through the windows, knocked on the front entrance, went around the side of the building to see if she was trying to sneak out the back. He returned to the front of the building. He put his ear up to the threshold. There wasn't even one floor board creaking.

He turned around leaned up against the door and slid down onto the seat of his pants.

"Know you're in there..."

"Am not..."

"Are so..."

"Am not..." Hazel was leaning her back against the other side of the door.

"Must be hearing voices then..."

"Crazy as a quilt, what I've been saying..."

"How come I can hear you?"

"Because you hear voices..."

"Understand your man's left town."

"I don't have a man."

"Well, whatever that thing is... that thing has left town."

"It won't ever work..."

"Might..."

"No might, or even a maybe to it."

"How come you know so much?"

"When a man wrestles a woman's father to the ground..."

"I didn't hurt that man."

"Might as well pulled a knife out and stabbed him in the chest."

"Hazel Harwood, he's always come between me and you."

"Keefe Kenny, you've always come between me and you."

"Why don't you open this door and we can sort things out like man and woman ought to do?"

"Why don't you leave and go away like a normal ex-husband?"

"You're going to sit still and let this town fall apart?"

"Bambalina changed my world when she kicked Ranger."

"He lived to tell..."

"Might as well have kicked him where the sun don't shine..."

"I'd have given that burro my blessings."

"Well, was a curse, kicked him so hard in the head his other parts haven't worked since."

Keefe tried to stifle his laugh but it only grew worse.

"I don't know what you think is so funny," Hazel said.

"Ranger's private parts keeling over like an un-watered flower..."

"Second time in my life you have got in the way of my sex life..."

"I'm feeling like I could make peace with you finally."

"I was making my new peace."

"Well, I got peace in me bigger than the best peace in the wide world; and it has got to have you, and nothing but you, from this day out and until the end of never."

"I don't know what you're talking about. You're not even good in bed..."

"I'm better than good; what do you mean no good?"

"You're some kind of human ice cube."

"Hazel Harwood, I'm a blast furnace..."

"You're worse than dry ice..."

"Was nothing but steam heat coming off us..."

"You were the deep freeze, ice chest with a lock on it; had to take my clothes off and run around like some pole dancer before the light in those britches of yours went on."

"You do have a talent for naked fun; I got to give you that..."

"I didn't have to do any dancing for Ranger. He was plain normal."

"I aim to go out of this world married to you and I'm planning on you and me having a sex life second to none."

"You just weren't any good at lovemaking, rubbed me like you were sanding a piece of wood. Now Ranger, he wasn't much of a conversation, but get him buck naked and I'll tell you he wasn't done until the project was completed."

Keefe was sitting shaking his head. He jumped in with both feet. "Hazel Harwood, we had us hot sex any night we wanted."

Hazel huffed. She shook her head back and forth whispering in spite, "Keefe Kenny is the curse of my life." She sniffed her nose and raised her voice, "I'll tell you what a good sex life feels like. It feels like you are alive. Man comes in the room and you're not invisible. Touch so tender, clothes go missing, knows what a woman is for."

"I know what a woman is for..."

"You don't know how to play along." Hazel said.

"What's that supposed to mean?"

"Means you're supposed to have secret plans and try and get me, even when I'm not even in the mood."

"You were always in the mood."

"See that? I didn't want to be the one that was always in the mood. Wanted a man that was always in the mood. Girl likes it when a man pleads for it."

"I begged you for the good stuff plenty."

"And another thing, Keefe Kenny, a bed's not the only place to have sex."

"So where else do you do it?"

"Bunch more places..."

"A bunch more of places?"

"And then you can have a bunch more sex, and doesn't go stale."

"If you'd open this door, Hazel, we could have an experience of the first order..."

"Problem is Dad hates your guts..."

"He'll break that fever, get over things, have to..."

"Fact is, I don't have a lick of faith in you. You'll never be the kind of man I'd want to be in bed with ever again."

"Doesn't sound too tough..."

"Never going to happen, divorce is final."

"Make love to you right here, right now," Keefe started unbuttoning his shirt.

"On the front stoop of my business...?"

"Shirts off," Keefe started removing his boots. "Make love right here, or take me inside, I'll do you on the floor..."

"Keefe Kenny, I am going to put a shell in my shotgun..."

"Buckles off, zippers down..."

Hazel turned around and pushed the mail slot in the middle of the door, "You are going to be the ruin of my life..."

"I'm feeling like I got a sweet tooth for living!"

"You never had a tooth for nothing..."

Glenna had come around the corner and was stopped dead in her tracks. There Keefe was in front of the door hopping back and forth barefoot, preparing to pull off the last of his garments and unveil the naked truth.

"What are you doing?"

Keefe wasn't ashamed of a thing, "I'm getting ready to make love to Hazel Harwood..."

Raising her voice so as to be heard from the other side of the door, "Is not..."

"Told you, see that, she's talking to me..."

"Hazel have you been encouraging Keefe Kenny?"

"Encouraging him to have a heart attack..."

"See there? Hazel Harwood doesn't have even one kind word for you." Glenna was smiling.

"Wasn't chest pains; it was love pangs. Woman goaded me into taking my clothes off... she was going to open the door and we were going to have a reconciliation right here, right now!"

Hazel shouted through the door, "You going to put your faith in your best friend or trust that man's lying ears?"

"I'm believing you, Hazel." Glenna picked up Keefe's underwear and stuffed them into his hands. She pursed her lips and narrowed her eyes, pointed with her finger to put his clothes back on.

Hazel took one more look through the mail slot, then said, "An ex-husband isn't something anyone should believe... not a word... they don't know how to tell the truth... ex-husbands are nothing but driving the wrong way down a one way street."

"You're afraid because I'm ready to do you on top a pile of your handmade first place ribbons." Keefe was hopping on one foot while kicking his leg back into his jeans, "Going to give you a real prize... take our sweet loving time... I'm holding back and let you have a first place finish."

"Hazel, I'm taking Keefe down to the Brewery for impromptu town hall."

"We're leaving right now," Keefe added.

"Good riddance," Hazel said.

"Walking down the street..."

"My prayers have been answered..."

"Won't have to pretend to not be talking to me one more second..."

"Get, before I go get my gun..."

"Hazel Harwood, I love you with all my heart... I aim to make you mine."

"Will be a cold day and lightning bolt out of the heavens aimed to strike me dead before that will ever happen," Hazel screamed.

Glenna tugged on Keefe's arm. He had a big smile on his face, "I'm riding into the eye of that storm. I miss you, Hazel Harwood. You are my kind of wife."

Hazel kicked the door with the heel of her foot. She screamed...

Glenna couldn't help herself. She had to put her hand up to her mouth and bit her finger. She got serious about tugging on Keefe and dragged him off into the night.

"Glenna Goddard... feels like I've been sitting by my phone all my life waiting for her to call. You don't know when she's coming back, or if she'll be the same when she gets here. All I know for sure is loving Hazel's never done me any harm, losing her temper doesn't count, she never means it, part of who she is and I love that part too."

They took about five paces then Glenna let go of his arm and made a fist and slugged him hard as all get out. "You know what is wrong with you?"

"No?" Keefe said.

"You try too hard..."

"I was that close..." Keefe claimed.

Glenna slugged Keefe in the arm again, "I wasn't supposed to see how excited you are about how close you were..."

"I was pretty excited, wasn't I?"

Glenna slugged his arm.

When they got back to the Brewery, seemed most of the whole town had squeezed into Rory's. Gig and some of the men from the Chamber were having useless words with men's ears that were closed, and minds all made up.

Glenna bought two pints. She handed one to Keefe. She looked in the mirrors behind the bar down the other side of the saloon. "That's the man driving the Mercedes..."

Keefe drank up. He set his pint glass down, looked into the mirror same as Glenna. "Didn't know we had a Mercedes in town."

"Dotty told me on break today," Glenna said, "me and the girls walked back to work and detoured and there it was set parked in front of the Sundial."

"Man looks like he drives a Mercedes." Keefe said.

He was groomed and shaved; clean as a whistle. He dressed as simple as the next man, but cut of his shirt and crease of his pants wasn't anything like anyone in Meadowhawk ever wore.

"Meadowhawk's curse... there's not a thing a soul gets to slide by with, when they come drifting into this town."

"Nothing but nosey ears and idle chatter as far as an eye can see..." Glenna clinked her pint against Keefe's. "Either you or me is going to have to go get his story."

"Might be right woman for the job," Keefe inspected her up and down, "a man with pair of eyes in his head could pour his heart out to a refined woman like you."

"He's got a wallet, good looks, earns the privilege of a younger woman." Glenna said.

"Thought you were a younger woman..." Keefe was baiting.

"And I thought you knew how to keep your clothes on..."

She made a fist. Keefe put his hand up to protect the arm she'd been slugging.

Glenna bucked up and smiled. "I'm going to see what I can see."

"Not going to get any answers down at this end of the bar."

She started to cross the room. She stopped turned to Keefe. Glenna unfastened one more button down her blouse, "Most of the time they'll do the trick."

"Can't hurt," Keefe said regarding her low cut blouse, "gives a man some hope..."

"Does it now?"

"They make a man feel the world is a better place, like blue sky, warm day, being with your two best friends..."

Glenna looked down to check how she appeared, "Great, now they're a weather forecast."

The stranger was reading a text message off the screen of his phone.

Glenna approached; she interrupted, "Any good news?"

The man said, "Same as ever, world's still falling apart."

"We're trying to keep Meadowhawk's crime blotter hushed up."

"This tavern's more than a murmur tonight."

"Tourism is picking up," Glenna said.

"Only corner of the bar has any peace is right here."

"Ruin our town's reputation, if we let someone pass through and have a peaceful visit. Can't have that."

"I'm Jace Brandt." He was easy enough, broad shouldered, athletic, bald with gentle eyes, kind expression, graceful. He took Glenna's hand. She had a grip. They shook.

He got off his stool. "Take my seat."

"No, I try not to sit at the Brewery. You can end up trapped on a barstool in this corner of Nevada." She smiled.

"I know all about trapping." The man said.

"You spend any time in small towns?" Glenna had a manner of keeping an eye on a person she was speaking to without that person ever feeling as if she was even looking at them.

"I've made time stand still in a few," the man said. "Thank god for this joint, it beat sitting in my room down at the Sundial watching the cable."

He wore a wedding band. Glenna didn't catch his eyes trying to steal a peek. She intentionally crushed her chest against his arm, "Must have family nearby?"

"No, just got into town; I'm here all alone. Have some business to tend to, and then I go home."

"You don't look like a door to door salesman."

Jace Brandt smiled, "I'm in private enterprise."

Glenna smiled, "Private enterprise; isn't that everybody's business?"

Jace shook his head, smiled. "What I enjoy about a small town; everybody knows more about your business than you do."

"Meadowhawk is too quiet. We like taking turns plying strangers with beer. Loosen our new friends up; then we can quench a few curiosities."

Jace smiled at Glenna. "I promise, if I do any business, you'll be the first one to get the memo."

"That's not how it works," Glenna smiled and winked, "you're in Meadowhawk. See trick is for us to find out your business before you finish your first beer."

There was something of a commotion over at the Chamber's table. Garrett Harwood got up off his seat. "Well, I'm done here." He slapped the table with his hand, set his white straw Stetson cocked sure off to one side of his head. "Time I get home."

Since the dance at the fair, he'd been wearing his aggravations out loud. He was broadcasting his leaving, the whole time ignoring Keefe or Fletcher. As far as he was concerned, those two men didn't even exist.

He picked his way across the saloon. He began walking down the line of stools at the bar. He stopped when he got to Glenna. Her extra unfastened button caught his eye.

"How are you tonight, Miss Goddard?" Garrett asked.

"Want you to meet town's newest tourist. Jace, this is Chamber's President, Garrett Harwood."

"Pleasure," Garrett said.

Jace stood and the two men shook hands.

"I understand Deputy Sheriff paid Fletcher McCrea's turquoise mine a visit today." Garrett kept looking at Glenna's unfastened buttons on her shirt.

"Didn't hear a thing," Glenna looked Garrett up and down same as he did her. "See that, Jace, see how Meadowhawk's citizens are?"

"Never run from the truth, unless it's a bill collector knocking on your door." Garrett fake laughed and shook his head, "Was overdue, ordered him to keep that burro up at his mine and out of town."

Glenna explained. "See Bambalina's kind of famous, some say, even notorious now, since she kicked a man."

"Kicked the man my daughter was dating. . ." Garrett explained. "See that burro in town again, and first one to put a bullet through her head will have the law on their side."

"I know," Glenna said, "you saw that they put up the for sale sign at the fairgrounds today?"

"Might be this town can make some progress now," Garrett said.

Glenna noticed Jace picked up his beer. He took a long drink.

"Garrett and Chamber are big privatizers, like to see government get out of the town's business," Glenna said.

"Hopefully, whatever happens, it turns out all to the good," Jace said.

"Why everyone is here," Glenna said. "Most of us want to try and save the fair."

"Most of us want to save the town," Garrett interrupted. "Some people feel otherwise, don't know a thing about how the world works. Biggest menace to free enterprise we have here are ideas some folks in town hold."

"Chamber's happy about fairgrounds being sold off," Glenna explained.

"Might be that committee to save the fair can fold their tent and go home now," Garrett said.

"Mr. Jace Brandt," Glenna asked, "you think closing down the fairgrounds might improve our little town?"

Jace measured his words, "I wouldn't dare hazard a guess."

"Town's founders, century ago, put a fairground here, smack dab in the center of Meadowhawk." Glenna said. "Most of us like that choice."

"It's time for the town's committee to save the fair to give up. Fair's days have come and gone. Time's come to move out of the way." Garrett smiled. "Might be town can make some progress." Garrett was full of brew, brimming to the rim with his brand of certainty. "Was a pleasure to meet you," Garrett tipped his finger at the rim of his Stetson. "Glenna..." he looked Glenna up and down one last time, "Might be we can start growing again. Citizens here have forgotten what made our country great. Freedom, that's what we need; you see, we are a free people living in the land of opportunity."

Garrett took no more time, spoke to no other person. He walked down along the row of bar stools, past Keefe, ignoring Fletcher, went out the Brewery's front doors.

Fletcher stood up from his chair at the table, he hoisted his pint, "Time we call this saloon to order..."

"Why we all came out tonight," Keefe piped in.

Glenna said, "Might stick around. See how citizens in town feel about things."

Jace finished his beer, "I think I'll let your town folk have their meeting."

Glenna followed Jace down the bar. She said, "Before you head back to the Sundial, want you to meet Keefe Kenny."

The men shook hands.

Glenna said, "Keefe's Hot Spring is about ten miles out on the foot of Pipe Dream Mountain."

"You got to come out for a soak; join us at the café for dinner."

"You're kind of famous," Jace said. "Heard about you; you're the man that got blown up and didn't find a thing wrong with you."

Keefe smiled, "Sounded like big news if you were from a small town."

Glenna said, "He's something of a miracle."

"Are you just passing through?" Keefe asked.

"I'm taking care of some business."

"Don't get a lot of businessmen stopping here. Might want to try out our new 'naked night' at the hot spring."

Jace smiled big, "'Naked night?'"

"Told you," Glenna said, "small town's all about the truth, the whole truth, and don't you know, nothing but the naked truth."

Jace got a big smile on his face. "How's 'naked night' business?"

Keefe grinned, put his arm around Glenna's waist, squeezing her tight, kind of helping all that sunny weather come shining out the top of her blouse. "'Naked night'. . .? It's been a revelation. . ."

chapter

TEN

Keefe's days were chock-full. He'd wake up; go downstairs at first squeak of the café's screen door hinges. He'd pour a cup of coffee, fret with Sal, gossip with Mitzi, eat breakfast and then get cracking with his chores in the greenhouse.

Hot house basil was thriving. Keefe had all manner of recipes planned for the tomatoes. So far he'd stopped flies, moths and ants dead in their tracks using homemade chili and garlic spray. There was not a problem that couldn't be licked. There were fresh grown new shoots sprouting from here to Sunday. Green beans, squash, kale, carrots were coming up hale and hardy.

Day by day, the hot spring's garden gathered momentum. Sweaty air dripped from this leafy oasis. Soon the hot house would be bursting with fruits and vegetables. As it stood, the building manifested abundance framed cheek by jowl. Growing a vegetable garden right smack in the midst of the Great Basin set possibility against 'no way- no how.' Folk in town spoke about the emerging sense of prosperity. Expectations were ripening and growing impatient for the picking.

Resignation letters began accumulating on Garrett Harwood's desk. Some of the Chamber's most loyal members were quitting. It wasn't hard to understand why. Most folks in Nevada found the notion of following orders was nothing but capitulation. The folks that made this place home were guided by sagebrush wisdom. It was rooted into their *set in stone* souls. People didn't need leading, didn't want to follow, and were by disposition insistent about making up their own minds. The tea party patriot rallies Garrett Harwood attended this last year had been a healing event, a true joyous outburst of pure revulsion of a kind he had not felt in how long he could not recall. His outrage had been all to his good. He was sure. He would quarry no doubt. When he listened to a speech about how second amendment remedies were a constitutionally enumerated right, the words rang in his ears like answered prayer.

Garrett Harwood was a man of years. He had no patience for compromise and had come to believe, in his heart of hearts, that there was simply no other way a right minded person could see things. So, while he thrived upon his unregulated anger, the resignations from the Chamber cut to the bone. And when stress builds, palpitations can set in. The tensions grew all the worse the more he remained in denial. Garrett wouldn't allow the bastards the pleasure of seeing he had even the slightest qualms. Whether it was a clinical form of arrhythmia, or just plain heartburn mixed with unacknowledged regret, a man of Garrett's kind held that the right thing to do was blame his aches and pains on the traitors in his midst. Grievance was his genius. It was their damn fault. He was a reasonable man, and because he was an open minded man with a keen sense of self-preservation, he did the prudent thing and made an appointment at the clinic.

The doctor had the stethoscope against his chest, "We're all dead eventually..."

"I get tired of eating the same things."

"It's what you're 'believing' seems to be the problem."

"I'm 75 years old; I'm wearing out."

"You just don't have any... left."

"What's that, Doc'?"

"Happiness..."

"Don't mince words."

"You are about the most miserable son of a bitch in Meadowhawk."

"Why do I have chest pains?"

"Ideology, that's what you have."

"So, you got a pill for that?"

"Man your age needs his happiness."

Garrett stood up, began buttoning his shirt.

"When was the last time you enjoyed the company of a woman?"

"I'm not attracted to women my age. And the ones I am attracted to, they're not attracted to a man my age."

"You got a mind locked shut tighter than a Texas oil drum."

"What do you know?"

"I take care of those women."

"So..."

"I can count any number of older women could take your breath away..."

"...Naked on a bed, nothing but their jewelry on?"

"You don't know the difference between a dirt clod and a diamond..."

"Know dull and I know when something shines."

"An angry man's a dead ender… got to learn how to appreciate what you have, stop bellyaching…"

"I got a good life…"

"If you had a good life, you'd be allowing men coming up behind you to take the helm."

"Not a man in Meadowhawk can do what I do…"

"Time to get out of the way, Garrett, time for the next generation to figure things out."

"I got a lot of life in me still…"

"Garrett," Doc tried to be sincere, "you have to open your eyes, love the things you find right here, right now, before the time God gave you ends up being spent on things won't add a lick of joy to your sour puss."

"Well, what do I do when my chest starts to hurt?"

"I took the Hippocratic Oath. If you were my mortal enemy, I'd still be duty bound to treat you…"

"So, what are you going to do?"

"I'm going to put you on low dose of aspirin and, if I'm right you'll be fine. If I'm wrong, won't matter; you'll be dead before your head hits the ground."

Garrett said, "You don't have to sound so happy about that…"

"It would be lot easier, if you weren't the most obstinate man in the whole of Meadowhawk."

Bero and Mirari were headed up Pipe Dream Mountain. They tooted their horn and Keefe dropped everything and just like that they were beating Bero's truck up a forest service road to higher elevations.

"I can have pine nuts for basil pesto right through the fall?" Keefe asked.

"Every day, my friend…"

"They'll keep?"

"They can keep; best if you keep them refrigerated."

"That's all pinion tree right along the ridge?" Keefe asked.

"Piñones, yes, and some *ipuruk*, you say juniper…" Mirari said.

A plume of cotton-ball-shaped thunderheads had been kicked up by the prevailing winds on the lee side of the peak. The clouds were born innocent but, as the afternoon passed, they turned gray to near black. Pipe Dream Mountain had moods. Up top on her peak isn't the same as the weather down in the valley.

"I've never picked the cones from pinion trees…"

"It is hard work; it tests you. You pick, you gather, you have to haul the harvest back to the trucks." Mirari held a branch with one hand and picked a cone off with the other. She twirled it around, inspecting the cone; it was still immature. She handed it to Keefe. He began counting trees. The dirt road ran straight up through a vein of pinion. Keefe walked along a footpath on the hillside. He went alone. He continued counting, estimating the number of cones, and how many nuts. He hadn't gone far; he'd seen enough.

Keefe hiked back. He asked Mirari, "Anybody harvest commercially?"

"You want to pick up here on the mountain?" Mirari smiled at Bero. She said, "Maybe we do."

Keefe smiled, "Maybe we harvest?" His eyes got wider, "maybe we do."

Jace Brandt had come out to Keefe's hot spring café for dinner. He chose a table on the deck still in the sun. Dining guests could regale upon the fresh cut bloomed couples, lumbering in the thrall of new love back and forth from their honeymoon suites to the hot spring's soaking pools. It was almost better than watching hummingbirds fighting at a feeder.

Keefe spotted his new guest. Jace started to stand up.

"Sit down, take a load off," Keefe said.

"Never been out to a hot spring resort..."

Keefe was proud of his enterprise. "You ever do any hot spring honeymoon spotting?"

Jace looked off toward the soaking pools smiling, "No, I'm a first timer."

Keefe smiled, sat down across the table, "Honeymooners bring a dedication to a marriage bed..."

"I bet they do," Jace said.

"They're the epitome of the truth that practice makes perfect."

"Is that what they're doing?" Jace looked out toward the soaking pools and sunset.

"Getting this new part of their married life all figured out, so that it can work real slick; like first time every time." Keefe was half teasing.

"I don't think I've ever been to a resort that's set up for honeymooners."

Keefe finished his beer, "We have a quality control program. Why we're so popular. I spent a whole week's labor figuring out a way to stop a bride and groom's headboard from slapping against a wall."

"I'd imagine there is a real craft to hospitality services," Jace said.

"We put in dimmer switches for the lights so that, when the groom starts his seduction, it's guaranteed to be a consummation. We want things to go extra slick. There's deluxe soundproofing and double glazed windows. What we're trying to do here is make a path to romantic feelings."

"I imagine honeymoon business has got to be competitive."

Keefe spotted Mitzi. He put two fingers up for two beers. "First thing I learned, you got to have your own airport shuttle."

"Just like the fancy hotels," Jace said.

Faith had come out from Meadowhawk. She had her bare shoulder peeking out of her top; it was sure fire. She had a rendezvous with Fletcher tonight.

Keefe waved to her, stood and pulled a chair over from another table. Keefe gave Faith a hug, winked. "You met Jace?"

"No, but we've talked about him."

"Almost as good," Keefe said.

"Saw Dotty, word is someone's written an offer on the fairgrounds." Faith shook her head in regret.

"Garrett Harwood's got to have strutted all sanctimonious up and down Main Street." Keefe said.

"Hazel tried pretending she didn't care," Faith replied, "but, the girls, we can see it in her eye, she's rattled too."

"Sad day in Meadowhawk when the fairgrounds is sold off," Keefe said.

"Can't be a done deal," Faith grabbed hold of Keefe's arm. "There's got to be inspections before seller and buyer come to terms."

"How much is it?" Jace asked.

"There's all hell to pay for that piece of land," Faith explained.

"Like buying the heart and soul of Meadowhawk," Keefe said.

"Might as well put what's left down on a long shot..." Faith was disgusted.

"All that money, never make up for what that land means to us," Keefe tapped his finger on the table, "you'd still have lost the best thing about Meadowhawk."

"Keefe," Faith said, "you're not a man inclined to give up at the first roadblock."

"Mr. Kenny," Mitzi said arriving with the menus and handing each a beer. "Miss Faith."

"Thank you, Mitzi," Faith had sympathy for the old woman's hard work.

Mitzi yanked on Faith's sagging sweater to cover her shoulder. Sweater fell off again.

Keefe told Jace, "She's got one of those shoulders makes a man say his prayers before bedtime."

Mitzi rubbed Faith's exposed shoulder with her hand.

Keefe said, "Good enough to chew on..." He took a bite.

"Keefe Kenny," Faith said, "if you break your habit of teasing me, my life will be a dull stretch of lonely road."

"Your bare shoulder's best rope trick I've ever seen."

"I work up the nerve to come out here for 'naked night' my shoulder's going to be the last piece of me you'll be eyeballing."

"'Naked night'....?" Jace wondered.

"Like sprinkling slander on top of best day of a man's life," Keefe said.

"Me and the girls are all talk about coming out," Faith said.

Jace said, "Come out here tonight for dinner, and wouldn't you know, I end up with an education on the finer points of the honeymoon industry."

"Lot of science involved when you put lovers into an extended stay package out here in the middle of nowhere." Faith said.

Keefe added. "Got the ladies to help me sort out the love making supplies we provide to our new married folk."

"We went to Las Vegas. We got Keefe all setup."

"I bet I paid twice as much as you spent for your Mercedes," Keefe said.

"We bought skin creams, body oils, and high priced glycerins; some of the girls got tighteners, prolongers and pleasure balms."

"Pleasure balms?" Jace asked.

"There is a lot of technology in the honeymoon business; in this day and age, people expect certain things." Keefe said.

Faith continued, "Got the fun stuff: lip glosses, edible oils, and girl's favorite secret weapon...delay sprays!"

"Delay sprays?" Jace was shaking his head smiling.

"You haven't been to the edge of excitement until you get your hand on that thing." Faith reached out into the air with one hand and got ahold, then took her imaginary bottle in her other.

"Idea is to squirt one of those delay sprays on it before all hell breaks loose..." Keefe cracked.

Faith said, "It's all in the instruction manual. We put a book together, tested everything out firsthand except the married part."

"Fletcher was their Guinea Pig."

"Put the instructions and how to use everything right below the Gideon's Bible." Keefe said. "Got the good book right above the better book..."

Blake parked the shuttle down in the lower lot. This was his first chance he had to get a close-up inspection of Jace's high performance Mercedes-Benz. He knew right off; it was the twelve-cylinder. Blake circled the machine. He had a worry on his face. This fine automobile parked in a dirt lot covered in dust, it was a desecration is what it was. A world class machine of this pedigree was a thing to go out of your way for. You keep it clean, stay on pavement, and garage it at night.

Fletcher was driving his International back out the Hot Spring Highway. He'd run errands in Meadowhawk. Lark had hitched a ride. He came off the road and rattled up the dirt lane. Fletcher pulled up next to Blake.

"Is it for sale?" Fletcher asked.

Lark got out and came around the other side.

"You know what this is?" Blake asked.

"Yes, I do." Fletcher put his arm around Lark. "That is a bucket of bolts."

"This is one of the finest machines the Germans have ever made."

"And this one comes ready to go wherever the driver's got the dream to take her."

Blake looked twice at Fletcher then at Lark and asked, "You come out to Keefe's for a soak?"

"I thought I might go to the airport with you..." Lark looked confident.

"Four hours of nothing to do..."

"I don't have nothing to do right here..." She widened her eyes.

"What do you say?" Fletcher asked Blake.

"You want to ride along?"

Lark shook her head, smiled, "As long as I get to pick what we play on the radio."

"You two... Like waiting for the water to boil," Fletcher said poking Blake, "and, Blake, try to pretend you like the music she picks."

Dusty whistled from the office. They had three couples going back. The guests had flights to catch. All this slow motion chitchat wasn't going to get the job done. Dusty whistled a second time.

Blake walked to the receptionist's desk and took two pieces of luggage. He was going back and forth out to the parking lot and putting the honeymooners' bags into the shuttle.

"We're going to miss you all," Keefe said.

One of the new husbands said, "We're coming back..."

"Telling our friends..." another new husband said.

Faith had come out to the parking lot. Fletcher gave his lady friend a wink and took hold of her hand, "Heard the news about the fairgrounds?"

Faith explained, "Just told Keefe."

"I'm aching to go find a spot where we can go be rotten and bitter about it together," Fletcher said.

"Maybe pretend you're heartbroken over me…"

Fletcher put his palm on Faith's cheek, looked her dead in the eyes. "There's no fooling; more than once on account of you, I've ached inside so hard sleep wouldn't come."

Faith wasn't having any of it, "Fletcher McCrea, what in the devil has gone wrong with you?"

"I haven't had a beer…"

Faith doubled down on that look she was giving Fletcher.

He said, "Let's go eat; afterwards I'll take you up the mountain, show you what the Milky Way looks like."

"Fletcher McCrea, you are going to need your strength."

Blake hauled two more pieces of luggage out to the vintage Chevy airport shuttle.

Keefe was on the other side helping the three couples into their seats. "We're proud of our hot springs, prouder still you decided to give us a shot," Keefe stood at the door. "Buckle those seatbelts…"

"Don't want to lose those new wives," a husband said.

Keefe had a smile, "Now that you got them all broke in…"

One bride said, "We're not broke in, they're all wore out…"

"Either way, never going to find replacements for the love of your life," Keefe was helping the women up into their seats. "We've got champagne in the cooler on ice. We want you happy about coming and plain rue the day about going."

One new wife said, "We are inconsolable; didn't want it to ever end."

"Best honeymoon we could have ever dreamed of," the husband added.

"We vowed to be married until death do us part," another wife said.

"Had such a powerful honeymoon," her husband said, "we've decided we're changing our vows..."

"We're staying together for all eternity." The wife kissed her husband on his cheek.

"See that," Keefe said. "Hot spring honeymoon will put a wiggle in a life."

"We were so nervous," another wife said.

"You walk up to the cabin, you open the door, take your bride inside... from that moment on, nothing's ever going to be the same..."

Keefe interrupted, "Okay, okay, now raise your hands, if you had the best time in your lovemaking life."

All three wives and all three husband's hands shot straight up into the air.

One husband claimed, "I had to hold on for dear life..."

"By the time he was done," his wife said...

"I threw my hands up and I was pretending I was riding a roller-coaster..."

"See what a wife you're all in love with will do for you?" Keefe said.

"I haven't had so much fun since my mother gave up asking me what time I'd be home..."

"He was all over me..."

"Begging her for more..."

"All night..."

"And all day long..."

"Came as a complete surprise."

"Hot spring can grow an appetite," Keefe said. "If you got any friends getting married, you tell them we got a resort that'll work better than perfect for them too."

Keefe shut the shuttle doors, "Okay, everybody, Blake, they're good to go."

Blake touched the key and the shuttle's motor rumbled to life. Lark was seated, country style in the middle, snug up against Blake. A pair of raven haired innocence is what they were. Blake put the vintage stretch shuttle into gear, Lark tuned in the country music on the satellite radio receiver, and they rolled off slow out of the parking lot down toward the Hot Spring Highway.

Dusty had come out to wave goodbye. "Breaks a girl's heart," Dusty said. "Come on out here to the resort, living the dream, then back to where they come from and all they got is a sink full of dirty dishes."

"Dusty," Keefe said, "you're day's coming."

Dusty smiled, "Men I share my bed with drink too much, sleep too late, and want me to promise to be the kind of woman they can't have."

"Sound like a fine bunch of men you're driving crazy..."

"I open with hard to get and close with impossible to keep..."

"Dusty, come on..."

"Put a dress on and try it yourself," Dusty smiled, "why I like living here. See working at a prison beats being locked up for life pretending you're happy in bed with some fool. I'd almost rather be put to death."

"You don't mean that Dusty..."

"No, you are probably right, I wouldn't do that. I'd get a divorce."

chapter

ELEVEN

"Who do you think Jace Brandt works for?" Keefe asked.

Rory leaned over the bar and in a low voice said, "Can't be anything good."

"Why would anyone come out here and stay at the Sundial Motel?" Fletcher asked.

"I can understand pulling in for a night," Keefe said.

"You think he's sleeping with someone?" Fletcher liked that notion.

"Almost impossible to imagine," Rory said, "ladies that live in Meadowhawk are an acquired taste."

"Rory," Fletcher said, "a man will sleep with near any kind of woman. Hell, a good woman from the Great Basin gives a man twice the fun for half what a big city lady would cost."

"I'm a brewmaster and barman, Fletcher McCrea. I suppose acquired taste or not, I know men, know what they'll do with their last dollar… small town or big city, in the end it don't matter."

Gage walked down to the Brewery after work with Dotty. The bar's windows were aglow with neon lighted beer advertising signs. Blake was sitting at a table reading over instructions in a shop manual for installing and adjusting a distributor for a Studebaker Superhawk.

Keefe tapped the bar with the tip of his finger. "I say a few of us, we go down to the Sundial, see what we see."

"I'll go," Rory said.

Fetcher tapped his finger on the bar, "I'm in."

"Blake, Gage, you coming?"

"My other man can hold things down," Rory said, rubbing the back of his hand against the beard on his chin.

The five conspirators were quick out the front door. Keefe hustled into the middle of the street. From where he stood he could see the back end of Jace's Mercedes.

Keefe raised his hand, fanned it downward, wanted quiet. "He's there," he pointed with his finger signaling his reconnaissance group to slip silently toward the Sundial.

The five men scrunched together. Rory, one of the older men, kept looking back like some kid making sure nobody was following them.

As they passed the Bakery, Gig came out the shop door. "Now, where are you all sneaking off to?"

Keefe and Fletcher looked at one another, then to Rory, Gage and Blake. Keefe spoke for the group, "Going down to the Sundial to see what we can find out about who this Jace Brandt is."

Gig untied his apron. He tossed it in the doorway. "I'm going too; don't like my news second-hand."

The closer they got, the more up on the tips of their toes the men crept. Rory twisted his head looking back, nothing worse than being snuck up on, while you're sneaking up. The wily pack halted all at once at the edge of the two-story Nevada Power and Light brick building. The Sundial parking lot opened up beyond the shadows they were pretending to conceal themselves in.

"From here on out there's no hiding." Keefe rubbed his unshaved chin considering how to approach things. He whispered, "There's only one light on."

"That's his car," Fletcher said.

"Got to be his room," Gage added.

The drapes were flickering. "He's watching TV," Gig said.

"Don't go near the Mercedes," Blake advised, "set the alarm off and won't be a thing to do, or a place to hide."

"How do we do this?" Keefe asked.

"Rory, Gage and Gig… You stay here," Fletcher instructed.

"Blake, you and me go," Keefe said.

"Keep an eye out," Fletcher bent down picked up a small pebble. "Throw this if you see someone coming."

Keefe took about two steps and stopped, "What do we say if something goes wrong and we get caught?"

"Tell him we all came down to invite him out to 'naked night' at the hot spring?" Fletcher said.

"'Naked night'…? Fletcher, you been putting table salt in your pickling brine again…?"

Gig poked him with his finger. "We don't need explanations about a man going naked hot spring soaking because he's in midlife crisis; what we need is a story."

"Something that makes sense," Gage added.

"Boys," Keefe said, "if we get caught, we'll say we come down to invite him to a poker game."

"Always use a high roller at a card game," Fletcher said.

"Poker playing, men play cards all the time."

"Mormon's don't..." Gage said.

"Give a Mormon half a chance," Fletcher said, "and they'll be most hung-over rooster crowing at sunrise."

"Enjoy a game twice as much," Keefe said, "and be three times as ashamed."

Rory kept checking for anyone coming up or down the street.

Keefe said, "Plan is set. We get caught. We all stick to the same story. Just come by to ask him to play cards."

The three men scrunched up into a tight pack. Rory, Gage and Gig remained behind.

Keefe, Fletcher and Blake skulked on eggshells along the front doors of the Sundial and then down to the middle of the vintage motel's frontage to where the window with the light on was.

Keefe peeked in from the side, extra cautious as he did.

Fletcher in a hushed tone asked, "Everything alright?"

"He's in there," Keefe whispered.

This time Keefe and Fletcher peered into the room from the edge of the window. Blake was mesmerized by the Mercedes.

"We got us a live one," Keefe whispered.

"What is it?" Fletcher asked.

"He's watching Fox Television," Keefe said.

"Must like suffering," Fletcher replied.

"Think he's dangerous?"

"He's got the wing-nut business bible on his bed," Fletcher said.

"There are too many of his kind in this world," Keefe said.

"Probably card carrying member of the Mormon Church..." Fletcher said.

"Doesn't strike me as the red meat type," Keefe was sure.

"Yeah, when I talked to him he smiled, acting like he was happy about life."

"Acted like he had an open mind," Keefe replied.

"Maybe he's just watching Fox so he knows what the other side's thinking..."

Jace drew down the zipper on his slacks, reached in and scratched.

"Got jock rash?" Keefe whispered.

"Probably getting ready for a date," Fletcher said.

"If he goes on a date, we're leaving."

"How you going to go on a date with yourself, while you're watching Fox Television?" Fletcher had no idea.

"Men get turned on by tough talk," Keefe said, "push a horn-dog right off ecstasy's edge."

Fletcher looked in through the curtain, "Never underestimate a man's imagination."

Jace finished whatever business he'd been tending to and zipped back up.

Fletcher was idle chattering, "Mormon girls sure do have the prettiest hair."

Keefe shot his elbow out into his friend's side, "Quiet, McCrea..."

Jace Brandt's phone rang.

"God damn television set," Keefe couldn't hear.

"He's picking up his remote," Fletcher said.

Jace muted the sound.

The men leaned toward the window even more, listening as hard as they could.

They heard Jace say, "Right on schedule."

Jace had a set of blueprints leaning against the wall. He picked up the bundle, placed them on top his bed and rolled the plans out flat.

"What the hell is that?" Keefe asked.

Jace replied to the caller, "Meadowhawk? Bunch of Great Basin loons, nothing but dirt roads and sagebrush," he picked up a beer from the desk, he took a swig, "bunch of old guys driving beat up pickup trucks, running around with a bunch of divorced women."

"What's he talking about?" Fletcher was angry.

"Chamber's on our side," Jace said, "man by the name of Garrett Harwood. He's all in."

"Garrett Harwood?" Fletcher had an angry look in his eye.

"Put the offer on the table," Jace said, lifting his bottle of beer high, "they signed this afternoon in Carson City. We're under contract." He completed the toast and drank up.

Keefe and Fletcher looked at one another eye to eye. Keefe whispered, "They're buying the fairgrounds."

"Right out from under our noses," Fletcher looked at the drawings on the bed. "Whatever that is, it's going to be big."

Keefe lost his cool, "Shit..." he said too loud.

Jace stopped his conversation, "I'll call you back." He set the phone down.

Keefe, Fletcher and Blake turned, but it was too late. Gage tossed the pebble. It hit the Mercedes. The alarm went off. As Jace opened his door, the Deputy Sheriff sped into the Sundial's parking lot, switched on his red revolving emergency lights, aimed his spot light at his suspects; Keefe, Fletcher and Blake were caught dead to rights. The Deputy jumped out of his car, he aimed his flashlight out on Rory, Gig and Gage while he approached his prime suspects.

Jace looked surprised, "Keefe..?"

"Jace Brandt. We come looking for you."

The Deputy Sheriff, recognizing everyone, didn't draw his gun, but he was suspicious by nature, had a nose for guilt. "I'm getting tired of seeing you, Fletcher McCrea."

"Everything alright...?" Jace asked.

"Everything's just dandy," Fletcher said.

Jace silenced the Mercedes alarm with the button on his key fob.

"You boys," the Deputy said pointing his flashlight at Gage, Gig and Rory, "want to step over this way."

Keefe was scratching the back of his neck.

"You boys line up against that wall," the Deputy ordered. He started back toward the patrol car, "I'm calling the Sheriff on this one,"

"No need," Keefe said. "Sheriff doesn't need to get involved."

"We come down to speak to Jace. That's all we were doing," Fletcher said. "Man like Jace, all alone, stuck in Meadowhawk night after night at the Sundial..."

"Broke our hearts knowing he was here sleeping all alone," Rory said.

Fletcher slapped Keefe on his butt, "We're a fun loving bunch of men..."

Keefe, stunned by Fletcher's fanny pat, explained. "We all bet Jace was the kind of man who likes to play our kind of game."

The Deputy stood with the microphone in one hand and his flashlight in the other, pointing the light at the men as they bantered.

"We're playing poker down at the General Store," Fletcher said.

"High stakes, gentleman's game," Keefe explained.

"High stakes, down at the General Store?" the Deputy asked. "Maybe the Sheriff might like to be invited to that game."

"Just a friendly game," Fletcher argued.

"Friendly game...?" Deputy replied, "Probably drink some tax-free whiskey, smoke some of those Cuban cigars Gage thinks Sheriff's Department don't know about..."

Jace jumped into the middle of the back and forth, "I'm sorry boys; I'm not going to be able to play cards tonight."

"Maybe later this week," Keefe said, "we play cards all the time."

"See that," Fletcher, changing the subject, said, "better answer than we figured we might get."

"I had my doubts," Gage said.

"Me too," Gig added.

"You go ahead and keep on doing whatever it is you have been doing," Keefe said.

"Because whatever you've been doing is none of our business," Fletcher added.

"Don't want to know what you've been doing," Rory said, approaching the Deputy, "and honestly, officer, we're just all going back down to the Brewery."

"None of us is going to drive home drunk until your shift ends anyway," Fletcher said.

"Because we have respect for the law," Keefe winked and smiled at the Deputy Sheriff, who wasn't having any of it. "Come on, buck up, good cop knows obedience and rascals just aren't true friends."

"We're just playing cards," Gage said.

Fletcher said to the Deputy, "We don't even have time to wonder what a man like Jace Brandt is doing out here in the middle of Nevada with nothing to do and not a friend to his name."

Keefe put his arm around Jace, "Sure you're not one of those famous escaped fugitives they put up at the Post Office?"

Fletcher put his arm around Jace too, "Maybe you're in trouble from bouncing checks..."

"Battered your wife... jury tampering..." Keefe squeezed Jace tighter.

"No need to explain nothing to us," Fletcher said.

"Where you got all the money needed to buy your car is none of our business," Keefe said. "Probably got a printing press hidden out here in the mountains somewhere," he looked off toward the nearby hills.

"Gold mine operator," Fletcher knew something about that.

Glenna, Faith, Tallula and Jolene had worked late at the Award Ribbon Company. They were walking toward the Brewery. They spotted the Deputy Sheriff's emergency lights and crossed the street.

"You boys having a party?" Faith asked.

"Poker party," Keefe said.

"Down at the General Store," Fletcher added.

"I'd like you women to stand back until I finish here," the Deputy said.

Jolene smiled broadly. She was looking fine tonight, dressed up in her tightest fitting denim trousers, sheer white blouse, dark lacey see-through red bra gleaming through the see-through fabric, all on account of her plan to pry a 'yes' from Fletcher McCrea's lips. "Deputy Sheriff, you know it would break our hearts not to stick our nose into your business."

"Jolene," the Deputy complained, trying not to take his eyes off her eyes...

She kept a steady gaze on the Deputy Sheriff. She took a deep purposeful breath in, wanted to wield some swelled woman parts as a distraction.

"Jolene," the Deputy concentrated with all his might on her eyes, "I'm not falling for any of your honeybunch tricks. I know you Hazel Harwood women, the whole lot of you, got an advanced degree in a pouring gasoline on a man's desire and then lighting their fuses off; that's what you do, preying upon man's weakness just so you get your own way."

She put her hand on her hip and swung it off to the side smiling, "Deputy Sheriff, why I feel almost strip searched," Jolene turned like a flamenco dancer, looking down her backside. "A woman is a harmless creature in a world of hungry desperate men searching for that perfect meal."

Faith approached Jace. Keefe winked at her as she did. She knew Jolene had dibs on Fletcher. "Maybe Jace would like to enjoy a beverage at the Brewery with a single woman?"

Jace was amused, "I'm sorry, Faith," trying to play along, "I got too much work to do."

Faith looked inside his motel room, "Can't be fun working all alone. Maybe you need a secretary help you out tonight."

Dotty and Elena come down the street and joined the meet up in front of the Sundial.

"Gig, what are you doing?" Elena asked.

Jolene leaned with purpose toward the Deputy Sheriff, "Looks like you keep those lights on a bit longer, whole town come out to find out what's going on..."

"Sure could be fun," Faith said putting her arm around Jace's waist, "I do make a red hot secretary. I got an outfit I put on and when I do, turn sexual harassment into company sanctioned fringe benefit."

Jace smiled, "I'm sure, if I needed a secretary, you'd do fine."

Deputy put the whistle to his lips and blew it hard as all get out, "Everybody, listen up, all of you. Want you all to get out of this parking lot; I want you all to get back to whatever you were doing."

Tallula come up the other side of Jace, put her arm around him too, "Faith doesn't know a thing about being a secretary; might be you need some real front office help."

Glenna stepped toward Jace's door. The blueprints were still spread across the bed. Keefe saw her looking into the room. She glanced at Keefe, caught his eye, she scratched the tip of her nose, pulled on her earlobe. Keefe looked at Jace fending off the two women. He looked back toward Glenna, tossed his head, she nodded back. She'd seen enough.

"Fletcher McCrea," Glenna called out in a loud voice, even had an affectionate lilt to her tone.

Jolene, Faith, and Tallula were stunned. Glenna, ordinarily, never ever even said Fletcher McCrea's name unless it was in private, and she wanted to cast aspersions on the town's most eligible womanizer.

"Deputy Sheriff has a job to do," Glenna said, "I thought you might walk me down to the Brewery..."

Fletcher figured Glenna was playing a game, so he went along, "Be my pleasure to escort you down Main Street to Rory's..." Fletcher took Glenna by one hand and with his other hand patted her fanny, testing it for the first time ever; he had the most annoying contented smile, "...even going to let you buy me my first beer..."

"That is a privilege I have never dreamed of having..." Glenna looking back behind where his hand was rubbing, "It's like having my intimate parts rubbed with such tenderness for the first time in public... almost like you'd think it was the perfect time and place..."

Fletcher lifted the cuff of his denims, pulled his whiskey flask out from where he kept it stowed down inside his boot. "Best whiskey you'll ever taste..." he took a nip from his monogrammed silver flask, offered it to Glenna.

She winced, "I'll try to resist temptation, at least until we get back down to Rory's."

"Glenna Goddard, what do you think you are up to? I know for a fact," the Deputy Sheriff said, "that you have never once, in all the years I have known you, to have had even one good word come out of your mouth with regard to Fletcher McCrea."

Keefe approached, "I'll have a snort," he plucked the flask from his best friend's hand. "Oh, that tastes near as smooth as the tender places kissing the satin on Glenna's French lingerie," he handed the flask back to Fletcher.

Glenna gave Keefe a look. She knew what Jace was up to. She blended her annoyance with a signal, eye contact, Keefe picked up on it. She wanted to get out there so they could speak.

There was near total shock in the group. Keefe got hold of Blake's arm and started following, "Come on, young man, we got a shuttle to operate, hot spring to run, beer to drink, poker to play, and aspirin to take before we see any sleep before sunrise…"

Fletcher took one more nip, "Well, I'm blessed, you've unlocked the truth inside your feminine nature."

"The truth has been freed," Glenna tried to smile.

"Even as headstrong a woman as you are, sitting home night after night, knowing deep inside your aching bones, that there was a turquoise miner, the one true man in all of Meadowhawk, a man that possessed a power so stupendous," Fletcher was getting carried away, "that his life force would eclipse every single solitary man interest you have ever fallen under the spell of over the course of your love life."

"Fletcher McCrea," Glenna smiled and drew her eyes tight, "I knew a turquoise miner would possess a talent for digging holes. It is hard to even imagine taking the shovel from such a talented hard rock miner's hands."

Jolene knew what Glenna had been up to, "He does have a gift." Jolene put her arm around Glenna. "And even if tonight was supposed to be my special night," Jolene said with mock sincerity, "Glenna Goddard, I will forgo my own satisfaction so you may taste firsthand the thrill of surrendering your feminine charms to the best devil you'll ever dance with."

"Well," Glenna said, walking with her arm around Jolene, "I can't wait for that dirty devil to give me his personal tour of his little hell."

Gig and Elena, Dotty and Gage, Rory, Tallula, Faith played right along and followed.

As was so often the case, Fletcher McCrea was bringing up the rear. There he stood, Meadowhawk's anointed, honest to goodness, true last bachelor, taking one more nip from his flask, stuffing it back inside his boot, and then joining the processional back to the Brewery.

Jace didn't know what had hit him. Deputy Sheriff stood next to his patrol car watching the crowd disperse.

Jace walked back to the door of his room, looked at the drawings sprawled across his bed. He turned back around, "It's going to be an interesting town to do business in."

"So how fast you had that car up to?" Deputy Sheriff asked.

"You'd have to arrest me, if I told you."

chapter

TWELVE

According to Fletcher McCrea's family tree, his great grandfather had married a Zuni woman. After a lively back and forth among the concerned, Fletcher was volunteered to perform the cave consecration. Whether or not his lineage qualified him to act as the ceremonial shaman was something of a puzzle that depended upon intimate magical experiences. Fletcher's lovemaking was art to those that knew, a carnal gate unmasking his warrior spirit, a revelation of both body and soul.

"I am not a sacred type being..."

"Fletcher McCrea," Keefe argued, "you are just what the good lord needs."

"I don't even go to church..."

"Everybody knows that," Keefe said. "What's even better, there isn't a soul in town less likely to invoke a sense of the divine."

"I should stick to what I'm good at."

"The last thing we need is someone actually pretending to be truly sacred come out here and muck everything up."

"My talent is in talking a woman into bed."

"Everyone knows there's nothing outright evil in seducing a woman into saying 'yes,' so long as when they dig in and say 'no,' a man has the good manners to honor their wish. It's just how things go sometimes; weakness of will is a two way street. Probably why you're not thought of as the best person in town, but then again you're not the worst. I think most folk think of you as marginally deplorable."

"Takes everything I got to be that good."

"And everybody knows that," Keefe explained, "and it's why everyone trusts you. We all know you wouldn't steal a thing from nobody, but you'd probably have to fight off the temptation twice as hard as an average person."

"You think that's what qualifies me for the job?"

"Sure it does... You got as much passion as you got regrets, and that's just exactly the kind of shaman this cave consecration is going to need."

"Why I enjoy taking care of my burro."

"You make people feel so much better about themselves, that they can be proud about judging you so harshly."

"We're both rotten to the core."

"But we're trying hard as all get out to not let those parts of our nature escape and do anyone any harm."

Bero had been tending to his sheep up on the mountain. He trailed a portable parlor up above the tree line so he could milk his sheep, but still keep them grazing on wild meadow grasses. It was up there in the high country that accounted for the prized flavors found in their sheep's cheese. He'd deliver the raw milk down the mountain every day during the peak of the summer season. Mirari and her crew handled chores back at their cheese making room. After the consecration ceremony, the cave would receive Bero and Mirari's first wheels for a stint of yearlong aging.

The field at the cave entrance was filling up. The citizens of Meadowhawk considered the event one of this year's most important. There were two rows of four- wheel drive pickups and sport utility vehicles lined up one after another at the edge of the bluff near the entrance to the cave.

Extra hands helped set up picnic tables in the field along the lower edge of the bluff. After the consecration they'd celebrate the cave's official opening in a more community oriented fashion. They'd pour some of Rory's beer and sample Bero and Mirari's fresh made sheep cheese. Group had swelled to more than fifty citizens.

Lark hitched a ride along with Hazel and Glenna. Since Keefe was going to be there, Hazel parked on the Hot Spring Highway. Lark hiked over to the cave alone.

Keefe spied Lark as she approached and set out to meet her in the field, "Is Hazel just going to sit out on that highway?"

"She doesn't want to have words with you."

"What's so hard about being around someone you used to be married to?" Keefe asked.

"Hazel said a divorced man can't know how annoying he can be."

"Maybe a woman's annoyed because of how she feels about the man."

"Her being annoyed is not in her imagination. . ."

"What is it then?"

"Women get annoyed because we give you everything we got," Lark said. "At least that's what Hazel and Glenna told me."

"So what's the problem?"

"She said that just about the time a woman gives herself to a man, the man stops appreciating it."

"I'm out of my mind crazy for that woman."

"And she's afraid the next time she's nice to you, that'll be the end of that."

"You mean for us to be mad about each other, we can never be nice to one another?"

"Personally, I believe Hazel feels the most passion, when you get her all worked up."

"I do too, and I want us to throw that on the fire."

"She's mad about the fire; she just can't stand you."

"And so you're telling me, if she wasn't so darned mad..."

"She told me, if she stopped being so angry, it would be the same day you'd lose interest."

"How in the world are we going to work that out?"

"She said you're never going to work that out; why, if she didn't stay mad at you, it would be like giving up on life."

"I want her fire in my life. That hot headed, short fused, ready to go off next time I say something stupid... Lark, being perfect isn't anything. Hazel Harwood is a lovable mess, and trust me, I've been on this good earth awhile, and an honest to god real woman isn't anything that needs improving..."

Lark smiled and shook her head, "Mister Kenny, you know how much time is left after we get it all figured out?"

"You get the rest of your life..."

"I have a lot of respect for maturity, but from twenty-two going on twenty-three, it's looking like only some of us get to have an honest to goodness adulthood."

Keefe lost the cheer in his eyes. He turned and dragged his sorrows through the dirt. He knocked on the cave entrance doors, "You boys ready?"

Fletcher was still lighting votive candles along the back wall. "Hold your horses, one more minute..."

Last chore was to light and hang a third lantern on a bamboo tri-pod.

"Sal, you'll stand on top this crate," Fletcher said, "you be ready when I give you the signal."

Fletcher unlatched the doors from the inside and pushed. "Okay, everybody..."

Keefe walked one door around while Fletcher opened the other; between the two vintage barn doors, the entrance was near twenty feet wide.

"Make a darn good looking shaman," Gage said as he passed Fletcher.

"First miracle of the thing... I can squeeze into Blake's riding leathers."

Fletcher's shaman looks stunned his women. He had a black plush velvet vest over a red silk blouse that Jolene had loaned him. It was a lace up affair with billowy sleeves accented with tight wrist cuffs.

Elena winked at Fletcher as she walked in with Dotty. Women from the Harwood Award Ribbon Company could not get over Fletcher.

Sissy said, "Fletcher McCrea's got his feminine side showing today..."

"You give the term 'lady's man' whole new meaning," Sharlene smiled.

Fletcher mock scowled. "You'd be surprised how many parts I got hidden inside."

Keefe and Fletcher closed off the light of day, when they sealed the doors. All at once the lanterns and candles seized hold of the captive audience's eyes.

Back out on the Hot Spring Highway...

"I think Keefe's been talking about you," Glenna said to Hazel.

"The man doesn't know how to quit a thing," Hazel complained.

"Sure you don't want to go on in for the consecration? You don't have any obligations. You don't have to answer to anyone. You're your own woman," Glenna said.

"This seat suits me just fine, right here. I'm happy as happy can be."

Glenna knew a whole lot of hooey when she heard it, "Well, if you can have all this fun out here, then I'm sticking with you. I know a good time when I see it."

"Glenna, go on. I can't go in, but I'm not leaving."

"I'm staying right here where I belong. You know and I know, Fletcher McCrea's shaman act by heart. After patting my fanny at the Sundial in front of everyone, acting like I was one of his women, man's nothing but a witch doctor putting a curse on a woman's self-esteem."

"I think we're overdue for a long weekend in Las Vegas..."

"Something we'd never be able to talk about," Glenna smiled.

"If we do anything we have to keep secret, we'll have got our money's worth."

Fletcher made his way to the front of the altar in the center of the circle. He stood motionless, facing the assembled with his eyes solemnly shut. Sal stood perched atop his crate with his flute rising to his lips. It was a genuine tribal flute, fashioned from walnut and maple, small tether of deerskin was knotted and dangling around the instrument. The flute was wired up to an amplifier. It had a built-in electronic processor that added a New Age reverberation to the wind instrument. This was the vital part of the sacred set-up.

The haunting melody Sal began to play infused the cave in a mystical atmospherics. The part-time shaman's short order cook's claim on the sacred was sealed with each soulful note. Mitzi was never more in love.

A bundle of sage had been placed in an abalone shell on the altar. Fletcher held the bundle over a candle until the herb began smoldering. Then, holding the abalone shell below and the smoldering sage above, Fletcher stepped processional style from one side of the circle to the other. From the look in his eyes he seemed able to see a soul's aura. He'd stand in front of a member of the assembled and gaze off beyond the edge of the person. He'd pass the sage all around this invisible part of their being. He said things like, "your soul walks with the wind," then he'd move down the line to the next member of the gathering and say, "may the coyote dance in your heart." And he meant every word of it.

When Fletcher got to where Jolene stood, seemed her lineation was distempering the shaman from his ethereal duty. So while he was working the sage up around her one side and down the other, her human contours had all at once appeared out of the smoldering mists and were visibly luring him back into the physical realm. Jolene had spent the better part of her life refining her God-given temptations.

"Shaman derives his powers from many places and many people," Fletcher said.

Jolene thought Fletcher looked extra special androgynous sexy in her red see-through blouse. She looked around at the ladies from the Award Ribbon Company. She raised her hand. She'd been moved as if she'd seen an apparition. "May I say something?"

Fletcher peacefully closed his eyes and nodded his head to approve.

"Our shaman is an out of the blue revelation, providing his believers a religious experience not a soul could have foretold."

Mitzi figured Jolene and Fletcher were likely going to have to go say prayers and worship after services. Of course, Sal was giving Mitzi feelings and notions of her own. His role in the affair was beyond just an ordinary surprise. His mystic flute playing was revelatory. It had been decades since she'd blushed over being publicly aroused by her husband's aura.

After smudging the audience, Fletcher went around the other side of the altar to the rear wall in the deepest part of the cave. With his back to the assembled community, he smudged with the sage, high and low, allowing the smoke to waft into the cave's walls.

When a shaman sets up shop in the spirituality trades, he'll want to plan to have a few extra-special effects, a thing a shaman can never have enough of. At the right moment, Fletcher stepped with his foot on a hidden device, triggered off a flash pot he'd pre-loaded with a tablespoon of black gun powder. The pyrotechnic effect created a surprise flash of light and a rising cloud of smoke.

He exclaimed at the right moment, "May the gods bless our new cheese cave... bless us Vishnu, bless us Shango, Bumba, Shiva, Luna and Baku. Give us strength Thor, luck Loki, and Baba-yaga the courage to prevail when we know not where else to turn."

Blake and Lark were stunned into a post-adolescent silence. Everybody but Dusty, a hard boiled type woman, thought the moment something they would not soon recover from.

Fletcher walked back and stood in front of the assembled audience. The valance for the altar was made up of chiffon and taffeta square-dancer petticoats. They'd been strung together into an awe inspiring kaleidoscope of turquoise, ruby, and purple laces and satin sheers, intended to tickle an eye. Undergarments for this shaman were near where sublime and sacred might meet. He gleamed in the candlelight, a bird of prey perching upon a nest of fine ladies' lingerie, a complex matrix of turquoise miner, town's most notorious lover and now the biggest miracle of all... a virgin shaman. His spiritual powers were a mask removed, a soul revealed.

Bero and Mirari's consecration was an ordained destiny. Fifty of Nevada's finest citizens gathered here and, of all places underground on the side of this bluff. With the smell of sage and the gentle trickling sound of the battery powered water fountain, a spell had come to be cast. It was all so Meadowhawk miraculous.

Fletcher picked up a large mallet that set on top the altar. He waved it back and forth in front of the four-foot-in- diameter etched copper Korean gong. The thing was hung from an ornate wooden stand. Sal hovered on top of his crate on the other side. Fletcher settled upon the location of where he intended to strike the gong. The turquoise mining shaman took a few practice swings, same as professionals might do at a tournament. Then, he finally let go and gave the instrument a measured strike with the mallet. Never in the wildest wonderings of the citizens of the Great Basin had it been thought that such a celestial service would come bless this inconspicuous corner of their world. The spiritual leader waited for the gong to cease its reverberations before entering into the formal part of the consecration ceremony.

Fletcher had wrapped his favorite Belgian beer glass in aluminum foil. Keefe approached with a fresh brewed bottle from Rory's. He twisted the cap off. Fletcher stood with both hands extended, eyes closed muttering a miner's prayer beneath his breath.

Keefe emptied the sacramental brew into the glass. He stepped back, bound by ceremonial rites, respectfully facing Fletcher at all times. Keefe believed that you ought to never turn your back on a shaman with a beer in his hand.

"We gather here, of one mind, one heart, and one hope." Fletcher drank from his glass, draining every drop. His eyes closed, resting the glass easily upon his chest clasping it with both hands. "We give our sincere wishes and fervent blessings, for here in the dark, cool, spore-filled air, mother nature and father time will age these new cheeses, artisanal cheeses, crafted by Bero and Mirari for markets near and far."

Gage, Dotty, Gig, and Elena seemed moved by Fletcher's words more than they had preconceived. Even Fletcher's sweethearts found themselves at a loss to explain the powerful feelings welling up inside. There was something riveting about the common man carrying out a sacred duty.

"And so here we are, a new enterprise, hope filled with hope, destiny turning like a wheel, if I can find turquoise in these mountains, Keefe can find hot water, and Bero and Mirari can make cheese, then we are fulfilling our responsibilities for nurturing the abundance that abounds before us all." Fletcher looked to the heavens above and concluded, "If only we maintain the strength and courage to discover what is here before us, may God bless Meadowhawk, God bless Bero and Mirari's cheese cave, and God bless our people."

For good measure Fletcher picked up the mallet and went ahead and struck the gong again. The doors behind the assembly opened letting the light of day into the cave and Sal cranked it up one more time on his flute and reverb unit, while everyone moved back out into the sunshine and sagebrush.

The audience filed out of the cave into the field where refreshments were waiting. Keefe dashed ahead. He wanted everyone to have a glass of sparkling wine in their hands. He got up on one of the picnic tables.

"Want to say first off, congratulations to Bero and Mirari. All of us want to wish you a long life and all the success in the wide world."

"I'll second that," Dusty shouted out.

Bero was wearing boots, denim and dust. He had a broad smile peeking out beneath his moustache. He put his arms around his beloved bashful, Mirari. The more the assembled audience applauded for the Basque couple, the more Bero cinched his wife in and squeezed her tight. Mirari set her hand over his shirt atop his heart and patted her exuberant man; her blushing grew all the more with all those eyes on her.

Sal was last out of the cave. Mitzi had saved a glass of sparkling wine for her miracle of a man. He arrived in time to lift his glass into the air with everyone.

"Next off," Keefe said, "we got some big news. We are official-ly announcing that we are forming a cooperative. Now, as you all know, the fairground has been sold. They're planning on building a big chain store right across the street from Dotty and Gage's."

The whole lot of Fletcher McCrea's women from the Award Ribbon Company all patted Dotty with their hands, consoling her.

"Well, that's just horrible news," Tallula said, "right on top of bad news."

"Well, we're not going to just sit frozen like a frog in an irriga-tion ditch, waiting to get gigged." Keefe said.

Jolene was having none of it. "If they think they're going to come to this town and make our money theirs...!"

"Bunch of slick operators out of Salt Lake City, Utah," Bunny said.

The spiritual feelings in the community were a fleeting state of mind.

"So, here's what I want you to know," Keefe had a genuine smile and confidence beaming from his eyes, "we're going into the pinion pine nut harvesting business. Every single solitary one of you that can hear my voice is invited up to Pipe Dream Mountain, to the pine groves. We'll start picking this week, and pick right up until the first snow." Keefe raised his hand and pointed, "Fletcher and Blake going to build the machines that do the tumbling and shak-ing; going to have a proper processing facility."

"Got a peak crop ready this year," Fletcher said.

"I bid on a tract and we won a lease," Keefe added, "called the biologist helped me with my greenhouse. He left me with the idea all our lives and bank accounts will be changed when we get the nut crop to market."

Keefe poured another glass full with the sparkling wine. He hoisted his glass one more time. "A cooperative... it's what they call fair and square capitalism. Idea is to take what we earn, keep as much as we can right here in Meadowhawk and use what we make for our own good. Not shipping our profits off to some fat cat who's hiding his money in the Cayman Islands."

"We got our sights set on scuttling the fairgrounds sale," Fletcher said.

"Besides picking, we're going to need a place to get the harvest ready for market," Keefe said, "and the exhibition hall on the fairgrounds is exactly what we need."

"So, we did a back of the envelope figuring," Fletcher said, "pine nut business isn't rocket science. Best we can tell, if we can bring a good harvest in, keep the equipment working, we can make a go of this enterprise."

"Jace Brandt and his kind got nothing to offer us," Keefe raised his arm over his head and then pointed it straight down to the ground, "they got nothing but minimum wages and bellyaching about how high their taxes are,"

"So, we'll do the nut processing right in the heart of our town," Fletcher said.

"We'll use a portion of the proceeds to buy the property." Keefe looked every citizen dead in the eye, one by one, his jaw never more square. "Plan is we'll keep the county fair open same as ever and, even better than that, we'll keep food on all our own tables."

"I don't believe his kind is ever going to agree to sell something he's just bought," Jolene said.

"We'll have to find a way of changing his mind..." Fletcher McCrea said.

"Man like that doesn't change his mind..." Dusty said.

"Meadowhawk starts changing a mind the day someone sets foot here..." Keefe said. "Raise your hands if you ever had Dotty and Gage give you credit."

Near everyone raised their hands.

"Look around..." Keefe said, "You see, Dotty and Gage. They made a life in Meadowhawk because they fell in love with the people here, and they know who their customers are, and what their customers mean. It's about us sticking together instead of all of us being picked apart."

"What is that man doing?" Hazel asked.

"He's making an announcement."

Hazel turned and gave Glenna the eye, "I know that."

"They're forming a cooperative," Glenna said. "They're planning to go into the pine nut harvesting business."

"That's a backbreaking business..."

"Well, that's what they're doing, going to process nuts at the fairgrounds. That's the plan."

"My father and the Chamber won't put up with it..."

"There's no way the Chamber and their big money boys stand a chance against folks who feel threatened about the place they call home."

"Keefe's picking a fight he can't win."

"The only fight Keefe hasn't won is the one between him and you."

"I'm not ever going to give up on myself, and give in to him." Hazel was getting fired up again.

"I wouldn't bet my last dollar on it," Glenna said, "don't know when, don't where, but that ex-husband's going to find a way to peel those britches off and light you up like a harvest moon."

Hazel squinted her eyes at Glenna, "He'll be kissing the dead, not now, not ever."

"So, last thing I want you to think about, is about joining us," Keefe pleaded.

"We've got a lot of good ideas," Fletcher said.

"Keep our town headed in the right direction."

"Main thing to know is we can make a go of life here," Fletcher added.

"On our own terms," Keefe said, "taking care of what we decide we want to take care of."

Jolene spoke out for the Award Ribbon women, "One thing me and the girls have a talent for is changing how a man sees things."

"Teamwork, that's the whole idea," Keefe said.

"Me and the girls are ready to do whatever needs being done." Jolene shot her fist into the air.

"Sal and I, we're ready..." Mitzi said.

"We didn't come here to just sleep with Fletcher McCrea," Jolene was being as honest as she could. "We ended up living in Meadowhawk, because we didn't much care for how the world was changing out there."

"This isn't pie in the sky," Keefe lifted his glass to toast, "to Meadowhawk and the people who love her, and for mercy on the misguided souls who try to stand in our way."

chapter

THIRTEEN

Bugs swirled around Jolene's porch light. Fletcher found a note tacked on her front door. He trudged through the garden path, dumbstruck, walked back to the street, stood on top his truck's running boards. It was a first. He looked around the front yard. Jolene's place was dead as a doornail. Meadowhawk had a way of tricking the hopeless and trapping a bedroom bound man in expectation.

He drove past the Harwood Award Ribbon Company on the slim hope he might find Jolene working late. Might be she'd changed her mind. She more than liked Fletcher, appreciated his companionship. After intimate relations Fletcher and Jolene, more often than not, let their guards down. They'd cuddle, dote, tickle, nuzzle and twirl their fingers in each other's hair. It was a mutual transitory belonging, momentary and then the closing off.

Rory and a knot of Chamber types were all that were drinking at the Brewery when he took his seat at the bar. Rory had a towel and wiped the counter in front of the stood up turquoise miner.

"You already done and leaving...?" Rory asked.

"Jolene wasn't home. Something come up." Fletcher was at a loss. "All I can figure..."

"Probably went to Carson City..."

"What's the use?" Fletcher asked.

"Jolene and the girls, they said they were going to go wrangle a change of mind out of those men, take some pictures, compromising pictures."

"Is that where they are?" Fletcher smirked; couldn't believe she didn't even call, "First time she's ever stood me up."

Rory leaned over the bar, "I had two girlfriends going at the same time. Found out that they both had just as many."

"That's always a good sign," Fletcher had a sincere look in his eye.

"Pissed me off," Rory picked up clean glasses and turned around and set them on a shelf behind the bar.

"If it was good for you, then it's got to been good for them."

"They liked that other man in their bed. What pissed me off is, I didn't."

"But you could, couldn't you?" Fletcher asked.

"We sure do go to a lot of trouble to make certain we're spending time with someone different."

"It is that 'dang thing' that happens, when you start seeing the same woman every day."

"I don't mind," Rory laughed. "But then I'm not seeing anyone right now; and if I was, I'd probably start feeling that 'dang thing.' And it only goes from purgatory to eternal hell from there."

"Something goes missing."

"Fletcher McCrea... Life's got slow parts, fast parts, fun parts, regular working day parts."

"When they start feeling strong feelings, that's the worst; they're boa constrictors, when they go getting emotions for you. I can't breathe... feel all boxed in... feel wiretapped..."

"All your women friends have strong feelings for you."

"I got strong feelings for them, but I got strong feelings about commitment too."

"One of them has got to be a favorite. I mean Jolene and Bunny both got so much woman packed into their clothes, pretty much keep a man busy 'until death do we part.'"

Fletcher laughed, "Rory, they all prettiest thing you ever saw, until you see the next one."

Jolene appeared in Fletcher's headlights. She was on the other side of a barricade set up in the middle of the dirt road that headed back up to the mine. She was teetering atop high heels. She had denim pants on, no shirt and for extra special effect was squeezed into her European imported, French made, fire truck red brassiere.

Fletcher stuck his head out the door of the International, "Didn't know there was going to be a sobriety checkpoint out here tonight."

Jolene was all glitter and Great Basin glamour, puffed up hair, puffed up bosom, and matching flame red lipstick and nail polish. She had one hand on one hip and the other stretched out. On offer were handcuffs.

Jolene slow walked. She was play acting. Fletcher was under the spell of a self-abetted-hormonal bum's rush. As she approached in the headlights, she swung her hips with exaggeration side to side. If she had a band accompanying her sashaying, the drummer would have been hitting rim shots off his snare drum. Her lip gloss gleamed in the headlights, and the steam in her eyes had a chili hot flavor. She was primed, game faced, there was no getting away.

"Fletcher McCrea, I want you to pull your truck off to the side of the road."

He looked Jolene up and down. "I have always believed that a man should do whatever a woman in a red brassiere tells him to do."

She locked one cuff onto his wrist. "That's right, time you did what you're told."

Fletcher regarded the restraint. "Jolene, I am under your charge."

He got off the road and set the parking brake. Jolene opened his door. "I need you to step out of your vehicle."

"I should have got you the Deputy Sheriff's uniform so you could play the part."

"Anything you say may be held against you..."

Fletcher hopped out of his truck. Jolene had a look in her eye like she was going to kiss him. They were face to face, inches apart.

"I want you to turn around, real slow..." Jolene was laying down the law.

Fletcher looked at his favorite with her flashy blonde hair, blue eyes, ruddy cheeks, and fine posture. His hands up, he leaned in and brushed the tips of her lacey red brassiere with his chest as he turned. That woman was something else.

Jolene was acting all huffy and puffy. "Give me that other wrist."

He put his hands behind his back, gazing up into the heavens imagining what might be next. He said, "You'll just have to do what you have to do..."

"I got him, I got him," Jolene shouted.

Out of the darkness rushed the Harwood Award Ribbon Company women. Sharlene and Tallula took hold of one arm, Faith and Bunny got his other. Sissy was behind and Jolene guarded him from the front.

"Fletcher McCrea, you're not getting away. Not tonight." Sharlene said.

Jolene grabbed hold of Fletcher's shirt, looked him square in the eye, "You're in way over your head, Fletcher McCrea. We're putting your bachelorhood into the fire tonight..."

Fletcher hadn't quite caught on yet, "You'll just have to do what you have to do..."

"You hush up, Fletcher McCrea."

The women hauled their captive handcuffed down a trail.

"You sure there's enough of me to go around for all of you?"

"We are going to find out just how potent a man you are," Sharlene said.

Fletcher smiled, "I only hope I am up to the test..."

They came to a campsite. Sissy tossed two more logs on the fire, setting off a swirl of crackling sparks into the night. The rest of the women marched the handcuffed Fletcher to a bentwood chair they'd brought to the camp.

"You'll sit down," Sharlene put her hand on top of Fletcher's head and pushed him down onto the chair.

Sissy had a fierce look in her eye. She got hold of his shoulders from behind and held the man in place, while Tallula and Sharlene got hold of his ankles and started duct- taping them to the chair legs.

Behind Fletcher, at the edge of the trees hidden in the darkness, were Glenna and Lark.

Glenna said, "Fletcher McCrea is about to come face to face with the uncomfortable truth."

"I don't know if I'm old enough to be watching this," Lark said.

"Going to see firsthand how much courage a bachelor's made of," Glenna said.

The Award Ribbon Company women all gathered on the other side of the fire pit, the glow of the campfire gleaming off their faces.

One by one they circled around to the other side of the flames to speak their piece.

Jolene strutted around first. She was buttoning up her flannel shirt, rolling the sleeves up to her elbows, the bark from the logs in the fire pit were popping and snapping. "Fletcher you know, he has a way of making each of us feel like we are the first flower he's seen in his garden since the last time he watered." Jolene got her lips right up next to Fletcher's.

"Because you all are..."

Jolene looked into Fletcher's eyes with a lustful fiery anger. "You hush up, Fletcher McCrea. We got some girl talking to do, and don't need your conniving confusing us..." she circled back around to the other side.

Tallula jutted her jaw out. She walked around the other side of the fire pit, skinny in jeans, smallest woman of them all, "I remember, first off," Tallula unfastened the top three buttons on her shirt, "you started dating Sharlene, and one night you came knocking at my door, you called out through the screen all innocent like, pretending as if you didn't know exactly what you were doing, you said, *'Sharlene's not feeling so good,'* that's what you said, *'maybe we might sit on the sofa, have a beverage, and talk a while, before I go home.'* Those were your exact words. I'll never forget."

Sharlene was on the other side of the fire pit with the others, "thought it was the right thing to do. I wasn't in love with Fletcher, not yet."

Fletcher's eyes shot toward Sharlene's.

Tallula sat side saddle on Fletcher's lap. "Next thing I know," she's running her fingers through his graying hair, "I've got my lips on Fletcher's lips..." Tallula was looking longingly at his mouth... she turned and looked across the fire at her girlfriends and concluded... "and then it's all adults only entertainment from there on out."

All the women on the other side of the fire pit grumbled and shook their heads in disgust.

Tallula stood up. Fletcher stared at her swishing bottom as she walked back around the fire pit. "No man's ever made so much fuss over getting to play with my skinny little ass." Tallula confessed, "The man had me hooked, head over heels, first time I ever had a man that made me feel like I was something worth taking to bed... me and Sharlene started passing Fletcher McCrea back forth like we was borrowing a cup of sugar."

All the other women laughed, caught themselves and resumed their game faced glaring look at Fletcher.

Sharlene said, "I figured if I was going to keep him around, might as well accept the fact that he was going to fool around."

Bunny was tall. She was the only woman that preferred false eyelashes. Everything was bigger on her. She came around the fire pit. "Rest of the girls went on a shopping trip to Las Vegas." Bunny stood behind Fletcher and bent down; she whispered into Fletcher's ear, "I went out all by myself for a drink at the Brewery."

"Remember it like it was yesterday," Fletcher said, gazing into the amber flames. It was like he was looking at Bunny waiting naked on top of her bed.

"I figured two of you letting Fletcher McCrea have privileges was plain wrong," Bunny tried to mean it, "and three of us would be near as evil a thing as any of us could ever do."

"She fought me off, telling me 'no,' over and over again, almost said 'no' until dawn."

Bunny stood tall and walked in front of Fletcher and said, "What I am ashamed of, was how doing something I shouldn't have been doing got me so worked up; felt like I was about to rob a bank. I'm being honest; that's what I thought was exciting."

"We both had our reasons, and we never told each other anything but the truth."

Bunny turns and points at the accused tied up to his chair. "He starts in on how my blue eyes remind him of a reef he'd dove in off the Kona Coast..."

"All of us with blue eyes heard the Kona Coast line, same as you," Tallula said.

"Could have been the Caribbean, maybe a lagoon in Tahiti," Bunny complained. "It is just too small a town," Bunny said to the women, "for all of us to end up with blue eyes that reminded Fletcher McCrea of the same snorkel spot." Bunny walked away disgusted.

"That's the problem right there," Jolene said. "If you're going to be as good in bed as Fletcher McCrea, you're going to need to be even better at thinking on your feet."

Faith with her one shoulder peeking out of her top came around the fire and bent over, grabbed hold of Fletcher's jaw. "All your fancy pillow talk," she noticed Fletcher looking down her blouse. He was relentless. "All your sweet considerations, remembering my birthday, calling me up while you're still in bed, after having your way with Jolene and telling me you can't wait for tomorrow night, then buying me Valentine's... birthday cards... box of chocolates..."

"That's what a single man is supposed to be doing," Fletcher replied. "Married man forgets all those things. They're so damn busy mowing lawns and paying bills, no time left for entertaining."

"But you're buying cards and chocolates a half dozen at a time." Faith turned and looked at the assembled jury of women. "So, you don't tell us," Faith shouted, "Dotty breaks the news, after all the bragging we did, like we were something special. How's that supposed to make all your lovers feel?"

"Dotty wasn't supposed to be snitching. I told her it was just between her and me." Fletcher objected.

Faith stomps off back to the rest of the women.

Sissy was scowling, giving Fletcher the eye; she came around the fire. "I go over Sharlene's one day." She holds her blouse with one hand leans over searching for any sign of remorse in Fletcher's eyes. "She's cleaning the floor to ceiling mirrors in the bedroom, chirping like a newborn meadowlark. A week later I'm over at Faith's, she's polishing her mirrors like the best thing she ever had happen might have been what she saw Fletcher McCrea do to her in that mirror." Her face went limp. She shook her head back and forth.

Jolene's right behind Sissy, "Tuesday at work I learn what we tried on Friday was same thing you and Tallula did Monday."

Sharlene's right behind Jolene, "I thought it was something you dreamed up all on your own; I didn't want to be performing a lovemaking trick on Wednesday Faith had taught you on Tuesday."

Sissy, Jolene and Sharlene all got their hands on their hips, waiting to hear what Fletcher McCrea had to say for himself. "It's not like any of that," Fletcher tried to defend himself. "All I was doing was what came natural."

"That's the problem right there," Jolene said. "It's not your lovemaking. It's your human nature that's causing all the trouble."

"But I've been happier than any other time of my life. All the chocolates, candles, cards and fun we all had. Best bachelor years I could have ever hoped for. I swear to god I've woken up so many nights these last six years to find my sweet lovers curled up fast asleep dreaming and cuddling with me, sharing a peace on earth that I didn't know could exist."

"Trouble with you," Bunny said, beating her false eyelashes for emphasis, "is you're too damn good at what it is we been doing with you."

"You're so happy about it," Faith complained. "Don't get jealous, never get worried. I hate when Fletcher smiles, and then he says *that it's just fine with him,* and he'd say *that's how the world works, if I go out and end up in bed with some other man,* and then he'd really stick the knife in and say, *wouldn't be first time that's happened."*

"Hasn't got any fetishes," Jolene said.

"Likes my skinny little figure," Tallula complained.

"And gets just as excited for his plus sized girls," Sharlene said, as she stuck out her bonus sized bosom.

"If you were a normal man," Jolene said, "you'd prefer one kind of woman or another. But not Fletcher McCrea, any kind of woman will do, so long as she doesn't want to have a relationship."

"Nope, nothing about a woman that doesn't turn him on," Bunny said. "Gets turned on by big butts or tiny tits..."

"Only thing that turns him off is commitment..." Jolene said.

"Thinks we're all some kind of feminine miracle..." Tallula said.

"It's what I see, when I look at the world," Fletcher pleaded. "You're all the most beautiful human beings, and things you've done for me, things you've shared, filled me with a sense of wonder I never dreamed I'd live to know. You are the most generous women I've ever come to care for."

Glenna took hold of Lark's hand. She leaned her cheek up against Lark's ear. "You need to see what Fletcher McCrea is. Spare you the grief of waiting for a man that's never going to change the spots he was born with."

"I didn't even know women did things like this," Lark was in over her head.

"It's his fault. It's always the man's fault. Fletcher McCrea's started it. And his bachelor's run is coming to an end," Glenna explained. She took Lark's hand. She whispered, "Come on, let's get a close look at what a man caught up in his own mess looks like." They crept up behind the chair Fletcher was tied to.

"And that's why this affair is going to have to come to an end," Jolene said, glancing momentarily at Glenna and Lark, then she turned and looked away.

Fletcher for the first time began struggling to break out of the duct tape. "Losing all of you is going to break my heart ten directions to hell and back. You'll have to pick up my shattered hopes and rush me to the emergency room."

"Well, we only got to find the strength to get over but one of you," Sharlene said.

"We've been trying to get the strength up to do this, since the first day we fell into your sweet talking trap," Tallula said.

"You'd think it wouldn't be much of a trick to find a man with enough courage to love one stinking woman with his whole heart," Bunny added.

Faith came around the fire and bent down right in Fletcher's face. "But, so long as we're giving you privileges, we don't get out and try and do anything about finding a good man that's got the courage to match the pleasures we provide with a promise he needs to keep."

"Worse than that," Sharlene said raising her chin in pride, "When we do try another man, that man's got half the imagination of our hot shot, Fletcher McCrea. You get Fletcher naked and get him going and he makes the nighttime fly and dawn come too soon. Sad truth is all those other men just aren't rotten enough for women with appetites like ours."

"He's ruined us all," Jolene said.

"Bachelor scared of his own shadow," Sharlene said, "makes love like the executioner's waiting for him at sunrise and we're his last meal."

"So, Fletcher McCrea," Tallula said, "we've all got our heads locked on the same notion. No more picking us apart, one weak willed woman at a time. It's been one day a week, month after month, for too stinking long."

Jolene had a steely look in her eye. "So, we've talked it through. Made up all six minds the same, and we've all agreed. Swore on our fathers' graves, that next time you make love to any one of us, then you'll have to live with that fact, and that's who you'll have for a partner."

"That's the story of your new love life," Sharlene said, "You'll either quit that one woman, leave Meadowhawk in disgrace, or fall over dead."

"And we don't much care whether you quit or die. The rest of us are going to move on with our lives..."

"We won't be waiting around for you to come knocking at our door..."

"Not no more..."

"Never again..."

"No more playing us off one another," Sharlene said.

"No more any of us finding out that what you need is a good 'this' from Bunny or some naughty 'that' from Tallula," Faith explained.

"There won't be any more this-and-thats," Jolene said.

"And all of us damn well know what a this-and-that is..." Sharlene said.

"And won't be any more card playing and sex talking with Sissy," Jolene gave Sissy a look.

Sissy was blushing; she tried to object.

"Jolene," Fletcher said, "you go easy. How she liked her sex is just not same as the rest. Sissy meant no harm."

"Sissy's promised she's not letting you talk her through an orgasm no more."

"She told us," Jolene scowled at Fletcher, "it turned you on near as much as her."

"And after everything we got in bed and did for you," Jolene said, "and for god's sake, you two sit at her kitchen table over a deck of playing cards, and do it without even touching one another."

"How do you think that makes us feel?" Sharlene asked.

"You all turn me on different ways..."

"Next time you take any one of us, might as well bring the wedding ring." Bunny said.

Now Fletcher began to struggle again. He shook his head back and forth. Jolene got hold of his jaw and stilled his shaking and bucking. It was a bitter pill they were forcing him to swallow.

Side by side the women lined up in front of Fletcher McCrea, Glenna and Lark silent and undetected behind him. Lark had no idea a man could set off so many women on a path into such a tangled web.

Once Fletcher stopped struggling, Jolene stepped back into the line with the rest of his lovers.

Jolene unbuttoned her blouse. Then Sharlene took her top off, then Tallula, then Bunny and then Faith. Sissy burned with a determined look in her eye. She resisted at first, and then finally began to unfasten her shirt buttons slow.

"You go girl," Faith was proud of her friend.

"You can do it," Bunny urged.

Sissy removed her shirt and wadded it into a ball and tossed it down in front of where Fletcher was tied up.

Jolene spread her arms out, hands down, palms facing toward Fletcher, "Take your last look, Fletcher McCrea."

The rest of the women followed Jolene's lead. They all turned to the side, and then faced away from Fletcher. Bunny wiggled her fanny back and forth. Then, like a line of showgirl dancers, they all turned to the other side, and finally they all faced him once more.

"Fletcher McCrea," Jolene and rest of the women were glassy eyed, "might be one of us, might be none, but not ever going to be with all of us ever again."

Fletcher's eyes were glassy too. "I've never ever been anything but faithful to my better self."

"Then, you can go find turquoise somewhere else," Jolene said.

"Start all over from scratch," Tallula added.

"Probably find another town of women willing to play along for a while," Sharlene said.

"Or, just maybe," Jolene took hold of her girlfriend's hands, she stepped nearer to where Fletcher was tied up, "it's time our sweet talking turquoise miner..." Jolene leaned forward, and then Sharlene, Tallula, Bunny, Faith and finally even Sissy surrounded their captive with their breasts hovering so close to his lips, they could feel their handcuffed lover's warm breath on them... "It's time you find the spine to make a life with one of us."

Fletcher had a mournful yearning look in his eyes. It was a close-up view of the sanctuary he'd been hiding out in these past six years. And now the biggest nightmare of his bachelorhood life had arrived.

He pleaded, "I have loved each and every one of you best I could. Idea of giving up five of you to find love with one of you, I don't know if I'm man enough to face up to those facts. I'm just no good for that." He closed his eyes and shook his head. He had a sorrow on his lips choking the hope right out of rest of his best days.

"You are going to pick one of us for the bedroom, the rest for friends," Faith said.

"Going to break my heart six ways to Sunday," Fletcher said.

"Going to miss you too," Jolene replied, "but we're going to make the best of it. We're going to take pleasure watching you change into the kind of man a woman can use."

"Might be, one of us gets an honest to god relationship out of the thing," Sissy said.

"I'm going to spend the rest of my days afraid to close my eyes for fear of seeing things I'll never get to do again."

The women all kneeled down in front of Fletcher. One by one, each woman took a turn placing their hand over the top of Fletcher McCrea's private parts, and as each woman removed her hand, she'd turn, look at the friend next to her, and then that woman would reach out and place her hand in the same place.

"How'd we get so mixed up?" Fletcher wanted to know.

"Only one way to get from here to a life fulfilled," Jolene said.

"I wouldn't even know where to start looking for the courage to be a faithful man."

"Best place to find your best self might be located on the other side of a lonely and empty life," Sharlene said.

The women got up off their knees. One by one they stood, put their shirts back on.

"We don't want to do your laundry," Jolene said, "don't want to make you curtains."

"Not going to fix you dinner," Bunny added.

"And not going to let you forget to put the toilet seat back down when you are done standing there doing your business." Sissy had that look in her eye again.

"Falling in love doesn't take courage; takes resignation." Fletcher groused.

"Thank Hazel Harwood for helping us find our spine," Jolene said.

"At first it seemed like it was trash talking," Tallula said.

"Fact is, it was more like truth telling," Bunny added.

"Hazel slapped the hard truth out of our gullible faces." Sissy was angry. "She said, you are not a man to go along with, you are a man to swear off, that we had to find the strength to put a stop to this sorry chapter in our sex lives."

"Take your last look," Jolene said. "Next time you see us, Fletcher, might see your better self and true love in the eyes of one of us."

"Don't do this..."

"It's going to be a revelation," Jolene said.

"It's going be a beautiful thing, all rice, and rings, and altars." Faith claimed.

"Oh, my god," Fletcher said.

"Vowing," Sissy added, "until death do us part..."

"This isn't a kidnapping; might as well have water-boarded me," Fletcher was frightened.

"Got to put you to the test, find out if you're a lifelong bachelor," Jolene said.

"...Or what...?"

"Or, maybe we find out you don't have the guts to try taking a bite out of the beauty to be found in true love..."

Glenna backpedalled with Lark into the darkness at the edge of the campground. She whispered, "Come on, time we hiked out of here."

"I didn't know a man could get so mixed up inside," Lark whispered.

"See the trick is to cool a stud down while you turn the sex you're giving him into a love he can understand."

"How's a woman know how to do that?"

"Exercise your prerogatives. You say 'no' to things for a spell, until the man's willing to find a 'yes.'"

"Men never do that..."

"Getting a man to change his mind is the second most important thing a woman can do with her life."

"And what's the first thing?"

"Bringing his child into this world..."

"Fletcher's too old to start a family..."

Glenna put her arm around Lark and smiled. She said, "But, Blake's not..."

chapter

FOURTEEN

It was a dead calm sticky dusk. The General Store was closed. Meadowhawk had come to a crawl. Town ached with silence. This was small town Great Basin beauty. Glenna and Lark sat out front on the bench seat. It was the right moment to spot nightjars hunting on wing for bugs hovering around the glow of street lights. A *sold* placard had been slapped across the fairgrounds *for sale* sign. Red plastic ribbons tied to survey stakes had been set in place on the front lot. Jace Brandt had been out of town. He'd shown back up today. His Mercedes was parked out front of the Sundial.

Keefe came in from the hot spring in his Ford pickup. He rolled into town at a crawl. He was on patrol, always a chance he'd bump into Hazel; that was right at the top of his life list. He let off the gas. He hit his brakes. Keefe saluted with one hand. Glenna and Lark both waved.

Keefe pulled into a parking space, killed the motor, hopped out of his truck; he looked up and down the block.

"Hazel's nowhere to be found," Glenna said.

"She's here. I can feel her." Keefe turned around and spotted the survey stakes, "Nobody called and told me about this." Then there was the gall of the *sold* sign right there in front of Keefe's face. He'd stomached all that bad news as best he could, and turned back around to face Glenna and Lark.

"Keefe Kenny, the fairgrounds are sold, and Hazel Harwood is lost. Anything else I can tell you that you won't hear?" Glenna was mock scowling at her friend.

"I like it when you talk like that," Keefe said.

"You're licked and don't know when to quit."

Keefe grit his teeth, gave Glenna a long eyeballing, turned and looked up into the dark sky. He could feel the touch of night in the breeze against his unshaved face. Meadowhawk's last days of summer had the sweetest touch. He reached inside his truck for a sack, picked it off the seat, and kicked his door shut with a flick of his butt.

"You got dreaming on your mind tonight?" Glenna asked.

"You got to get over it, Glenna, time to face facts," Keefe handed Glenna the sack, sat down next to Lark. He put his arm around her shoulders.

"What facts are we facing?' Lark asked.

"I got an open mind, always room for a better idea," Keefe said, pointing to his head, "but my heart isn't giving up, even if Glenna Goddard tells me it's not ever going to happen."

"You're just going to need to be sad for the rest of your days," Glenna laughed.

"At least we'll eat good food, while we wait for our fortunes to change."

Glenna poked around looking through the grocery bag. "Looks like we're going to have a well fed misery..."

Keefe sat down on the bench, "Picked dandelion greens, basil, red leaf lettuce, cherry tomatoes, and green beans."

"You're still not yourself. I liked you better when you were more rotten than you are." Glenna poked around the sack of produce, "Have you and Lark over for a barbeque. Maybe talk Blake into coming." Glenna got up off the bench seat. "Come on..."

"Where you off to...?"

"You too," Glenna offered Keefe a hand.

"We're walking down to Blake's garage," Lark said.

"You started picking yet?" Glenna asked pulling Keefe up to his feet.

"I was up the mountain with Bero; he organized a crew."

"How'd it go?"

"Did good; hauled two truckloads off the mountain."

"So, what's that mean?"

"Means, when I marry again, I'm having a great big family wedding. Going to take Hazel Harwood and we're going to go to Paris for our honeymoon, and I'll have the money to take her."

Lights were on at Blake's. Roll up doors to the Quonset hut were open. You could hear the police scanner over the tow truck's external speaker. Inside a custom racing bike was strapped onto a hydraulic motorcycle lift. The aerodynamic fiberglass body had been removed and set, piece by piece, on the shop floor. Blake had a work light dangling on a cord from the rafters. His tool box stood near as tall as he did and had been rolled up next to where he was working. He had a pry bar in one hand and box end wrench in the other. He'd mounted a dial-indicator between two sprockets. He was setting the chain tension to the supercharger.

"Lark, you want to hold this light right here?" Blake asked.

"Oh, you do have a way with women," Glenna said.

"What is this thing?" Keefe asked.

"It's a Honda motor, custom frame, tricked out. I'm running it out on the Salt Flats. This is my ticket to membership in the two hundred mile an hour club."

"Aren't you luckiest young lady in Meadowhawk," Glenna said.

"That's what men do, they make a woman worry," Lark said. "That's what Hazel said."

"They make a woman worry?" Glenna shook her head. "The worries are just warm-ups."

"You'd have to be worried about not being worried," Keefe said.

Glenna gave Keefe a look, and then she spoke, "Blake, haven't you got enough danger in your life?"

"I don't think of riding a motorcycle as something to worry about; it's more like something to worry about not doing."

You got a death wish or a stubborn streak." Glenna said.

"Leave him alone." Keefe understood. "It's his one life, and Blake gets to choose how he wants to spend it."

Blake picked a shop rag off his toolbox, wiped his wrench clean and set it back in its drawer.

A crackling voice came up over the police scanner radio speaker. There was static. "Meadowhawk sheriff department," there was a moment of silence, "Meadowhawk sheriff department," there was another pause then, "This is Nevada Department of Transportation Ely, over..."

Lark was looking at Keefe, then at Glenna. Keefe and Glenna were looking at one another and listening intently.

"Go ahead, D.O.T. Ely, over..."

There was a break in the radio transmission, then another hissing sound and a voice said, "We got a D-10 on a lowboy coming in at 5 a.m. verifying you're ready on your end?"

"I saw the rig," Blake said.

"Where...?" Keefe asked.

"Parked out the Hot Spring Highway, north at the *Last Arrow*..."

Keefe looked at Glenna. He looked back at Blake and said, "Let's go..."

Blake unzipped his coveralls. He hustled. "We're taking the Jeepster."

"What's all that about on the radio?" Glenna asked.

"There's a bulldozer on a truck parked up at the *Last Arrow*," Keefe said.

"I don't know what that means?" Glenna asked.

"It means there's a bulldozer headed here to the fairgrounds. That's what it means."

"We're going too," Glenna pushed the front seat forward; she and Lark hopped in the back.

After racing north in Blake's Jeepster, they pulled over on the side of the road. They were a mile off from their destination. Glenna and Lark unfastened their safety belts, got a grip on the roll bar and hoisted themselves up. The solitude of the *Last Arrow's* illuminated flashing business sign landmarked the high desert way station.

"I count five big rigs and four pickup trucks," Keefe said.

"Lark, you and me, we'll go inside and we'll create a distraction," Glenna said.

"Give Blake a chance to do what he's got to do," Keefe added.

Blake pulled back out onto the highway, then shut his lights off, cut his engine and rolled up at the edge of the *Last Arrow's* parking area stealth like. The only sign of any life came from the flashing advertising lights on the *Last Arrow's* billboard trailer.

Glenna was brushing out Lark's windblown hair. Lark was fixing her lipstick in the Jeepster's side door mirror.

"Maybe you should do the distracting," Keefe said.

"I can slow a man down, but Lark can stop them."

Lark took a deep breath, her palms were sweaty, "Ready..."

"I'll do the talking; you do the flirting." Glenna was in charge.

Blake was focused on the bulldozer. His mind was ticking off his list of mischief he was about to make.

"He's probably young and handsome." Glenna teased, "Might be one, might be a whole room of them."

"Lucky me," Lark said, "probably whole room of Fletcher McCreas."

"One last look," Glenna inspected her head to toe, "turn around." She regarded Lark's sure fire figure. In the right hands it could lure and confuse. "What do you two think?"

Keefe was jumpy, "Lark's prettiest young woman a man could ever hope to come walking their way."

Blake glanced up and down, "I hope you know what you're doing."

"I'm sorry," Keefe said, "sorry I got you two kids all tangled up in this."

"It's alright," Lark said. "Sometimes doing the wrong thing is the right thing to do."

"If we showed up in Salt Lake City with a bulldozer, you think they'd let us knock their fairgrounds down?" Blake said.

Keefe was grateful, "You two..."

"Suck that tummy in," Glenna said. She took another notch of Lark's belt. Glenna stood back and then unfastened one more button on her shirt, tugged it open a bit more. "Not even going to be a fair fight."

"Lark," Keefe approached, "all you're doing is stopping the world long enough for Blake to do what he's got to do."

"Come on," Glenna grabbed Lark's hand. They hustled across the street to the roadhouse. At the entrance a patron leaving pushed the door open.

Glenna used her smile to stop the man, "You're not leaving already?"

"I'm afraid so," he smiled back easily, when he looked at Lark, he tried acting as casual as he could. He looked back at Glenna, then looked at Lark one more time. "Nothing like a pair of aces appearing right out of the night..."

"You part of the team hauling that bulldozer?" Glenna asked.

"That's your boy right over there."

Glenna spotted their mark, "Well, you drive careful out there."

Keefe and Blake stood off in the darkness on the other side of the Jeepster.

"You got a plan?" Keefe asked in a whisper.

"Wait for that driver to leave," Blake said. "Then, I'll fiddle with things..."

Glenna stood with Lark at the door. She sized up the room. She dug some change out of her pocket, said in a low voice, "Go put some Patsy Cline on that jukebox; pick a few ballads."

"Then what do I do?" Lark asked.

"Act like you'd throw the night away, if you could only find a man in the saloon worth the trouble."

"How do I play that card?" Lark wasn't at all sure what Glenna meant.

"Pretend...make believe... be something you've never been before."

"I wish I had your experience," Lark said beneath her breath.

"It's your good looks that're going to do all the work for us," Glenna was keeping an eye on the men at the bar, "just play along, a man isn't a complicated thing."

Glenna walked across the roadhouse saloon to the bar. She had to keep an eye on her driver without looking at him.

Lark picked a song, punched the code in, and out came, "If you got leaving on your mind..."

Glenna turned and went out of character, extra big, and called to Lark, "Honey, that boyfriend is done breaking your heart..."

Lark fed more quarters into the jukebox, picking more songs, swishing her hips side to side, bobbing the bait, waiting for the men in the room to take a bite of the lure.

The driver was thin. He had black sideburns and a sun-beaten face. He reeked of tobacco smoke.

Every man in the roadhouse had swung around on their bar stools, subtlety wasn't a long haul driver's game. The mark wasn't half bad looking by Glenna's eye.

When Lark turned, she played her moment nonchalant, cool, pretended as if she was at her job taking care of business at the clinic. She looked around the room, ignoring everyone else, but for the driver, she saved that look in the eye for him, looked away after counting one, two, three, under her breath, feigning modesty, smiling about a thought running through her mind, brushed her black hair off the side of her face, and tried to use a style of walking she'd seen on a televised fashion show. Lark figured the moment had come in her life to audition her version of the showboat. Her desperate-for-a-man's- attention act seemed to be working, so far at least.

Glenna turned and said, "She's heart broke; the bastard walked out on her for another woman."

Driver looked at Lark; could not believe his eyes, "Threw her back?"

"She's not for the weak or timid." Glenna stood up and offered her bar stool to Lark.

Lark was growing more skillful by the moment. She took the seat, brushed her long hair off her cheek and cocked her head around. She was determined to close the deal. Lark surrendered her smile to the driver. Looked him up and down, acting as if she had thoughts about what she might let him do.

Glenna circled around, "Barkeep, two vodka stingers."

Lark turned and faced forward; her hair hid her closed eyes. She lip-synched to the jukebox music. She arched her back and stuck her butt out. She was drawing feminine lines with her instincts. Lark kept her shoulders down and let her chest fill full of air.

Glenna was waiting for the drinks and caught the driver stealing looks. A man, as Glenna had long ago learned, if nothing else was a predictable creature.

Glenna put her arm on his shoulder and placed her other hand down on top the wrist he held his pint glass of beer in. "Not too many drivers in this life ever come to the *Last Arrow* and have an honest to god, real live chance to do some Patsy Cline two-stepping with a pretty, 'heartbroke,' young thing."

Lark had her arms crossed over one another, leaning on the bar pushing her bosom up, playing the part. She turned her head, looked the driver up and down and when the driver looked her up and down the same way, she dropped her eyes in false modesty, then lifted them up and flashed her eyes at the object of her deception.

Glenna swatted the driver on his backside right on top his wallet. "Go on, you two, life is for living and Patsy Cline's for dancing..."

"You want to dance?" the driver asked.

Lark spun around on her stool, stepped off and glided with her new swishing hipped walking style out to the floor.

Glenna spun around. When the driver stepped off his stool, she restrained him with a grip around his waist, "I'm going to tell you a secret," she leaned up toward his ear, "my girlfriend has a tender heart and open mind. I know when she likes someone."

The driver looked at Glenna. She widened her eyes and swatted him on the behind once more.

Lark and the driver gripped one another and began two stepping. Lark pulled the driver closer to her than she'd ever dared to do in her life before.

The driver and Lark danced tight as a tick. If there'd been a chaperon and this had been a school dance, they'd have been pulled apart, parents would have been called, and they'd have been sent home for acting shameless.

"Don't seem like you're going to be missing your boyfriend for long…"

"I hope not," Lark said. She was way in over her head now.

Glenna walked across to the jukebox. She looked at what else they might play. She turned around. The bartender and customers were feasting their eyes on Lark and the luckiest truck driver this side of Pipe Dream Mountain. There was a spell cast at the *Last Arrow*. To a man, the notion that a willing woman could come blowing into a roadhouse and go, cheek to cheek, with a companion parched driver, left every single solitary one of those dreamers all tangled in their own foolish Great Basin delusions.

Glenna walked over to the door. Nobody paid her any attention. She stole a glance through the window. Keefe and Blake were walking back toward the Jeepster. The pupils in Glenna's eyes grew. The expression on her face was wiped clean off and replaced with another look altogether different.

Glenna rushed out onto the dance floor. She got hold of Lark's arm and tore her away from the driver, "What in god's good name are you doing? I told you we're not like that. Not anymore."

Lark didn't see it coming.

"I'm sorry," Glenna said, "I thought she was a better woman, but some people never change," Glenna grabbed hold of his wrist and lifted it up, "…You missing anything?" she asked the driver.

The driver grabbed hold of his wrist. Glenna reached into Lark's jeans pocket and pulled out his watch.

The driver looked at Lark shocked.

"You better check your wallet," Glenna said.

He pulled it from his back pocket.

"Go on," Glenna urged, "I'm ashamed of you," she said to Lark. Glenna raised her hand. It was his cash she was holding.

"You're not fit to love a man," Glenna started dragging her out of the *Last Arrow.*

"Where you going?" the driver got hold of Glenna.

Glenna didn't struggle. "I'm saving you from the biggest mistake of your life."

"I'll make my own mistakes," the driver wasn't ready to give up on his plans for Lark just yet, "I know how to handle a woman."

"Are you the man bringing that bulldozer to Meadowhawk tomorrow morning?"

"That's me..."

Glenna wiggled her wrist out of the driver's grasp, "I got a girlfriend twice as pretty and three times more trustworthy."

The driver found that impossible to believe.

"That's the trouble with a pretty face," Glenna said, "man like you ought to have a good woman. You don't need this trouble."

Lark grabbed hold of the driver and squeezed him in close to her. He began getting confused, and then Glenna grabbed hold of him too, and put her hand down and pressed against his wallet.

"You won't do yourself any good," Glenna said, "Might be fun for an hour or so, but then you won't have anything but a bad decision to show for it when you wake up." Glenna looked as sincere as she could at the man, while she held Lark's arm tight with her hand.

Lark fake tugged, pretended to be trying to break her grip, "Let go of me," Lark said.

"I'm sorry it turned out this way," Glenna said, "A man handsome like you... you deserve the company of a real woman..."

The driver tried to speak, Glenna interrupted, "Nothing to say." She opened the door. Glenna pushed Lark out first. She scanned the room. The men were frozen in place. "It would never have worked out," Glenna smiled at the driver, "she's nothing but weakness and bad habits." Glenna backed up toward the threshold, "we'll see you tomorrow; I'll introduce you to the lucky side of Meadowhawk. I guarantee you. You can hang that promise with a magnet on your truck's dashboard."

Glenna waited for the door to shut. She looked through the windows. The drivers were all twisting their heads looking at one another.

Glenna turned and stepped quick to catch up with Lark. Keefe and Blake were waiting, the engine was idling.

"Honey," Glenna said putting her arm around Lark's waist, "that's using what you got to get what you want."

"And I thought we were the poor, weak, defenseless creatures..."

Glenna laughed, "Most all men are a one trick pony, and they're just waiting to be taken for their first ride."

chapter

FIFTEEN

The front bonnet to the big rig had been tipped open. The driver wiped the sweat off his forehead. "I don't know. I tried to turn the motor over and nothing..."

"If anybody can get the rig running, Blake's the man," the Deputy Sheriff said.

Blake positioned his repair truck alongside the big rig and unlatched and folded down the compartment doors for access to his tools. He climbed up on the front tire. A car was approaching from the south. Jace Brandt's Mercedes was making a beeline on the highway from Meadowhawk.

The Deputy Sheriff walked toward the approaching Mr. Jace Brandt. He sped into the *Last Arrow's* parking lot, kicked up a mess of dust, rolled his window down.

Garrett leaned his head down in line of sight to the Deputy. "Any luck?"

"None yet," the Deputy Sheriff said. "Blake just got here."

Jace loosened the knot of his tie. "Let's get this thing rolling. . ."

Garrett got out of the Mercedes. He walked over to the rig. He knew a thing or two about diesel motors, removed his sunglasses for a better look. "What happened?"

Blake was pumping on a lever; he had opened a valve. He answered, "Air in the fuel system." Blake snapped his fingers, "These motors are famous for eating injector pumps."

"Simple enough, if it's air. But if it's the injector pump, I don't know," Garrett said.

"Might just be air," Blake's voice was unsteady. "I can rebuild the pump if need be."

Garrett looked up and down the row of convoy vehicles. There was a pilot truck parked first, chase vehicle at the rear, and the big rig with the bulldozer on top the low-boy trailer, in between.

The Deputy Sheriff said, "If Blake gets this rig fired up, ought to be in Meadowhawk by noon."

"We got a crew ready to break ground," Garrett said. "We want the fairground cleared. There's a store to open, nobody's got time to wait for tomorrow."

Garrett climbed back into the passenger seat. Jace turned the Mercedes back onto the Hot Spring Highway and mashed the gas pedal.

Blake figured he'd dilly dally as long as he could. He maintained an earnest expression on his face, acted like he was doing everything he could.

Glenna had her leather shoulder bag next to her seat. She reached down, opened it, and removed an alarm clock. "I want you to put this in the honeymoon suite..."

"A clock radio...?" Keefe asked.

"Clock radio with built in camera, going to take a picture or two, at the right moment, of guests doing what people do when they think nobody's looking."

"Glenna Goddard!" Keefe looked at the radio trying to figure out where the lens was hidden.

"The girls are coming out for 'naked night' and have us a time."

"You're coming out for 'naked night?'" Keefe asked.

"We're going to have strong feelings for one of the guests."

"What are you going to do with those pictures?" Keefe had a sly look on his face.

Glenna resolved. "Change how a person thinks..."

"Help him see the error of his ways?" Keefe asked.

"Finding a way to changing a man's mind isn't necessarily done by playing around with what he has between his ears," Glenna said.

"A lot of men do their most penetrating thinking by way of another part of themselves altogether," Keefe said.

"I'd say that holds true for near all the men I've ever known," Glenna said.

"I can see how a good photograph could be a breath of fresh air in a stale mind." Keefe smiled and had a faraway look in his eye...

Glenna got a stoic expression on her face, "He's a nice enough looking man and when the time comes, and if he picks me, I'm aiming to play the part..."

"Can't be evil, if you end up saving the fairgrounds..."

"Might just do the trick," Glenna said, "every time I've climbed into bed with a man it's been for either love or fun, haven't tried doing it for my civic duty. That could put a whole new wrinkle on the thing."

"Of all the no good lousy luck," Fletcher McCrea griped. He'd struck it rich about the exact moment he'd fallen on the hardest days of his life. His heart wasn't in it anymore. He tried to cheer up. He cooked up his favorite recipe of sour cream pancakes. Even put sliced bananas on them, real butter and covered them with genuine maple syrup. He choked them down like he was eating a leather bound copy of the Bible.

Bambalina was worried near to death. Fletcher wasn't even 'kind of the same' man. If he'd kept working, even at this pace, unfortunate as it may have seemed, Fletcher McCrea was going to be stupid rich and rock bottom woeful, all at the same time. That kind of paradox could shatter the soul of even the most skillful womanizer. The saddest part was the burro could see Fletcher didn't much care for his life any longer. Worse still, Bambalina could smell that he wasn't even bothering to shower. There was no need. He wasn't going into town, and not one of his women was driving up to spend the night up here at the turquoise mine. He wasn't even getting drunk. He didn't even have enough sorrow for that.

Since the kidnapping, he'd worked the sudden end of his sex life over and over in his head. The same answer to his problem spit out every time. Fletcher McCrea could not conceive of there being any method or means to his being faithful to one woman. It was not natural to his inclinations. He knew that once he was on pledge that he would be incapable of keeping his good word. For Fletcher's sex life to work right, he needed to be all tangled up with one woman, but just for the night, and then best thing was while he was with that one, he'd see another he'd have to have, and then he'd start dwelling on the other while he was having intimate relations with the one. His women all knew that. His way of turning his sex life into some kind of relay race was an adaptation, a coping mechanism. It wasn't fair. It wasn't kind. It was simply the best he could do. It was incomprehensible that when Fletcher McCrea looked out from Pipe Dream Mountain across the open wild Great Basin bottom lands, he was looking as far as any man's eye could see, and there wasn't in eyesight another bunch of women ready to take over where all his former girlfriends had left him off.

What was even more treacherous now was the risk of suffering a relapse; one wrong move and he'd end up right back in the same predicament he'd found himself in. Only this time, if Fletcher went to town and lost what was left of his self-control, and he fell into the carnal spiral of lust, it would be an irreversible act. And he'd already surrendered any notion that he'd be able to consummate a simultaneous reconciliation with his six sweethearts. And even if he could perform such a miracle, it would only be a matter of time before discontent set in, and monogamy was again floated as a means to the end of all this sordid suffering that this other arrangement was the cause of.

Bambalina stood in her corral and watched in disbelief as Fletcher McCrea took a shower, shaved, put on fresh clothes, walked down the hill, climbed into his truck, and started out on the dirt road heading into town. Then, the next thing she knew, the burro could hear the squeaking brakes, the truck being shifted into reverse, and Fletcher backing his rig up to the lower lot, and then his getting out, slamming the door, cussing like there was somebody there to cuss at, and hiking back up to the mine, getting out of his clothes, pouring a glass of whiskey, sit on the deck out front of his trailer, mutter, knock a few shots back, have one more cussing fit, shake his head, back and forth, and then go flop on top his bunk in the trailer and collapse into a fretful sleep.

One of these days Bambalina feared Fletcher McCrea would finally make it all the way to town, and then who knows what would come of her?

The work at the Harwood Award Ribbon Company had been proceeding accordingly and at the usual pace. The last of the season's first, second and third place fair ribbons were all boxed up and ready to ship. Hazel and her crew were right proud of all the little lives they'd change. All those teenage barrel racers and future farmers they'd make proud. And don't think for a moment that Hazel wasn't working hard for her own tomorrows. Hazel had been breaking in new product. They were making rosettes that decorated funeral parlors, and they had other new products for altars for customers that were taking their nuptials.

Bero and Mirari called. They were looking for help with the pinion pine nut harvesting. After lunch Hazel stayed behind to do paperwork while she sent her crew up the mountain to help pick.

"I have never worked so hard in my life," Jolene said.

"Look at me," Bunny declared. Her hair had sap stuck in it. She was covered in pine needles.

"I worked for Del Monte one summer," Faith explained, "and that was the hardest job I ever had until I tried picking pine nuts."

"We got nothing better to do," Sissy said.

"Sex life is over," Tallula complained.

"I miss that sweet talking turquoise miner throwing me down on my bed then jumping on top of me," Sharlene said.

"Got no sex life," Jolene said, "shouldn't have done it."

"All we were getting was scraps," Bunny said.

Glenna was hauling her basket in along a trail. She heard the women grousing. "Now's not the time to lose your will..."

"Glenna, you don't know nothing, on account of you weren't willing to go in on the thing with us," Faith said.

"The only way to ever find a good man is to get rid of the wrong man," Glenna said.

"We figured Fletcher was helping us get ready," Sharlene said.

"Ready?" Glenna asked.

"The problem was, Fletcher was too good at his job," Tallula said.

"We never faced the facts," Jolene said, "and the truth is, none of us want a man around all the time. Pretend like we do."

"Now, look. We have picking to do, plans to make," Glenna showed her mettle. "First things first. After the dust settles, things go right, somebody's going to find Fletcher McCrea come crawling on his knees, back into her life."

"After he finds out what we are going to do?" Sissy asked.

"There is no shame. We are performing our civic duty," Glenna said.

"I'm proud of all of you," Jolene said. "Proud you're willing to put yourselves on the line."

"Jace Brandt doesn't look like hard work," Tallula said.

"It is something to look forward to," Jolene said.

"I don't know if I got the guts," Sissy was blushing.

"Honey, might be a healing for you," Jolene said.

"Seven of us with just one of him," Sissy said.

"I'm scared to death," Glenna said, "but I trust you all..."

"Good god, girl, we're planning on having an orgy!" Bunny's fake eyelashes froze wide open.

"There's a first time for everything," Glenna replied.

"Might be last time any of us have any fun," Jolene added.

"What is going to happen to the rest of us?" Tallula wanted to know.

"Look, we got a fairground to save." Glenna said, "Tomorrow night we make our move; save our town. Night after that, I'll have you all over to my place, and we can put our heads together and come up with a plan on how to put a little spark back into our sex lives."

The following day the convoy from the *Last Arrow* arrived in Meadowhawk. They parked on Main Street in front of the fairgrounds. The driver shut the truck's motor off. Next, he climbed up onto the trailer into the bulldozer's cockpit seat, and right on cue, just as Blake had planned, the thing wouldn't fire up. The driver cussed.

Blake tried to look surprised. He got a wrench and shop towel and climbed up on the treads to the machine and banged on the injector pump. He acted sincere and swore. They drove the big rig over to Blake's repair facilities.

Glenna met them there. She walked the driver down to the Brewery. Rory poured the driver an example of his fresh made lager. Then at the right moment, the plan was for Sissy to come on in and hang all over the man, keep him busy, rattle his cage, keep him confused. That way Glenna looked to keep her word, serve up one of the girls on a silver platter just the way she said she would, and then, when push came to shove, Sissy could break out her deck of playing cards and, just like that, she'd get what she wanted without having to give that driver the thing the driver thought he wanted. Sissy going off over a game of cards was a sight to behold.

Blake's plan was to tinker with the D-10's fuel delivery system. He'd pull the injectors. He'd put them on a racking mechanism. He'd bench test each one. When that didn't fix the problem, he'd pull the fuel pump, take it apart and put it back together. It was all plausible deniability, stall for time. He aimed to work his side of the game while the women worked their side. Thinking ahead, Blake figured to get the thing running, and then do like a lot of politicians of certain persuasions do, pretend like you're being helpful, while in fact, all you are doing is really getting folks to look one way, while you go the other. The idea behind this approach was to let them believe they were going to start bulldozing down the fairgrounds, when in fact the next thing they were going to discover was that the hydraulic system was all goobered up. The only question in Blake's mind he didn't have an answer for was, how long would it take for Garrett Harwood to catch on?

Up on Pipe Dream Mountain Fletcher McCrea had once again shaved, showered and dressed. Bambalina watched the whole thing, and couldn't believe her ears when there was no squeak of the brakes, no sound of the truck being put into reverse, and that her keeper seemed to have finally got up the gumption to drive into town, to tempt fate and plant the seeds of regret. Bambalina knew that her life hung in the crosshairs of Fletcher McCrea's self-control. She got so worked up, seemed to her, that Fletcher could be at risk of causing an irreversible harm to his reputation. There would be no escape. A hypocritical turquoise miner was akin to being a tone-deaf lounge singer, a freak of saloon nature. She was sick with worry that the loss of his willpower to fight off the flesh-induced temptations might well lead this pillar of bachelorhood to his own self-inflicted bitter end.

Bunny fluttered her fake eyelashes then dug her elbow into her girlfriend. Faith had come dressed with one of her shoulders peeking out of her sweater. She slid her chair back as Jace Brandt tried passing behind her. Faith shot up out of her chair and beamed and glowed, smiled and heaved a big breath. It was her celebrated breathless woman technique that she used on the man.

She grabbed hold of her earlobe. She looked down, "Must have lost my earring on the floor."

She sang that line like it was a note perfect song. Faith bent forward in front of Jace in such a way as to allow the stretched out neckline of her sweater to sag forward. She had put on tonight, for purposes of the entrapment, a 'no fooling around black as sin' bustier. It squeezed her breasts into an underwire cupped floral lace affair. Make matters even more enticing, it had fine pink ribbons decorating the tender edges of where her breasts bulged out from beneath the Lycra-stretched front panel.

While Faith was distracting Jace, it was Bunny's job to assess the degree of weakness and thirst the man displayed, after getting a good look see at her girlfriend's puffed up chest parts. His ears turned red and his eyes twitched. Bunny figured he'd taken the bait. All of the women stood up, all at once, they had the same knowing look on their faces, and they all cocked their heads off to the side.

"Jace Brandt," Jolene said, "if you aren't a breath of fresh man air in a town gone stale with dog days of summer."

Sissy pushed her chair toward Jace, "Have a seat..."

"Buy you a beer?" Sharlene said.

Gig walked over to their table, "Aren't all of you looking like a brand new box of my favorite cereal? My god, I haven't seen this much glitter and glow since last time I watched fireworks."

"Well, that's mighty sweet of you to say," Jolene replied.

"Half of what I am," Sharlene stuck out her chest, "is on account of that baked bread I can't help leaving the bakery with. If I took a man home as often I do a loaf of your bread, they'd say I was married."

"I eat twice as much as Sharlene does; and look at me, nothing..." Tallula complained, "My daddy said it's not what you bring to the fight, but how much appetite you have for one."

Gig laughed, "I'm buying the beer at this table tonight." Gig lifted his hand and gestured to Rory for a pitcher.

"I think he likes you," Tallula said to Faith.

Faith had Jace squeeze in next to her at the table. Sissy with all her Italian ancestral might was leaning against him from the other. Of all the women, Sissy and Faith had particular skills. They could dote and fondle a man in such accidental fashion that it wasn't even fair. Jolene and Bunny would have been too much woman for a man not to see he was being hunted.

Glenna was pacing up and down the block. The palms of her hands were cold. She put them together. They felt clammy. She grabbed hold of the door handle, put a silly grin on her face, and went inside the Brewery.

"What are we waiting for?" Glenna said.

"We're all but ready," Faith said.

"Only question is if Jace Brandt's ready too?" Sissy wrapped her arm around Jace's.

Jolene poured the beer Gig ordered into eight glasses, enough to wet everyone's whistle, "If we're going to make it out to the hot spring for 'naked night,'" Jolene said lifting her glass, "best make it an adventure."

"I think what she's saying," Glenna explained, "we'd like you to join us tonight."

Jace's eyes got wide, "...me!" he laughed nervously, "I'm afraid that's a bridge too far."

"Bulldozer's not going anywhere until Blake fixes it," Jolene said.

Sissy and Faith leaned in on Jace, trapped his arms in their grasp, they continued utilizing their covert tactile persuasive technique with their other hands. Sissy put her arm around his shoulders and tickled the back of his neck, "Jace Brandt, there's nothing but harmless fun waiting for us tonight."

"Then it's settled," Glenna said, "Come on, up we go, everybody..."

Faith and Sissy pulled Jace up from his seat and started tugging on him to come along, he resisted. Jolene put her arms around his waist from behind; Bunny got in front, while Glenna held the door.

"'Naked night' at Keefe's Hot Spring," Jace said looking into Glenna's eyes, "I guess I'm going to find out what I need to know, before I know whether I need to know what it is I'm going to find out."

"It's not what you know," Glenna said, "it's what you live to tell." She raised her eyebrows and twisted her head, finished it off with a wink.

The women poured out of the Brewery, and before Jace had a chance to come to his senses, and in all the chaos, it seemed that the whole lot of them piled into two cars and headed pell-mell out the Hot Spring Highway.

Fletcher parked on a side street a block from the fairgrounds and set out on foot. He was a mess. He came around a corner and flinched when he saw his own shadow caught beneath Meadowhawk's vintage street lights, set there back in the days when the town and her city fathers still believed she was a place with a future and on her way up.

In the chaos of getting Jace into the car, Glenna had slipped off alone. She couldn't do it. She'd lost her nerve. She was slumped on the bench in front of the General Store. Glenna was ashamed. She was a deserter. She was supposed to be out at the hot spring. Her friends might need help.

Fletcher spotted Glenna and froze in his tracks. He figured if he was going to be safe around any woman, it had to be her. He approached. "What's wrong with you?"

"I lack the courage of my convictions," Glenna said, shaking her head back and forth.

"Saucy woman like you..."

"Shut up, Fletcher McCrea." Glenna said, "They took Jace Brandt out to the hot spring."

"Who took Jace out to the hot springs?"

"Jolene did... Sharlene, Tallula, Faith, Bunny, Sissy, I was supposed to go too..."

"For 'naked night'...?"

"For one last bite of the apple," Glenna said. "Try to save our town."

"I lose six girlfriends and Jace Brandt ends up with the whole lot of them out at Keefe's?"

"We weren't taking Jace to 'naked night' because we thought it was fun. We were taking him there so we could get him up to his eyeballs in hot water, take a few pictures at the right moment, and maybe get him to see the world the same way we do."

"I didn't know skinny dipping was criminal behavior." Fletcher said.

"He's married. What's that man going tell his wife?"

"First thing you do is say it isn't what it looks like."

Glenna looked at Fletcher, "Really? So, what does it look like?"

Fletcher searched the nighttime sky, "I suppose there's no explaining, catch that man doing the deed. Going to break a wife's heart and shatter their lives."

"If he'll do what we say, his wife will never need to know."

"That's the whole problem right there." Fletcher started coming around to his bigger concern, "A married man's not free to embrace opportunity."

Glenna turned and looked at Fletcher. She opened her mouth.

Fletcher looked inside, "I know it's in there..."

Glenna closed her eyes, shut her mouth, and shook her head.

Fletcher smiled and looked off into the darkness of the night, "I've got a knack for leaving women speechless."

Glenna clinched her hand into a fist, gave him that look, the eye, and then she socked Fletcher on the shoulder, "You've been hiding up at your mine, afraid to face the facts of life."

Fletcher shook his head. He looked off in the distance, his eyes lost in thought, "You ever get lonely?"

"Only when I'm around you..."

Bambalina paced back and forth in her corral. She could not stand there and do nothing. It was 'for better or worse' and 'until death do us part' as far as Bambalina was concerned. The time had come to exercise her prerogatives. Life was about making choices. The tamperproof latch on her gate had been engineered to impede the escape of the common barnyard animal, but the same foolproof latch is nothing much for a burro to defeat. Oh, Bambalina never let such thoughts go to her head. She wasn't the kind of animal that believed in superiority of any kind. She had as much respect for the mind of a horse as she had for that of a human being. She knew she was twice as clever as near any horse she'd ever met, still she admired a horse for being blessed with good looks and gifted with a temperament half as stubborn as hers.

Bambalina did what she had to do. She opened the gate. She stood at the steep edge on the mountain and looked out into the distant valley below. She knew what she was doing. She knew she was taking a chance, that she ought not to be going into town, but Fletcher was in a perilous fix and saving the man from himself was a risk worth running. Bambalina set off, worried sick, ears spiked straight up; she was going to go find Fletcher McCrea and stop him before it was too late.

chapter

SIXTEEN

Jace was in the upper soaking pool. Sissy, in a white terrycloth bathrobe, exited the women's dressing room. She held the door open. Stepping in unison out of the doorway wearing white robes, Faith and Bunny were followed by Sharlene and Tallula. The women had swaddled towels over the tops of their heads. Hidden behind the women was Jolene.

Sissy closed the door. The entourage of 'naked night' hot spring soakers walked with a ceremonial pace; synchronized in lockstep, the bevy approached the pools. Faith and Bunny parted, each woman raising an arm and pointing back to the next. Sharlene and Tallula parted and gestured back to Jolene who stood motionless, immaculate, pristine; she'd come from the locker room with her game face on. Jace didn't know what in the world he was in for, but the moment stood out, the woman cast her spell.

Jolene was wearing her flashy high heels. Her blonde hair had been gathered up onto the side of her head. A pair of gardenias had been bobby-pinned into the swirl. She stared at Jace and smiled easily. Sissy reached around from behind her and unknotted the sash on her bathrobe.

Sharlene spoke for all the women, "We decided that since you came on out here to 'naked night' at the hot spring, that the best way to enjoy tonight might be to keep things simple, not get overwhelmed. Might be better if you had the chance to enjoy the company of one woman. If you can handle Jolene, might be second one of us will come swap favors with you…"

Jace was caught off guard, "I…"

While he was objecting, Bunny was pouring sparkling wine into two glasses.

Sissy pulled the robe off Jolene. She was a fair skinned, smooth as silk woman, and the fact was, she possessed the best figure of the bunch, at least best looking in the nude with no gimmicks, no fancy lingerie, pure and simple, stark naked standing on the edge of the pool. Jolene was as close as some kind of perfect gets. Her human flaws were hidden out of sight of an aroused man's appetite. These imperfections were beyond what a testosterone-fogged mind might be able to detect with a naked eye. Jace Brandt's tongue was tied and mind emptied. He had entered a state of wanting, and this wanting, had stolen his reason.

Jolene slipped her feet out of her high heels. She did the removal act one foot first, then the other. She gave it drama. The barefooted Jolene marked Jace's last chance. Jolene took the two glasses from Bunny and stepped down into the hot spring pools.

Her girlfriends slipped away without so much as another word; they tiptoed down to the lower pools. They left Jolene and Jace to trace with lips and fingertips upon body and soul the simple pleasures that come of mutual attractions.

"Perhaps a toast is in order," Jolene suggested.

"What do we toast to?"

"Change..." Jolene pinched the ring on Jace's finger. "I hope this isn't going to get in our way."

Jace said, "I don't think this ring changes anything."

"Maybe tonight changes everything," Jolene said.

"People are people; what you see is what you get," Jace smiled in all his glorious nakedness.

"Maybe what's the same is that every day you're different, and there's not a thing a soul can do about it."

Jace touched his glass against Jolene's, "I believe that's true..."

Jolene looked Jace in the eye while she sipped her sparkling wine.

"The hot springs, the sparkling wine... Tell me, this isn't a trap?" Jace asked.

"It's not a trap." Jolene said. "It's human nature."

"Tell me about this human nature, what is that?"

Jolene couldn't help herself; she pressed in against Jace, wrapped her arms around him, crushed her chest against his, "I'd say something is knocking at my door."

Jace blushed. He gazed down into the dark mineral pool, "Oh, no controlling that, has a mind of its own."

"Do I answer the door?"

"Here, right now?"

"There's a honeymoon suite, room for two,"

"I thought we'd come for a soak."

"We've come to do whatever we want to do."

"Are you giving me permission?"

Jolene squeezed in tighter against Jace; she smiled, twisted her head, readied to kiss him, "You have my permission to find out..."

The Brewery had been desolate. Garrett Harwood was last to leave. Hazel's women had gone out to Keefe's for 'naked night.' Even if Hazel's employees didn't much care for Garrett's company, just their being around was lively enough to give sport and spirit to the Brewery. Rory locked the door behind him.

"Good night now, Garrett." Rory said.

Garrett steadied himself. "You take care..."

The Chamber President cocked his best white straw Stetson off to the side and strode atop his boots with a long legged swing and a clunk of his heel, dug them into the cracked pavement like spurs. He prowled the night, a watchman guarding over his empire.

Still, he was ornery. After two blocks of slow walking through the silence, he saw the work lights spilling out of the doorways of Blake's repair shop. He got that sour look on his face. He was losing his patience. He was not a man to be trifled with. He wanted that fairgrounds demolished and the sooner, the better.

The whole while he walked toward Blake's, he groused. You couldn't hear his words, but if you could read lips, seemed to look like, "Now what in the name of good god is that boy doing with that bulldozer?" And, "I swear to high heaven, if Blake doesn't have that machine running by sunrise, there will be hell to pay and ass to kiss."

"Lark," Blake said, "get me the next size up..."

She took the wrench out of Blake's hand; she was frozen, didn't move.

"Something wrong?" Blake asked.

"You didn't even notice me when I came in..."

Lark had combed her hair out; took extra care tonight. She'd put just a touch of eyeliner on, fussed with her mascara. She was wearing Glenna's midnight blue gabardine shirt, and tallest heeled boots.

"I see you," Blake said.

"Well, go over to your sink; wash your hands."

Blake scrubbed his hands and arms up to his elbows. He got a fresh shop towel and dried them off.

"I get on edge, when you get this way," Blake said.

"It's your fault," Lark said. "If you tried kissing me, we might have kissed by now."

Blake was blushing, "I wanted to kiss you at the dance."

"That didn't work out; something else has to work out; and it's going to have to work out soon."

Blake put his hands on Lark's hips. He didn't have the nerve to look her in the eye. He turned his head. "Put a wrench in my hands and I know what to do..."

Lark set her hands on Blake's hips. "Put a woman in your arms and guess what, slick, don't even know where the ignition is..."

"Lark, when I'm not with you, I play pretend about being on a picnic and nobody's there but you and me and I'm not nervous..."

"That has to be make-believe..."

"I close my eyes and I've got the courage inside me to do whatever I want."

"I told Fletcher McCrea, two shy people don't have a prayer of ever getting together."

"What if I did kiss you and it wasn't so good?" Blake asked.

"Better to be disappointed twice..."

"Twice...?" Blake asked.

"Once for not trying to kiss me, and second time after you do."

"I'm not scared of nothing until you touch me..."

Lark tilted her head off to the side, "We're just going to have to figure this out."

Blake looked up into Lark's dark eyes. He swallowed, turned his head off to the side. "Are you going to close your eyes?"

Lark closed her eyes. She dug her fingers into Blake's hips.

Blake closed his eyes.

Garrett came around the corner of the building, "For god sake, Blake Varela and Lark Lockwood, what on earth are you two doing?"

Blake and Lark separated.

"You got this thing running yet?" Garrett asked.

"Close," Blake said.

"I'm not looking for close; I want done, finished, ready to go."

Blake wasn't so good at deceit, "Well, Mr. Harwood, I'll be up until the job is done."

"Lark, you go on home… get, go on now… a man can't keep his mind on his business unless his mind is on his business."

"Maybe our business is none of your business," Lark stood her ground.

Garrett looked right through her, "Blake, you get this machine running by sun up, then if I were you, you might want to go find a woman doesn't sass a man, never mind how pretty she is. Nothing pretty about a woman doesn't know her place in the world."

Garrett had the glowering expression on his face. He was all boot and hat, red faced and full of his imperial self. He turned and strode off on his old knees into the hours of the early morning, into the darkness of Meadowhawk's empty streets.

Bambalina heard footsteps. Her nose picked up a disagreeable scent. She knew that stink. She took off trotting toward the bad smell. She picked up her pace to a canter at the sound of footsteps. Then, when she came around the corner, she came to a halt. Half a block away, she saw the one man she could never forgive.

Garrett was taken by surprise. He froze.

Bambalina wasn't wearing a halter; there was no corral. This wasn't going to be no cheap shot. This was going to be one on one, fair and square. It was a beast of burden facing off against mister big shot. She had a bone to pick and circle to square. She walked, then trotted cocking her head.

Garrett backpedaled, keeping his eye on Bambalina, as she closed in on his position. He thought to run for a porch. He could pound on a door. Might be that someone would let him in before it was too late.

"Easy now," Garrett pleaded.

Bambalina stopped just beyond his reach. She steadied her gaze at her adversary.

Garrett flinched and Bambalina leaped to block his retreat. Garrett went flatfooted. Bambalina was snorting. She brought her ears back. She was so disappointed with this man. Garrett jerked one way then tried to flee the other. Bambalina blocked his path a second time. She began scratching the pavement with her back hoof.

Garrett took a deep breath, "For god sake," he was pitiful, "easy now..."

Bambalina looked fast one way, then the other, up and down the desolate street. Apparently Garrett wasn't going to get his wish; wasn't anybody going to save this bitter old pill of a man. It was just between the two of them and wasn't even going to be much of a fight once it got started. The only question was whether Bambalina would quit the brawl before she'd brought the man to within an inch of his life.

Garrett stepped back. He had his hands stretched out in front of him. "Easy now, Bambalina, that's a good girl..."

Good girl? Bambalina stepped toward Garrett. *Who did he think he was fooling?* Every time he took a step, she took a step too.

He turned and, feeble and old as he was, he tried to run. Bambalina got her teeth on the belt of his britches, clinched down and halted his escape right then and there.

Garrett shot his hands up like he was at a mugging. "Okay, okay... I won't run, I promise, I promise, I won't run... damn it, animal, let go of me, let go..."

Pleading was music to Bambalina's ears. She let go of her grasp of his belt. He almost fell to the ground stumbling forward.

Garrett swung around. He couldn't help himself. He got that hateful look in his eye. It infuriated Bambalina. She lunged forward. She could have struck him. Instead she made a false charge toward her opponent; she stomped her feet, then snorted.

"I'm sorry, I'm sorry," Garrett pleaded, "I'm an old man, forgive me... please."

A screech owl called out in the darkness; swooping in on wing, the bird alighted upon a fence post. The altercation between a man and burro was a curious thing. The bird made its living off small rodents caught unaware. She had no sympathy for weaker creatures; they were her supper.

Garrett looked quick to the right. He spotted the owl. He re-trained his gaze on Bambalina. The owl took to the wing. The nocturnal bird's mind was made up; instincts took hold. She knew whose side she was on.

Bambalina spun and sent her hoof past Garrett's jaw (she could have nailed him, had she wished) while the owl sailed over Garrett's head and with her talons snatched his fine white straw Stetson off the top the cowering man's head.

"Don't..." he pleaded, "don't hurt me..."

The owl soared across the street to the limb of a cottonwood. The animal perched, balanced on one foot, with Mr. Garrett Harwood's hat clasped and dangling in her clutches in the other.

Garrett searched the ground. No hat. The owl screeched. Garrett startled. He looked from where the call had come from. The animal was in the tree. She had his best hat.

Bambalina was disgusted. Her adversary was pathetic, spineless, not even a worthy opponent, and say what the world will about the animal kingdom, rare if ever does an animal fight simply for the sake of a fight.

Bambalina and the owl traded a knowing look. They knew a man was no match in a real brawl.

Garrett slunk back. The old man turned and trotted away. He was not her equal. He ran for his life.

The owl screeched. The bird leaped from the limb of the tree and swooped low across the ground dragging the Stetson along. The bird stroked its wings and landed on the next fence post. The stealth night hunter wanted to go eye to eye, close-up with the burro. Bambalina paused near the post. The owl twisted its head, looked off in the direction of the frightened Garrett Harwood, and then back the other way. The owl looked into the burro's eyes. Bambalina met the bird's piercing yellow-orange eyes with a steady gaze. The owl grabbed the rim of the hat and clinched it with its beak, tried tearing a piece of the rim off, gave Bambalina another look, and at last let the hat fall to the ground. Then, in an instant, the bird let out a call, her screech, and then into the night the owl took wing.

Bambalina approached the white straw Stetson. Looked up and down the street, she regarded the hat, and then in one vengeful blow crushed the crown with her hoof. Bambalina never the sentimental trophy hunter gave into her weakness and plucked Garrett's Stetson from the ground into her teeth. It was too much the temptation; the least she could do. The score felt settled. And then, like that, she was off to find her better half, her lost miner tangled up somewhere in this town, likely about to plunge into the abyss of things he ought not to do. She was worried sick Fletcher McCrea would spoil everything, do something he might regret for the rest of his mortal days on this good earth.

Keefe's door opened. He stirred in bed. Steps could be heard on the floor crossing the room.

"Keefe," Glenna nudged him, "Keefe..."

"Glenna Goddard..." He sat up, turned on the light next to his bed.

"Did they get Jace in the honeymoon suite?"

"Jolene's been in there with him," Keefe looked at his watch, "been in there for three hours."

"That should have been me in there..."

"You...?"

"I froze up, got scared... When everyone jumped in their cars at Rory's, nobody even noticed that I went missing."

"How's Glenna Goddard go missing?"

"Keefe Kenny, I'm old news; I promised myself I'd find a place where I could start all over."

"Being Hazel's best friend has been a good thing you've done," Keefe said. He got out of bed naked and went over and opened up the doors that looked out over his hot springs. "I lost Hazel five years ago." He rubbed his head, "and I don't recollect if I had a girlfriend..." He looked at Glenna, "Did I have any girlfriends?"

Glenna handed Keefe his bathrobe. He put it on. He surrendered his shoulder. Glenna socked it.

"Sorry," Keefe said.

"It's more information than I need."

Keefe turned and opened his bathrobe. "Looks like good news to me..."

"Keefe Kenny!" She leaned on the rail and looked around at the still of the early morning.

"What did I do wrong?" Keefe asked.

"You were too busy building this to have the time to do that..."

"And so what's your excuse?"

"I guess I never believed in the thing," Glenna explained. "Figured after the thrill wore off, the men I enjoyed were going to move on, so instead of waiting for a man to walk out on me, I figured I'd beat them at their own game."

"Look at us, aren't we a pair?" Keefe said.

"Jolene has got the courage of her convictions."

"Is that what it is?"

"There's only one good reason to go to bed with someone..."

Keefe laughed, "I guess all those lousy reasons work too..."

"True enough," Glenna said. "But a good sex life is about as rare as finding a thoughtful man at a tractor pull."

"A woman has it pretty tough."

"You have no idea..."

Fletcher McCrea had wandered to town for no purpose. He didn't know what he was doing. The evening started out with his getting tipsy, and then devolved to a full blown bender. Sentimental, stubborn, empty, the forgotten man... The loss of six lovers in one fell swoop was his cross to bear. He had an urge to relieve himself. That took him onto the fairgrounds. He walked out to the back lot. After making room for more of what he'd clearly already had enough of, he collapsed in a sorrowful heap upon a bench. Fletcher McCrea unbuttoned his denim trousers while he was serving himself up another nip from his hip flask. He considered taking this moment of privacy to provide self-serving personal relations with himself. He hadn't had reason to extend such a kindness in so long, he couldn't remember last time he'd even tried.

Fletcher took another nip, closed his eyes, and took a tender grip onto the talk of this little town. Then in his mind's eye, the passing parade marched by, and to his horror the band played nothing but tunes of lonely roads and heartaches. It took no time at all before he had to open his eyes and save himself from a set of big busted hopes and endless torment. The only thing that came to his mind were his six Award Ribbon Company women, and that only made things more doomed than they already were.

He was determined. He figured he'd try doing the deed again, but this time he'd imagine other women. He tried a few movie stars. There was a woman that worked at the post office, he put to the test. Resorted to Dotty, Elena and Mirari, they all took a turn and passed through his mind, but a married woman wasn't any kind of solution, even if it was only in the privacy of his own imagination. Lark was against everything he believed. She was too young for a man so long in the tooth. The mere suggestion provoked a convulsion of guilt and shame. About the only woman left was Glenna Goddard. She wasn't married. She was about the right age. She had a fanny on her he'd been contemplating for so long, it was almost hard to believe how much time he had wasted in his life dwelling upon a thing he would never have the privilege of enjoying firsthand. So Fletcher went ahead and he closed his eyes again and this time he tried with all his might to bring some self-salvation to the misery and loneliness he was feeling so deep inside his aching heart.

Things had never been easy between Fletcher and Glenna. She'd never be a consenting partner. So, Fletcher decides he's going to have to play the scene rough. He throws her down on his bed. He stands there all smug and tough. Then he starts unbuckling his pants. If she wants to play hard to get, he'll show her what hard to get looks like. Of course trouble with this approach is that Fletcher wasn't that kind of man, didn't have it in him, and then the imaginary Glenna started pushing him around, wanted him to say he loved her, make a commitment to her, wanted him to be her steady, the whole thing started careening out of control, even in the privacy of his mind's eye, that wasn't the kind of lovemaking that was going to bring him a Merry Christmas and a Happy New Year.

Bambalina had seen the whole thing. Standing there with Garrett's hat clinched in her teeth. She'd been peeking from around the side of the horse barn. She felt bad for her miner. The human species, as far as Bambalina could figure, was probably hurt more than helped by that big brain of theirs.

Fletcher couldn't stop his thinking and the more thinking he did, the worse the things he was thinking about got inside his mind. From what Bambalina could tell, the penetrating depths of deep thought seemed to lead a man to more agony and less happiness. She waited. Fletcher gave up. He'd put that thing of his away, and not a moment too soon.

Fletcher took another nip from his flask. He felt like such a loser, such a failure. He was so lonely. He had more turquoise than he even knew what to do with. He was stinking drunk. He'd had his pants open and could not believe he'd embarked on some kind of failed experiment in self-pleasure. This was the bottom of the barrel. Nothing he tried worked. The whole project was appalling, a terrible step down in class from the life he had made.

Bambalina waited.

Fletcher sat up on the bench and buttoned his trousers back up.

The time had come for Bambalina to reveal herself. She stepped out from the side of the horse barn into view.

"Bambalina...?"

His burro approached. She didn't care about anything but Fletcher.

He tugged on the crushed straw western hat, yanked it out of her teeth. "You know I'm going to have to give you a whipping for this?"

No he's not. Bambalina had heard that sorry act so many times, but Fletcher McCrea was all bark no bite, and it was why she remained faithful to this man. The sarcasm and snide commentary was part of something bigger than the both of them. His popping off was why she held her keeper in such high regard. It is one thing they understood about each other. She dropped her head down and placed her cheek against Fletcher's. He wrapped his hand around her head and pressed it tight against his. Her heart was pounding and she exhaled. Her warm breath had a tender caressing feel against his neck. A mutual contentment inside Bambalina and Fletcher arose in the early morning air.

Fletcher patted her cheek. "Sorry I wasn't there; would have enjoyed seeing that red faced excuse for a man lose the fight."

Bambalina nudged her head against Fletcher's, she nodded up and down the least bit, with a truthful tenderness, enough to sign an acknowledgement; she wanted Fletcher to see, that she knew that deep inside he hurt, and that she was the one living thing in this whole world that would stand by her man through thick and thin. . . until the bitter end.

chapter

SEVENTEEN

Dusty was up at the first light of day. Her mother had arrived last night. She'd driven down from the Big Snowy Mountains in Montana, first time ever, to see her daughter. Besides fetching supplies in Lewiston where she lived, Dusty's mom hadn't been out of Fergus County for 'no reason whatever' since the years before her husband had passed. Dusty and her mother had got up, put robes on, and gone to the upper soaking pools. Dusty's mom, her first name Ruth, was a little bitty thing. Scraggy, tawny sun damaged skin, white haired, square jawed. She was a 'no nonsense' kind of woman. She knew her mind and wasn't bashful in the least about giving anyone within earshot a piece of it.

"Drove two days to get here," Ruth said.

"We're going to have fun," Dusty promised.

"I don't need fun." Dusty's mom bellyached, "I need you and time. I want to be with my baby girl."

It was like that between Dusty and her mom. They soaked and bantered back and forth. Dusty's Montana friends from her youth, most of them had scattered, some remained, labor was hard, lot of hay crop work, livestock management, and a long winter.

The air was tinged with a sulphuric odor, then hint of sage and musk of dirt. The creak of the cabin door opening startled the browsing sparrows. The flock scattered; was nothing but tail feathers ducking for cover. There was the dripping of water, over-flowing the rim of the soaking tub, draining back into the sluice channel, and then flowing down toward the hot house. Dusty heard the sound of the door. She wasn't in on last night's mischief.

Jolene sat on the edge of the porch. She was wearing a t-shirt knotted up at her waist and a red and yellow batik sarong tied to her hips. She sat with her bare feet on the steps. Jace was in his pants barefoot. His rumpled shirt was unbuttoned, the tails not tucked in. He leaned against a post that held up the porch roof. Jolene turned and looked Jace up and down. She grinned. He met her blue eyes, held them and wouldn't let her go. They had a streak of luck sparkle; and after last night's affair too little sleep in them. They both looked out over the sprawling miles and miles of high desert fading into a distant horizon marked by where a blue sky merged with a sagebrush soaked landscape.

Jace spotted a lizard basking on a rock in the sunlight. He stepped down off the porch. He improvised his steps on a makeshift trail in the brush stalking his prey. Jolene followed.

"We used to catch them across the street from my house in a field," Jace said.

Jolene coiled her arm around Jace's arm. "You caught collared lizards?"

The foot long reptile ticked its head one way, then back. It flicked its tongue out.

Jace turned toward Jolene and put his free arm around her. He closed his eyes and clinched her tight. When he relaxed his squeeze, he opened his eyes and gazed up toward the peak of the Pipe Dream Mountain.

Jolene had turned and rested her cheek against Jace's heart. He had the smell of sweat from their lovemaking on his chest. She opened her eyes. The lizard hopped off the rock. The animal scurried away into the brush.

Jolene lifted her head from Jace's shoulder and pointed. The swift lizard lifted off its front legs and dashed away on its back feet vanishing into the sage.

Jace rubbed his hand against Jolene's fanny.

Jolene looked Jace square in the eye. "Well, it's either we have more of that or we go over to the café."

Jace's roving hand slid off. He raised it up and with the back of his knuckle scratched the cheek on her face. "Coffee....maybe something to eat..."

"I can go get us coffee..."

"No," Jace said. "Mitzi's going to grill you, if you go alone. I'll go too; might as well. They're going to find out; probably know already."

"I don't know if this town's ready." Jolene smiled and shook her head back and forth.

"They're going to be talking," Jace said.

Jolene's face melted to serious, "I thought this was a one night stand." She pushed him away and tried tiptoeing toward the porch as quick as she could before Jace could catch her. She dashed into the cabin, leaped for the bed and rolled over in time to catch Jace landing on top of her.

"That's it; that's all it was," he said.

"I knew it..."

"Why would I want to turn my life upside down?" he said.

"I wouldn't..."

"I've had a good time... I've a great time, but I never had anything like what happened this time." Jace studied Jolene, first one eye, then the other, then both all at once.

Jolene was trying to maintain her game face. "We're compatible; that's what it is." She giggled.

"I guess I better get your number..."

"We already got each other's number," Jolene explained. "Got each other's number; punched each other's buttons. Is there something else we need to know?"

"Are you making fun of me?" Jace asked.

"I'm telling you the truth..." Jolene rolled Jace off her. The silence took hold again. Jolene looked into Jace's eyes, then down to his lips, the day old beard, then his teeth, and back to his eyes.

Jace closed his eyes momentarily, then opened them and gazed into Jolene's eyes. He said, "I wasn't thinking Meadowhawk was the place I'd find a woman that was going to turn my life inside out."

Jolene smiled, "Oh, you know how it is. They sprinkle men and women all over the world... a little here, a little there. It can happen."

"I found you about as close to nowhere as nowhere can be."

Jolene sealed the banter with one more kiss.

Glenna snuck around the other side of the hot springs, careful to keep out of sight.

"I got a table for you two, right here, on the front deck," Mitzi said.

Jace helped Jolene with her chair.

"Two coffees," Jolene averted Mitzi's prying eyes.

"Two coffees," Mitzi knew something was up right off. She looked over toward Jace. He was looking at Jolene. They were both too smug for their own good.

"Okay, two coffees," Mitzi said. "If you got any appetite left..."

Jolene had satisfaction written on her face. "We're hungry; bring us two menus." Mitzi was standing still studying the moment, too careful for her own good. "Well, go on, Mitzi." Jolene waved her hand in the air trying to get Mitzi to go away.

Mitzi looked at Jace and said, "Those hot spring honeymoon suites. Go in one kind," then she looked at Jolene, "and next morning, you come out another. World's not even the same the next day."

Jolene's face became stoic, "Mitzi, coffee, okay? We already know about how new the next day is."

Glenna circled back around to the rear door of the kitchen.

Keefe was waiting for her. "How does it work?" He asked.

Glenna pulled the memory card out of the base of the clock radio. "Here..."

Keefe slipped the card into the reader on his laptop. He opened the files.

Glenna picked up Keefe's reading glasses. She clicked on a thumbnail version of a photograph and enlarged it.

"There they are," Keefe said.

"Hard to describe that as a platonic relationship..."

Glenna clicked and closed the image on the computer screen. "We got what we need."

Mitzi hustled from the kitchen with two coffees. Sal, Keefe and Glenna peeked through the cut out in the kitchen where the hot plates were set. They could just make out Jace Brandt at the table on the front deck.

"Here you are, coffee," Mitzi stalled, she was still sniffing for clues. The old woman looked back and forth, first at Jace and then Jolene. Each took the cup to their lips. They continued looking into one another's eyes.

Mitzi turned and rolled her eyes at Keefe. "So, you both liked the honeymoon suite?"

A puckish twinkle lit Jolene's face. "Did we enjoy ourselves?"

"No..." Jace winked at Jolene.

Glenna and Keefe walked out onto the front deck at the café. The instant Jolene saw the expression on Glenna's face, she slid back in her chair.

"Jace Brandt," Glenna said, "it's time we talk to you."

"What's wrong?" Jace said to Jolene.

"Buying the fairgrounds is what's wrong." Glenna said.

"What's that have to do with this morning?"

"Don't do it..." Jolene said.

"You wanted to save the fair too, didn't you?" Glenna said. "We got it. We got him."

Jolene put her hand to her mouth. Tears filled her eyes. She ran down the steps off toward the upper hot spring pools to the women's locker room.

Mitzi didn't know anything about the pictures. "I'll go, Jolene will talk to me." Mitzi hobbled off on her old knees.

Jace stood up from his chair, "What's the matter with you people?"

Glenna wasn't backing down. "We set you up, Jace Brandt. We have pictures of the whole thing."

Keefe said, "I'm afraid so."

"Jolene was in on this?" Jace asked.

"Only one that didn't know was you," Keefe said.

"You give us the fairgrounds and we'll give you the pictures. Keep your little tryst a private affair," Glenna said; "your wife will never need to know."

"My wife?" Jace raised his hand. He pointed to his finger the one he had his wedding band on. "My wife would have given me her blessings."

"One way or another, you're not going to ruin our town," Glenna said.

"I've made my plans." Jace rushed down the steps. "That deal's done." For a moment he thought to run to the upper pools for Jolene. Instead he turned and walked as fast as he could to the lower parking lot.

"You go see what you can do for Jolene," Keefe ran off toward the lower parking lot.

"Hold up a minute, Jace..."

"I've got nothing to say to your kind..."

"Jolene, Jace Brandt, you got feelings for that woman?" Keefe said. "You had a time of it last night. I mean you both really had a hot time."

Jace was aghast. He put his hand on his forehead. He swung sharply. Keefe stepped back. "What happened last night, what I found, turns out I ended up getting carried away with a woman who got me into bed, so she could set me up. I thought maybe something else happened. Won't be the first and won't be the last time a man is made a fool. I was wrong."

"And if something did happen, you wouldn't want to ruin best part of what Meadowhawk is; you'd be wanting to figure how to make this a better place for you and that thing you found."

"We bought the land... we're tearing the fairground down... we're putting in the store."

"We're not going to let you do that."

Jace opened the door to his Mercedes. "You don't have that choice."

"What if we've got a better plan?" Keefe asked.

"Town's had a hundred years to work on a plan..."

"Then your wife is going to have a rude awakening." Keefe said.

"Well, you'll have to wake the dead. My wife was killed in an accident last year."

Keefe reeled back. "I'm sorry, we didn't know."

"She always hoped; said it many times to me, if one of us went before the other, that we shouldn't spend the rest of our life alone. That's the character of the woman I was married to."

Keefe regarded Jace's eyes. "Your wife, she'd have wanted us to turn those buildings at the fairgrounds into a processing facility."

"I own the fairgrounds now and those buildings are going down."

"We'll pay you. There's plenty of money. Nobody needs to lose here."

"I made a mistake last night. Same stupid mistake any man will make when he stops using his mind. I thought I had found a woman that I could trust. Wouldn't you know it? I was wrong. I don't plan on making the second biggest mistake of my life so soon."

chapter

EIGHTEEN

Glenna glided down the Hot Spring Highway in her Ford station wagon. It was her bone stock 1969 model with faded light green paint and faux wood siding. The front seat was plush as a living room sofa. Glenna eased off the gas, as her "ain't made like they used to be" wagon sailed over the cattle grate, smooth as butter, didn't even know it was there. Glenna was aiming to parade right through the center of Meadowhawk.

"Brace yourself," she said to Jolene, "time's come to speak truth to power."

Glenna reached across and got hold of Jolene's hand. The women both lengthened their necks and slapped their game faces on.

"Ready or not," Glenna said, "there's no veering off."

"We're not hiding on some side street," Jolene said. "It's time Jace Brandt faced our music."

Glenna said, "We're going to open the secret door of torment, and that man's going to be left wandering in a world of wonder."

Jolene still had hold of Glenna's hand and gave her friend one more squeeze.

Dotty had come out of the General Store. Across the street Jace Brandt and Garrett Harwood were standing in front of the fairgrounds. Jace had his building plans rolled out on top the hood of his Mercedes.

Glenna braked and stopped smack in the middle of Main Street, squeezed right between the fairgrounds and the General Store.

"Dotty," Glenna greeted the town's merchant. She spoke loud and clear.

"Looks like you two are late for work," Gage said, walking out the front door.

Garrett turned. Jace remained face down studying his architectural plans.

"Jolene got a slow start this morning." Glenna said. "I swear I couldn't get her out of bed."

Jace stewed motionless, looking at his plans, listening to their every word.

"Hazel's going to dock your pay," Dotty said.

"Hope whatever it was that was keeping you up all night was worth it," Gage said.

"Fletcher McCrea must have lost his nerve and broke down and given in." Dotty was being sassy.

Jolene said loud as she could without it sounding as if she was shouting, "Only wish it had been Fletcher McCrea. At least you know what that miner's made of."

Glenna chimed in, "They don't make a man anymore. Just make quitters and takers..."

Gage said, "Quitting and taking is for fools and losers, but it sure isn't a man."

"It's near criminal," Glenna said, "I mean to allow a man privileges his character does not deserve."

Garrett set his hands on his hips, listening to Glenna shouting out her window to Dotty and Gage. Garrett twisted his head.

Jace was frozen. He had his hands on the hood of his car pressing against the drawings. Jace squeezed his eyes tight. The muscles in his jaw were flexing, his ears had near heard all he was willing to stand still for before his indignation snapped.

"Well," Gage said, "any old jackass can knock a woman off her feet, but it takes a spine and heart to get up the next day and be true to what you've found."

Jace Brandt turned and set his hands on his hips. He had a scowl on his face.

"That kind doesn't exist, not in this day and age, not anymore," Glenna let off the brakes and the station wagon crawled down the street. The Harwood Award Ribbon Company women were going to work.

Garrett said, "Glenna Goddard might be easy on a man's eye, but it's getting harder to swallow what comes out that mouth of hers."

Jace said, "They know exactly what they're doing."

"Town doesn't appreciate how much risk a businessman has to take," Garrett said.

"It's the nature of the game," Jace said.

"You can never back down," Garrett Harwood blustered, "not ever... Stand your ground."

Jace looked across the street. There was Dotty sweeping the walkway in front of the General Store. He looked down the street in time to see Glenna's Ford station wagon turn off Main Street.

Garrett said, "A businessman's got to square the risk of going into business. A man's got to stare that straight in the eye."

"You buy a new straw Stetson?" Jace asked.

Garrett took his hat off, he regarded its shape. "I like a new hat. My old one was stained with sweat."

Jace looked at the General Store. He turned back to the plans on the hood of his Mercedes, "I don't like to sweat, why I don't wear a hat. And I don't make reckless bets. I've learned the hard way. Tomorrow isn't promised to anyone."

Glenna parked her car around the back entrance to Hazel's. She sat there in the driver's seat. She said, "It happens about once in a lifetime."

"Feels like a flashflood after a hundred year drought," Jolene was daydreaming dead ahead at the misery inside her.

"It's always the one that's never going to work out," Glenna said.

"Best moment of my life slipped right through my fingers."

"You'll get over that man."

"What if I don't? What if I can't? What if he's the one man in this whole world I was meant to be with?"

"There's got to be more than one man, at least two or three."

"It's when you're not looking that it finds you," Jolene said. "Fletcher McCrea, first time I let that man into my bed I knew right then and there, in my heart of hearts, maybe we were friends, neighbors with privileges, but that's all we were ever going to be."

"Been a long time since I let a man into my bedroom," Glenna said.

"You're going to let your life pass you by," Jolene said. "It's never going to happen, if you don't open that door you got locked and let a man back in."

"Jolene... every time I start feeling the itch, I pour myself a glass of whiskey, I put on some country music, listen to some Miss

Patsy Cline; I like being lonely with that woman. I feel like she's singing songs written just to me. When I wake up in the morning, the mood's passed; I find lonely isn't so awful, beats sleeping with a man that doesn't know how to keep what he's found."

Jolene opened her car door. "What about the kind that loses the woman he loves? What's that man to do? How does he ever work his way back to love?"

"Give it time, Jolene. It's like a rock in a boot," Glenna said. "Jace Brandt might still come 'round."

"After what we did?" Jolene got out. "All of us here in Meadowhawk, we all know how to do lonely," she shut the car door, "I'm ready for whatever 'not lonely' is."

Glenna got out of her station wagon. "You can go get lost all by your lonesome seven days a week in Las Vegas." She shoved her door shut. "Lonely is all gridlocked, stuck in a car, dressed to the nines and nobody's noticing, it's a rush hour-happy hour, can't even bring yourself to finish the drink, only place you got to go is to an empty house and a cranky cat to feed."

"I'm scared to death." Jolene said. "I had my hands in the hair of the man I wanted."

Glenna walked around the other side of the car. "One thing a Hazel Harwood Award Ribbon Company employee can do is stubborn. We've made an art out of making up our minds and never changing them."

"Stupid and stubborn is going to be the ruin of our lives." Jolene said.

Glenna hugged Jolene. "There's no fixing stupid and no cure for stubborn. Jolene, that's not who we are." Glenna leaned back, looked Jolene in the eye. "Or maybe, it's just how it feels until change arrives."

Jolene walked toward the Award Company's employee entrance. "I'm done driving down dead end roads, Glenna." As she grabbed hold of the door knob, Jolene turned, "I'm ready to keep my promise. I remember the day that girl I used to be crossed her heart and hoped to die. I am ready to get on with it. I'm going to live my life big, bright and loud. I may fail, but I won't, from this day until ever, I will not quit."

Blake had the diesel idling when Garrett and Jace pulled up in front of his shop.

"Engine's ready," Blake said, then pointed to the front blade, "everything's good to go. Last thing, the hydraulic system's got the wrong oil."

Garrett climbed up onto the bulldozer opened the door to the driver's compartment and settled into the operator's seat. Blake followed him up. Garrett got hold of the electro-hydraulic control stick. He throttled up the diesel. Any direction he wiggled the stick controlling the front blade, nothing happened.

"Pump's toast. I'm bleeding the system, ordered new seals." Blake had to shout over the motors roar.

"Sure it isn't the electronic control?" Garrett could not believe how much trouble this machine was causing.

"I'm going to bleed the thing. Got the right replacement fluids coming in from Ely; take two hours to get her done." Blake was hiding behind his sunglasses.

Garrett looked right through Blake. "I'm getting tired of all your bad news. Time you told me something I want to hear."

Garrett climbed back down off the beast of a machine.

Blake killed the diesel's motor.

Jace walked into the Quonset hut. "I didn't know bulldozers could be so difficult."

"The thing is more trouble than a bad marriage," Garrett said.

"What do you do with this motorcycle?" Jace asked.

"Running it at Bonneville," Blake said.

He walked across the shop to the sand rail, "And this?"

"It's for dirt and sand."

"Your sand buggy and motorcycle, they both start and run better than new, but the bulldozer won't?" Jace asked.

"Yes sir. . ." Blake said, "I'll get her running."

Jace looked Blake up and down for a clue. "Luck of the draw, same as a woman. . . some work, some won't." Jace walked out of the shop. "I want this bulldozer working first thing tomorrow morning."

Garrett smelled trouble. He looked at Blake, "You got that? You get her done. I don't want no more excuses, no more problems. I want that bulldozer knocking down that fairground, and not tomorrow; I want that done yesterday."

There was a blast from the horn of her car. "Fletcher McCrea. . ." It was a woman's voice. Again a blast from the horn shattered the silence. "Are you hiding up there?"

Bambalina walked over to the edge of the arch above her gate on the corral to see who the woman was that was making all that noise. Nailed atop the arch dead center of Bambalina's fiddle proofed gate was her trophy straw Stetson.

Fletcher walked out of his trailer, stood on the deck and looked down the mountain at where his truck was parked. "Glenna Goddard, what did I do wrong now?"

"Putting you to the test. . . right here, right now. . ."

Fletcher was of no mind to be lectured to by Glenna Goddard, "School teacher, and what is it we're studying that I'm supposed to be taking a test for?"

Bambalina looked down at Glenna, then, she looked at Fletcher. Bambalina turned and slow walked toward the water trough. Out of the corner of her eye, she spied a mustang lurking in the trees above the mining claim. The wild horse had been loitering, making a pest of himself the last few days, giving the demure burro the eye. Bambalina was having none of it. She hated how stallions had a way of acting like they were in charge of everything.

Glenna reached into the front seat of her car, pulled a bottle of sparkling wine out and set it on the hood of her station wagon. She looked up the mountain. There was a steep footpath up to where Fletcher's Airstream trailer set perched. She started unbuttoning the sleeves on her shirt. "We're going to find out what kind of man you are this afternoon."

"You just stay down there, Glenna Goddard. You already know what kind of man I am."

She shouted back. "If I'm sleeping with a man, that man's going to have to keep his word, pledge to make his bed with me, and not another soul gets what I'm getting."

Fletcher got a worried expression on his face. "I got six ex-girl-friends who already got my answer. Not sleeping with anyone no more, not if I have to give up everything I am."

Glenna started unbuttoning her blouse, "Maybe, that's what comes popping out of your mouth from up on top of that hill when you are all by yourself, nobody to test whether your word is true or if your mind is made up."

"You just leave that shirt of yours buttoned, get back in that car and drive on out of here," Fletcher advised. "You come up here and anything happens, you got nobody to blame but your own fool self."

Glenna tossed her shirt onto the front seat. "I don't believe you know a thing about fools, or how to be your true self." She unzipped her pants, pulled her boots off, next she removed her pants. Then she put her boots back on, grabbed her bottle of sparkling wine, and looked up to where Fletcher was grandstanding out on his deck. "We're going to have some sparkling wine, and then I'm going to drag you, kicking and screaming into that trailer, and we are going to find out if I like having you being my beau."

"I don't like being a beau, and I don't much care for a woman arriving on my doorstep peeled down to her underwear, ready to go, not willing to give it a fight."

"You want romance?" Glenna said. "Put on some music; light a candle. I'm coming for you, Fletcher McCrea, and you are going to surrender what I've come for."

The mustang had worked his way down along the ridge above the mining claim. He kept peering between the trees, listening for Bambalina. The stallion couldn't make any sense of all the commotion going on between that turquoise miner and the woman that'd come hunting him. Bambalina walked toward her keeper and then she gazed down the mountain as Glenna struggled with the steep trail up from the lower parking lot.

Fletcher dashed inside the trailer. He looked in the mirror. He cracked the bottle of mouthwash open, took a nip and rinsed. He bent forward and spit. He looked dead on at his likeness in the mirror. He said, "This is your life, Fletcher McCrea. No woman's going to tell you what you can and cannot do. It's going to be her-own-sorry fault."

He came back out onto the front deck. He shouted down to the approaching Glenna. "You peeling down into your French lingerie and your slick high-heeled cowgirl boots, I swear on a stack of Gideons, you don't want a fair fight. Trying to ensnare me in my own weaknesses. I know your kind; you'll have nothing and nobody to blame but all those temptations you're trying to weaken my will with."

"If I was you, Fletcher McCrea, I'd start washing my hands and combing my hair." Glenna gestured with her hand, "End of your bachelorhood's not even fifty yards away."

"Glenna we never had two kind words for one another, not once, not ever."

"I wasn't ready and either were you. Time's come, Fletcher McCrea. I'm skinning you like a squirrel and stewing you in a pot."

The higher up the trail she climbed, the more the sweat on her skin shined in the light of day. The cheeks on her face, the top portion of her bust on account of the steep climb up the hill glowed red. Her full hips, Fletcher thought that they were something, they flattered her trim waist line, and the shapes of her long legs vanishing into her cowgirl boots, oh poor Fletcher McCrea, they made for a kind of sexiness a man of his character would regard as near heaven on earth alluring.

Fletcher had had it. "Why can't you have something I can pick on? This would go a lot better for the both of us, if you were more repulsive."

Glenna stopped her hiking up the hill. She put her one hand on her hip and the other clutching the bottle; she had the biggest smile on her lips she'd ever shared with this bachelor man, "You sure do know how to sweet talk a girl."

"I'm not sweet talking you."

Glenna held up her hand, "I did my nails special for this occasion." She pointed to her eyes, "Put on favorite eyeliner... put it on, just on account of I know how you like a woman to look."

She was out of breath, between all the shouting back and forth to one another, and climbing up the hill. She turned around and looked out over the valley.

She had all kinds of plump sculpted woman shapes. She kept wiggling her hips side to side, that bountiful tail of hers swung first one way, then the other. She was near all the way up the hill, when she pulled her man trick stunt. He knew she was doing it on purpose, so as to untether a man's resolve.

"I know what you are looking at," Glenna said with her back still turned.

"I wouldn't have to be looking at it, if you didn't have to keep pointing it at me."

Glenna turned around and faced Fletcher, smiled and raised her bottle of sparkling wine. "You got two good glasses?"

"If I go into my trailer for two glasses, I'm going to lock my door."

"I knew you'd be scared to death, why I brought the bottle, calm you down. Fletcher McCrea, don't you be nervous; I don't want you getting any performance anxiety. You're going to do just fine, once I get my hands on you."

"I'm not scared of you touching me; I'm scared of what you expect of me."

"Fletcher McCrea, you're scared of yourself." Glenna was up the hill and stepped up onto the porch. She set the bottle down on the picnic table. "You are ten miles by pavement, six by dirt road, hiding out up on this turquoise mine, worried sick to death about being asked to be faithful." Glenna approached. She was beaming. She looked right into Fletcher's eyes. She got hold of his shirt with her hands, grabbed him and pulled him toward her. "I don't know if I want to be faithful to you either. Haven't tested that proposition in more than ten years; last time I tried, I wasn't that good at it."

"Well, maybe so, but I know I'm no good at it..."

"Under the right circumstances you might be better at loving someone than you know."

Glenna began to fiddle with Fletcher's buttons. She pulled his shirt off of his shoulders and once clear in one fell swoop she yanked it 'clean' off of him. Glenna reached around and unfastened her bra. She slipped one strap off one shoulder, and then the other. She tossed the lacey French brassiere onto the picnic table.

"It's all your fault," Glenna explained, leaning in and putting her arms around Fletcher, crushing her chest against his. "For the last ten years I've been putting up with you looking at me like you knew what you wanted to do."

"I wish I had never set eyes on that thing of yours," Fletcher was squirming, trying to break Glenna's grip.

"Night you rubbed my bottom in front of the Deputy Sheriff," Glenna was clenching Fletcher tighter, "until then I didn't know nothing about nothing. And I've let my fair share of men, I am ashamed to say, go ahead and have a touch, but that night you got hold of me, I went home, I looked in the mirror, and I had to admit, and don't think it was easy, because nothing about you is easy. But never mind, fact is, your sweet hand rubbing my ass, I'm sorry to say that it agreed with the woman I've kept locked up inside of me."

"I told you," Fletcher said, "it's always the man's fault."

"It's the nature of the beast." Glenna grabbed hold of Fletcher's hand and guided it down to her backside. She just beamed with happiness waiting for Fletcher to give her bottom a try. "There you go, Fletcher, that's my baby. . ."

Fletcher closed his eyes and was getting woozy.

Glenna had seen all she needed. "Why'd I know," Glenna said, walking over to the trailer's screen door, "that I was going to be making love in a vintage aluminum travel trailer? Hope this thing has hot water?"

"Hot and cold running water, shower, bathtub, you name it."

Glenna pushed Fletcher into the trailer. "Give you a bath, get you to shave," Glenna started unbuckling his belt on his denim trousers, "then we'll get that thing of yours out, give it time to get comfortable, don't want to make a man nervous, and when we're both ready, we'll find out what you're good for." She closed the screen door.

The mustang was on the move. The wild horse bolted, tucked its head in, and charged at the corral then hurdled over the top of the rail. The mustang's leap startled Bambalina. She trotted around the corral's perimeter. The mustang charged toward the burro cutting off her circling. She changed directions and moved out the other way. The fleet mustang cut her off a second and third time. Bambalina gave up and froze; she was panting, breathless. The prize was his.

The stallion nickered. He brushed his muzzle against Bambalina's cheek. He nibbled sweet equine nothings into her ears. He flinched, tossing his head back. He thought for sure she was going to bite. Bambalina regarded his forelocks and length of his mane. He was a handsome free and wild mustang. He stood next to her, a genuine force of nature. She approached her intruder and sniffed beneath his chin and near his throat. He had a scent that was the most strangely familiar, never before experienced aroma. In the whole of her life she could not recall ever having her nose tickled by such an overpowering temptation.

The stallion took a deep breath. His chest swelled. There was no mistaking the ambrosial hormonal aroma wafting in the air. Bambalina didn't have a premonition about what on earth all this was about. Her instinct had her on automatic pilot. There wasn't going to be another answer when the stallion put her to the test. This Jenny, when the moment came, could by way of behavior, answer his question with a surrender befitting her own kind.

The shine of the sooty-black-brown coated stallion stood in stark contrast to the gray top coated and white bellied burro. The mustang admired his petite Bambalina's black mane and white snout. She was exotic, entrancing... irresistible. He'd never had a burro before. Their offspring, with a bloodline of both Iberian and Nubian lineages, would be born here on the American frontier a stout, formidable and rare animal. Siring with Bambalina would add glory to the potency, legend and legacy of his prowess. The foal would be their masterpiece.

You could make out a faint groaning, the impatient stallion's hooves tapping against the packed soil. Bambalina pulled her long ears back, nervous, kicking out with her rear foot. Her hoof went flying in the air. The swift stallion dodged the blow. She was distraught; she so wanted the stallion and then didn't. There was little she could do, and resisting was an instinctive part of how her nature expressed itself. And if you had looked away for even a moment, it was in that fleeting bolt of time that there was a tussle, tapping of hooves, powerful lungs exhaling heaps of sweet fresh air and then... what they had done had come to pass and was over.

The stallion's demeanor was drunken; the wild horse staggered. His legs wobbly, the once noble countenance and his regal posture vanished. The weakened wild horse appeared spent. He was drowsy, drunk; he drooped. His head fell. He couldn't keep his eyes focused. He needed time to regain his strength, to rebound from the glory of this pairing's consummation.

It took one quarter of one human hour, what seemed like a blissful equine moment of life for the stallion to regain his stamina. He grew anxious. His desire was to be alone. He paced about the corral, tested the fence rail with his nose. He leaned against it measuring its strength. And like that, the great horse charged-leaped-cleared the hurdle and vanished into the vast unfenced beyond of the Great Basin.

It was all so much a mirage, a phantom, a dream. Bambalina kept listening for signs. She sipped water. She chewed some hay.

The screen door to the trailer was kicked open. Glenna, all rosy cheeked, stepped out onto the deck. She was snapping Fletcher's pearl buttoned western shirt over her naked body. She was barefoot. She had a glass of water in her hand. She took a drink from the glass, brushed her long brown streaked with gray hair back away from her face. Glenna gazed off into the unbound wild lands south toward Meadowhawk, then beyond. She was lost, untangling her feelings from her former conceptions, setting down some old baggage she'd been carrying all these years, holding what was packed in those bags against Fletcher, and now letting them go. Contentment rolled right through the center of Glenna. She could make out the glimmer of recognition in Fletcher's eyes... the sight of friendship. A happy bed with a man that was a trusted companion... Well she was getting a little ahead of things; time would test and character would tell. But, for a first time, seemed like to her there was the chance of their making a long time of the feelings they'd found.

"Hope you're not the jealous type," Glenna teased Bambalina. "We're going to have to learn to share."

Bambalina didn't understand a word that woman was saying. She was feeling herself again. *Hell, share that turquoise miner?* As far as that burro was concerned, she could have him.

chapter

NINETEEN

Pickup truckloads of pine cones were hauled off Pipe Dream Mountain. The harvest was destined for Bero and Mirari's. The sheep ranch barn had been transformed into a makeshift seed processing facility. After cleaning and packaging, the seeds were stored in refrigerated truck trailers ready to be hauled to market. Long-haul drivers out of Reno would transport the crop to a fine foods distributor in California. Meadowhawk's fledgling cooperative was in its birth-throes.

The Harwood Award Ribbon Company women had come to Bero and Mirari's to help with the harvest. Heartbroken Jolene was there, as was lonely Faith, dejected Bunny, a miserable Sissy, long-since-given-up-hope Sharlene, and the woman that had no more appetite for any kind of man, Tallula. Their boss, Hazel Harwood, had come too.

Half the crew worked the seed cleaning equipment, while the rest of the women operated the seed bagging machine. Each vacuum sealed bag contained one pound of clean processed pinion pine nuts; each box had 25 bags of seed destined for market. At least, they believed, they were making good use of their misery. Nothing about this was easy, but they were iron-willed and would not allow themselves to weep over their losses.

Hazel had stepped outside the barn. She put her hand up to shield her eyes from the late afternoon sun. "If it isn't the glory and the wonder herself..."

Glenna pulled into the ranch followed by a cloud of dust. She turned off the motor and sat frozen in her station wagon. She was late. Glenna's habit of going missing was catching up with her. She looked in her rear view mirror. She was trying to find the spine to tell everyone what had come of her trip up to Fletcher McCrea's turquoise mine.

Hazel and her crew, the whole lot of the Harwood Award Ribbon Company women, came out in front of the barn. Her girl-friends all at the same time had set their hands on their haunches.

Glenna wiped her extra lipstick off. She took a Q-tip and tried removing her eyeliner. She got out of her car. "I'm sorry," Glenna said, "I'm late."

Sharlene looked at the watch on her wrist, "Glenna's time is get-ting docked, all I know."

Tallula added, "We are a cooperative now and fair and square is how this works,"

Glenna approached in full blush.

"Glenna Goddard, where have you been?" Hazel asked.

Glenna was trying to get up her nerve. "Had an incident up on Pipe Dream Mountain at the turquoise mine."

"You didn't go up there with your shotgun?" Sissy asked.

"I went up there in my underwear."

"Any of us could have tried that, if that's what 'trying' looks like," Hazel said.

"I went up there and put Fletcher McCrea to the test."

"I thought, if there was going to be any testing, it was going to be one of us," Sharlene said.

Jolene approached. She had a sober expression on her face. She raised her hand and placed it on Glenna's cheek. She brushed Glenna's hair back. She could see nibble marks beneath her hair on her neck. Jolene turned and looked at her workmates.

Jolene said. "Raise your hands, if you were of a mind any time in the last six years to even think you'd be happy stuck in a relationship with Fletcher McCrea..."

Sissy raised her hand, "I might have tried..."

"Come on, Sissy, a steady diet of Fletcher McCrea would be a full time misery."

"What are you trying to tell us?" Faith asked.

"We are losing the fight to save our town," Jolene explained. "Going home after work, playing solitaire by our lonesome selves, that isn't a life."

"You speak for yourself," Bunny said. "You're just heartsick on account of you getting Jace Brandt in bed and not having the sense to keep your feelings from taking you over."

"I drove up Pipe Dream Mountain today," Glenna said, "took the road up to Fletcher's mine, and turns out I have a lot more feelings for that man than I knew."

Hazel burst out, "For the love of tequila and sagebrush, we've all lost our slaphappy brains."

Hazel walked toward her car; she turned and shouted, "Let's get to work here. I'm sick and tired of men ruining our lives. Every time I look up, I got a man looking down my blouse, trying to get his hands on my phone number."

"Where are you going, Hazel Harwood?" Sharlene shouted out.

"Got enough crew here; I need to go find my peace of mind and solitude."

Glenna ran across the lot toward Hazel. "I'm the one who's in trouble."

Hazel turned and looked her best friend in the eye, "My life is passing me by. I see it in Jolene; I see it inside you... And I want what both of you have."

"Me and Jolene...? We don't have anything you don't have."

"You have your feelings. Most times, how I feel doesn't mean much anymore; then every once in a while, once or twice in my life, I had what I see glowing in your eyes."

"We're getting too old for this," Glenna said.

"Lucky me... I'm just plain dead in the water. Haven't had a feeling pass through this chest of mine, and I'm scared; I'm not sure it will ever happen to me again."

"You can't love what you won't let yourself know," Glenna said.

Hazel put her Jeep into first gear. She had all the mercy in the world, for everyone else. "I'll try and remember that. Let the girls see that spark that I see; they'll understand... they're forgiving women. See, they know that there is a difference between that sparkle in your life and fool's gold."

Fletcher McCrea looked out over the vast Great Basin Desert. His mind was spinning. He was in the tightest corner he'd ever bumbled into. After Glenna left him, he set off on foot. Together with Bambalina, they walked off the mountain. He needed his time to gather his thoughts and come to grips with the Gordian knot he'd let come untied. He figured what he needed was a good long soak.

Fletcher spoke in earnest to his Bambalina, "Might be, we set out on foot and never come back. We'll just vanish into the desert."

The sound of those words rang a pang of new frets in his mind. Bambalina didn't understand a thing, but was sure he was anxious and figured Glenna Goddard had rattled her keeper's nerves.

Dusty met up with Fletcher at the front desk. "You hike down from your mine with Bambalina?" She checked outside. All she saw was the burro. "I've never seen you walk down from your claim before... something wrong with your truck?"

"There was a cave in," Fletcher said. "The whole thing's over... going to the upper pool for a soak, then, I don't know what I'm going to do." Fletcher looked out the door. "Where's Keefe?"

Dusty was examining Fletcher's face. "He's down at the greenhouse..." Dusty shook her head, "Must have been some kind of cave in you had up there. Did you know Keefe's bent on saving half of Meadowhawk from coronary artery disease?"

"I don't know one happy vegetarian," Fletcher replied.

Outside, Dusty's mother, Ruth, had untied Bambalina and was leading her to shade.

Fletcher came to the door, "Where you going with my burro?"

"Going to give her some water," Ruth was a nurturing mother type; she was also a scold. "You ought to know better than leave this creature suffering in this sun."

"I wasn't aware the sun was too hot today," Fletcher said.

"You have to take care of your livestock...show them respect," Ruth said.

Bambalina found that she was inclined to the old woman, preferred her tone of voice and thought she had a fine touch when she scratched her cheek. Ruth's demeanor had seasoning. The old woman knew how a burro liked to be doted on.

"Well, side of Dusty's cabin's fine. But she's not supposed to come down off Pipe Dream Mountain. Deputy Sheriff spots her and I don't know what he might do."

"You let me handle that man with a badge on his chest." Ruth was easily angered. "I'll kick that flatfoot right where the sun-don't-shine and the next day won't be the same."

"I'm just telling you," Fletcher explained. "I don't think the Deputy Sheriff is going to be in much of a mood to settle things, if you haul off and put your boot into his private parts."

Ruth got her arm around Bambalina's neck, "She's a fine animal. Ought to be free as the wind and treated fair as any kind of living being blessed with a life on this good earth."

Fletcher went to soak his sorry bones and turn his thoughts and feelings over, while his precious Bambalina and Ruth made brand new friends with one another.

Hazel rolled out to the Hot Spring Highway and turned toward Meadowhawk. She had a Bimini top stretched over her flat fender Jeep's roll bars.

Hazel drank in the sprawl of sagebrush. High up on the sides of the peaks, there were avalanche shoots. Alluvial fans of rock and rubble had poured down the creases; slow marching through geologic time, the mountain was fated to become valley floor. It is what comes of rock that is met by the force of gravity and water against epoch and era. This was to Hazel's eye the timeless place her heart called home.

Whenever she drove her Jeep, she would wear a ball cap. It cut out the snarls and tangles she'd get, if she let her hair go whipping in the slipstream, when she'd hotfooted it southbound down the Hot Spring Highway. She slowed up as she approached the turnoff that headed up Pipe Dream Mountain. Temptation stopped her dead in her tracks. It had been too long since she'd gone up to the high country. She turned around and checked her back seat. She carried two gallons of water. She was safe to travel off-road. Hazel hung a turn and rolled onto the dirt.

She got out, locked her hubs and hopped back into the driver's seat. She was ready to go wherever the Jeep would take her. She engaged the shifter to the transfer case, set it to 'high range.' Hazel reckoned to head up to where the air was sweet and, when she got there, if she was so inclined, she thought she might pick for a while… if she wanted.

Keefe was opening the ball valves that controlled the hot water that ran underneath the greenhouse. Nights were getting cooler. Keeping the soil warm would help with the autumn crop.

Fletcher soaked a spell. He'd given up any hope of finding Keefe. He was desperate for his best friend's wise counsel. Fletcher's nervous system was shot. He stretched out on a chaise lounge and fell into a fitful late afternoon nap. When he woke, he was in a world of worry. He had the jitters. Glenna had outwitted him, stealing his prized bachelorhood that he had vowed to go to his grave with. Fletcher was a broken man. It was like he had a fever. He was convinced that the sense of satisfaction and happiness he was feeling was a mirage he would not recover from. During his nap he had a nightmare; he'd dreamed he had grown tame and he had a ring in his nose and was being lead around on a rope by an old woman. The woman looked mean. She looked an awful lot like Ruth.

He asked Dusty, "Have you seen your mother and Bambalina?"

"I'm not my mother's keeper, Fletcher McCrea. She is where she is, and goes where she goes. She has always been that kind."

Keefe came hustling from down below where the greenhouse was set. He'd spotted Hazel's Jeep headed up the mountain.

"Where are you running off to?" Fletcher asked. "We got to talk. All hell has 'broke' loose."

"Not now," Keefe said. "I got a date with my future wife up on the mountain." He ran out to the parking lot and hopped in his Ford pickup truck. Keefe drove off on a tear. He was going to eat Hazel's dust all the way up the mountain.

Fletcher was standing there left to wonder where in the world his Bambalina had gone. He was sick to death sure that he was going to grind his teeth when he climbed into bed tonight.

Hazel four-wheeled off the valley floor to the high country. The top of the mountain, well above her and above the tree line, was veiled by late afternoon clouds. She passed the fork that headed for Fletcher McCrea's turquoise mine. Hazel kept wheeling higher. She began seeing more and more pinion and juniper trees. Two miles beyond Fletcher's fork, she pulled into a clearing.

She hiked along the hillside. The pinions closest to the road had already been harvested. She explored further along the trail.

Keefe kept his eyes peeled for any signs of tire tracks heading off either side of the forest service road. He came around one hairpin, then another, and there Hazel's Jeep was parked on the side of the road.

Keefe set his brake and put a rock behind his rear tire. She could have hiked off in any direction. Keefe tried reading the footprints in the dust. There were tracks made by shoes from other pickers. He couldn't make any sense of which direction Hazel might have lit out on.

This was one of those afternoons' best not to be caught up on the peak. A late in the day lightning storm, when all hell broke loose, could rattle the silver fillings right out of a hiker's mouth. Keefe thought of calling out, but by his reckoning, Hazel, if she heard his voice, most likely would hide.

Keefe turned and walked back to where their vehicles were parked. Thunder could be heard in the distance. He put his straw Stetson on to keep his head dry. He tried the other direction. Five minutes in along the trail, he saw signs of fresh tracks.

Keefe squatted and looked extra close. "That's her boot," Keefe said out loud, talking to himself up on the mountain. He looked off along the trail he'd been following. "Those are Hazel Harwood's boots."

Keefe stood. This was no time to ponder. It was time to go hunt her down, tracking the best thing to ever happen to him in his life. There was another flash, then thunder. In the distance, a veil of falling rain, ten miles off, a nasty squall streaked that piece of Great Basin sky.

Hazel had come upon an unpicked grove of pinion trees. Co-op workers had left their ladders, picking poles, and baskets. Tomorrow, the crew would start back up, right where they'd left off. Hazel spread out a tarp underneath a tree. She put her deerskin gloves on. She stood the ladder and figured she'd climb up and use the picking pole to shake out the cones on the tip of the tree. From there she could work her way down.

Keefe spotted her. He hid behind a tree. "Okay, Keefe Kenny," he whispered. There was another flash, more thunder. "If you are any good at anything, now is the time to be the best you ever were."

He had a lump in his throat, and the instant he got within clear sight of Hazel, a lump just the other side of the buttons on his denims began forming. Hackles ran down the back of his neck. Sneaking a look at Hazel stretched out reaching up over her head with the picking pole, the way her shirt rode up, and her belly showed, sent his blood sizzling all through his body. He'd been going to sleep since the accident, every night, and he'd imagine Hazel in bed with him, husband and wife doing and allowing from every angle and position, a kind of sex party that was near unspeakable to even talk about to friend or priest. And every night since he'd been blown up, he was down on his knees whispering a husband's prayers to his beloved Hazel, pleading against hope she'd see how much he'd changed and how true his feelings for her were.

Storm on top the mountain was getting stronger. Wind was whistling through the needles. Pinions were singing. First song of winter was in those gusts. Hazel kept reaching up with her picking pole and scraping the pine cones off the branches, and her belly beckoned Keefe and filled him with a wildfire.

Keefe approached. The cones were accumulating on the tarp. She had no idea she was being hunted. He got underneath the ladder and grabbed hold to steady it. "Hazel Harwood, I come to plead my case for you..."

Startled, Hazel looked down. She scanned the surroundings for other intruders. "I swear to high heaven you are nothing but a jinx. I can't get rid of you. Go on now, get, I got no use for your kind."

"I am the father of your children and a changed man. I can't eat, can't sleep, can't go a day, not an hour that I'm not thinking about how good every moment of my life was, being in love with you."

"Well, if that is what you want to do, I don't give one hoot. You go ahead and keep digging that hole, but I'm done. I'm painting a better picture. I'm making my life new. And the life I'm making doesn't include you..."

Hazel gave Keefe one of her time-tested 'I hate your guts' looks. She squinted her eyes, shook her head back and forth. She could not, for the life of her, understand why he wouldn't take 'no' for an answer. She reached up with her picking pole, tried to keep on working.

There was a crack of lightning. It was right above where Keefe and Hazel stood quarreling. The bolt sped across the sky. There were twenty-some tracks, shooting one way and the other, when one piece, of one bolt, found the end of Hazel's picking pole. The blast knocked her clean off the ladder. Last thing Keefe saw was Hazel's behind falling right at him.

The pinion tree caught fire. Hazel was out cold. It probably saved her life, when her fall was broken by landing on top of Keefe. He pushed her body off his. He rolled her over. He put his ear against her chest. She was breathing. Her eyes were fluttering. She had a knot where she'd cracked her forehead when she hit the ground.

"Hazel Harwood," Keefe said, "you can't die on this mountain. I got the rest of my life bet on being in love and married to you..."

The top of the tree was aflame. He got one arm under her torso and the second under her knees. He was trying to lift Hazel up, but she wasn't a petite thing. He gave up on moving her; she was nothing but dead weight. He got hold of her ankles and tried dragging her away from the burning tree. And that's when the widow maker fell and conked Keefe Kenny right on his noggin.

Keefe collapsed on top of Hazel. The end of the branch was smoldering. Flames had caught on the other end and were inching up toward where the two of them had fallen.

Hazel started groaning. When she opened her eyes, first thing she saw was the top of the smoldering tree. Keefe was dead out. His head resting on top her chest. The branch that fell set right across his back. Hazel Harwood pushed the branch off.

She rolled Keefe off her. She put her ear down to his chest. He had a heartbeat. She checked his breathing. He was alive still.

Hazel was kneeling alongside this strange comatose body. She felt her forehead. She wasn't sure where she was. She opened his eyelids. There was 'nobody' home.

"Who in the name of mankind are you?" Hazel shook her head in disbelief.

She stood up and walked ten paces, turned, and looked at the man. She approached and studied his likeness. "I have never in my life…" Hazel shouted, "Help… somebody…" She turned her head side to side listening… hoping against hope… there had to be someone that would come to this man's aid.

She kneeled down. She still didn't know what happened, who he was, what they were doing here. She straightened his legs, got her man-victim stretched out, made sure his neck and head were set in an unobstructed angle so he could breath.

Hazel stroked his dark brown hair, "Looks like we both took a good one," she said.

His hair and eyebrows were to her liking. She touched his unshaven face and found his day old beard handsome. He had an Adam's apple as manly as any she'd ever admired. She unfastened one more button on his shirt, and Hazel said, "If he doesn't have fine gray hair on his chest…" He was just about the right age for a woman of her vintage. He was strange, recognizable, but still, she wasn't sure who she had. She checked his wrists, his forearms, biceps and shoulders. He was hardy, strong, and unaccountably familiar. The man was appealing, a real specimen.

The fuel that consumed the tree had gone all up and the flames were near out.

Hazel leaned in and got as close to his face as she could and examined his lips, his nose's sharp straight ridge, the high cheek bones, lean neck; he was fascinating, rare, odd and common, yet different and somehow some kind of inexplicable perfect fit for something. She just couldn't quite put her finger on what it was about this man. She rubbed his chest. "Thank god," she muttered. He was still breathing.

"I wonder what your name is," Hazel said, doting over her new prize.

She ran her hand down his belly. She decided that the best thing was to unbutton his shirt another notch. The right thing to do was continue checking him for further signs of injury. If she found pleasure in her work, there 'wasn't nobody' there but her and her maker to judge the sincerity of her efforts.

Hazel found the whole affair to be unexpected; it had altered how she was feeling. She kept looking at this face before her, and something set so right in her mind about this unconscious man, that it was hard to reckon how much she felt just being in this face's presence.

Hazel felt across his belt buckle. She reached further south. And her hands discovered that unlike the rest of the man, this southern part was all inflamed and raging, in full glory. She tried touching this other part of who he was again. He was at the peak of his power. The thing just yonder of his trousers' buttons even pulsed some when she set the tips of her fingers over this swelled part and stroked it.

It was a curiosity. Hazel looked around, checking her privacy. "I am duty bound..." she said.

There arrived in Hazel's thinking, right or wrong, a suggestion that comported with the most private part of her rascal nature. Hazel felt she needed to know what she needed to know. She unfastened the buckle on his denims, undid the buttons down the front of his trousers and slid her hand beneath the man's briefs. Hazel took hold of this gift of nature. The man began to groan; he was coming to. And if he was coming back and her hold on him was what revived him, then so be it. Hazel would just have to do mercy's good work, and take no shame in whatever it is she found herself compelled to do.

She let go and plunged into the task, unbuttoning his pants in all due haste. He seemed to fall out again. Hazel got hold of the man and he groaned. She had determined in her own mind that, if he came to and she had revived him, her means might appear at odds with what is right, but indeed the results, she would argue, demanded she do what she deemed best under exigency's circumstance. After all, this was a matter of life and death.

She got a firm grip on this sweet thing's best part, and he groaned, not as if he was in pain, but like he was whispering something, he was calling out.

"What is it?" Hazel said placing her ear next to his lips. "Who are you? What do you want?"

All Hazel knew was that the more she ran the tips of her fingers up and down this fine looking piece of humankind, the more life stirred. She lay down alongside him, stretched out with this mystery, head to toe, and continued to thrill and be enticed by anything and everything; she tried in her sincere efforts to bring him back from death's door.

She was pulled by the immutable duty of sacrifice and service into helping him more and more… whatever she could do, whatever it took… and she knew deep inside, right from wrong, that he might be married, might have a woman in his life, but if his light went out and his life ended, and if she had not done everything in her power to save him, what wife or lover would blame her for not doing everything that circumstance demanded? Anything she might try from this moment forward was born of necessity. She'd try whatever, doing what she must, under these uncertain conditions, high on this mountain, in this wilderness. She would not let herself feel ashamed. She was coming to his rescue. Even if it was in service of her self-pleasure, the goal of his resuscitation was in the end the only thing that mattered. At a moment of this kind there were no more physical boundaries, no more time for moral distinctions.

Simply put, there was life and there was death. She was ordered by the higher powers to be obedient to what fate demanded of her.

Hazel unsnapped the pearl buttons on her western shirt and crushed her chest against this man. She rolled him on his side and it was, near as she could tell impossible to believe, right then that his open mouth hovered over the tips of her breasts and he clamped hold and there was an insatiable, intimate groaning and she begged for guidance as the last straw of her will crumpled on the tender touching of his lips upon her.

"Oh, dear god, forgive me, if he is a married man..."

The beams of sunlight fell through a hole in the clouds. The mottled light and shadows danced across the ground, first shadow, then, spots of light in the surrounding forest. Hazel pulled his boots off, first one foot, then the other. She was convinced the right thing to do was to make him as comfortable as was humanly possible.

Hazel's instincts were in full glory. She could only do what she had to do. She threw her shirt off. She unfastened her pants and kicked them off. Her bra already unfastened she tossed on top the pile. She got down on her knees next to this man and she examined him head to toe. The whole time she had hold of his singularly defining part, this most handsome piece of man she had ever in her life set eyes on. The magnificence and glorious erectness was a natural wonder to covet; it was a true wonder of wonders, the utter pinnacle of a man that could be used to tickle glory's most tender spot deep inside her. That seemed here and now, as odd as fate's circumstance seemed, the method and means for Hazel Harwood to perform God's good work.

Hazel straddled this man whose life she was desperate to revive, and she felt the most earnest, most sacred action she could take was to show generosity and mercy and do whatever was required of her to bring this man back from the brink. "Eternity can wait..." Hazel said.

She leaned down and put her lips on his ears and with her one hand on his swollen golden spur and other hand tickling her own fully bloomed wayfarer's highway, Hazel's body convulsed to the challenge and plunged his almighty part to the sacrosanct task.

"There is too much of life in you for the heavens not to part and this miracle healing not to work..."

There came to this moment high on the mountain an intimate silence in the pinion pines, the woman renouncing the last fragments of any sense of shame, plunging into the task at hand until there were no hands at all, and there weren't only his sweet muffled murmurs emanating from his throat, but there was Hazel's melody matching his. She surrendered herself to the task of his salvation, knowing in the eyes of creation that her soul would be forgiven for any physical liberties, resolved as she was by the depths of her glory, in her heart of hearts there was a righteousness to a woman's dominion over this gateway for life not yet born or a life to be saved.

Keefe was groggy. He didn't know where he was. He had this notion it was Monday night, that he'd had one too many; he was on his sofa, the kids were asleep. He and his wife were fooling around as they often did back in those days. It was almost like that. When he opened his eyes, as he was returning from death's door, the newborn sight in pasture's paradise dangling before him was heaven's bosom. There was a blinding opalescence, a shining, sweating... each orb more celestial, bound by the force of attraction, the whole of the universe was hovering in his mortal orbit, both golden as grain, each possessed with an intrinsic, delectable corpulence.

"My beloved, my wife, the wonder," Keefe whispered.

Hazel's eyes were closed. It had been too long. She was working with such abandon on the best thing to happen in her life, that the sound of this man's voice, a sound she knew by heart, did not snatch her from the precipice she had promised to leap from. She was at the threshold of a purpose, the wonder and the presence was near.

Hazel took hold with her hand and made in this moment a physical offering. Keefe latched his lips upon her breasts' tender tips. Reminded of the willfulness of his own hands, and that he had the power to place them upon this moment's fortunes, he reached for his paragon's posterior. When first caressing one, then her other, synchronizing this squeezing, a rhythmic touch-squeeze-release, and then a sharp sweet tender slap, first one side then the other, in then out, faster and faster, finally Hazel Harwood let out a scream the likes of which she herself had never in her whole life heard before. Why it had the melody of the sweetest song blended with the beat of a brigade-sized military band. The lightning strike had shattered the gates of her being to a promise she had never dreamed of unlocking. There erupted from deep within her a soul's sense of the infinite.

In sympathy with this apparition, this dream, this confounding inexplicable 'who in the world, what in the world, why in the world is this happening to me' moment, Keefe, still awash in a thousand uncollected pieces of consciousness, followed the path opened before him, racing frantically to meet this fortune with his own sterling exclamation point, and it was then, that there appeared in his mind, a clear and singular purpose, a known point from which a multiple of millions of willing volunteers would be sent off in search for the truth of what kind of man he was. When the moment came and his chance arrived, he yelped like a wounded helpless soul at the joy that comes from finding a way through time back to the center of his most pure inner self, arriving like a fallen leaf upon the garden's path in the midst of a drought-ending welcomed balmy fog-shrouded rain... It was life...

The lightning-struck tree smoldered. Hazel clasped hold of Keefe's wrists and with each pulsing he made, she squeezed hold of him tighter and tighter. The two lovers fell off into a post intimate drowsiness. Together they slipped into a satiated sleep. It was some

kind of retrieval they had shared. The two of them were still con-
joined. Keefe opened his eyes. He smelled smoke from the tree. His
stirring woke his other. Hazel was unsure of where she was. She felt
the stickiness. Sweat had formed between her chest and this man
she was on top of. She was coming to her senses. Keefe was so elated
that the part of his excitement that could rise to the moment was
beginning to swell against all odds.

Hazel's eyes grew wide. She pushed herself up, "Oh, my god…
what are you doing?"

"What are you doing to me?" Keefe said.

"I'm not doing anything to you," Hazel said.

"I'm afraid you're holding me down." Hazel still had a grip of
Keefe's wrists.

"You forced me into it," Hazel deadpanned.

"Never did a thing in your life you didn't want to do."

She tried to squirm out of the fix she found herself in. Keefe
poked her good with his poker, enough so she flinched. Made her
angry; he gave her another good poke. Her eyes glazed over like
she'd just been staggered by a knockout blow.

Keefe's mind was clear as a glass of spring water. The next time
he poked Hazel with his fully realized man poker, she climbed
down her stairs and met the man in the hallway. Her eyes fell closed
and she shook her head back and forth. Hard to grasp what she was
saying 'no' to, as on account of most of the rest of her was saying
'yes.'

Keefe got bold. He rolled her over. "We're getting married…"

Hazel's eyes shot open. The cooperation she'd volunteered
ceased and she froze.

Keefe slowed up, but he kept on his persuading her. "It's going
to be Mr. Keefe Kenny and his wife, Hazel Harwood Kenny."

Hazel glared at Keefe. She got her one hand free and started pushing Keefe away. He leaned against her hand and he kept

providing a conjugal persuasive tender encouragement that he knew she wasn't against, even if she was pushing him away with her one free hand, it was the last gasp before she unbridled what she feared and welcomed what she'd hoped for.

Keefe leaned toward Hazel and he pressed closer toward her until he was a mere breath's wisp from her face. He adored Hazel, her ruddy red cheeks, the riot of curly brown hair, when he looked he saw a child's eyes, the eyes of their children, the eyes they had created, his offering was the color, hers the shape, ghostwritten on the faces of their offspring by their love all those many years ago, and then her hand collapsed and she sped up her part of the two part rhythm and he kissed his ex-wife, and she socked him in the arm, then she got hold of his ear, then she pulled his hair, and finally gave up and gave in, and declared, "you may never break my heart, not now, not until death do us part, not ever..."

chapter

TWENTY

Jolene had settled in for a one woman pity party on the fair-grounds' dance hall steps. She'd been waltzing her way through the better part of a six pack. "...Of all the lousy, no good, rotten luck," she was shaking her head disgusted. Then she'd take another swig from her bottle of beer and shake her head back and forth again. "Why's that man feel so good to my touch?" Then another gulp of the brew and she looked up into the heavens and griped, "What do you want from me? Why can't I have one regular, normal, ordinary man? Is that asking too much?"

All of this beer drinking and heart-aching was the best a woman could do. She couldn't eat and couldn't sleep. Misery of this kind can hijack the mind and send it speeding down dark roads a soul will never find its way back from. That's how life can go from bad to worse.

Jolene had got herself so worked up, so fixated upon the feelings in her heart that she wasn't in her right mind; she was seeing and hearing things. They were all hers, all made up in her head and tearing at her tattered hopes. The fact was that the bellow of a twelve cylinder diesel's rumble in the distance didn't even register. Then the metallic clanging of tractor treads slapping against asphalt went undetected too. This distant rumble was getting closer and closer; the racket it was making might have started off as nothing but was fast becoming impossible to ignore.

Jolene stood up on the steps of the dance hall, drained her bottle of beer dry, entranced and lost in her own thoughts looking at the area of the street between where she stood and the General Store. That's when the bulldozer with Garrett Harwood at the controls rumbled up in front of the fairgrounds on Main Street. Garrett pivoted this beast right in her direction.

"You are a miserable old toad..." Jolene said, near almost slurring her words, "you want to try a woman's hell on for size, Mr. Chamber of Commerce President, come on, menace me with that thing, give me your best shot, 'cause I'm not budging and you sure as hell aren't going to knock this dance hall down, not so long as I have a breath... you will not succeed."

Garrett opened the door to his cockpit. "You get the hell out of my way, Jolene."

She threw her beer bottle as hard as she could. "You sorry excuse for a rooster, you'll have to go through me and answer to your maker, before I'll let you ruin this town."

Lark ran down the street to the Brewery. "Come quick, Garrett Harwood has lost his mind, and it looks like Jolene's drunk and fighting him off with a beer bottle..."

The whole room poured out of the saloon and ran down the street toward the fairgrounds. Sal and Mitzi were last, like always, hobbling as they always would toward the commotion.

Garrett was ten feet high inside the cockpit yelling at the top of his lungs over the racket made by the big Cat diesel motor. Standing between what he had in mind and the fairgrounds was one pissed off woman; she didn't care, didn't have anything to live for and she wasn't budging.

"You get the hell out of my way," Garrett shouted. "All you are is some kind of trinket of a thing for a man to play with. Go on, get, go... Back into the gutter to wherever your kind goes..."

"You shut that thing off. Just walk away." Jolene was not going to stand down. "You walk away right now and I might not carve my name with a pocket knife on your forehead."

That trash talk riled the old man. Garrett engaged the transmission and the machine inched another foot closer to Jolene.

Jolene was ballistic. She had a grit and fire in her eyes that not anyone had reckoned ever seeing before. She ran back to the stoop on the dance hall, grabbed another empty beer bottle, turned and heaved the thing hard as she could. This one crashed into the impact resistant windshield on the bulldozer. "You can rot in a sea of hungry leeches, Garrett Harwood. You are a disgusting excuse for a bloodless creature. They'll toss your ashes in the dump; the world will celebrate your miserable soul's end."

He dared to stick his head out the cockpit door window, "You will give your life for a lost cause," Garrett shouted. "Now get the hell out of my way before I climb down off this machine and drag you by your hair over to the Sheriff's Office."

"This is our place, our town, and this is our fairgrounds." Jolene turned and pleaded with the gathering crowd.

Jace had come quick with the folk from the brew pub. Jolene looked right through the man. She picked up a third empty from the stoop, didn't know who she wanted to throw the bottle at more, Jace Brandt or Garrett Harwood. They both deserved a beaning.

Jolene walked straight up to the big blade of the bulldozer and shouted, "Not going to let anyone, I don't care how much they're worth, ruin what this town has fought its whole life to preserve," she cocked her arm back, but didn't let the bottle fly.

Dotty yelled, "Garrett Harwood, you got thirty eye witnesses here."

Garrett glared at Dotty. Gage stood in front of his wife to protect her from this man's contempt. Garrett noticed a figure trotting toward them. They were riding straight down the middle of the street, right over the top of the center stripe.

Dusty's mother, Ruth, was mounted and approaching quick, coming in from the north. She'd been out meandering through the Great Basin, riding on Bambalina's back. That burro had a nose for trouble and knew that mischief was afoot.

The expression on Garrett's face changed.

Deputy Sheriff was highballing in from the south, emergency lights and siren blaring.

Garrett turned and yelled at Jolene, "I'm telling you, woman, you move out of my way or I will not be responsible for what happens. This fairground is closed, sold and it is coming down."

Ruth wasn't in any mood to have an old gizzard like Garrett bully 'nobody' or nothing. She climbed off the back of Bambalina, all 95 lbs. of spunk and grit packed into riding boots and denim jeans. The woman strode through the crowd shoving everyone and anything out of the way. Bambalina followed behind this dervish of a woman.

"Who is that sorry excuse for what passes as misery?" Ruth wanted to know.

"That's Garrett Harwood. He is Meadowhawk's Chamber President..."

"Chamber President?" She fixed her eye on the man. "Garrett Harwood," she shouted, "you are giving old age, wrinkles and white hair a bad name." Ruth marched right up to the track of the bulldozer. She pointed with her finger. "You get your sorry little ass down here on the ground or I will come up there and kick it so hard they'll find it lost in a field and wonder how it got there."

"I don't think I have to do anything some half-witted gray haired old woman says," Garrett sassed back, "don't believe a little bitty thing like you could force me to do anything I don't want."

Dusty had never in her life ever heard anyone talk back to her mother. And the few times anyone ever tried...

For seventy-five, this old gal from Montana could do near anything she set her mind to and nothing set her mind to a doing like a stubborn, insulting, peapod-brained wacko of the kind Garrett was.

The Deputy Sheriff stepped into the middle. "Ma'am, you let me handle this."

Garrett gunned the diesel and the beast of a machine lunged toward Jolene.

Jace couldn't take it. He broke through the crowd and approached raising his hand toward Garrett, gesturing toward him to hold up.

Jace stoic, serious, got within a foot of Jolene, standing between the blade and her. "What are you doing?" Jace asked.

"I'm saving this town from the likes of a man like you." For emphasis, she threw her bottle into Garrett's windshield. Glass splattered and rained down onto the street.

Jace swung his head away like he'd been slapped in the face. He twisted his head back and looked at Jolene. "Somebody's going to get hurt here."

"Somebody already got hurt," Jolene said. "That pain won't kill me. Giving up on this town could."

"You think I don't hurt too?"

"My life's already over," Jolene said. "All I got left is a town to save. Looks like the lives of the people I love... turns out they are all in my hands now."

"What in the name of Meadowhawk do you want?" Jace Brandt asked.

"Same thing you do. I want what we have."

"I had what I wanted and she's dead and buried."

"Says you, and maybe I'm the second bite of the apple, maybe I'm forever, might be..." Jolene said. "Could be; might be what she wanted for you was for you to have one more chance."

"Don't I get a say?" Jace asked. "Maybe I don't have it in me to take one more chance."

Jolene stuck her finger right into the spot on Jace's chest where set his heart. "I believe you already said everything I need to know. In fact, I know I heard you loud and clear. I am no young thing, those days are in the rear view mirror, but no man, in all my life, ever touched me the way you did, never, not even once, and I know a thing about touch, and when a man touching me rings true." She poked her finger first in his chest and then into her own. Jolene looked dead into Jace's eyes. "So what are you going to do about that, Mr. Jace Brandt?"

Jace stared into Jolene's ultimatum. The assembled crowd leaned in; everyone was waiting. "I don't want to be in the pine nut business. And I don't want to have my heart broken again."

"And I don't like my fairground getting bulldozed down."

"We're both too old to start a family..."

"Might already have one in the oven,"

Jace stared dumbstruck. "And you're drinking beer, throwing yourself at bulldozers, and heaving beer bottles at Garrett Harwood?"

"I'm fighting for a future, and right now I don't have one..." Jolene stuck her finger in Jace's gut, "And what are you going to do about that?"

Jace scrunched his lips tight, and cocked his chin upward and looked down his nose like it was a barrel of a rifle at the off chance he was looking at the mother of his child.

"I don't like 'nothing' about this," Jace complained.

Jolene didn't even flinch. "You haven't even tasted my barbeque yet."

"You want a boy or a girl?" Jace asked.

"I want a family," Jolene shot back, "and I don't want to just be in love with the man who gives me that family, I need to live in a place where we're both part of something bigger than all that. You fancy city types don't get it. I don't live here because I have to. I threw my lot in and live in this old town because I wanted to."

"Get out of my way," Ruth shot an elbow out and it plowed right into the gut of the Deputy so hard, knocked the wind right out of him. She marched, pounded one boot heel into the ground then the other and launched herself up on the bulldozer's track; she got hold of the door handle and yanked it open quick as quick can be and like that she was eye to eye with this sorry excuse for a man.

"I am sick and tired of old men howling like wounded dogs, pointing their fingers at everyone and everything, complaining about how they know so much about life and everyone else knows so little; nothing but a bunch of worn out and weary testosterone with nowhere to go and nothing to do." Ruth raised her hand, and was ready to deliver a blow, "I'll give you the back of my hand, scratch your eyes out, and throw what's left of you into a fire full of Rocky Mountain oysters. You'll be singing soprano, somewhere in the hereafter, you don't shift this thing into neutral and stand down."

Garrett didn't know what to make of this thing yapping at him like she had the deed to his ranch and the certificate to their marriage locked up in a safe deposit box. Ruth slugged him in the arm. And it hurt.

Garrett was infuriated. He tried getting hold of Ruth's wrist with his hand.

Ruth started laughing, playing keep away, teasing her adversary. "I never met a man who could keep up with me." Ruth cackled. She smiled. She looked Garrett dead in the eyes, "You are a handsome old man, look awful good to this woman, but this bulldozer doesn't do a thing for you."

Garrett tried getting hold of Ruth's wrist as she pulled the kill switch. Garrett visibly winced. He got a look of fear in his eye. He let go of her and put his hand across his chest. "Woman, you are giving me chest pains."

"I hope I do." Ruth looked a might compassionate at Garrett. "You are too handsome and too old to be acting so mean and nasty."

Garrett began slouching clutching at his chest.

"You stand up. I want you down on the ground." Ruth demanded. "...Time for change in this world, and best place to watch that change is from a chair on a porch in your front yard."

Garrett kept clutching his chest. "My days are numbered..."

"Then time's come to make the best of the few you got remaining..."

A pair of headlights rattled over the cattle guard. It sped up, the thing screamed toward the crowd. It came in fast and skidded to a halt. All four doors popped open, and out came Glenna Goddard from behind the wheel of her station wagon. Fletcher riding shotgun opened his door, behind him Keefe Kenny and from the other door Hazel Harwood. They all stood at their doors assessing the fix the town was in.

The four of them approached the assembled citizens of Meadowhawk.

Garrett Harwood at the sight of his daughter sprung back to life. "What in the hell are you doing with that man?"

Jolene flung a full bottle and it shattered and beer splattered everywhere.

"Shut up, daddy," Hazel said, "time you started showing more respect for the father of your grandchildren."

"He'll ruin you; wreck this town," Garrett said.

"I'm not going to tell you but just once. I'm my own woman; I got my own life. Time we make peace over that."

Ruth got hold of Garrett's arm, "You be still, old man, a daughter has a right to her own life; they are sovereigns, same as you and same as me..."

Keefe was stitching this mess together in his mind. He got hold of Hazel's hand, Fletcher took Glenna's and they approached. They joined Jace and Jolene in front of the bulldozer's big blade.

"Jolene," Keefe bowed slightly to the woman, "Jace... How is everybody doing tonight?"

"Waiting on how we're all doing right now." Jolene said. "We're waiting on an answer."

Fletcher surveyed the circumstances, and ventured a guess, "Jace, I happened to find something new in the book of bachelor wisdom. I found that there comes a point in life when the best thing a man can do is the thing he promised himself he never would."

"Why is that?" Jace Brandt asked.

Hazel put her arm around Jolene, and she gave her friend a tight squeeze, "Because what the two of you have is better than anything you can ever have on your own."

"But, I don't even like pine nuts," Jace Brandt said.

"You'll come around," Keefe said laughing.

"Deputy," Garrett shouted, "there is a law breaking turquoise miner standing there, and that burro's not supposed to be in town no more."

Bambalina gave Garrett a look. It put a shiver up his spine.

"That's enough of your sassing everybody and everything," Ruth said. "I want you off this bellyaching binge you been on, and down at that brew pub. I aim to have you buy every thirsty soul in this town a beer. Why, by the time I'm done with you, I'm going have you singing sweet little nothings to this cowgirl's ears."

Garrett hesitated. Ruth scowled. Garrett backed down.

"What are you doing?" Ruth asked.

Garrett had started walking toward the Brewery then turned around. He could not get over how abusive this woman was.

"A real man offers a lady his hand when she's walking with a gentleman."

"And why would I do that?" Garrett asked.

"I can give you a licking right here in public, or I can give you the time of your life in private."

"What makes you think I have any interest in a woman your age?"

Ruth looked dead through this man. She looked around the crowd; she reckoned, there wasn't a thing to lose. "When was the last time you were in bed with a real woman? I'm talking about one that can give as good as she gets." Ruth sniffed the air around Garrett, "I don't think you know what 75 and a last hurrah even feels like."

"What the hell is a last hurrah?"

"If you got one in you, I'm going to squeeze that sweet thing out of you. . ." Ruth grabbed hold of Garrett's arm and yanked him out of the crowd toward the Brewery. "Come on, you get; we got no time for any more of your nonsense."

On cue and on instinct, Garrett froze when he came face to face with Bambalina. Ruth looked at the burro, then at Garrett. She reached out with her hand and scratched the burro on her chin. "Look at that. How can you not love a face like that? Sweetest little pack-animal the world's ever known."

"That burro's a danger."

"I'm dangerous too, unless you treat me with good manners, so buy me a beer, crack that heart open, get your wallet out, start talking to people like you have respect for them, and next thing you know, tonight might turn out to be the luckiest seventy-five year old night of your life." Ruth winked at Bambalina and walked toward the Brewery.

Bambalina stepped one hoof, then the other toward Fletcher and Glenna. The burro came to a halt. Looking as she did, first at Fletcher, then Glenna, next Keefe and Hazel, and finally she looked at Jace and Jolene.

Something about Jolene rang a bell. Jolene met Bambalina's eyes with her own, the two shared something, had a common bond between them. Bambalina knew what she knew, and she was sure Jolene and her were fated to carry to term hopes for a future Meadowhawk.

"Come on, everybody," Keefe shouted. "Garrett Harwood's buying."

"What are we celebrating?" Jolene asked.

"We're going to celebrate changing a man's mind," Glenna said.

Fletcher put his arm around Jace and his other around Keefe. Fletcher said, "There's nothing a man can do. One day, there's not a woman you can't have, and the next, there's not a way out of the corner that woman has worked you into."

"And the pine nut business," Keefe said, "don't you lose one night's sleep over your new business venture."

Jace grew stiff and froze.

Keefe looked sincere. "I know pine nut business isn't music to your ears, but it will make the till sing and the town thrive. If things work out way we all reckon, you could be the first human being ever to be dragged kicking and screaming into the best thing ever to happen to a businessman."

Hazel and Glenna had hold of Jolene and they followed.

Hazel said, "He'll come around; I can see it in his eyes. He's as good as yours."

Blake had come down the street unnoticed. He climbed up on top the bulldozer. Lark had heartache and disappointment written across her face.

Glenna let go of her two friends; "I'll catch up..." She approached Lark.

"Nothing's ever going to happen," Lark said.

"Nothing ever happens until all hell breaks loose. It happens in a riot of the moment. Never sure it's done, until it's over."

"Might as well give up and move to Las Vegas..."

Glenna got hold of both of Lark's shoulders, "Don't do that; we got a life right here in Meadowhawk. He'll come around..." She pinched the tip of Lark's chin. "He hasn't got a chance against a woman like you."

Lark searched Glenna's eyes for hope that there was some truth in what she said. She turned, grabbed hold of Glenna's hand and began scuffing her feet walking back toward the Brewery. "Blake's running out of time, Glenna. I don't know how long I can keep playing this waiting game."

chapter

TWENTY-ONE

The daredevil had come to Meadowhawk. The thrill show performer's private motor coach was parked on the fairgrounds. Daredevilry brings sauce to the boil on a life's stove. And when you get a whiff of the scent, and have a taste for the finer cuisine that is associated with the men who chance their lives for the public's pleasure, why it is a kind of bait hard not to get hooked on.

Dusty was still sprawled on top Karl's queen-sized bed reeling from the lithe Bulgarian's private one man show. And after his spectacular feats of intimate daring do, the legend himself got up to check on his precious, his one, his only, his pachyderm… he called her Hattie. She was his goldmine. An elephant ride was a real moneymaker.

Karl had slipped into his off-stage jumpsuit. Dusty reckoned his thin hips and broad shoulders made him near as sexy a man as

she has ever in her life had the pleasure to share a queen-sized motor coach bed with. And the way he slipped his feet into his clogs,
like he was preparing to walk into center ring... Then he opened
the door, and hopped out of the tour bus. The showman never saw
the hole that a ground squirrel had burrowed, and it was right there
that the unforeseen event occurred.

Dusty heard her daredevil's plea. She scrambled to put a bathrobe on, burst out of the trailer; found him crumpled on the ground
clutching his ankle.

"Oh, no..." Dusty ran for help.

The great showman groaned and agonized, "It's broken. I know
it is."

The Harwood Award Ribbon Company women all had rendez-
voused at Sharlene's. They had come over for libations and swap-
ping in and out of each other's dance outfits.

"I heard," Sharlene said, "friend of mine up in Elko, she told
me there were cowboys, who are off the rodeo circuit now that summer's passed, planning on coming in for the dance."

"I know at least four more coming from Tonopah," Bunny said.

"Nothing like a man with nowhere to go and nothing to do for
a winter," Tallula said.

"We're going to need as many cowboys as we can get," Faith
said. "Fresh as the last shower they took... as far as a saddle will
take them... as hungry as a girl's figure can make them..."

The daredevil was seen by the doctor at the clinic. "I want you
to take two pills every four hours."

"I've got a show tonight," Karl said.

"I'm not in your line of business," the doctor was filling out a prescription, "but I am hard pressed to see how you can perform."

The daredevil was in a removable cast, "I've never missed a show in my life, never. It's the code."

"What code's that?" the doctor asked.

"The show must go on..." the daredevil said.

Dusty steadied her new partner with her arm around his waist. Karl was on crutches. They were headed back out to the parking lot.

Lark was shaking her head. "I don't see it. He needs to be in bed."

"Well, go on." The doctor removed his reading glasses. "See you at the dance tonight."

Come dusk between the fairgrounds and the General Store a half dozen self-powered World War II carbon arc searchlights were lined up along Main Street. They were painted fire engine red. The operator, dressed in color coordinated coveralls, cranked the motors up, punched this button and threw the switch that brought the searchlights to life. They scribed to high heaven bright beams into the emergent nighttime sky... "Come one, call all..."

Gig and Gage had put on suits and ties. Elena and Dotty wore long sleeved white blouses and paisley print skirts. The two couples had spent all day baking a three foot tall multi-tiered cake for the evening's festivities.

The short Sal and his bride of 60 years, Mitzi, were proud attendees.

Rory had closed the Brewery and, along with his hired hand, had volunteered to pour lagers and ales at the dance hall. The joy of free beer was its own reward.

With Garrett's retirement there was a new head of the Chamber. And with fresh blood in leadership the Chamber had come to celebrate.

"My name is Tip Top Tom, I come down from Wyoming to play for you tonight, boys are dressed in finest collection of bolo ties you'll see this side of the Utah border." And like that, pedal steel guitar, fiddle player, drummer and the rest of the High Country Haymakers tore into the first song on the evening's set list.

Fletcher opened Glenna's car door. He helped her up from the seat of her station wagon.

"All this time, pretending like you didn't know what to do," Glenna grasped hold of Fletcher's hand.

"I'm counting on you putting a real shine on my personage," Fletcher laughed.

"You know, we don't have to stay together forever," Glenna said.

"There is that." Fletcher replied.

"Chances of us making it are slim to nil," Glenna said.

"I hope you're right..."

"So, what's your problem?"

"I got no problem. That's the problem... I'm happy."

Glenna smiled at Fletcher. "I make you happy?"

"I'm cleaning my trailer, washing my dirty dishes, and worse than that, I want to..." Fletcher shook his head in disbelief.

"I'm going to make you buy me a house and move into town."

Fletcher reached down, pulled the cuff on his pants up, and snatched his flask he carried and took a toot. "Now let's not get carried away..."

Glenna put her arm around Fletcher. Then she grabbed hold of his flask. "Carried away?" She screwed the cap to the flask back on tight. Handed the flask back, "You, definitely; me, maybe a little..."

Glenna started walking toward the dance hall.

Fletcher was standing still. He'd got his eyes on Glenna's behind. "I could live in town and go to church with that."

Glenna turned around. She'd caught where his eyes had been aimed.

He smiled, "I love that thing of yours..."

"Do you?" Glenna walked back and put her arms around Fletcher. "What is that thing of mine you are so in love with?"

Fletcher met Glenna's eyes, held them in his embrace. He was admiring her spunk, "Glenna Goddard..."

"Fletcher McCrea..."

"I think I'm in love with you."

"See that," Glenna smiled, "wasn't so hard now was it?"

"Did you know I'm having a hard time eating? I can't sleep like I used to; all I do is lay in bed at night looking at the ceiling worried you might up and leave me. I'm a mess..."

"You'll get used to it," Glenna laughed, swat him on the butt, "it's good for you."

Keefe and Hazel had been laboring all day in the kitchen at the rear of the dance hall. Out back they'd been slow cooking a whole pig on a spit. Keefe had brought salad makings from the hot spring greenhouse. Bero and Mirari donated some of their finest examples of this season's fresh made sheep cheese.

Keefe was wiping his hands with a towel. "I swear, watching you in a kitchen is a sight to behold."

Hazel had been bent over spearing potatoes in the oven. She turned and gave an indifferent look to Keefe and tried to pass by. He latched hold and spun her around and got her in his arms.

"We've got food to cook," Hazel said.

"We're going to have to learn how to cook food and make love on the same stove and in the same kitchen."

Hazel, with her wild curly head of hair and a complexion that could shine bright red when she was happiest, said, "You are doing your darn best."

Keefe squeezed Hazel tighter. "It's what you do with the days you have left."

"Kids said they're coming out in November for the holidays," Hazel kissed Keefe.

Garrett Harwood walked in on his daughter and son-in-law. "Are you two cooking, or are you two *cooking?*"

"Cooking up plans for your grandkids to come see us here in Meadowhawk," Keefe said.

Garrett Harwood eyes were a glassy rife. He swallowed.

"Town's on the mend," Hazel said. "The family is too."

Garrett turned and tried to get away. Hazel and Keefe stopped him as he got to the kitchen's swinging door.

Garrett wouldn't turn and look at them. "Leave me be." Garrett said. "I'll be alright. I'll get used to you."

Keefe let go of Garrett's shoulder. The old man went through the doors.

Hazel put her arm around Keefe's waist. "He told me he didn't know how to tell you."

"Tell me what?" Keefe said.

"How sorry he is."

"I think second chances are something to believe in. I do I believe this world is made of them."

"Underneath that nasty temper there is buried a good man," Hazel said.

"It's how our family comes wired. We run hot." Keefe smiled then twitched his eyebrows at Hazel and gave her that sly smile.

Hazel got a mean look on her face, "How many bullets you figure you got left in that thing?"

"You know, when you give me that look it's like putting one in the chamber."

"I swear on pile of pine nuts, you are not to be underestimated." Hazel said, "Come on, Mr. Hot Shot, I'm your biggest believer."

Jace came quick through the swinging doors from the dance hall. He had been jittery all week. Meadowhawk's newest citizen had been on the phone with a contractor who was breaking ground on the new home he'd ordered. Then, between all the truck traffic hauling in the pinion pine nut crop and all the special event staff that had been busy getting everything ready for tonight, well, Jace Brandt, on account of his new life, was wearing out.

"You just settle down now," Keefe said. "Everything's going to be fine."

Jace tugged on the cuffs of his white shirt, "I hope so."

The two men peeked out the doors into the main dance hall.

"See look, that's Meadowhawk and a whole county full of friends and neighbors right there..."

Bambalina was sulking. It was Fletcher she was perturbed by. That ornery miner understood how much she loved being around the dance hall. But Bambalina knew the score. Glenna had him eating out of the palm of her hand. His old faithful burro wasn't on his mind, not anymore. Glenna Goddard had thrown the book at her keeper, had her turquoise miner right where she wanted him. Capitulation was a pathetic sight.

Ruth had walked out to the back end of the fairgrounds. She had an apple in her hand. "Come here, you're being too high strung for a lady-burro living on the first rung of the ladder."

'*What is that supposed to mean?*' Bambalina never could get over how confounded the human species was about pecking orders.

Blake walked over from the Quonset hut. First time in his short life he'd polished his boots twice in a row. He'd been talking to himself in the mirror while shaving. He was all butterflies and extra clean fingernails. He was at the end of his rope.

"Young man," Ruth said. "Give me your arm. I'm going to trip over something out here in the dark; help me back out to the front of the fairgrounds."

Blake hesitated.

"Well, come here, I'm not asking you twice..." Ruth had given up on Bambalina. She wanted to play hard to get? That was fine by Ruth. She'd meet that stubborn old burro more than halfway on that score.

That was the last straw. Bambalina ratcheted up a breath, then a second, and she let out a classic heartfelt burro's call of such desperation probably would have broken a wine goblet, if there had been one to put to the test.

"What?" Ruth froze in her tracks. She turned around. She asked Bambalina. "You are nothing but spoiled and rotten, and if you weren't so much like me, I don't believe I'd have the least bit of pity on you." Bambalina's lip began quivering. "Get her lead." Ruth said. "Well, go on, get..." She lifted her boot and kicked Blake on his backside.

Faith and Sharlene were walking out to the front lawn with a couple of cowboy dancers. Faith said, "Look at Miss Lark." She was wearing a sleeveless dress. "And I thought I had the prettiest shoulders in town."

Sharlene said, "Lark's are first place shoulders; they're also twenty years younger..."

Lark blushed and waved them away, "Go on, you two..."

Jolene had come looking for Jace. She found him in the kitchen.

Jace grabbed Jolene by her hand. "Come here..."

He walked her out the kitchen's back door out to his car. He opened the glove box. He handed her a small red velvet jewelry box.

Jolene's blue eyes jumped from the box in Jace's hands and then locked onto his eyes. "First, you steal my right mind and now you are set to put me in a fix I will never find a way out of."

"You are in a fix of your own making." Jace handed her the gift box.

"My daddy told me the man that wanted me was likely going to try and bribe me to stay." Jolene looked at the box then she looked at Jace.

He turned his head and looked off into the Great Basin night. "I am sorry for your father's loss..." Jace had his own grace and strengths...his chin and eyes alert and at ease.... "I will do my best to be as kind and caring."

Jolene pressed her thumb against the spring loaded velvet lid. Inside was lined with deep blue satin and set into a slot was a triangular shaped pendant hewn of precious metal. Attached to the golden charm was a delicate thin gold chain.

"That's you," Jace said pointing to one corner of the triangle, "that's me," he said pointing to the other corner, "and that's whatever life brings..." he said as he touched the tip of his finger to the highest of the three points.

She turned around and held her long blonde hair up. Jace fastened the clasp to the chain. Jolene turned. She put her arms around Jace. "What do you know about love?"

"It shows up one day, on its own, uninvited; can't see it until you stop looking."

Jolene smothered Jace with a long kiss. Then she leaned back. "Would you take me to the dance?"

Garrett Harwood got all tangled up talking to his friends from the Chamber. He'd been swept away on a sea of idle chatter. He'd lost track of where he was or who he was with. It was fifteen minutes before he'd looked around the room for Ruth and realized his petite fireball had gone missing. As hard as it was to pull himself away from talking to his friends, he thought it might be the better part of smart to go looking for her before she came and hunted him down.

Glenna and Fletcher had walked out on the lawn in front of the dance hall. Dusty was standing with her hobbled daredevil. He had removed his temporary cast, and you could see where his ankle had been taped up. He'd swallowed twice as many pain pills as the doctor had advised. The injured stuntman wasn't feeling any discomfort, but then he wasn't feeling like he was in any shape to get shot from a cannon either.

Garrett walked out of the dance hall and for a split second froze. He wasn't nothing but seventy-five years of bad habits. Ruth knew, as soon as she saw that look in his eye, that he didn't approve of her bringing Bambalina out from the back lot. Garrett shook his head, caught himself and laughed.

"Oh, would you hush," Ruth said as she approached with Blake and Bambalina. "I'll go borrow that elephant hook and drag you around this fairgrounds and make you do tricks."

Garrett was penitent, "I'm sorry there, young lady."

"Don't you smart talk me..."

Garrett scratched Bambalina's ear kindly. "I'm trying to get used to the idea that I got an appetite and this skinny woman out of Montana doing the cooking is making me hungry."

"You hold your tongue or you'll be sleeping on the sofa in the living room."

"Are you ever going to be nice to me?"

Ruth winked, "After the dance, when nobody's looking."

Garrett gave Bambalina a worried look. Then he smiled. "She'll come around."

Blake stood frozen out front of the dance hall. His pulse quickened at the first sight of his night's ambition. Lark was in a magenta hued chiffon dress. Glenna had picked it out special for her.

"...Must have cost a week's worth of wages," Lark said.

The fabric wasn't even as thick as a piece of tissue style wrapping paper. It was as close to see-through as a woman would dare to wear in a Great Basin small town. Beneath the dress Glenna had given Lark an intense, ruby colored bra and matching embroidered style panties. The intimate garments had been imported from Paris. The floral appliqué stitched into the lace was the naughtiest lingerie Lark had ever worn in her life. The undergarments glow flickered like fine lined suggestions; her silhouette etched explicit delineations beguiling the chiffon fabric, intoxicating the eye, and weakening a man's will. Glenna made Lark promise she'd wear her velvet high heeled ballroom dancing shoes. Black hair, black shoes, and in between stood all the woman a prayer could ever hope to answer.

Lark got hold of Blake's eyes. Blake tried looking at her. Panic set in. It was worse than ever before. Lark's likeness flickered in his mind's eye, not another woman in his life had ever looked like that. Not ever. No woman.

Tip Top Tom and His High Country Haymakers ended a song and invited everyone outside for the big event.

Ruth could see Dusty was trying to steady her new daredevil friend. "You go help them," Ruth said to Blake, "I got Bambalina."

Recorded marching band music was cued up and coming out of the built-in speakers on the daredevil's shiny polished aluminum cannon.

Blake kept his eyes locked on Lark. The searchlights were sweeping through the star encrusted sky. Blake remained transfixed on Lark's gloss red lipstick, flickering and gleaming... she stunned the man. Lark had grown up. She glowed with an inner radiance. He could feel her.

The big moment had arrived.

Dusty had hold of her showman on one side and Blake provided a shoulder for the other.

"You sure you are good to go?" Dusty asked.

"I got to be," the daredevil replied.

"I don't think he can do it," Dusty said.

Blake looked down at his ankle. Lark had Blake near all the way at the end of his rope. "You can't do this."

"I can't afford not to..." the daredevil said.

"Dusty," Blake said, "you seen me on the springboards at the hot spring?"

"Yes, I have."

"Can I do a one and half?" Blake asked.

"Every time..."

"You ever see me do my one and a half with a full twist?"

"Yes, I have..." Dusty said.

The daredevil looked Blake up and down. "How much do you weigh?"

"I'd say about the same as you..."

"Let's get him back to the motor coach," Dusty said. They helped him up. The coach door closed.

Keefe and Hazel had just walked out of the dance hall. Everyone had been invited outside to watch the big stunt.

The door to the motor coach opened. First one out the door was Dusty. Next was the daredevil dressed in his human cannonball jumpsuit, and behind the daredevil, the last man to climb out of the motor coach, with his ankle taped up and still on crutches, it was... it was the daredevil in his street clothes.

"What is he doing?" Keefe asked.

Lark put her hand up to hide her mouth.

Glenna said, "What's wrong?" Then she looked.

"I'll go talk to him." Fletcher crossed toward Blake.

Keefe followed.

"Sure you know what you are doing?" Fletcher asked.

"Doing what I do best; I'm taking my chances."

"Keep your knees bent slightly, keep your feet flat against the bottom of the barrel," the daredevil said. He strapped Blake's helmet on tight.

Blake jumped onto the fender of the truck the cannon was mounted on. He climbed on top the tip of the muzzle, turned to the crowd and the daredevil flipped a switch. The end of the cannon ceremonially began to rise, taking aim on its target. Blake teetered waving his arms to keep his balance; he wrapped his foot around the tip of the barrel until the great gun reached its preconfigured position. The cannon stopped. It seemed set to an improbably steep angle.

"You'll clear the roof of the dance hall," the daredevil said. "Put your goggles down. Keep your eyes open. Keep your chest up, hold your hands out like you're doing a swan dive, and once you spot the net, start arching your spine, bring your ankles up over the top of you, and they'll turn you so then you'll land flat on your back on the net..."

Glenna had her hand around Lark's arm and Hazel held her other.

"You don't have to watch," Hazel said.

"You should have kissed him for good luck," Glenna said.

"She should have kissed him goodbye," Hazel said.

Lark had a look on her face. There was a sorrow in her eye.

Blake, his two feet clad in calve high red-leather-made boxing style shoes, slipped them into the barrel, then slid down until he was waist deep at the muzzle. He was wearing tights and had a red, white and blue sequined top, and lacquer sprayed helmet that matched.

Tom's drummer had brought his snare out and began to do a drum roll.

Lark broke free of Hazel and Glenna's grasp and ran toward the cannon.

"You are going to kill yourself, Blake Varela," Lark said, "and ruin the life we were going to have."

Blake didn't know what words to say.

"I will never forgive you," Lark said.

Blake looked down from the muzzle of the cannon. Everyone and everything else vanished. There was nobody else there, but Lark. "I won't make it, if you don't forgive me."

Lark spun around and bolted five paces. She turned back around the chiffon dress whirling away from her body. There was temper in that turn. There was spunk and the flash of her panty clad body. "You are going to break your neck, ruin our lives."

Glenna ran up and got hold of Lark, "Let him go."

"The only man I want, and he volunteers to go get killed. And turns out to be on the same night I was going to give him every reason in the world to want to stick around."

"You can ask a man, but you can't tell him," Hazel said.

"Lark Lockwood," Blake hollered.

"What, what do you have to say..." Lark said.

Blake swallowed. He tried finding the words, even opened his mouth. Best he could do is point with his finger right into the eyes of Lark. "I'm counting on you kissing me after I land on the other side of this dance hall."

Fletcher was stunned. He stepped toward Blake, "Getting pretty brave for a man might not have much of a future."

Lark turned and began walking away, "You go find some other woman. I'm not made strong enough for a fool like you."

The daredevil pointed to the drummer. He started to play the drum roll once more. The daredevil pointed to Blake. He vanished into the muzzle down into the pitch black depths of the barrel. The daredevil lifted his head to check one last time that the wind was still calm. He lifted his hand and counted with his fingers, each finger met with a rim shot by the drummer and when he got his whole hand opened, he pointed to the drummer. There was silence...

Next, a loud boom... there was smoke, then a blur, the sparkle of sequins, then the eyes of the crowd caught up with sight of a man flung into the night. Blake shot out a record breaking one hundred feet up in the air and he was still rising higher; he was half way over the top of the dance hall. Blake continued to gain altitude until Lark couldn't stand still one single second longer; she changed directions, broke out running and she ran toward the net where he was going to land. Everyone broke at the same time... everyone running, shouting, screaming. Blake flew through the air swift as an arrow, and then beyond the net he was targeted to hit, and that's why everyone set off running... and then there was a crash... he slammed into the exhibit hall, went right through the aluminum roof and vanished... only thing to see was the hole he made when his body smashed through the roof.

People were hollering. "Someone find the doc," a voice shouted, "hurry."

Nobody ran faster than Lark. She skid to a halt, pulled the door to the building open. In she dashed, seemed like the whole town poured in behind her. The exhibit hall filled with processed seed, the seeds must have been piled 8 feet high.

Looking up Lark could see the hole in the ceiling where Blake had crashed through. She waded into the harvested seeds. She struggled. She fought her way across, waist deep in the seeds, fighting her way until she got her hands on Blake. He was flat on his back.

Lark looked down at Blake. She held him by his shoulders. "Blake..." she said.

Blake opened his eyes, "How'd I do?"

"Anything broken...?" Lark asked.

"I hope not." Blake said.

"Wiggle your toes," Blake moved his toes.

"Turn your head," he turned his head.

"Put your arms around me," he put his arms around Lark.

Lark looked around to everyone crowding in. "Get the doctor," Lark said.

"Sometime when you can, maybe you can explain a man to me," Glenna said.

"It's hard to know..." Fletcher said.

"A man is the same as a woman, except the woman comes with a shortcut and the man has to take the long way around," Keefe said.

Hazel said, "Well, one day you finally get here..."

Jace and Jolene, Ruth and Garrett, the Hazel Harwood Award Ribbon Company women and their cowboy dancing partners all come crushing inside the pinion pine nut seed storage shed. Then there was Gage and Dotty, Gig and Elena, Bero and Mirari, Dusty and the daredevil. The doctor and Deputy Sheriff were at the back of the pack, and as always Sal and Mitzi were last. Bambalina couldn't help herself and got to the door and peeked in too.

Lark unfastened Blake's chin strap. She eased the helmet off his head. She kept looking him up and down for signs of injury. "You want danger in your life?"

Blake didn't know what to do with Lark so near him; her dark dramatic eyes and black hair lured him into a world turned upside down. He started to try and say something.

Lark placed the tips of her fingers over his lips. Blake was gathering his wits with each passing moment. His eyes traced Lark's face, first one eye, then her other... he looked at her lips, and his mind went off, same as it ever did... his eyes began swirling around Lark's lips... and the sight of her lips so near his own knocked him clean out of whatever else in the world had happened.

Lark had her eyes aimed on Blake's lips too. They'd both had the same idea for far too long to have not done what they should have taken care of some time ago. Being shy is hard on a soul. Lark leaned closer and hovered right over Blake, then she collapsed and surrendered to his lips. As she kissed Blake, Lark pressed her lips and the whole of her body against Blake; it was the longest kiss, her head tossed side to side, back and forth... she was frustrated... they were stuck together, and if you didn't know they'd never kissed, seemed like a tempest, a cloudburst, and they both seized the other's hair and Blake swung his other arm around Lark and squeezed her tighter, she groaned, he came to his senses, let up, and when he did she pressed harder and shook her head, squealed and she didn't stop and wouldn't until she felt sure he understood how it was between them, and when the feeling of that moment was mutual, even though they'd never had that moment ever before, just after there came a mutual release, and their kiss began to come to an end.

Lark eased up. They both had their eyes closed. They came apart, but she punched her lips against his staccato style. First kiss she never wanted to ever come to an end.

Lark took a deep breath. She opened her eyes and met Blake's as he opened his too. She wanted to know, "You want to do something dangerous with your life?" He almost spoke too soon. Lark touched the tips of her fingers on his lips. Blake's eyes grew wide. Something happened. Lark said, "Try loving me..."

About the Author

Dana Smith studied Theater Arts and English at Santa Clara University. In 1981 he finished his first novel, *Highway Home* on his trusty Smith-Corona manual typewriter. In 2005 he returned to the manuscript and over the next four years revised and completed this book. In 2009 he launched work on a second, *Pleasure Craft* and completed it in June of 2011. In January 2012 he embarked on the drafting for his third novel, *Hot Spring Honeymoon*. The novel, a comedy was finished in September 2013.

www.ingramcontent.com/pod-product-compliance
Lightning Source LLC
Chambersburg PA
CBHW020536020726
47494CB00006B/1789